Thank you to Jadylu, for allowing me to base Zoë's journey on your hopes and dreams. Thanks also to Joss, for sharing the hilarious stories from your days as lead singer in Black Widow, and to Matt, the Smoke Feathers frontman, for the insight and for the incredible music. (Fans, take note: they are going to be huge.) Dick, thanks for your words of wisdom and good luck with *Bat For Lashes*. You're a fantastic manager and I swear I didn't base Louis on you. Cliff, if I ever need a music lawyer, I'll know where to come. You are a fountain of knowledge and a great person, too. Paul, the authority on all things radio, thanks for the steer. Ashlea, you were the brains behind the Q gigs and you will be sorely missed. Thank you, Mischa, music reviewer extraordinaire. Tom, thanks for exposing the grubby insides of a certain record label that shall remain nameless. Thanks also to James and everyone else at Absolute Radio. I'm extremely grateful to both Sammia and Kesh at Avon for their patience and editorial expertise, and of course, to Chris, for always being there.

To all the unsigned artists out there.

Prologue

Hutchinson cocked his head to one side and made a clicking noise with his tongue.

'All right,' he said eventually. 'Show us the DVD. But no promises.'

The large American rose from his seat as quickly as was possible for someone of his size and stature. 'You'll like this, I'm tellin' ya,' he said in his irritating, mid-Atlantic drawl.

The head of the label didn't reply. Nobody told Edgar Hutchinson, President of Vicinity, one of Universal's most successful commercial labels, what he would or wouldn't like.

After much button-pressing, the blinds slithered down and a fuzzy image was projected onto the far wall. The American man sank back in his chair like a proud parent waiting for his child to appear in the school play. Slowly, the resolution improved and after a few seconds it became obvious what they were all looking at.

Hutchinson raised an eyebrow, taking in the long, denim-clad legs of the lead singer. Her dark hair was cut to chin-length and she had that doe-eyed, Keira Knightley thing going on.

'So . . .' He looked around at the other men, waiting for something to happen on the screen. 'Do we have sound and light on this thing, or is it just a fancy photo frame?'

The American rolled his eyes. 'Give it a mo.'

Hutchinson looked back at the image, letting his gaze roam

1

over the rhythm guitarist, a gypsy type with dark, wavy hair and cat-like eyes. Then he saw the blonde on bass and laughed. 'Who's that – Britney Spears's little sister?'

'Hey,' said the large man, twisting round in his seat and waggling a sausage-like finger. 'Wait 'til you hear 'em.'

Several seconds passed. Hutchinson looked at his watch.

'Look, Louis, I really don't have time for a Girls Aloud remake or whatever this is. You know I don't do girl-bands. They're expensive, high maintenance and they don't sell any records outside the UK.'

The American was shaking his head, poking buttons on the remote control like a baby with a new toy. 'Huh. Looks like I had it on pause.' He held the device aloft as he tried again. 'No, believe me, this is *not* a girl-band.'

Suddenly, the room was filled with a very loud humming noise and the screen was filled with a wonky shot of the girls on stage. Hutchinson grimaced.

'It's a live recording,' the big man explained.

'God help us,' muttered Hutchinson.

He was picking at the strip of skin by the side of his thumbnail when something made him look up.

Despite the background hum on the recording, it was just about possible to make out the vibe of the song. It wasn't pop, exactly. Nor was it rock, or indie. Post-punk, maybe. Whatever it was, it wasn't the sound he had expected to come from these cutesy chicks. For a start, the singer could *sing*. Hutchinson didn't like to think of himself as sexist, but the fact was, girls didn't usually make good musicians. This, though . . . It sounded like The Killers or The Thrills or something. There was, as the American had irritatingly pointed out, nothing girl-band about this group at all.

The guitarist's quick-fingered solo was good. And he liked the way the buxom, blue-eyed drummer kept peeping out from behind her raven-black hair as she kept the beat. Even the mini-Britney was doable, too, if you were into the young girls thing. But Hutchinson's attention kept flitting to the lead singer. She had the looks all right – porcelain face, bee-stung lips, long, Bambi legs and a decent rack on her, too – but better than that, she had presence. You could feel it, even by watching the shoddy, amateur recording.

'Okay!' he cried, looking away from the screen. The perpetual zooming in and out was making him feel seasick. 'That's enough.'

The DVD was switched off and the room became silent.

'So . . . ?' said the American, after some time. 'You wanna think about signing them?'

Edgar Hutchinson exhaled noisily and started tapping his fingertips on the desk. He did this for some time.

Eventually, he looked up.

'No.'

'What?'

'No. I'm not going to sign them. I've got a better idea.'

1

'This is an insult to my ears.' Shannon angrily stuffed her earplugs into her ears and downed the remains of her beer.

Zoë persevered with tuning her guitar as the distorted noise continued to grind through the walls. She was concerned by the number of empty bottles at Shannon's feet, but knew better than to aggravate the feisty Irish drummer when she was like this.

'I'm sure we'll be able to turn down these awards nights when your amazing campaign starts to pay off,' Kate remarked quietly.

Zoë closed her eyes, waiting for the inevitable retort. They'd been cooped up in the grotty backstage cell for nearly an hour and nerves were evidently beginning to fray. The promoter had lied about the timings. It was the usual stunt: goading the fans to arrive early and then forcing them to hear acts they didn't want to hear whilst spending money in the overpriced bar. All gigs were a sham – even these so-called awards nights.

'What did you say?' snapped Shannon, removing an earplug and staring at Kate's bowed head.

The bassist shrugged anxiously. 'I just meant, I hope it was money well spent.'

Shannon sighed loudly and shook her head, looking at Zoë. 'Did you hear that?'

Zoë held out her hand in a gesture of peace. 'Let's not—'

'She has the cheek to criticise *us* for our efforts!' cried Shannon.

'Look . . .' Zoë watched uneasily as the drummer began taking ever larger mouthfuls of beer.

'Miss *Sit-back-and-see!*' Another swig. 'Like *your* efforts are going to propel Dirty Money into the global spotlight!'

Kate flashed a look of aggression that didn't quite mask the pain in her eyes. Shannon's remark was unfair. Kate did a huge amount to help promote the band; she just didn't make a lot of noise doing it. However, for the promotion in question, it was fair to say that the bassist had played no part.

It was hardly surprising that Kate disapproved of their latest ploy for attracting the attention of major labels. She had never been one for taking risks – especially when money was involved. Ever prudent, the bassist liked to stay well within her safety zone. Shannon, however, had never been inside a safety zone.

The plan, executed by Zoë, as usual, was to send copies of their demo CD to the heads of the key record labels, along with photocopies of the review that had appeared – in microscopic proportions – in *Mojo* the previous month. The controversial part of the operation was the inclusion of a used ten-pound note (a fiver for indie labels) in each mailshot, representing 'dirty money'.

Shannon's thinking was that no self-respecting label manager would dare pocket money from an unsigned band and that nobody would bother to post the cash back to them. Which meant that the recipients would feel obliged to at least play their CD – and that was the critical hurdle; most promo packs went straight into the recycling bin.

The promotion, which had set them back nearly three hundred pounds in tenners and fivers, had gone out eight days ago. Zoë kept telling herself that no news was probably good news. Kate clearly wasn't so sure.

It was the fourth member of the group who eventually curtailed the row.

'There's not a lot we can do about it, anyway,' Ellie muttered quietly from behind her wavy locks as she strummed her un-amplified guitar. 'Let's just see what happens.'

Shannon looked over, drew a breath to respond, and then shut her mouth.

Zoë smiled. It was typical of Ellie to suggest that they do nothing, that they put their faith in fate. That was her mantra for life. *See what happens.* It wasn't apathy; it was more of an unwavering belief that good things would come to them in the end. Ellie wasn't one for setting herself ambitious targets.

Glancing across at Kate, Zoë felt her smile fading. The bassist Kate was staring at the floor, unblinking, expressionless. She was clearly upset, but Zoë suspected that it wasn't down to the argument. Kate was well versed in dealing with Shannon; she could hold her own in a row. Apart from anything else, Kate had the advantage of being right, most of the time. No, the pursed lips and watery blue eyes could mean only one thing: She had been dumped. Again. Zoë laid down her guitar and crossed the room, catching her eye. Then the door burst open.

'Evening all!' cried the short, wiry man with spiky ginger hair. It was Jake, their overzealous and underachieving manager. 'How's me girls?'

Zoë switched on a mechanical smile and allowed their eyes to meet. 'Fine, thanks.'

'Ready to rock the joint?'

She grunted. Jake Gordon-Spencer was one of those people who lived in blissful ignorance of the irritating effect he had on others. His accent, which had been cultivated through years of expensive schooling and then years of half-hearted rebellion at Daddy's expense, was presumably supposed to appeal to the geezers of the industry. In fact, it had the opposite effect; Jake was known as The Mockney Dickhead across the London scene. However, he had one saving grace: his cousin, Dan, who came as part of the package and who was one of the city's best booking agents. Without Dan, Dirty Money would never have made it

7

this far. He was diligent, well connected and commercially savvy. He was also unfathomably loyal to his cousin.

'Record number of fans 'ere to see you,' Jake reported as they trooped along the damp corridor towards the stage. 'All my hard work paying off . . .' He tilted his head to one side, like a market stall holder clinching a deal.

Zoë glanced at him, wondering whether the manager really was deluded enough to believe that he had been responsible for the audience numbers tonight. *She* had gone round with a clipboard, collecting email addresses at their last umpteen gigs. *She* was the reason they had twelve thousand friends on MySpace, the reason they'd been nominated for the Indie Awards tonight.

The girls assembled themselves in the wings while the compère rallied the crowds. Zoë leaned forwards, catching a glimpse of the curly blond locks of their most loyal fan, Crazy Jeff, just in front of the stage. Whooping and catcalling, his skinny arms were flailing like wind turbines in a gale. Jake had been right. Tonight was a record for the band. There were probably four or five hundred bodies crammed into the sweaty pit, a good proportion of them rooting for Dirty Money. With a bit of luck, thought Zoë, they'd have this award in the bag.

'*It was only seventy-five pounds each,*' Shannon whispered loudly.

'They're loud, they're dirty, they're sexy . . .'

'*Seventy-five pounds we could've spent elsewhere,*' Kate hissed back.

Zoë glared at each of them in turn. Now was not the time to be bickering. They needed to focus. They needed to win an award tonight.

'. . . our final act of the night, please welcome . . . Dirty Money!'

2

Zoë kicked off her office shoes and dumped her bag on the doormat. The mouthwatering smell of roast chicken was wafting through the flat.

'Hey,' James called out, holding out a glass of red wine, like a carrot for a donkey.

Zoë smiled, kissing him and then sipping the wine as she tugged playfully at her boyfriend's untucked shirt.

'Good day?' he asked.

She rolled her eyes, taking a sip of wine and not bothering to reply. Good days at Chase Waterman were few and far between. 'How was the trip?'

James shrugged and stooped down in front of the oven, peering through the layer of grime to see what was going on inside. 'So-so.'

He never complained. Zoë couldn't remember a single time in the three years since they'd graduated that he'd really had to let off steam. James worked in the marketing department of one of the UK's leading home insurers. His work was mundane, often involving last-minute assignments, late nights and tedious trips to the Norfolk headquarters, but he never seemed to have cause for the explosive rants to which Zoë was prone.

'Another ten minutes, I reckon.' He nodded in the direction of the lounge, grabbing both drinks as he went.

It was impressive, how easily James seemed to have made the transition from student to young professional. Six years ago, he'd been the tall, lanky stranger with the piercing blue eyes and dirty blond, messy hair, loitering at the back of the sticky-floored hangout where Dirty Money had first performed, drinking pints with all the other Goldsmiths undergrads. It was his scruffy, rebellious streak that had drawn her to him. He was as devoted now as he had been then – work permitting. But now, with his military crop and slick Moss Bros suit, he looked like a different man.

'So.' He topped up her glass as she drew her laptop towards her and logged onto MySpace. 'Did you win, the other night?'

Zoë took a large sip and groaned quietly. She had been trying to block the Indie Awards from her mind.

James raised an eyebrow.

'Shannon got drunk before we went on and Kate wouldn't let up about the dirty money campaign . . . then it all kicked off on stage. Shannon messed up one of the songs, Kate tried to correct her, then next thing you know, Shannon's chucking her bass pedal at Kate. It knocked out the power for the whole venue.'

James drew back his head, eyes wide. He was clearly impressed by the new level of absurdity achieved.

'So, no, we didn't win.'

Zoë sank into her wine, trying to dispel the image of the angry woman with the headset, sweeping them off the stage. 'Shannon stayed 'til the end and said some bunch of drunk, teenage boys took the award. We came third. She reckoned we were penalised because we were girls.'

'Not because she smashed up the stage and tried to decapitate her bass player?'

Zoë managed a meek smile. 'Oh, and then Jake walked out on us.'

James expelled a jet of air from his mouth. '*He* walked out on *you*?'

Zoë nodded. She needed to have a proper word with the girls. Shannon had called, as she always did, muttering a vague apology and then quickly moving on to her next harebrained scheme. She remained happily ignorant of the trouble she'd landed them in, even after Zoë relayed her conversation with the promoter about the damage to the stage equipment. Kate had called, too, admitting that she had been partly to blame. The storm had blown over, as it always did, but the consequences remained very real; Dirty Money no longer had a manager.

James watched over her shoulder as she edited the details of their upcoming gigs. Then he sat up and looked around the room. He had a very low boredom threshold.

'I was wondering,' he said, staring up at the ceiling. 'D'you reckon Axl Rose spent his evenings fine-tuning the details of his promotional packs, in the early days?'

Zoë smiled. 'Oh, I'm sure he did. You know, Slash and the other guys were like, "Come on Ax, let's get fucked and smash up some hotel lobbies," and he'd say, "I'll catch you up, I've just got to change the font on this title track."'

James laughed and reached for the TV remote control.

They'd had similar conversations before. James knew how much things had changed since the eighties. If a group from thirty years ago had been reborn and expected to 'make it' all over again, they'd probably sink before they'd even cut their first track. Back in the day, all you needed was a bit of talent, an attitude and a lucky break. If you happened to be playing in the right place at the right time, you'd get picked up by a manager, who, over a couple of lines of coke and a hooker, would sweet-talk some A&R rep into taking you on. Then, assuming you had enough decent songs inside you to fill a couple of albums, you were made.

Not any more. These days, there were more acts to go around. The internet was awash with talent. There were literally millions of artists pumping out tracks – something for everyone. Even the fan bases of the mainstream acts were carved up into smaller pieces. The days of bands like the Beatles, whose appeal reached from brickies to housewives, were long gone. As a lowly unsigned act, Dirty Money had to shout as loud as it could to stand a chance.

Settling for *Cook Me Famous*, a programme about deluded nobodies trying to batter and fry their way into the history books, James kicked off his shoes and drew his own laptop towards him. Zoë knew he was trying to make a point, sitting beside her and mirroring her exact posture, but the MySpace page was a priority, and nobody else was going to update it.

> Thanks for asking, she typed. We actually have a gig in N London in 2 weeks' time – check out our schedule! DM x
> Hi M, yes we do play private gigs – for a fee! Let us know what you're thinking and we'll get back to you. DM x

It was a laborious way of reaching out to fans, but it was the only way. Zoë removed the usual smattering of lewd postings about bizarre sexual fantasies involving the members of Dirty Money and their instruments, scanning the page for other requests. As she did so, an email alert appeared in the corner of her monitor.

> Dear lead singer,
> I just wanted to tell you how much I admire the way you work that stage. I would be truly honoured if you could spare some time to spend with me at some point in the next few weeks to celebrate my appreciation of your work.
> Your adoring fan x

Zoë smiled.

> Dear Adoring Fan, she typed.
> Thank you for your kind words. It's always nice to hear from admirers. In terms of spending time together, what were you thinking?
> Zoë

She flicked back to the website and checked through the outstanding messages. There was always a slew of requests for dates – most directed at Shannon or Kate, some both at once. Ellie attracted a different type of guy altogether: the black leather, pierced flesh, greasy hair variety – mostly guitarists themselves. Zoë looked again at the bottom of her screen where the alert had reappeared.

> Dear Zoë,
>   Thank you for the quick response. I was thinking along the lines of dinner. Might you have an evening spare for me to take you out? Around Valentine's Day, perhaps?
>   Adoring Fan x

Zoë leaned forward and tapped out her response, feeling a shiver of excitement at the prospect of a proper date.

> Saturday 11th then?

A moment later, James turned to her, eyes twinkling. 'Sure you can spare me the time?'

Zoë smiled. 'For my Valentine, of course.'

3

'It's hardly a *ban*,' scoffed the ruddy-faced man to her right. 'All the coppers round our way are too busy galloping after hounds to make any arrests!'

He hooted at the apparent irony, prompting a ripple of false laughter along the table. The woman who had brought up the subject of fox-hunting looked at her lap, blushing.

Zoë was regretting her late arrival. Had she arrived at the Inns of Court at six-thirty, as stipulated by the glossy, gold-edged invitation, she would at least have been able to sit with her parents. Not that she'd usually relish the prospect of their company, but this evening it would have been preferable to that of the slack-jawed buffoon.

Zoë leaned sideways as an array of colourful vegetables and finely cut veal appeared in front of her, trying to blot out the drone on her right. The hall looked like the inside of one of King Henry VIII's castles: dark oak panelling, carved buttresses and glinting chandeliers on chains that stretched all the way from the raftered ceiling down to the long, wooden tables along which they sat.

Up on High Table, as it was apparently known, her sister sat, chatting away, her curly hair splaying out over the fur-lined gown that seemed to be compulsory attire for all of the part-qualified barristers. Even some of the guests were wearing gowns, she noted, including the pompous cretin she was sitting next to. It was another world. A world she could have inhabited herself, had things turned out differently, and now, more than ever, she felt glad that they hadn't.

Zoë let the man talk, nodding when the moment seemed right. People like this, she thought, were evolutionary anomalies. They were so focused on themselves and their own activities that they should, by rights, have become extinct years ago – eaten by a bear whilst regaling others with their tales of bravery. But somehow, they lived on to tell their dreary tales.

Zoë watched as her sister surreptitiously slid her profiteroles onto a neighbour's plate, glancing about as if worried that some-body might be watching. Their eyes met briefly and Tamsin cast her a guilty smile. Zoë winked back, thinking about all the times she had flouted laws and bent rules in the last few weeks.

A month ago, she and Shannon had had the brilliant idea of performing a gig wearing hard hats, on a stage decorated like a road works site: traffic signs, cones, flashing orange lamps . . . Of course, they had planned to return everything after use. It was only when Shannon appeared on the night with the pièce de résistance – a large set of temporary traffic lights – that the promoter had put his foot down and threatened to report the girls to the police. It seemed obvious, thinking about moments like this, that Zoë wasn't destined to follow in her sister's footsteps.

They were similar, in many ways. They had the same drive, the same sense of determination and resilience. They were both bright, hard-working and ambitious, but they were motivated by different things.

For Tamsin, it had always been about following the path but walking it quicker and better than everyone else on it. She had excelled at school, acing her exams and easily over-coming hurdle after hurdle. That was how she had ended up here, a trainee barrister at one of London's most prestigious chambers.

Zoë had never cared about following the path. For her, the

further she got from the path, the better. She knew, having lived in Tamsin's shadow for twenty-four years, that she was the outlier. She understood that her parents couldn't understand her way of thinking. That was why she compromised. She had gained a degree – albeit not the one her parents would have liked – and she had found herself a respectable job. But inside, she knew she could never be satisfied by her traditional middle-class existence.

'And what about you?' asked the man, poking his pitted nose in Zoë's face. 'What do you do?'

Zoë straightened up and looked at the man. 'I'm at Chase Waterman.'

'Ah!' he cried. 'You're a bean counter!'

'Well,' Zoë averted her eyes. She wanted to defend her role at the UK's largest independent auditing firm, but she couldn't think of anything positive to say about it.

'Didn't you fancy your chances in law?' He tugged proudly at the navy gown that engulfed his ample frame.

'Something like that,' Zoë replied, deciding that now was not the time to admit that she'd failed to make the grades for her first choice of degree. Looking down the table, she watched as her father became embroiled in a debate with a man in a green tweed jacket.

'You'd be surprised,' her father was saying. 'Misconduct has existed in top-level sport since long before it all went commercial.'

The man, who appeared to have far too much hair for his age, squinted at Zoë's dad. 'Is that so?'

'It is.'

Zoë smiled wryly. They were trying to out-sport one another. Her father would put up a good fight, she suspected; he had once played rugby for Hertfordshire. He was also one of the most highly-respected defence lawyers in London.

'What sort of misconduct?'

'The England rugby squad in the nineteen-eighties,' Zoë's father replied. 'There was plenty of match-fixing, even then.'

The man drew his head back, frowning. 'How could you possibly know that?'

'I trained with them. I was offered a place on the squad.'

Zoë nearly yelped. *Her father had nearly played rugby for England?* How did she not know this? And why had he turned it down? She looked at her phone. It was eight fifty-two. The questions would have to wait.

Still reeling, Zoë leaned back as the waitress poured coffee into her bone china cup. She would slip out now, pretending to visit the ladies, and then by the time everybody adjourned to the room with carpet on the walls for drinks, they'd all be too sloshed to notice her absence. She felt bad about leaving her sister, but there wasn't really an alternative. She could hardly skip up to 'High Table' and explain that she was abandoning one of the most important dinners of the legal calendar to go and rehearse with her band.

Out of the darkness came an unmistakable Irish shriek.

'Over here, you eejit!'

Zoë followed the sound to where Shannon was parked illegally in the middle of High Holborn, honking and yelling through the open window.

As a drummer, owning a large car was a prerequisite, but there was something about the battered old Volvo estate that particularly suited Shannon. The car was like the vehicular equivalent of its owner: noisy, colourful and unreliable. It had transported Shannon and all her belongings, including the drum kit, from Limerick to East London six years previously – miraculously, only breaking down once along the way.

'I've had an idea,' said Shannon, winding up her window and swerving into the fast lane. 'Fuck off!' she yelled as the driver behind them made a gesture with his hand in the glow of the next car's headlights. 'We should get some celebrity endorsement.'

Zoë gripped the fabric of the seat, glancing at the silhouette of the angry man in the wing mirror. 'What d'you mean?' she managed to ask. Rides with Shannon were not for the faint-hearted. Kate refused to get in the car unless there was no alternative.

'Well, we've got fans all over the world, all over the internet, but none of them are *famous*. If we could get a big name to say, "Hey guys, I think you're great", we'll be made.' She yanked the steering wheel round and pulled a sharp left, provoking more sounding of horns.

'Mmm, maybe.' Zoë nodded, grabbing the door handle to keep herself upright. It was hard to focus on promotional strategies and staying alive at once.

'That's what Ladyhawke did,' Shannon went on, flicking on the internal light and checking her hair in the rear-view mirror. Zoë watched as a fearless motorcyclist approached them on the outside. 'Apparently Courtney Love left a glowing review on her MySpace page.'

'Right . . .' Zoë tried to control her breathing as the motorcyclist slipped into Shannon's blind spot. 'And don't you think maybe that might have been a PR stunt by Ladyhawke's management? Watch the bike, by the way.'

'I don't know. Don't matter, does it? If it's a stunt, then we need to be doing one too. Jesus! Where did he come from?'

Zoë breathed a sigh of relief as the motorcyclist emerged, seemingly unscathed, in front of them. 'Um . . . yeah, although it might not be that easy. I bet if you look closely, you'll find that Ladyhawke's on the same label as Courtney Love, or her management knows Courtney Love's management or something like that. It's not so easy when you're unsigned.'

Finally, Zoë began to relax her grip as they made the last turn onto Shannon's road. It was always tricky explaining realities to Shannon. In many ways, it was great that she was so up for anything. It made a welcome change from the attitude of most of the people Zoë dealt with on a day-to-day basis. Shannon never saw problems, only ideas. Masses and masses of ideas. The hard part, for Zoë and the rest of the band, was bringing her back down to earth.

Their rehearsal studio, which was actually the front room of the West London flat that Shannon shared with three or four other girls (it fluctuated), was just large enough for the drum kit, three small amps and four people standing, as long as Zoë half-perched on the armchair and Kate stooped inside the upturned sofa. Sometimes, when the girls scraped together enough funds or they had an important gig coming up, they'd book a slot in the Shoreditch studio but most of the time, they made do with the drummer's lounge.

Flattening herself against the wall to let Ellie pass, Zoë thought about how she was going to broach the subject of their Indie Awards fiasco.

'Great, we're all here!' cried Shannon, 'Let me tell you my news!' She thumped the bass drum with the newly-purchased pedal.

'Hold on.' Zoë held up her hand. 'I just want to say . . .' She bit her lower lip, not wanting to come across like a bossy head-mistress. The truth was, though, she *was* the boss. If she didn't say it, nobody would. 'We really messed up, the other night. And now, because of that, we don't have a—'

'Who cares? We don't need—'

'One sec,' Zoë pleaded. 'We don't have a manager, we don't have a booking agent, we didn't win the award and I think it's safe to say we won't be asked back to the Camden House for a while. I think we need to start—'

'For Christ's sake!' yelled Shannon. 'We don't *need* Jake or Dan any more!'

'What?' Zoë asked cautiously.

'Well . . .' Shannon bowed her head and performed a drum roll that seemed to go on forever. Zoë watched, willing it to stop. 'We have a new manager!'

The three girls looked at Shannon, who beamed back at them triumphantly and whacked the cymbal for effect.

'Who?' asked Kate.

'Aha.' Shannon carefully balanced her drumsticks on the rim of the snare, her movements deliberate and slow. She rubbed her hands together, like a magician warming up for a trick. Zoë sighed impatiently. Finally, the drummer looked up. 'The guy I met in the bar, after the awards night. He's called Louis Castle. Ring any bells?'

Three faces looked back at her blankly.

'Okay,' Shannon shrugged. 'Maybe he's not that big over here. But he's from LA and he's managed bands like The Anglers and Domino Scene and . . . and Tepid Foot Hold!'

Zoë glanced at Kate's face, then at Ellie's. There were no signs of recognition on either. 'Tepid Foot Hold?' She frowned. 'Sounds like the name of an IKEA flat-pack.'

Shannon growled. 'They're big in America. Massive.' She rolled her eyes. 'Anyway, this guy has his own management company and he wants to manage *us*! He'll sort us out with a booking agent and everything. I mean, seriously. He was talking about stadium gigs!'

Zoë exchanged a quick, apprehensive look with their bassist. Kate's expression said it all.

'Well, don't all thank me at once!' Shannon cried loudly. 'I've only gone and put us one step closer to world domination!'

Zoë tried her best to look enthusiastic. The problem was, they'd been here before. Shannon was always making Useful Acquaintances. She seemed to have a natural magnetism for lonely, lecherous males who – either by calculation or misunderstanding – ended up in her address book when it was perfectly clear to everyone else that they simply wanted to get in her pants.

'Oh, and I forgot the best bit!' Shannon's eyes were wild. 'His company, Blast Management, has some sort of connection with Universal. Universal!'

Zoë's ears pricked up. She glanced at Kate.

As a general rule, Kate's expression served as a good sanity check. She was naturally cautious – to the extent that she chopped up her old credit cards and scattered the pieces in different dustbins around the country – and as such, tended to stand in the way of Shannon's more ludicrous schemes. Kate was still looking sceptical.

'Not . . . BMI?' asked Ellie, smiling dreamily. 'Maybe he's going out with an air steward.'

Shannon tossed her long, black ponytail over her shoulder.

'Look, I'm telling you, this guy is a hot-shot manager from LA. He's seen us perform a few times and he *loved* our set at the awards.'

'Did he love the bit when you threw the bass pedal at Kate?' asked Zoë. 'Or when all the lights went out?'

'Shut up!' cried Shannon, her accent full strength. 'If you don't want a manager, then fine. But if you ask me, this is our big chance. And to be honest, we haven't got a lot to lose right now.'

'Okay,' said Zoë, thinking for a moment. 'You're right. How did you leave it with this guy?'

Shannon cleared her throat melodramatically. 'He wants to see our demo DVD.'

'Our what?' chimed Zoë and Kate in unison.

'I know. He said it needs to be visual.'

Zoë pulled a face, wondering what 'visual' meant, and whether Shannon might have got the wrong end of the stick.

'Not like *that*,' the drummer clarified. 'And don't worry, I know a guy who'll do it.'

Zoë looked at the others and laughed. Shannon always knew a guy. Whatever the challenge, there was always a man from Shannon's past who would fit the bill.

'Can your guy come and film our next gig?'

Shannon smiled coyly. 'I'm sure he could be persuaded.'

Zoë rolled her eyes and switched on Ellie's amp, nodding for her to play. After a quick tweak of strings, they were ready.

'Shall we?' said Shannon, holding her sticks in midair, ready to launch into their first song.

Over the years, the band had built up a repertoire of about thirty decent songs. Two albums' worth and five extra songs, to be precise. Not that any had been officially released. The tracks, having been recorded in a studio belonging to a sleazy millionaire acquaintance of Shannon's, had been uploaded to various places on the internet, but never released. It was a deliberate move. The girls had considered the idea of self-releasing – burning the tracks to CD and flogging them to friends and fans – but had rejected it on the grounds that no proper label would want to release a rehash of an album that had photocopied sleeves and handwritten inserts. Dirty Money were waiting for the real thing.

Most of the tracks on their first unreleased album were either cheeky reflections on events or incidents in their lives, like 'Run Boy Run', a song about Shannon's man-eating attributes, or flippant takes on the world around them, such as 'Man Made', a song about an increasingly materialistic society.

Over the years, their lives had changed and so had their music. Recent tracks included 'Sensible Lies', a frank exposé on the double life Zoë found herself leading, and 'Clap Now Turn Around', a song that hit back at the endless stream of identikit girl-bands who stripped their way into the charts, only to be pushed back to obscurity when the next set of grinning dolls came along.

They bashed through a few of their old favourites, experimenting. They never needed to tell one another what worked or what didn't. If Ellie discovered a new set of chords that improved the sound, there might be a nod or a smile, but if the new bass line was off, nobody would bother to point it out.

It wasn't always like this in a band. As a teenager, Zoë had sung, or rather, shouted, in a head-banging metal group that consisted of two tone-deaf guitarists and a drummer with a limited sense of rhythm. Being in Dead Canvas had been the exact opposite of Zoë's experiences in Dirty Money. With the boys, their rehearsal time had been spent alternately yelling at one another and passing round joints. The girls were different. They had an understanding. Perhaps because they'd been friends for over half a decade, ever since their early Goldsmiths days, they never needed to state the obvious.

Six years ago, Zoë had been lugging a battered old suitcase up the concrete steps of her first-year halls of residence: a drab, flat-roofed monstrosity that filled the gap between the A20 and the ugly sprawl of New Cross Gate. She had two guitars slung over one shoulder and a rucksack over the other – a consequence of her own stubbornness, having declined her parents' offer of a lift, following a row over her A-level grades.

Ironically, Zoë's 'shockingly poor results' (her mother's words) were both the product and the cause of her unrelenting passion for music. Looking back, her memories of sixth form involved jamming, songwriting and lying around hatching plans to become a big-time musician. With the benefit of hindsight, her grades shouldn't have come as a surprise to anyone. But they had done.

Expectations had been running high, following Tamsin's straight-A performance. There was a sense that Zoë would follow in her sister's footsteps. She was bright enough; in previous exams she had matched Tamsin's results, sometimes even beating her older sibling. But the motivation hadn't been there. Maths and history and economics had slipped down in her priorities, while music had climbed to the top.

Even with her father pulling strings from his chambers in Lincoln's Inn Fields, there was no way Durham would accept her into their hallowed law department. Which, as it turned out, was a blessing in disguise. Had Zoë never set foot on those concrete steps that led to the Goldsmiths first-year halls of residence, she would never have made friends with Ellie, and consequently would never have come into contact with Shannon or Kate.

Ellie had offered to help carry her belongings up the steps, which, of course, had led to a conversation about how they both played the guitar. It turned out that the girls' box-like rooms were on the same floor, so in the first few weeks, while everyone else was making spurious friendships and trying to find their way, Zoë and Ellie were hiding away in their poky student bedrooms, trying to find their sound. By the end of the first term at Goldsmiths, they had become inseparable.

Ellie probably would have been happy to go on like that: Jamming, singing, chatting and jamming. But by the second term, they had written some songs of their own – songs that were too good to keep hidden amongst the chocolate digestive crumbs of Rooms 5a and 5d.

Zoë put up ads around college for a bass guitarist and a drummer. The intention had never been to form an all-girl quartet. It was only when, during the informal audition in Ellie's bedroom, Kate had quietly introduced herself – she was studying Finance, the same as Zoë – that the idea of a female ensemble had presented itself.

Finding a drummer had been the problem. Decent female drummers were rarities. They did get a call from one girl, but then when they'd all met up, having chatted at length about the prospect of forming an all-girl group, it had transpired that the drummer's repertoire consisted solely of the thumping beat to 'We Will Rock You'. It just wasn't going to work.

Eventually, they had taken on a young man called Hans, a sweet-tempered foreign exchange student from Denmark. He was only around for the remainder of the year but he sufficed as a stopgap. Zoë had arranged for them to play at the Goldsmiths spring ball and it was there, in the middle of the beer tent, that Shannon had made herself known. Making use of her low-cut silk dress, she had talked Hans into stepping down for one song and shimmied her way into his seat. Three minutes later, it was obvious that they had found their drummer.

'Hold on!' cried Shannon, stopping midway through their newest song and poking her drumsticks behind her ears. 'I heard something.'

The other parts trailed off and for a moment, there was quiet. Then they all heard it. *Thud, thud, thud.*

'Mrs Costello,' they all said, in unison.

Mrs Costello was the downstairs neighbour. For someone who lived beneath a bunch of noisy Irish girls that included a drummer and a DJ, she was a tolerant woman. But when the broom handle started banging, the girls knew it was time to stop. It was a small price to pay in comparison to the studio fee.

Waiting for Ellie and Kate by the door, Zoë checked her phone. One missed call from her mum. She dialled to hear the inevitable voicemail.

'Hello dear, only me. Lovely to see you tonight. Pity we didn't get a chance to chat. You seemed to arrive late and then you, er, disappeared . . . Anyway. I wanted to ask, I'm having a bit of a clear out. You didn't want your old guitar, did you? I'm taking a carload to the charity shop.' Zoë let out an involuntary squeal. 'There's a . . . speaker-thing, too. You know the one I mean? Black . . . sort of square, lots of holes in the front . . . I'm not sure whether it'd be any use to anyone. Perhaps I'll get Daddy to take it to the tip. Oh and that jar of old plectrums – can I throw that away? We're trying to make the spare bedroom look a bit more presentable. Let me know. I'll see you soon. Byeee.'

Zoë growled angrily and deleted the message.

'Your mum?'

Zoë looked up. James was standing in the doorway. He must have driven round to give her a lift home.

'Hello.' Zoë tried to match his smile. 'Yeah, my mum. She's trying to throw out my old guitar.'

Shannon and Ellie poked their heads round from the front room.

'What?'

'What?'

'And my old practice amp. And you know that little pot of plectrums I collected at uni?'

'*Sacrilege*,' hissed Shannon, shaking her head.

James was frowning. 'Um . . . Perhaps I'm misunderstanding, but if you haven't used these things in the last two years, do you really need them?'

There was a collective gasp. Zoë drew a breath to explain, but Shannon got in first.

'It's not a question of need, James. It's a sentimental thing. You can't throw out your first guitar.'

'Oh. Right.' James nodded, nonplussed. 'And . . . the amp?'

'Okay,' Zoë nodded reluctantly. 'Maybe that can go.' The connections had always been a bit loose anyway. 'But the *plectrums* . . .'

Kate raised a hand and slipped out. 'Sorry – gotta go.'

James looked into the darkness and quietly called out to her. 'Chin up, eh. I'm sure it'll work out.'

The girls looked at one another; presumably Kate had been telling James all about her latest rejection by Henry or Hugo – the names blurred into one.

'You gotta have words with your mum,' Shannon said firmly. 'Make her change her mind.'

Zoë nodded, handing her guitar to James and stepping outside. The truth was, she had to change her mother's mind about a lot more than the fate of her old guitar.

'Oh and Shannon?' she said, poking her head back into the warmth of Shannon's flat. 'Nice one on the Louis Castle thing.'

Shannon grinned back at her. 'Tepid Foot Hold, I'm tellin' ya. Go check 'em out.'

4

'I think that covers everything,' Brian Aldridge concluded, much to Zoë's relief. Her balding boss was blessed with a gift for all things numerical, but he was also an incredible bore.

'Don't forget,' he called out as people morosely filed out of the meeting room. 'Rigorous Accounting Practices. RAP!'

The most irritating thing about Brian, thought Zoë, was that he genuinely believed he was interesting. His way of spicing up a presentation was to pepper it with his own acronyms, which just made you want to throw something at his shiny head.

Zoë found herself nodding as she passed through the door. It was a reflex she had developed at university for dealing with tedious lecturers.

'. . . this afternoon, Zoë?'

Zoë faltered. She had no idea what he was talking about.

'Or have you already done it?'

'Uh . . .' Zoë thought about answering, but decided against it. 'Sorry, have I done what?'

He looked at her, brow deeply furrowed. 'The British Trust audit.'

Zoë masked her mild panic with another smile. The British Trust was turning out to be something of a can of worms, largely because the charity was run by a bunch of sweet, well-meaning grandmothers who were incapable of using an abacus, let alone a spreadsheet.

'I've done the first run,' she replied.

'Could I see a copy, please?'

Zoë didn't like his patronising tone. 'I'll email it to you now,' she replied, leaving the meeting room and striding back to her desk.

Hoping she hadn't left any gaping holes, Zoë dispatched the email and looked at her watch. Twelve forty-three. She was meeting Ellie at one. It didn't seem sensible to get stuck into a spreadsheet with such little time. She opened a browser and typed three words into Google.

Results 1-10 of about 2,400,000 for 'tepid foot hold' returned the search engine. Zoë stared at the hits: The official TFH site, a couple of YouTube videos of live performances, a Last.fm profile, a MySpace page . . . even *Q* had a page for the band.

Zoë clicked on a couple of links. The country-rock fusion act had had seven top-ten singles in America and two platinum-selling albums, both making the top forty over here. Their lead singer, a guy called Toby Fox, was originally from London but now lived in LA with his model-actress girlfriend. Through Tepid Foot Hold he had won two Mercury awards, an *NME* award, a Grammy . . . Zoë squinted and reread the line. He had won an Ivor Novello award. An *Ivor Novello*. That was the ultimate achievement. It was more impressive than filling Wembley Arena or headlining on a bill that included the Eagles and Sheryl Crow – which, according to the articles, Fox had also managed to accomplish. Ivor Novellos were the musical equivalent of the Oscars. They were for real songwriters.

She was about to search for 'Louis Castle' when her survival instinct kicked in, telling her to revert to her spreadsheet.

'Getting through it?' asked Brian as his middle-aged paunch drew level with her desk.

'Mmm . . .' Zoë squinted hard at a formula, following her manager's progress through the office. It was ten to one. She set her screensaver to 'Never come on' and stood up, draping her coat over her guitar as she eased it out from under the desk.

'Are you going outside?' Eric, her annoying neighbour, asked loudly. Several heads turned. 'Can you get me a Coke?'

'Ooh, Zoë, can you buy me a sandwich?'

'Will you be going anywhere near a newsagent?'

Zoë pulled an apologetic face. She didn't want to admit that she'd be gone for a full hour. Hour-long lunch breaks were frowned upon, especially during January.

'I'm, er . . . I've got to run a few errands,' she explained. 'Sorry.'

'Is that a guitar?' asked Eric, even louder, as though wanting his colleagues to appreciate his powers of perception. There was something about the pointy-faced auditor that Zoë found exasperating. He managed to turn every conversation into a competition.

'Oh, er, yes.' Zoë looked down at the case. 'That's the, um, the errand. Gotta drop it off somewhere.'

A minute later, the revolving glass doors spat her onto the pavement and Zoë fled north, towards the barren wasteland of Shoreditch.

Ellie, it turned out, was running late. Ellie was usually running late. Her whole routine, if you could call it that, was set in a fluid version of time: one that was infinitely stretchable and infinitely compressible. Sometimes, she was early. Very occasionally, her clock coincided with Greenwich Mean Time and she arrived at a place exactly when she was supposed to. Most of the time though, Ellie was late. The only other person on the planet who inhabited the same time zone was Ellie's boyfriend, Sam.

Sam and Ellie lived in a caravan by one of the Thames's tributaries that ran through Hackney. Purchased five years ago from a group of travellers, the shack had initially served as a summer stopgap; a place to stay during the two months between first-year halls and their second-year student house. As it turned out, neither Ellie nor Sam made it as far as second year. Sam had been offered a choice by the college: to repeat his first year or to relinquish his place on the design course – which, truth be told, hadn't taught him much other than how to design the ultimate spliff – so he took the easy option and walked out. Ellie decided that she liked the vibe in the music shop on Denmark Street, where she had found herself working that summer, and dropped out as well. Five years later, Ellie was still at the shop, still living in the caravan with Sam, still smoking weed for breakfast.

'Hi!' cried Ellie, skipping across the road in front of a car, seemingly oblivious to its screeching emergency stop. 'Sorry I'm late!'

The car zoomed off, its driver glaring angrily at their embrace.

Zoë checked the time on her phone as Ellie let them in. 'I've got about forty-five minutes. I had to tell work I was running an errand.' She pulled a face.

Ellie smiled placidly. She had no idea about the pressures of corporate life. Fortunately for her, at Desmond's Strings there was no sneaking around behind colleagues' backs, no faking enthusiasm for mind-numbingly dull tasks, no bullshit. Ellie enjoyed stringing guitars and chatting to the Led Zeppelin enthusiasts who passed through the doors of the shop. In fact, it was thanks to Desmond that they had this pseudo-rehearsal studio at their disposal.

They messed around with the fragments of vocals that had been floating around Zoë's head for the last few days. *We say we will, we say one day / There's never time, it runs away / The beat, it's here, but do we care / We're out of time, we're out of air . . .*

Zoë felt herself loosening up, drifting away. Ellie's chords changed the whole sound of the song. After a week of hearing her own imaginary backing parts, it felt as though the melody was finally coming alive.

'This sounds great,' she said excitedly. 'D'you reckon we could get this polished in time for The Mad Cow gig?'

Ellie lifted her slender shoulders. 'Sure.'

The Mad Cow was Shannon's local pub. Run by an Irishman,

staffed by Irishmen and frequented by an eclectic mix of Irish, Caribbean, Polish, Russian, Indian and probably others; it was difficult to make out the accents above the din of the high-wattage amps. In fact, that was probably why everybody got along so well; nobody had the faintest idea what anybody else was saying.

'It'd be good if we could get this on the DVD. Maybe this one and the six on our main set list.' She was thinking out loud. 'I wonder whether we can ask Eamonn for a longer slot . . .'

'Good idea.' Ellie nodded, trying out an alternative riff.

Zoë trailed off, smiling. Ellie never got involved in the planning. Brilliant harmonies and guitar solos were her fortes; turning up on time and helping with logistics were not.

'Oh,' she said, remembering something else. 'I looked up that band Shannon mentioned – Tepid what's-it. It looks like they're really big in the States.'

'Really?' Ellie looked up, finally pulling herself away from the strings. 'How big?'

'*Big*. Google them.'

'Wow.' Ellie's eyes were wild with hope and unfulfilled dreams. She didn't care about the details; details were for somebody else to deal with – usually Zoë. She only cared about the dream. For Ellie, it was just a matter of time before a major record deal landed in their lap.

Zoë watched as she began to pluck at the strings, improvising. They had so much in common, in a musical sense. They both loved to play, to sing, to listen, to get swept up in its powerful, intricate harmonies . . . But what they took from it was very different.

Ellie's world was filled with a select group of people, namely Zoë, Shannon, Kate and Sam. She only welcomed those privileged few, not caring what anybody else heard or didn't hear. Zoë, on the other hand, felt claustrophobic in that world; she needed an outlet. Having created the music, she had to share it. The more people it reached, the quicker it flowed from her and the better she felt.

31

Zoë knew she had changed since the early days. She couldn't pretend that the dainty office shoes and starched suit jacket were the only consequences of her lifestyle. Her choice of career path had had an impact on who she was and she resented that impact. She didn't like having to answer to Brian, having to fit in with the other po-faced clones, having to skulk around pretending to run errands . . . She didn't like living a lie. But at the same time, she knew that the changes had made her stronger.

Every day, the resentment inside Zoë piled up a little more. The day job, her parents and even some of her closest friends seemed to be doing their utmost to bring her in line. But Zoë was determined to escape. And the exit route, which seemed to be looking clearer every time she gazed at it, was the success of the band.

'Awesome,' she said, as they found themselves back on the chorus. 'That works. We'll try that next week.'

'Let's.' Ellie nodded, still playing. She got so wrapped up in the music; sometimes it was hard to pull her out.

Zoë looked at the clock on the wall and felt something plummet inside her. 'Shit! Is that right?'

Ellie glanced at her bare wrist as though half-hoping to find a watch there. 'Um . . .'

'Bollocks,' Zoë muttered, having found her phone and confirmed that the time was indeed nearly half-past two.

She rammed her guitar into its case, yanked her coat on and stuffed her notebook and pencil into one of the pockets. Ellie watched her with a perplexed expression.

'Gotta go!' Zoë said, flinging herself at her friend in a hasty farewell gesture. 'See ya!'

Ellie was shaking her head as she leapt towards the door. 'Honestly, Zoë . . . You'll give yourself a hernia.'

Zoë laughed and rushed out.

Brian was standing at her desk when she got back, rubbing a palm over the top of his shiny head.

'Ah, there you are.' He caught her eye, glancing down at her heaving chest and the guitar-shaped coat in her hand.

Zoë eased herself into her seat and waited for the inevitable reprimand. Her boss looked very serious.

'I've been looking through your British Trust figures,' he said, placing a print-out of her summary on the desk and wheezing a little. 'Now, what do you see here?'

Zoë frowned. 'Er, my summary?'

He pointed a stubby finger at the revenue line. '*Here*,' he said, looking at her.

'Um . . . Four million, one hundred and sixty-two thousand, two hundred and eighty-five pounds, fifty-five pence?'

Brian cleared his throat. 'Anything . . . strike you as odd?'

Zoë shrugged as politely as she could. 'Is it a prime number?'

Brian closed his eyes briefly and shook his head. 'It ends in five, Zoë, so no.'

She nodded slowly, pretending to give a shit. There was nothing odd about the figure, as far as she could tell, but then Brian had evidently spent longer thinking about the matter than she had.

Finally, he enlightened her.

'Decimal points, Zoë! Pennies! We don't need two d.p. in the summary, do we?'

Decimal points, she thought, pointing a trigger-finger at her boss and faking a smile as he started to bang on about RAP and obvious mistakes. *Decimal points*. This was what her life had come to.

5

'Okay, so red for record, black for stop, and this slider thing does the zoom. Got it.'

'No, you don't need to press the black at all. Just use the red for record, then it's the same button for stop.'

Zoë glanced warily at Shannon as they ran her friend through the controls one more time. It didn't bode well.

'Drinks, girls?' the towering landlord called out from behind the bar.

At six foot ten, Eamonn Gallagher was, according to some websites, officially a giant. After thirty years' serving pints in a bar of normal proportions, he had developed a permanent stoop, which, along with the gout-inflicted limp and the gnarled fingers, scarred from too many closing-time brawls, gave quite a fearsome first impression. But the girls were long past first impressions. Shannon's local had become something of a second home in the last year and they all knew Eamonn on first-pint-on-the-house terms.

'Can you get me a coupla beers?' yelled Shannon, above the din. The place was noisier than usual, thanks to a large group of half-naked Antipodeans celebrating Australia Day in the corner.

Zoë wasn't sure it was wise to ply the cameraman with drink before he'd even worked out how to operate the device, but there was nothing she could do. Sometimes, no matter how terrifying it seemed, she just had to put her trust in Shannon.

'Nothing for you, Zola?' called the landlord as she passed the bar. He always called her that, after Zola Budd, the Olympic athlete from the eighties. He claimed that Zoë rushed around at the rate of the record-breaking runner.

'No, thanks!' Living up to her name, she pushed through the crowds to the backstage door. They were due on stage in twenty minutes.

Gigs at The Mad Cow were different from all the others. At most gigs, the girls were performing for a reason: because their manager wanted them to, because a certain A&R rep was supposed to be turning up, because the promoter was well-connected . . . Every stage was a potential stepping stone onto a bigger and higher one. But The Mad Cow was no stepping stone. They played here for one reason. Well, two if you counted the free drinks.

Six years ago – for reasons most likely associated with Shannon's plunging cleavage – the landlord had granted them a Saturday night slot, when the band had been barely more than four girls with instruments and a few ideas for songs. They had played out of time, forgotten their set list, stood around discussing what to play next . . . It had been too soon for them to perform in public. But Eamonn had allowed them to see out the set and since then, Dirty Money had gone from strength to strength, outgrowing pub gigs like The Mad Cow. They were at a level where they could play every night if they wanted, anywhere on the London circuit – with the recent exception of the Camden House. Now a slick, well-oiled rock machine, they turned down many of the gigs they were offered – but never The Mad Cow.

'So,' said Zoë, squeezing through the narrow door of the closet that served as their dressing room. Kate was sitting on the upturned mop bucket, tuning her bass. 'Are we playing "Out of Air"?'

Kate shrugged anxiously. She raised the instrument to her ear and repeatedly plucked at her E-string. 'New songs are always a bit of a gamble . . .'

Zoë needn't have asked; she already knew how Kate felt. Kate was all about preparation, rehearsal and control. It wasn't that she didn't enjoy spontaneity; she got a kick out of being on stage just like everyone else. She just liked to *prepare* for the kick. She wanted every performance to be perfect.

'I think we should do it,' Zoë declared.

Kate nodded blankly. 'Okay.'

Zoë squatted down next to the upturned bucket. 'What's up? Is it what's-his-face?'

'Tarquin?' Kate turned her head, finally making eye contact. 'No, I'm totally over him.'

Zoë tried not to baulk at the name. Really, it was no wonder she'd been having problems. 'So what is it?'

Kate exhaled shakily. 'It's work. My boss.' She looked into Zoë's eyes. 'Oh, it's everything.'

Zoë shifted her weight, her knees beginning to ache. Kate was training to become an actuary. Nobody knew exactly what that meant, except that it was something to do with measuring risk – something Kate was ideally suited to – and that the qualification process culminated in a series of mind-blowingly difficult exams that only about twenty per cent of applicants passed. The only other thing Zoë knew about the profession was that it ranked even higher than auditing in the tedium stakes, which was saying something.

'Is the revision getting you down?'

Kate looked up at her through wisps of fine blonde hair. 'No, it's not that.' She smiled ironically. 'In fact, that's the only thing that's going well. I'm good at exams. It's the job I can't do.'

Zoë shook her head. 'Don't be silly,' she chided. Kate was smart and hard-working. Although Zoë had never seen her in a work context, she could imagine her being good at her role. What was lacking, however, was self-confidence. 'What can't you do?'

'They want me to stand up and *present!*'

Zoë looked at her. 'What d'you mean, present? Like, in a meeting?'

'Yes!' cried Kate, highly distressed. 'My boss is this high-flying guy called Mark and he's insisting I do it, but I can't! I just can't!'

Rocking onto the balls of her feet, her knees in new leagues of agony, Zoë reached for Kate's hand. 'How many people?' she asked.

'Four or five – maybe six. They want me to stand up in front of clients.'

Zoë looked at her. 'Kate, you're about to go on stage in front of two hundred sweaty, jeering louts. Why are you worried about a couple of clients?'

Kate baulked as though she couldn't believe Zoë was making the comparison. 'That's totally different! Out there, I'm just playing an instrument. I can hide behind my bass. It's impossible not to look good with a bass. You just rock up, play the notes and walk out. There's no talking or answering questions . . .'

Try being lead singer, thought Zoë. Working the crowds was the most thrilling part of her role, but it was also fucking terrifying.

'I could never do what you do,' said Kate, as if reading her mind. 'I wish I could, but I'm just not *like* that.'

Unable to feel her legs any more, Zoë pushed herself up from the floor and squeezed Kate's shoulder.

'Look,' she said, looking down at her friend. 'We've all got things we don't like about ourselves.' She hesitated for a moment, thinking about her own cowardice. She was too weak to even talk to her own family about her ambitions. 'You've just got to live with them. And to be honest, most people wouldn't even notice your flaws.'

Kate looked up with a grateful smile.

'Hey, guys!' Shannon bounded through the door, her mate in tow with the camcorder haphazardly slung over his shoulder. 'Say something for the camera!'

Zoë smiled wearily. 'Hi.'

Kate raised a shaky hand.

The cameraman gave up on them and swivelled back to Shannon, who was tipping back the remains of her pint. She swallowed, then looked around. 'Where's Ellie?'

Zoë looked at her watch. 'Good point.' The camcorder spun back to her. 'She's cutting it fine.'

'Probably gazing at the Hackney skyline with Mr Pot-head,' said Shannon. The recording equipment swooped back across the room.

As Shannon's mate sought out the next piece of footage, the door swung open again and Ellie drifted in.

'Hi, guys!'

'Ellie, this is Gavin,' Shannon explained, as the camcorder was pushed into her face.

There was a bang on the door. 'When you're ready, girls!' It was Eamonn's cousin, the promoter.

Zoë tried to hurry the group along, shooing Gavin back into the crowd and hoping that Ellie's missed sound-check wasn't going to matter. There had only been one gig where they'd had to stop playing to ask the sound engineer to turn on her amp. It wasn't that Ellie didn't care about the gigs; she was as desperate as everyone else to make a success of the band. She just couldn't get the hang of time management.

With a quick nod, Zoë led them out from the darkness. After several hundred performances together, they knew the routine. She walked to the centre spot, adjusting her guitar strap as the noise rose up from the room around them.

'Get ya kit off!'

'Girl-band!'

'Tits out!'

One of the Australian revellers in the corner stood up and lobbed a beer-soaked flag at the stage, before toppling sideways and being removed from the premises in the crook of Eamonn's arm.

Zoë looked round at the girls, smiling with anticipation. They were used to this. With an all-female cast, they had to work doubly hard to prove themselves, particularly in a place like The Mad Cow.

They kicked off with their rockiest number, 'Delirious', Zoë pouring her heart into it, watching as the hecklers slowly lost their nerve. A rush of pure, concentrated emotion coursed through her. It was moments like this that Zoë lived for. Offstage, she had an ordinary existence, but on stage, she became extraordinary. It no longer mattered who was listening. It didn't even matter if nobody was listening. She was surrounded by and absorbed in the music, feeling more alive than she could ever feel in the day. No stomach-churning fairground ride, no skydiving trip, no surround-sound cinema experience could ever match the exhilaration she felt as she emptied her lungs into that microphone.

By the third song, the doubters were few and far between, but Zoë knew they'd be silenced by what was to come. Ellie's guitar solo had that effect. Complete strangers had been known to throw themselves onto the stage, likening her nimble fingers to those of the masters, Jimmy Page and Jimi Hendrix. It was at times like this, when Ellie disappeared into a frenzy of movement and sound, drowning them in the beauty of her improvised tune, that the band came into its own.

A few weeks ago, they had featured on an obscure page of the Kerrang! website thanks to Shannon's brief relationship with the online editor. The review summed up their sound perfectly: *Loud and hypnotic, with an edgy disco beat beneath sweet, twisted lyrics, Dirty Money combine elements of The Strokes and New Order with frothy but powerful feminine vocals.* When she sang, she could see those words dancing in front of her eyes: Loud. Edgy. Powerful. That was Dirty Money. They were pop, but as another, less renowned reviewer had once put it, 'more Killers than Kylie'.

'That was amazing!' yelled Gavin, beating his way through the crowds afterwards, still shouldering the camera.

Zoë thanked him quickly, her mind already on the bigger picture. 'Did you get it all?'

He frowned at her. 'What d'you mean, all?'

Zoë's throat tightened. 'All . . . the songs. The gig.'

Gavin stared gormlessly for a moment, his mouth hanging open a little. 'Oh my God . . . I didn't realise you wanted the whole thing. I just got – you know, the first one? Where the guys were doing that thing with the flag?'

Zoë closed her eyes, cursing herself for letting Shannon take responsibility for something so important. They *needed* this demo DVD.

It was only when she opened her eyes and spotted Shannon, suppressing a ridiculous smirk, that she realised that the joke was on her.

'Oh.' She smiled sheepishly. 'Very funny.'

6

'Dear, oh dear,' muttered Brian, hovering over Zoë's desk and grimly shaking his bald head.

Quickly navigating away from the band's MySpace page, Zoë looked up and forced a smile.

'What . . .' said Brian, bending down and scooping up a handful of papers from her desk, 'is this?'

'I think, um . . .' Zoë stammered. 'I think that's last year's audit for . . .'

'Clutter!' he screamed, triumphantly. '*That* is what this is.' He let the print-outs slither out of his hand and then, rather unhelpfully, picked off some random pages from other piles to make sure the paperwork was completely out of order.

'It's all organised in—'

'Ah!' he cried again, making sure most of the department could hear. '*Organised* clutter! Is that what it is?'

Zoë sighed quietly, watching as her boss picked off yet another sheet and put it down somewhere else. She knew what this was about. It wasn't just Brian trying to annoy her – although he was trying to annoy her. This was about the new rule that had just come into force across Chase Waterman.

Weeks earlier, the powers that be on the seventeenth floor had enlisted the help of some highly respected consultants, whose job it was to improve efficiency in the company. Following a lengthy period of consultation that included employee surveys and a series of experiments comparing staff productivity under different levels of ambient lighting, the troubleshooters had come to the revolutionary conclusion that auditors worked most efficiently whilst sitting in upright chairs, in silence, in natural light. But the beady-eyed consultants had also spotted another spectacular insight: *The best auditors tended to have clear desks.* It was this little gem that formed the seed of a new way of thinking at Chase Waterman PLC. They called it, imaginatively, the *clear desk policy.*

'Sorry,' Zoë said wearily. 'It's just, I like having everything to hand. It's all in piles. I know where everything . . .'

Brian silenced her with a raised eyebrow. 'ODOM,' he said.

'Sorry?'

'Odom,' he said again. 'ODOM. An Organised Desk is an Organised Mind.'

'Oh, right.' Zoë nodded.

'Let's have it clear by the morning.'

Zoë let her eyes glaze over as her boss strode off to persecute some other employee. She stayed like this for several seconds, waiting for the irritation to pass before she got back to pretending to work.

'There's no need for paper these days, anyway,' the weasel next to her piped up. 'You can just do everything electronically.'

Zoë's frustration ramped up a notch as her neighbour's spiky hair poked into view.

'Well, maybe I just like having piles of paper,' she said, wearily.

She jiggled her mouse to see the time. Thankfully, it was twelve minutes to six.

'What's that?' asked Eric.

Zoë quickly minimised the browser, annoyed that the oily-haired rodent had caught her out.

'The GM audit,' she replied in a monotone.

'No, not that. The website.' He wheeled himself up to her screen.

It was no good, she thought. He had seen it. And with a voice as loud as his, it was likely that most of the office would be seeing it if she didn't shut him up soon.

'It's just a band,' she shrugged, briefly showing him the page. Nobody at Chase Waterman knew about Dirty Money. It was her secret – her other life. Her colleagues wouldn't understand if she tried to explain how it felt to strut onto the stage – to belt out her songs to a roomful of strangers.

'Hold on! Go back.'

Reluctantly, she returned to the page.

Eric let out a low-pitched whistle. 'Fuck me!'

Zoë cringed.

'It's a girl-band!' Eric went on. He was practically salivating. Zoë could feel her breathing become shallow as she waited for the penny to drop.

'Look at – oh my God!' He slapped the desk with his palm. 'That's you!'

A couple of heads turned. Zoë rolled her eyes in an attempt to discredit his cry.

'You're in a girl-band!' Eric laughed, peering at the screen and noting the name. 'Dirty Money? Kinky, eh. What d'you sing? Are you like the Spice Girls? "Spice Up Your Life . . ."'

He continued to squawk, thrusting his shoulders left and right. '"Who Do You Think You Are . . ." Which one are you? Posh? Sporty?'

Eric was not to know this, but for a serious musician, there was nothing more insulting than being called a boy- or girl-band. There were key differences between the likes of U2 and, say, Westlife, the principle one being that U2 was comprised of people who could play instruments and sing, whereas most of the boy-band magic happened in the recording studio with session musicians and a fancy mixing desk. Being likened to a member of the Spice Girls was, for Zoë, a little bit like Michelangelo being called a plasterer.

'We're not a *girl-band*,' she spat, closing the browser and angrily shutting everything down. It felt as though a fuse had snapped inside her.

Eric let out a low *oooh*, gliding back to his desk and muttering something about Scary Spice under his breath.

Zoë marched over to the nearest recycling station and tugged it towards her desk, aware of several pairs of eyes nervously tracking her movements. In one swift action, she swept all the paperwork into the bin and then kicked it back into the gangway. She didn't care what her colleagues thought. They were a bunch of ladder-climbing executives whose idea of exciting was wearing a brightly-coloured Donald Duck tie to work. She would show them, one day. She'd show them what it was to succeed.

'A glass of wine,' she said firmly. 'A large one.'

'Good day?' asked her sister, grinning as she paid for the drinks.

They were perched on high, space-age stools, surrounded by well-cut suits and polished brogues in one of the many identical bars around St Paul's. Unfortunately for Zoë and Tamsin, their places of work were at opposite ends of the Square Mile, a district that accounted for more than ten per cent of the capital's GDP and a good proportion of its spending too – as was evident by the hundred-pound round that was going on beside them.

'It wasn't the best,' Zoë admitted, her mouth already watering as she drew the large, dewy glass towards her.

She didn't feel as furious as she had half an hour ago. The walk had done her good. Listening to angry music always calmed her down.

'Anything in particular?'

Zoë took her first sip. She thought about telling Tam about the incident with Eric and the MySpace page, but decided against it. On reflection, her reaction to the little imp's taunting seemed a little melodramatic. 'Just the usual.'

A collective cheer rose up from the men on their right and the girls shifted sideways on their stools. Padded shoulders jostling for space at the bar, the young men assembled themselves in front of a long line of pints, each one accompanied by a double shot of a viscous, brown liquid.

'Nothing's changed,' Tamsin remarked, rolling her eyes.

Zoë wasn't sure whether her sister was referring to the city boys or her attitude towards her career. Tam had never really understood Zoë's take on life. She was sweet and supportive, always there for her little sister, but the fact remained, she couldn't see why anyone would want more than a stable, well-paying job and a flat with a well-equipped kitchen.

'It was in here that I first met Jonathan,' Tam went on, clearing up the doubt. Zoë smiled at the thought of her sweet, sensible sister falling prey to the slick young predators in here tonight.

'Did he look something like that?' she asked, nodding towards the beer-drinkers, who were wandering the bar, bleary-eyed, wearing the shot glasses on their heads like small Russian hats.

'They all look like that when they get together,' Tam said, shaking her head. 'Herd instinct.'

Zoë laughed. 'Speaking of herds, how is life in the "second six" at the Inn?'

Tamsin took a large sip with closed eyes. 'Fairly similar to the first six, to be honest. I still get mistaken for the secretary, still get told off for walking on the wrong bit of grass, still get no respect from anyone else in the courtroom.'

'Oh dear.' Zoë cringed, thanking fate yet again for her abysmal A-level grades. The Inns of Court actually made Chase Waterman seem like a dynamic, forward-thinking place to work.

'I guess things have improved a little,' Tamsin conceded. 'I was invited to the Spring Croquet Tournament the other day, and I'm actually on my feet in the courtroom.'

'Wow. Really?' Zoë raised her eyebrows, feeling a rush of pride tinged with just a small hint of envy – about the courtroom, not the croquet. Whilst she knew she could never sit in those stuffy wooden halls, wearing that wig and ridiculous gown, it would still be an incredible thing to know that your words, in some cases, made the difference between freedom and imprisonment.

'Well, yes . . . Although typically, when the judge acquits our defendant he makes it very clear that he's acquitting him for reasons *other* than those outlined in my defence. I don't think they like the idea of a woman having influence at the bar.'

Zoë smiled. 'It's like being a musician. A few weeks ago I got ordered to leave the backstage area because it was "artists only". I tried to explain that I *was* the artist, but this guy was having none of it. He thought I was some dolled-up groupie.'

Tamsin smiled. 'How are things with the band?'

Zoë shrugged. It was the same every time someone asked. She always wanted to break some news, tell them that Dirty Money had been signed, that they were releasing an album, supporting some well-known act . . . But there was never any news. Not proper news, anyway.

'We approached a few labels a while ago, but haven't heard back. Oh—' Zoë smiled sardonically, realising that there was in fact some news – bad news. 'And our manager walked out on us.'

'Jake?'

Zoë nodded.

'He wasn't much good anyway, was he?'

'Well, no . . .' Zoë sighed. 'It's the booking agent we'll miss, really. But hey, we've had some interest from someone else – some American dude.'

Tamsin drew her head back, looking impressed. 'Sounds promising.'

'We'll see.' Zoë smiled. Her sister was trying to show an interest. She always did. She really wanted to help, but the truth was, she had never grasped her little sister's obsession with the band. She knew what it was to be driven; that was an attribute they shared. But she couldn't grasp the idea of public endorsement,

46

of eminence . . . of *fame*. There. She had used the dirty word. Zoë wanted more than the monthly salary and the well-equipped kitchen. She wanted recognition for the music she made.

Was that so wrong? Was it bad, her desire to see positive reviews in the *NME*? To fill an arena with fans? To hear people scream the lyrics to her songs? Her family seemed to think so. Rock music was not an acceptable pursuit in the Kidd family. Classical music was another matter. Had Zoë continued with violin lessons, practising her arpeggios and working her way through the ranks of the county youth orchestra, *then* they'd be proud. Had it been Mozart and Haydn blasting from her bedroom throughout her teenage years instead of Nirvana and Pearl Jam, then they might talk about her achievements. But perhaps it was better that they remained silent. In the words of one seventies pop duo, *some things were better left unsaid*.

'Hey,' Zoë looked at her sister, remembering something. 'Did you know Dad nearly played rugby for England?'

Tamsin spluttered, eventually swallowing her mouthful of wine and frowning. 'What?'

'Back in the eighties. He got accepted onto the squad. I think he turned it down for a place in chambers.'

'I didn't know, no.' Tamsin's brow remained furrowed. 'That doesn't surprise me, though. I knew he was good. I guess he just didn't want to take the risk. How did you find that out, anyway?'

'I heard him talk about it at your . . .' Zoë faltered. 'Your dinner thing.' She hadn't meant to bring that up.

'Oh yeah. What happened to you that night? I couldn't find you during drinks.'

Zoë hesitated, not sure whether to tell her sister the truth. Tamsin knew how important the band was to her. She would understand about the rehearsal and the gig and the demo DVD . . . But the question was: would she see it as more important than her own celebratory dinner? *Was* it more important than

47

the dinner that signified Tamsin's coming of age in the legal world?

'I . . .' Zoë tried to decide. She kept getting close to coming out with the truth, then chickening out. 'I . . .'

She was rescued by the sound of her phone. Quickly, she pulled it out of her bag.

'Hiiiiii,' came an unfamiliar, nasal drawl. 'Is that one of the lovely young ladies from Dirty Money?'

'Yes,' she replied, quickly lowering the wine glass from her lips and trying to shield the mouthpiece from the noise. 'This is Zoë.'

'Zoë, hiiiiii,' said the man. He sounded like a crank caller – possibly a fan from one of their less salubrious gigs. 'This is Louis Castle.'

Zoë's grip tightened on the phone. She could feel her heart rate quicken inside her chest. This was the man who managed Tepid Foot Hold's career. The man who had helped Toby Fox win an Ivor Novello.

'Hi!' she squeaked breathlessly.

'Just thought I'd drop you a line, y'know, t'say hi. I gat your demo DVD.'

'Right.' Zoë swallowed.

'And I kinda like it. Or at least, I like the music. The DVD's not gonna win any awards, is it?'

'No. Um . . . Right.' Zoë couldn't speak properly. She wanted to apologise for the poor quality of the recording, to explain that they were a lot better in the flesh than the footage implied . . . But her mind was swamped by the single question: did he like the music *enough*?

'So, I'm thinkin',' said the man, 'if you girls are up for it, we should meet up. Chat a little. Talk about a management contract.'

There was a pause, and Zoë realised she was nodding into the phone. 'Right,' she muttered, shell-shocked. Then she pulled herself together. 'Yes, great. Let's!'

Tamsin was looking at her strangely when she got off the phone.

'Is everything all right?'

Zoë forced herself to take a breath, then exhaled, slowly.

'I think,' she said eventually, to her baffled-looking sister. 'I think Louis Castle might want to take us on.'

7

'Beer for you . . . Beer for me . . . Whisky for Ellie, if she ever turns up . . .' Shannon slid the drinks across the table. 'Why're you on orange juice, Kate? What's up? It's not right to celebrate without a proper drink.'

Zoë took her pint and shifted sideways, beginning to realise the scale of the task ahead. It was becoming apparent that their drummer's feet had long since left the ground and it was going to be all they could do to keep her at the current altitude, let alone bring her back down.

'Strictly speaking,' she said, saving Kate from her explanation, 'we're not celebrating. There's nothing to celebrate yet.'

Shannon let out an exasperated sigh. 'Oh, party-pooper! We're just about to get taken on by the guy who put Tepid Foot Hold on the global rock map – who, by the way, have just had their latest album go platinum. That's reason to celebrate, if you ask me!'

Kate glanced anxiously at Zoë. 'We haven't even met the guy yet.'

'I have,' Shannon retorted.

'Yeah, after about twelve beers at the end of a long night.' Kate started manically stirring her orange juice. 'We haven't. He hasn't met *us*. He might not like us.'

'Of course he likes us!' cried Shannon, lowering her pint with such panache that the head sloshed all over the table. 'I mean . . .

50

Why wouldn't he?' On seeing the other girls' gazes drift upwards, Shannon looked round. 'Oh, hi!' She pushed the whisky towards Ellie as she drifted over.

Zoë sipped her beer as their drummer prattled on about other artists she intended to meet when they were up there with the biggest bands in the world.

'. . . the latest single by The Cheats. Have you heard it? It's *gorgeous*. I'm totally in love with the lead singer.' Shannon tipped back some beer. 'You know, Niall King?' she prompted, looking around briefly but not waiting for a response. 'He's Irish. Has the most amazing voice. Honestly, you *have* to hear him sing. Wouldn't it be awesome if we got signed by the same label?'

Zoë exchanged another worried look with Kate. This was getting ridiculous. They hadn't even got a manager yet.

'I wonder which label they're on . . . Ooh!' Shannon suddenly ducked under the table, emerging with her phone.

The others sipped their drinks while Shannon alternately fiddled and swore at her handset.

'No word from the labels, then?' Kate asked quietly.

'Not yet.'

Zoë felt guilty. She knew that the second word was super-fluous. Their dirty money campaign had clearly failed. If any of the label reps had been remotely interested, they would have called by now. The bastards. They'd probably pocketed the money and thrown the CD in the bin, along with all the others. Or worse . . . Zoë thought unhappily about the other prospect: they had listened to the CD and rejected it.

Sitting here now, waiting and hoping to get taken on by Louis hot-shot Castle, Zoë was beginning to realise that their little stunt might have actually set them back. If the heads of the labels had already turned them down, then no amount of schmoozing on Louis Castle's part would convince them to change their minds.

'Listen,' said Zoë, deciding to put the whole expensive operation behind them. 'I think, when we meet this guy, we should show him what we're all about.'

'Definitely,' agreed Shannon, looking up from her phone.

Zoë wondered whether she actually knew what she meant. 'He's seen us on stage,' she said, 'and he knows our music, but he doesn't know us. He doesn't know what we're capable of *between* gigs.'

Shannon was nodding, her brow creased in earnest.

'Our promotional capabilities,' Zoë explained. 'The way we can generate a buzz. The massive fan base we've built up.'

To say 'we' was generous, thought Zoë, given that she always did most of the work, but it was important that they felt like a team.

'Yeah!' Shannon agreed. 'We should show him what we can do!'

Kate winced. 'Please, not the Brent Cross gig . . . Don't tell him about that.'

Zoë baulked at the thought. A few months ago, they had been asked to perform a few songs during late-night shopping in the run-up to Christmas. It was the sort of gig they'd usually turn down, but the fee had been good and the promoter had guilt-tripped them into playing by telling them about all the orphans around the world who would benefit from the proceeds.

Their music had proved surprisingly popular with the shoppers and during their break, Shannon and Zoë had hatched a plan to make their final song especially memorable. At the time, it had seemed like a fantastic idea for Zoë to take the escalator to the next floor of the shopping centre, grab hold of one of the decorations that hung in the atrium and sing the next song whilst swinging, Tarzan-style, across the stage in front of the other musicians.

The decoration had supported her for long enough to attract the attention of most of the onlookers and a couple of burly but fast-moving security guards, at which point Zoë had plummeted to the stage via Shannon's drum kit, her landing amplified by her radio microphone. Surprisingly, they hadn't been asked back to Brent Cross Shopping Centre.

'Maybe not that one,' Zoë conceded. 'But Manchester,' she said, referring to a gig that she still maintained had come about as a result of an administrative error. They'd been supporting one of the biggest indie acts in the Northwest and the promoter had referred to them all night as 'Thirsty Money', but they didn't need to explain that. 'And Chiana.'

Chiana was a live music venue in Soho whose owner Shannon had somehow talked into letting them play. When it had tran-spired that a couple of minor celebrities were drinking there, Zoë had managed to engineer a photo that revealed not just the inebriated celebrities but the whole of the Dirty Money setup, complete with promotional backdrop, which, following a mysteri-ous 'leak', had appeared in one of the trashy free newspapers the following day.

'It'll all help, won't it?'

'Um . . .' It was Kate. 'Can we make sure we only tell him about the good stuff?'

'Don't be so—'

Shannon trailed off. A man was swaggering across the bar towards them, dressed in a giant, red and brown flecked shirt that must have been made to measure – possibly out of a set of Persian curtains. His garish, gold-buckled belt was only visible from the girls' low vantage point, due to the flabby overhang.

'Hiiiiii,' he called in a manner that Zoë recognised instantly from the telephone call. He had the type of face that had prob-ably once been handsome: perfect white teeth and an overly warm smile, but it was difficult to tell with all the chins. 'How are my adorable rock goddesses?' He opened his hands to them like a preacher addressing a congregation.

Zoë couldn't help glancing at Kate, who stared back at her, wide-eyed.

'Good!' cried Shannon, when it became apparent that nobody else was going to reply.

'Good? Good! So, what can I get y'all?'

The ordering process took some time, mainly because every time one of the girls said the word 'bottle', the American would repeat it four or five times in various accents, then pretend to forget what the bottle was to contain.

'Not funny,' muttered Kate, as Louis Castle retreated to the bar, relaying the whole conversation to the barman in a booming voice.

'Give him a chance!' hissed Shannon.

'At least he's not trying to flirt,' Ellie pointed out. They all cringed at the reminder of their old manager's sleazy ways.

'I gat you a double,' he said, pushing a bucket-sized tumbler of Jack Daniels towards Ellie. 'And here's a vaardka for you, in case that OJ needs spicin' up.'

The girls took their drinks and watched the enormous man arrange himself at the table, siphoning off nearly half of his pint with his first sip.

'So,' he said, looking at each one in turn, his eyes glistening behind the rolls of fat. 'Are you ready for the big time?'

'Yeah!' replied Shannon immediately.

'Mmm,' added Ellie, presumably because Shannon had pinched her under the table.

'Are you ready to *make it*?'

Zoë closed her eyes. Perhaps these lines worked on artists in Los Angeles or wherever he came from, but they really didn't wash with her. 'Have you got any ideas about labels?' she asked.

Louis looked at her, eyebrows raised. 'Woah!' He looked around at the other girls, grinning manically. 'You're quick outta the blocks! I only just sat down!' He pointed to his half-finished pint. 'Gimme a chance!'

Shannon laughed along with him, prompting Ellie to do the same.

Zoë forced a smile too. 'Sorry. It's just . . . We've been together for a while now and—'

'Hey,' he interrupted. 'I know. You've been around a few years, hoping to get signed and now you just wanna grab that deal and run, huh? Yeah. I've seen that before.'

Reluctantly, Zoë nodded along with him. She had been about to explain that their manager had promised great things and never delivered, and that they didn't want to end up in the same situation again, but Louis Castle had already moved on.

Zoë sat back and let the conversation flow around her. The manager quickly got onto the subject of his stable of successful acts in the States and his plans for replicating such success over here. Ellie and Shannon lapped it up, gasping and cooing and clapping their hands like small children. Kate, like Zoë, was doing her best to look convinced.

'When you say, "package us up",' the bassist ventured, 'what exactly do you mean?'

Louis turned to her, grinning enigmatically from behind his many chins. 'I'll tell you . . . over the next drink!'

Once again, he returned with a bumper round.

'So,' the large man began, returning to his seat and sinking into his next pint. 'What I mean, is make you "sellable".' He drew quotation marks in the air. 'Like a brand. We need to make it obvious what you stand for.'

'You mean, like our image?' asked Shannon. 'What we wear and that?'

'Exaaaaactly,' Louis replied. 'And that includes getting you out of those old hooded tops and jeans!'

Shannon laughed. Zoë and Kate glanced at one another.

'Don't you think,' Zoë said carefully, not wanting to offend the man, 'that the image thing is only really important for manufactured pop music? Boy-bands, girl-bands . . .'

He smiled at her pityingly. 'Honey, *all* acts have an image.'

'But . . .' she persevered. She wanted to explain herself. 'I can see why the teeny-bop artists have a certain look . . . They have to appeal on the looks front, because there's nothing more to them. But say . . . Coldplay? Razorlight? U2? It's all about the music for them, isn't it?'

The four faces flicked round to Louis.

'Zoë,' he replied, still wearing the sympathetic smile. 'It's *all* about the image, whatever the act. Why d'you think Brandon Flowers wears those cute little military jackets? Now, nobody's telling me *he's* not talented!'

Zoë nodded, annoyed that the manager had found an exception to the rule. As the conversation moved on to the subject of touring and festivals and broadcasting rights, Zoë started to consider the possibility that Louis might be right. If he really had pushed so many acts into the American limelight, if he really had nurtured a band like Tepid Foot Hold from small-town act through to global superstardom, he had to know a thing or two about the music business, didn't he?

It was a few drinks later, all courtesy of the prospective manager, when the subject of representation finally came up.

'So, you think you're ready to jump on board?' asked Louis, smiling like a fat schoolboy.

'Yes!' cried Shannon and Ellie, who, by this point, looked ready to jump into bed with the man.

Even Kate had mellowed a little, Zoë noticed, watching her try not to smile at the manager's dubious charm.

He was like a holiday brochure, thought Zoë: slick, enticing and full of promise. But then, she thought, watching her drummer crash her glass against his and throw back her drink, he was a man whose job it was to place artists with record labels. His job was to 'sell the package'. Perhaps being like a brochure was no bad thing.

'Yes,' she said, looking across at Kate.

Eventually, the bass guitarist nodded.

'Great!' roared Louis, reaching out and grabbing one of Shannon's hands and one of Zoë's. 'That is *fantastic* news.'

After a period of mutual congratulation, they rose to their feet and stumbled out.

'I'll get a contract over to you this week,' he said, crushing each girl's hand in turn. 'Then we can talk about recording a few of your tracks properly.'

'Plopper – properly?' Zoë was more drunk than she'd thought.

'Yeah, you know. With a producer.'

'We already have a producer!' cried Shannon, presumably referring to the creepy architect who had wormed his way into her affections, wooing her with descriptions of his in-home recording suite and persuading the girls to use him to produce their demo CD.

'What, Sleazebag Simon?' asked Kate, grimacing.

The CD had turned out all right in the end, but Shannon had clearly blocked from her mind the memories of what she'd had to do in order to retrieve the disc from Sleazebag's house.

'Sleazebag Simon, eh?' Louis chuckled. 'You won't be needing him any more. You're in another league now, ladies!'

Staggering across the road like a malcoordinated, eight-legged animal, the girls relived some of the cheesier moments of the night, all scepticism somehow having dissolved and been replaced with childlike excitement.

'We're heading for the big time!'

'*Big time*!'

'We're on the *fast train* to success!'

Suddenly, Shannon broke loose from the pack.

'Louis!' she called, waving her arms above her head as though she was drowning. 'I forgot to ask!'

In the bleary distance, Louis tilted his head to one side, his breath forming clouds around his face.

'Can you get us signed to Polydor?' she yelled.

'Why's that then?' he replied.

'It's my destiny!' Shannon shrieked. 'I've got to meet Niall King from The Cheats!'

It was almost possible, from where they stood, to see Louis's eyes roll in their sockets. 'I'll see what I can do,' he called, raising a hand, turning on his heel and walking off.

8

Zoë closed her eyes and let her head roll back on the velvet seat, imagining she was somewhere else. The sweeping string section built to a climax with a piercing blast of high-pitched brass and in her mind, the heroine held up the prize in her hands, victorious. Classical music always sounded like a soundtrack to her.

She opened her eyes again as the volume dropped to a pizzi-cato murmur, watching the polo-necked conductor as his arms jerked up and down like those of a Thunderbird puppet. The music was incredible, she couldn't deny that. But it didn't seem like something to be admired in its own right. There was no stage presence – no element of *performance*.

'Bravo!' yelled her father through the clamorous applause. He and thousands of others clearly disagreed with Zoë's judgement. 'Splendid!'

Presumably deciding that the thunderous ovation was not quite sufficient for an encore, the conductor disappeared from the stage, only to return seconds later with a camp flourish to take another set of bows.

'Magnificent,' muttered Zoë's father, nodding approvingly as they started to shuffle along the row.

Zoë looked at Tamsin and smiled. Their annual winter concert was nominally a treat for the whole family, paid for by their parents in lieu of Christmas presents, but the appreciation was always somewhat one-sided.

'Shall we go for a drink?'

Zoë nodded, catching her sister's eye again. Clearly the glass of wine in the pleasant café overlooking the Thames was their mother's favourite part of the evening. It wasn't that she didn't enjoy concerts or that she was overly fond of wine; she just couldn't relate to classical music. Debussy and Wagner hadn't featured on the Croydon council estate where she had grown up.

'It's such a pity you don't play anymore,' said their father, handing his daughters their glasses of wine. 'You were both so talented.'

As a barrister, Rupert Kidd, QC was an expert in extracting the response he wanted. Zoë had discovered long ago that her father, though now in his fifties and approaching retirement, found her no match in an argument. She had developed a mechanism to suppress her instinct to rise to the bait.

'Tamsin still sings,' their mother pointed out. 'You're still a member of the Inns of Court Choir, aren't you, darling?'

Zoë looked at her sister, torn between vindication and irritation. It wasn't jealousy that she felt; more just the sting of injustice. Tam, in their parents' eyes, could do no wrong.

'But the orchestra . . .' Their father wore a pained expression, which landed, predictably, on Zoë. 'It's such a tremendous thing to be involved with. Didn't you enjoy being part of the first violin section?'

'Of course I enjoyed it,' she began, glancing at her sister, who was looking intently into her wine. Zoë knew where this was leading. It was a trick question. If she replied negatively, she would be implying that all those evenings spent practising for her violin exams and – more to the point – all the time and money her parents had lavished on her musical education had been for nothing. And that wasn't the case. She *had* enjoyed playing the violin and she knew that her classical training was, in part, what made her the singer-songwriter that she was today. But if she said yes, she would face more questions about why she didn't still play the violin, why she insisted on chasing her silly dreams with Dirty Money. She didn't want to go there tonight.

'But not enough to stick with it,' finished her father.

Zoë took another gulp, willing herself to remain calm – to swim away from the bait. 'I . . .'

She fought to explain herself in a way that somehow avoided the subject of the band. 'It didn't feel right, just playing the dots on the page.'

Her father frowned at her, looking mildly amused. 'You would have preferred to play something *other* than the dots on the page?'

Zoë hesitated, wishing she could fashion an argument as quickly as her father. *She* knew what she meant. Watching the violinists tonight, their identical movements dictated by the flick of the conductor's wrist, had reminded her why she'd given it all up. They were like foot soldiers in an army, following rules and taking instructions – never thinking for themselves. Zoë didn't want to be part of an army. She wanted to fight her own battles.

'I'd rather have a chance to express myself,' she said, realising that she was sailing dangerously close to the wind. 'But I guess Tam still enjoys her music. Tam, d'you do concerts with the Inns of Court Choir?'

Without hesitation, Tamsin took up the mantle, sharing news of upcoming performances and swiftly moving on to the subject of her bumbling choirmaster and then the Inns of Court dog, Monty. That was why she made a good barrister, thought Zoë as she sank into her glass of wine with a grateful smile.

Conversation meandered through Tamsin's court cases, then on to Zoë's work, at which point people's eyes started glazing over. Try as her parents might, they couldn't show genuine interest in the inner workings of Chase Waterman Plc., no matter how pleased they were that she'd taken the role. There really was nothing to get excited about when it came to balance sheets and write-downs.

Zoë's father emptied the last few droplets of wine from the bottle as his wife rummaged in her handbag.

'There you go,' she said, handing Zoë a small plastic parcel.

Zoë unwrapped it and smiled. The label on the jam jar had faded, but the contents were still intact. There were probably over two hundred plectrums in total, collected by the members of Dirty Money throughout their university years. They came from all over: Gigs, friends, festivals . . . Some were freebies, some had been bought, some borrowed and never returned. Zoë turned the jar round in her hand, feeling suddenly emotional as the memories came hurtling back.

'Have you got my . . .' Zoë glanced under the table and then looked at her mum, frowning. 'Guitar?'

An awkward glance passed between her parents.

'Mum?'

'Well . . . no. I'm afraid we gave it to the charity shop.'

'Wh—' Zoë couldn't speak. She looked at her mother, then her father, then down at the table. This was no oversight on her parents' part. They hadn't accidentally put the guitar in the wrong pile. Zoë had explicitly asked them to keep it aside. They had thought about this and acted with the sole purpose of proving a point.

'We assumed you wouldn't mind,' said her father, raising his eyebrows as though nothing was amiss.

'You hadn't used it in years,' her mother added.

Zoë could feel her breathing quicken. She felt angry and hurt and sad all at once.

'I loved that guitar!' she cried, unable to keep the wobble from her voice.

'Yes, um . . .' Her father looked around the restaurant. 'Don't make a fuss, now.'

'You haven't even *seen* it in years,' her mother went on.

Zoë's chest was heaving, her bottom lip quivering ominously.

'That's not the point,' she managed, as the pressure built up behind her eyes.

They all knew what the point was. It wasn't anything to do with how much or how little she used that guitar. The point was one they'd been avoiding for years – the point that her parents refused to accept her for who she really was.

They saw her in a particular light – the light in which they *wanted* to see their daughter. They saw the successful young professional, a high-flying financier. They turned a blind eye to the traits they didn't like – or worse, tried to stamp them out. They detested her dogged resolve to take an alternative path. *That* was the point here, although Zoë couldn't say it because tears were choking her throat.

'You're getting all het up over nothing,' chided her mother, pushing a tissue in front of her.

Zoë blew her nose and dabbed at her eyes, determined to regain her composure – to not let them win.

'I wanted to keep that guitar,' she explained, her voice strengthening with every word. 'The band's going well.' She sniffed. 'I know you don't like that idea, but it's the truth. And you know . . . One day, I might want to look back and say, *that was the first guitar I ever played.*'

Her parents exchanged a dubious look but said nothing. Their doubt spurred Zoë on.

'We've got a new manager – a proper one. He's from the States and he looks after a lot of top acts over there.'

'Well, that's good news.' Her father smiled primly.

Zoë's blood started to heat up again. She knew what her father was doing. He was playing along, saying all the things that a supportive parent would say, but not meaning any of it. His words were hollow. This was his way, and it frustrated the hell out of her.

'How many acts does he manage?' asked her mother.

Zoë bit her lip. The sudden display of interest in her band was pathetic. It was all false. She wanted to scream and walk out on them, but she knew that they'd claim that as a victory so she stayed put.

'Lots,' she replied, preparing to recall some big-name Blast Management acts.

Her father started doing up the buttons on his coat, his expression clearly designed to imply concern about her response.

'What?' demanded Zoë. 'What's that look for?' She knew, deep down, that she should have just said her goodbyes, kissed her parents and thanked them for a lovely night.

'Well, I suppose *some* of his acts must become successful . . .'

A nasty feeling crept over Zoë, not just because her parents were playing games with her – implying that Louis took on hundreds of artists, of which only a handful got anywhere near the charts – but because she knew that they were probably right. Dirty Money *was* just one of thousands, maybe millions, of bands in the world that were fighting for attention from the masses. Even Louis Castle couldn't guarantee any sort of success.

For a moment, Zoë stood there, clutching the jar of plectrums and trying to formulate a smart response. Then she realised that nothing she could think of would outwit her father, so she gave up and forced herself to smile through the tears.

'Great concert tonight,' she said, kissing her dad on the cheek.

If he was surprised at the turnaround, he didn't show it. 'Lovely to see you too.'

Zoë hugged her mother, who gave her a guilty, awkward smile, then turned to her sister and buried her face in Tam's collar. She knew that Tam was on her side, even though she didn't fully understand what Zoë was trying to achieve. She knew what it was to be wrongly convicted.

Before the tears could well up again, Zoë raised a hand and

stepped out onto the South Bank, walking quickly, the cold wind bringing fresh tears to her eyes. She loved her parents, she really did. They were the sort of parents who had always tried to be 'right behind you, whatever you choose to do'. But they weren't. They couldn't help it. They were right behind Tamsin, because she was in the right place, but ever since Zoë had stepped out of line, they had resolutely failed to follow.

Her father's last dig was still ringing in her ears. He knew her so well; he knew exactly how to piss her off. He was a professional when it came to messing with people's minds – especially hers. Only a few hours after getting off the phone to Kate and agreeing to sign Louis's contract as soon as possible, here she was, doubting her whole future with the band.

The orange glow of the Houses of Parliament shone back off the surface of the Thames, Big Ben's face shining like a lighthouse at one end. Zoë stopped and pulled out her phone. There was something her father *didn't* know about her. All the years of playing in Dirty Money had created something inside her that even Rupert Kidd, QC wasn't aware of: her resilience. He was underestimating her.

It was late, but Zoë didn't care. In another industry, like auditing, nobody would call their manager at ten fifteen on a Wednesday night. But this was the music business. And this was important.

'Yeah?'

Clearly Louis hadn't added her number to his phone, thought Zoë, feeling slightly embarrassed as the thumping background beat pounded into her earpiece. Maybe Louis was busy signing another act. She hesitated for a second, then cast her doubts aside.

'Louis, it's Zoë. From Dirty Money.'

'Hiiiiii!' he yelled. 'How's it goin'?' There was a grunting noise that implied Louis was levering his body into an upright position.

'Not bad. Um . . .' Zoë faltered again, wondering whether this was in fact an entirely inappropriate thing to do. Then for a second time, she forced herself to go on. 'I just wanted to ask. How many acts have you got on your books?'

A loud 'phhhhhh' came down the line, temporarily drowning out the ambient hum. 'I guess, twenny? Maybe thirdy? I don't count them very often.' He laughed. 'Gin please, no ice,' he yelled.

'And how many of your artists are signed to labels?'

'Sung to Mabel? Who's Mabel?'

'How many of your acts are *signed*. You know,' she said, speaking loudly and slowly. 'Signed to a label.'

'Oh! Jeez. I dunno . . . about half, at the moment? A little more, maybe.' A rustling noise drowned everything out. 'Just a splash of tonic, thanks.'

Zoë nodded to herself, feeling a weight lift inside her. Half. That was a decent proportion. She wished she'd had such a statistic ten minutes ago.

'Why d'you ask?' cried the man, above the din. 'Not getting cold feet on me, are ya?' He laughed again.

'No,' Zoë replied. ''Course not. Just wondered.'

'Well, that's just as well,' said the manager, after a slurping noise and a smack of his lips. 'Because I got you lined up for making a demo track with Clive Berry next week!'

'Clive Berry?' Zoë repeated. She must have misheard. Clive Berry was a *name*. She had read about him in Q and the *NME*. He wasn't up there with Mark Ronson but he was definitely known in the industry. She had a feeling he'd produced the early tracks of bands like Suede and Placebo in the nineties.

'Clive Berry, yeah.'

'Cool,' she said, dumbstruck.

'Saturday,' he said, with another slurp. 'I'll bring the management contracts with me then, yeah?'

Zoë mumbled something, lost for words.

'See you there at nine a.m. Saturday, bright and early!' he yelled as the background noise swelled. 'It's Soho Studios, just off Tottenham Court Road.'

'Cool,' she said again, but she had a feeling Louis was no longer listening.

9

'Give the high-hat another tap,' said the producer, frowning earnestly at the myriad of dials and sliders before him. 'Mmm, that's better. Again?'

Zoë glanced across at Kate. They'd been in the studio since nine o'clock this morning and it was beginning to get dark.

'That's it,' declared the man, scratching his neatly-trimmed goatee.

'HALLELUJAH!' came the familiar sound of Shannon's voice, booming through one of the mikes.

Clive Berry gasped and swivelled back to the button marked Comms. 'Don't touch that!'

Zoë, Ellie and Kate, like meerkats, leapt up from their seats to see what Shannon had done wrong.

'WHAT, THE MIKE?' Shannon's voice boomed again.

'Yes!' cried the producer, irate. 'The mike that we've spent all afternoon positioning to give you the perfect sound . . . Don't touch it.'

Zoë was beginning to understand how the man made such impressive records. If he was this particular about the setup, she could only imagine what he was like with the mixing.

Finally, after the long-haired engineer had made the necessary adjustments to the microphone and skulked off again, Shannon was permitted to give it another go and the whole process started again.

Clive Berry was a man of few words. Or perhaps he just didn't have much to say to the members of Dirty Money. Zoë got the impression he wasn't particularly enjoying his day's work. Maybe he resented their manager for lumbering such novices on him for so many hours – or weeks, as it was looking likely to be. It was unbelievable how slowly and carefully everything had to happen.

Having spent most of the day squashed up behind the producer in the small, sterile booth, Zoë had had plenty of time to marvel at the pine-floored studio with its carpeted walls and faux-natural lighting. Expensive guitars stood on stands about the place and an array of gold discs hung at eye-level around the room.

Clive's fingers flitted about the gigantic control panel as though it were the simplest instrument in the world. Zoë was used to watching the engineers at gigs during sound-checks, and of course she'd seen Sleazebag Simon at work, but those mixing desks looked like Fisher Price toys in comparison. This setup looked like something from Starship Enterprise.

The door squeaked open and a rotund face poked round.

'How're we doing, guys?'

It was Louis.

Zoë, Ellie and Kate straightened up. The man, as of six hours ago, was now their manager. The demo recording was being made at his expense, so it didn't do to look bored or ungrateful.

'Getting there,' said Clive, without looking up.

'Mind if I . . .' Louis moved the rest of his sizeable self into the room and pulled up a chair next to Clive. Zoë sensed that the producer would have preferred to be left alone, but as the supplier in the relationship, he didn't have much say in the matter.

'OK, try that again,' Clive barked.

For what seemed like the hundredth time, Shannon bashed out the opening sequence of 'Sensible Lies', stopping at exactly the point Clive held up his hand.

'That's great. I think we've got it.' The producer nodded, playing something back in his headphones.

'WHADDAYA MEAN?' Shannon's voice filled the small room. 'WHAT ABOUT THE REST OF THE SONG?'

Clive looked at her through the glass. 'We'll loop it. You don't need to play the whole thing. Yup, we've got the ending too. You can come back this side.'

Shannon didn't move from her seat. She looked confused. Zoë glanced at Ellie, then at Kate. She too was surprised to hear that they wouldn't need to record the whole percussion track – that the hours spent positioning mikes and testing beats had all been for thirty seconds of capture – but that was clearly the way things worked.

'Maybe someone could go and get her?' suggested Louis, nodding his head at the crestfallen drummer, who was still on her stool, staring incredulously at Clive.

Zoë hopped off her seat and pushed through the double-sealed door.

'*Why aren't they doing the whole song?*' hissed Shannon as Zoë prised her away from her beloved kit. '*Idiots!*'

Zoë cringed at Kate through the glass. Clearly Shannon had forgotten that the studio was filled with microphones.

'It may seem idiotic,' Clive said calmly as they returned. 'But it gives a much cleaner beat.'

Shannon looked at her shoes, clearly not in the mood for apologising.

Suddenly, the tiny room became filled with the sound of the 'Sensible Lies' introduction. It was loud, throbbing and slightly hypnotic. The beat went on, and on, and on. There was something intriguing – addictive, almost – about hearing exactly the same bar, repeated over and over again. Zoë could feel herself being drawn in.

'Bass line?' Clive suggested, swivelling round.

Kate rose to her feet and reached for her guitar. Her hands were trembling, Zoë noticed.

There were further adjustments of microphones and appearances from the engineer, who crept in and out of the studio like a nocturnal mammal on a hunt for food. The headphones turned out to be too big for Kate's head, so the lank-haired young man had to improvise, fixing them around the bassist's forehead with a rubber band.

The first take was aborted when the rubber band snapped, pinging across the room and leaving the broken headphones to slither down onto Kate's guitar. The second take, performed with the engineer standing behind her, lightly clamping the headphones to her ears, was note-perfect.

'Nice,' said Clive, beckoning for Kate to come back to their side.

Ellie, as expected, rattled through her part in a single take. There was a bit of a discussion afterwards between Louis and Clive about whether her short instrumental, which was undeniably impressive but which had veered away from the metronomic click-track, would have to be rerecorded to fit with the click, but Zoë eventually convinced them that nobody else would be playing at that point, so it didn't matter whether there was a bit of 'rall', as the producer insisted on calling it. It was incredible, the care and attention lavished on each microsecond of sound.

'Was it OK?' asked Ellie, re-entering the cramped room, her guitar still around her neck.

The producer nodded without looking up. 'Very good.'

'Very, *very* good,' Louis added. 'There are not many people who can lay down a track like that so quickly, huh?' He looked at Clive for approval.

Clive nodded again, still fiddling with his dials. He clearly wasn't one for lavish praise.

Zoë felt a rush of pride, mingled with nerves. Even though the producer wouldn't admit it, she could tell that her band members were nailing it. Most artists, she imagined, would take hours to record a single track. She hoped she'd live up to their standards.

'Vocals?'

Zoë nodded. It was time to find out whether she would.

It was only as she positioned herself in front of the glass screen, allowing the engineer to tweak the angle of the microphone and make tiny adjustments to the height of the stand, that Zoë stopped to think about how incredible it was that Dirty Money was here at all.

A couple of weeks ago they'd been scrapping around, trying to work out whether their best chances of 'getting spotted' lay in Camden or Chiswick, dreaming up ridiculous ways of attracting the attention of label managers, and now here they were, having their sound immortalised by the most expensive equipment money could buy.

'When you're ready,' Clive's calm voice came through the headphones above the sound of the click.

Zoë glanced at the roomful of people and drew a breath. The beat was distracting. It was just a tick, every one exactly the same as the last. *Exactly* the same. It was disconcerting. It reminded her of being eleven and being made to practise her violin scales in time with the metronome.

Click, click, click, click.

'Everything okay?' asked Clive.

Zoë nodded. This was ridiculous. She was a musician. She was supposed to have an imagination. All she had to do was pretend that she was standing on a stage in front of a couple of hundred rowdy fans, spotlights on her face, Shannon's drumsticks counting one, two, three, four.

Finally, she did it. Perhaps it was the quality of the amps or the carpeted walls, or the fact that she'd consumed about eight cans of Diet Coke over the course of the day and her body was filled with sugar and caffeine, but Zoë's voice sounded stronger and more powerful than usual. She was enjoying it, too. It wasn't quite the buzz she got from standing up on the stage, but it was a thrill, nonetheless.

'That was great,' said Clive as she finished the first take. 'Hold on one sec.' He fiddled about for a while, twisting knobs, pushing sliders and pressing buttons. 'OK, it's in the can.'

Zoë grinned at the girls as she returned to the cramped, over-heated room. It was pitch black outside now and there was a strange sense of . . . well, perhaps comradeship wasn't the right word. It wasn't a bond, but there was definitely a *closeness* between them: the band, their manager and the producer. Even Clive and his greasy-haired assistant seemed to be warming to the girls now that they'd laid down their tracks so efficiently.

'So!' cried Louis, leaning back in the chair and making it creak rather ominously. 'Shall we press play?'

Obediently, the producer did exactly that.

Zoë looked at the other girls, her mouth slightly open with wonder. Everything about the track was pristine: the beat, the bass, the harmonies and her vocals. It sounded as though some-body else was singing her part. Pure and perfectly in tune, there was no shouting to be heard over drunken revellers, no missing words where she'd had to duck to avoid a flying pint glass, no white noise between the notes. The whole song was . . . utterly clean.

Afterwards, nobody said anything. The girls were too stunned and the men were looking at one another with narrowed eyes, as though subliminally discussing what could be done to make it sound even more perfect.

'Strings?' said Louis.

Clive frowned slightly but didn't disagree.

'Maybe just in the chorus,' Louis added, backtracking a little.

After a period of twiddling, pushing and pressing, the song came back on, this time with a sweeping string section beneath Zoë's chorus.

'Um . . .' Zoë wasn't sure what to say. The song sounded good;

there was no doubt about that. But it didn't sound anything like it was supposed to. The whole point about 'Sensible Lies' was that it was angry, with caustic lyrics that talked of the burning frustrations of living a double life. They were turning it into a happy singalong ditty.

'Amazing, isn't it?' said Louis, shaking his head at the wonders of the mixing desk.

Zoë glanced at the other girls, wondering whether they were thinking the same thing. Shannon just looked wildly excited, her earlier snub clearly forgotten. Kate was frowning, either in concentration or doubt, and Ellie seemed miles away.

'Maybe some sort of . . .' Louis looked at the producer and rubbed his fingers together. '*Tchyka-tchyka-tchyka-tchyka*?'

Zoë's expression turned to one of alarm. The noise coming from Louis's mouth was like the backing track of some boy-band ballad.

Again, there was some activity on the keyboard-like part of the mixing desk. Moments later, the song came back on, slightly slower than it had been before and complete with *tchyka-tchyka* beat. Shannon's part was almost inaudible beneath the electronics.

'I'm sorry,' said Zoë, rather louder than she had anticipated. She lowered her tone. 'But I think it sounded better before all the strings and everything.'

Louis looked at her, tilted his head, then turned to Clive.

Clive raised his brow, a look which Zoë interpreted as *I'm not going to say anything,* but which Louis clearly read differently.

'Let's go with what the producer thinks.' He smiled as though Zoë didn't really understand. 'We can fiddle about 'til the cows come home, later. No need to worry about it now. We got plenny of time!'

There was a brief silence in which Zoë nearly argued but then caught Shannon's eye and stopped herself. The drummer was clearly concerned about falling out with their manager on day one.

'Of course,' she said softly. 'Plenty of time.'

'The other two numbers?'

With her excitement only mildly marred by her frustration, Zoë sank back into her chair as Shannon prepared to lay down the beat for tracks two and three. After the recording of 'Delirious', an argument broke out that ran along very similar lines to the first one, so by the time they played back 'Run Boy Run', Louis and Clive had clearly forged some sort of alliance that meant they weren't going to meddle with the track – at least, not in the presence of the girls.

It was nearly ten o'clock by the time the four musicians fitted themselves around the cymbals, amps and drum stands for the journey home. The combination of hunger and exhaustion meant that emotions were running high.

'I see what you're saying,' said Shannon, shooting out at high speed from the parking space. 'But you can't diss the guy who's just taken us on as manager.'

'I can if he's wrecking our tunes,' replied Zoë. She couldn't believe the drummer was willing to sacrifice their musical integrity in favour of some bolshy hot-shot's ideas.

'I agree,' said Kate, her neck bent at an unnatural angle to avoid the snare drum that was occupying the space where her head should have been. 'That last version sounded like an early Boyzone number.'

'Boyzone sold a lot of records,' yelled Shannon, swerving frighteningly close to the kerb.

'But not *our* type of records,' argued Zoë, concerned that Shannon was focusing on the row and not the road.

'He's a decent manager! Look what he's achieved with other bands.'

'Decent managers leave the producers to do the producing,' Kate pointed out as Shannon embarked on an ambitious overtaking manoeuvre.

'He seems to know what he's talking about,' Ellie pointed out, blissfully unaware.

'Exactly!' cried Shannon, buoyed by the support. 'I don't think it would be a disaster if we ended up releasing something like—'

'I am *not* in a boy-band,' Zoë growled. Then she realised they were outside her flat. 'Oh, right.' She thought about making a final point, then decided it could wait. 'Thanks for the lift.'

'No bother. I'm sure Louis will run it past us before he sends the demo to the label guys, anyway. Right?'

Zoë eased herself out of the car. 'I'm sure.'

She slammed the door shut, patting the roof as it lurched off, trying to cleanse her mind before she entered the flat. She would worry about the CD another time. Burdening James with her Dirty Money issues was something she'd done too much of lately.

The place was in darkness. It was only as Zoë crossed the threshold that she realised that something was wrong. Not wrong, exactly. Just . . . amiss. It felt as though she'd forgotten to do something, or left something behind. She just couldn't work out what it was.

James, when she finally tracked him down, was sitting on the sofa in the glow of the small table lamp. His short hair was lightly gelled and glinting. As he turned, Zoë noticed something else shining out. Something on his wrists. Cufflinks.

'Why—' Zoë stopped and closed her eyes, suddenly realising what it was. 'Oh God,' she said, crumpling at his feet. 'I'm so sorry.'

It was Saturday the eleventh of February. She had forgotten about their date.

10

'You must be joking!' cried the brunette, visibly gagging. 'I mean, no disrespect to him or anything, but it's a *singing* contest. You can't win if you can't sing.'

'That's discrimination.'

'She's got a point though,' said the girl next to Zoë – someone she vaguely recognised from previous events James had brought her along to. 'JJ was a terrible singer.'

'Not true,' claimed another. 'He had a good voice; he just wasn't always in tune.' She downed the remains of her wine and readjusted the fashionable sack-like top that hung from her shoulders.

Zoë let the argument wash over her as she mashed the cheese-cake crumbs into the plate with her fork. They were, as far as she could make out, discussing the controversy surrounding the Talent Tout final, an event that had taken place more than two months ago. Over the main course they had dissected no fewer than six contestants' performances, ranging from Maureen, the cleaner from Norwich, to 4U, the boy-band from Salford that featured in its ranks an albino and a midget gymnast.

'Well, call me un-PC,' said the brunette, 'but I say the boy deserved to lose. Denzel White was by far the best act.'

'You're un-PC,' declared the girl at the end of the table. 'Denzel White is a dick.'

Zoë tried to recall something from the times Shannon had sat her down to watch the acts in their final rounds of auditions.

She remembered Denzel White; it was impossible not to. In the last few months of the previous year, the whole nation had gone crazy for the North London rapper – his pearly teeth shining out from billboards, his lyrical voice pumping out from the internet, his cheeky smile winking from magazine centrefolds. But the other finalists . . . Nope. Zoë drew a blank.

That, in a nutshell, was why she didn't believe in the merits of Talent Tout. It made great television, but it didn't make rock stars. She had never entertained the idea of subjecting Dirty Money to the ordeal. Her band deserved more than five minutes of fame. They deserved longevity and musical respect. They wanted their songs to *mean* something. They wanted to make their own decisions about what to wear and when to smile. Nobody got that from appearing on Talent Tout.

Denzel White was a prime example. He had been hyped to super-star status within the space of about three weeks, his background spun in a way that spectacularly endeared him to the UK public, and now what? He hadn't even released an album. He had enjoyed his brief accolade and then he had plummeted back into obscurity.

Kate was with Zoë on this; she understood that the show wasn't right for the girls. Shannon disagreed. She bought into the Talent Tout dream, swallowing it hook, line and sinker, seeing the show as the obvious route to stardom. In her eyes, the twelve million weekly viewers spoke for themselves. Ellie, when pushed, agreed with the drummer, which made for an ongoing rift between the two halves of the band.

Zoë glanced longingly at the other end of the table, where James and all the boyfriends of the marketing girls were engaged in a drinking game that involved a burned cork and a piece of cheese. Zoë wished she'd been smarter and manoeuvred herself into a better position when they'd all sat down. In fact, she wished she hadn't agreed to come out at all. If it hadn't been for her hideous Valentine blunder then she might have let James come alone, but that wouldn't have been fair. She owed it to him to be here tonight.

James had been quiet for the two days that followed their supposed date, making it difficult for Zoë to know how to react. For her, when something was troubling her, she let it all out, exploding with rage or misery or angst. But James wasn't one for confrontation. He just stewed, keeping his feelings locked up inside. She had apologised, of course, trying everything she could think of to make it up to him. She hated the fact that occasionally, her relationship ended up taking a back seat to her music, but she wasn't sure James understood that. She needed him to understand.

Tonight, as they'd set off for the restaurant, Zoë had seen the first sign that her message was getting through. James had slipped an arm around her waist and asked, quietly, whether she had heard any news from Louis Castle. Now, looking down the table at his merry, cork-charred face, it looked as though his sulk had been long forgotten.

'How d'you think that poor guy felt?' the first girl went on, like a dog with a bone. 'Being kicked out because he was deaf?'

'*Deaf*?' Zoë spluttered.

The girls whipped round, all staring at her.

'How could you *not* know JJ was deaf?' asked one.

'Well . . .'

There were gasps of astonishment and wary looks.

'I . . . I must've missed that episode,' she said sheepishly. It was as though she had confessed to not knowing of Barack Obama. She felt her phone vibrate in her lap and pushed the thick linen tablecloth aside.

Oh God. Just played it.
Boy-band-tastic. He's
taking it 2 Universal
this wk :-(Kx

Zoë closed her eyes momentarily and took in the news. Louis must have sent them all copies of the demo CD. He had got the tracks edited and without even telling them, set up a meeting with Universal. She felt deflated. How could he do that? *Why?* They'd written the songs; they knew how it should sound. If Louis was putting *tchyka-tchyka* versions of their songs in front of record labels, he wasn't showing them the real Dirty Money.

He was doing what he thought was best for the band, of course. He only made money if they made money – Louis took twenty per cent of whatever they got; that was the agreement – but Zoë felt he was making a mistake. She was worried that he would turn them into another homogeneous, straight-off-the-conveyor-belt pop act. They were better than that.

She sighed, just as the phone buzzed again in her hands.

Wow! Have u heard
CD? It rocks! + I had
gr8 idea 4 celeb
endorsement: I can
get us on Irish TV
with a star! Shan x

Her frown melted into a smile. Shannon always had a great idea. You couldn't fault her enthusiasm. Zoë wondered how the tracks actually sounded. Deep down, she had been half-expecting something like this. Louis Castle didn't consult his unsigned protégés when it came to dealing with big-time labels. He called the shots. And maybe, given what he had achieved in America, the girls should just put their trust in his judgement.

After several attempts to catch James's attention, she made contact with his sleepy blue eyes. He and the others around him had reached the hitting-wine-glasses-with-forks stage of the evening, which suggested that it might be time to go.

'Bus?' suggested Zoë as they wandered into the damp, night air.

James grinned hazily at her, trying to focus. 'Little . . . *black* bus?'

Zoë smiled. When James got drunk, he turned into a chilled-out caricature of himself. He became more . . . well, more like the old James. He always maintained a grip on reality, just a skew-whiff version of reality. So when he pushed open the door of their flat and found, behind it, a small brown parcel marked SOHO STUDIOS, he seemed to know exactly what it was.

'D'you think this is for you?' he asked, holding the package just out of Zoë's reach.

'James, please . . .' She grabbed at his long, muscular arm, stepping on a pile of junk mail and skidding to the floor.

'You want this?' he goaded, waving the brown box around as she crawled onto all fours.

Using the parcel, he led her onto the sofa where she collapsed on top of him, dizzy and panting.

'Will you put it on?' Zoë pleaded, as James unwrapped the disc, at arm's length. The note enclosed, which he eventually relinquished, was written in neat, female handwriting – presumably belonging to Louis's PA.

Hope you like. Will be meeting the Universal boys this week. Fingers crossed.
Louis

James reached back and switched on the hi-fi system. Stretching, he inserted the CD, raised an eyebrow seductively at Zoë and, with excruciating slowness, moved his finger across to the Play button.

Zoë sat up, straddling her boyfriend and starting to undo the buttons of his shirt. She wanted to hear the tracks but she also wanted a piece of James. His eyes were filled with mischief and she could feel his hand – the hand that wasn't controlling the stereo – working its way up her thigh.

The introduction to 'Delirious' started blasting out of the numerous speakers and she suddenly stopped. She could feel the colour drain from her cheeks.

'Oh my God,' she said, feeling instantly sober.

Fleetingly, she wondered why he'd put that track first, when 'Sensible Lies' was so much better, but there were bigger things to worry about.

It was like being punched in the stomach. She couldn't think about anything – couldn't articulate a response. All she could do was listen to this . . . this *sound* that was filling the lounge.

'It's fucking *disco*,' she spat, when the song got into its groove.

If James replied, she didn't hear him. Her ears were focusing on the clinical beat. She waited for Ellie's chords to come in, then the vocals. It was unrecognisable. Like listening to somebody else's music.

'Fuck!' she yelled, as her own voice sang back at her above the sanitised riff. She wanted to cry. 'What've they done?!'

The song finished and, transfixed, Zoë waited mutely to hear the next butchered track.

'Zoë?'

Zoë listened to the mutilated rendition of 'Sensible Lies'.

'Zoë,' James said again, propping himself up on the sofa and pulling her firmly towards him.

'What?' she asked, distracted by a cheesy key-change that had been inserted just before the second chorus. It was unbelievable what they'd done.

'I said, this is amazing.'

Zoë looked at him and frowned. They both seemed to have sobered up now but James wasn't making any sense. 'What, amazingly *bad*?'

'No,' he said, pushing himself up on the sofa so that she was sitting in his lap. 'Listen to it.'

In silence, they listened to the instrumental that preceded the final verse – ordinarily, Zoë's favourite part of the song.

'Seriously,' said James, wrapping his arms round her waist and squeezing her against his body. 'Imagine you've never heard of this band.'

Zoë closed her eyes in anguish, letting her head roll back on James's shoulder. She *had* never heard of this band. It wasn't hers. This was not the sound of Dirty Money.

Enveloped in James's arms, swaying gently to the unfamiliar music, Zoë tried to force herself to hear it afresh. She heard the pulsing beat and the harmonies and the catchy tune . . .

The song finished and the final track came on. 'Run Boy Run' was one of their most uplifting numbers. Zoë tilted her face upwards to tell James that he was right, that she was too obsessed with the band, that she was sorry for sometimes neglecting her commitment to him, that she really was grateful for his unwavering support. But she didn't get a chance, as James's lips were pressing against hers.

11

The phone rang for the second time in as many minutes.

'It's Brian again.'

Zoë's typing became even more frantic.

'The email still hasn't come through.'

'Uh . . . Really? That's weird.'

She scanned the main paragraph, trying to stem her internal panic. In fact, there was nothing weird about the situation at all. It was simply that Zoë had failed to complete the audit in time and was now shifting the blame onto the mysterious workings of the client email server.

'You did cc me this time, didn't you?'

'Yep,' she replied, quickly typing Brian's name in the cc box. She hadn't wanted to lie, but the client had called her this morning and launched into a long story about firewall issues at their end and it had slowly dawned on Zoë that they were assuming she'd sent the audit the previous week, and . . . well, it had just seemed simpler not to make the correction.

Brian grunted. 'Very strange. I'll get onto IT.'

'No,' she said quickly, knowing that even the cretins employed by the Chase Waterman IT department would spot that no email had been sent from her machine. 'I'll do it. I think it might be something to do with my computer anyway.' She checked the message one last time and pressed Send. 'Oh, it seems to be doing something now.'

'I'll leave it with you,' he barked.

Zoë slumped back in her seat and let out a heavy sigh. She didn't like disappointing clients, but it seemed to be happening more and more these days. Perhaps it was because of her workload. Nobody else seemed to have so many projects on the go at once – or at least, nobody else seemed to struggle with the volume of work. But then . . . She leaned forward again and squinted to check that the email had been sent. Nobody else spent hours every week taking calls from promoters, liaising with venues, updating websites or slipping out to write songs. Nobody else came in to work with a raging headache, their eyes bloodshot from the late nights in sweat-filled bars.

Maybe it wasn't possible to combine the two careers, Zoë conceded. Not that the band was a career, exactly. She didn't know the exact definition, but she had a feeling that 'career' had something to do with making money. So far, if you added everything up over the years, Dirty Money had probably lost them a few thousand pounds.

Her mobile phone started buzzing its way along the desk, flashing *Unknown number*. She snatched it up, preparing to explain to the client, yet again, that the email was on its way.

'Hiiiiii.'

'Louis?' she checked. This was surely the call they'd been waiting for.

'Yeah! How you doin'? What're you up to?'

Zoë pushed back her chair and sloped off towards the lift lobby. Good news or bad news, this wasn't a conversation she wanted to have in front of her colleagues.

'I'm . . . I'm at work,' she replied, not entirely sure whether Louis expected an answer or whether it was simply one of those rhetorical Americanisms.

'Oh yeah.' Either Louis hadn't wanted an answer or he had simply forgotten that most people, at half past eleven on a Wednesday morning, were at work. 'Where's that then?'

'Near Liverpool Street.' Zoë stepped backwards as a pair of suited men strode out of the lifts, resisting her urge to scream for an update on the Universal meeting.

'Great! I'm in Shoreditch. Not far at all. Can you meet me in half an hour?'

'Wh—' Zoë faltered. She wanted to know *now*, not in half an hour. Why couldn't he just tell her by phone? And how on earth was she going to round up the others at such short notice? Kate would be stuck in some important meeting about pension funds, Shannon was probably sweet-talking some media client over an early lunch and Ellie needed at least twenty-four hours to get anywhere. 'I can try and get everyone along,' she offered half-heartedly.

'No, just you for now.' Louis cleared his throat.

'R-right,' she replied hesitantly. If Louis had bad news then she didn't see why it was her job to deliver it to the rest of the band. She wasn't a spokesperson.

'Meet you in The Bathhouse at noon?' It was an instruction, not a question.

Zoë dropped the phone from her ear to check the time. As she took a breath to respond, she realised that the line was dead.

The following twenty-five minutes were not very productive. She couldn't concentrate on intangible assets when there were so many questions vying for attention in her head. Why did he want to meet her alone? What did he have to say that couldn't have been said on the phone? Was it bad news? Had Zoë's phone call the other night somehow damaged their relationship with the manager? Was he going to cancel their contract? Zoë stopped pretending to work and walked out. Honestly, she was getting like Kate with her worrying. There was no point in fretting over things that hadn't even happened.

From the outside, The Bathhouse looked like a miniature Russian church, complete with coloured tiles, dome roof and painted dovecote. Inside, it was a hip, candlelit wine bar with carpeted walls and sparsely-placed chandeliers. Zoë entered with caution, alarm bells ringing. Was it normal for managers to meet with their acts in such dark venues? She barely knew Louis Castle. Perhaps it was all a sham – perhaps he wasn't *the* Louis Castle she'd read about on the internet.

A waiter ushered her over to the alcove nearest the grand piano, where Louis could be seen, reclined in an armchair, his large, chunky hands clasped around a tumbler of amber liquid. Zoë's anxieties began to lift. It was obvious that for the manager, there was nothing unusual about this at all. Whereas auditing conversations were conducted under the harsh strip lights of seventh-floor meeting rooms with small cups of water, in the world of rock and roll, candles, sofas and whisky were still par for the course.

'Hiiiiii!' He was smiling as he heaved himself out of the seat, which Zoë took as a good sign. 'What can I getcha?'

Zoë tried to relax. Even in her paranoid state, it seemed unlikely to her that a manager would summon his act at half an hour's notice just to buy them a drink and then drop them from his list. 'An orange juice, please.'

Louis drew his head back in disdain, clearly waiting for her real answer.

'I'm working,' she explained.

He waved a hand. 'We're all working, honey.'

Zoë shook her head, grinning faintly as she slid into the leather seat opposite. To her knowledge, only one person had ever turned up at the Chase Waterman offices drunk. And he'd been a lapsed alcoholic in the throes of a nervous breakdown. Even at Christmas, people stayed sober. There was no way Zoë would risk even a sip of alcohol, knowing what her nosy neighbour was like. Unless . . . unless Louis's news was big enough to eliminate the need for the sensible career in auditing altogether – which, Zoë knew, was unlikely.

After a couple more attempts, Louis relented and allowed the waiter to take her abstemious order.

'So! I got some news for ya.'

Zoë leaned forward, her forearms resting on her thighs. She dug her fingernails into the flesh of her palms. 'Yeah?' she said as innocuously as she could.

'Two pieces of news, actually.'

Zoë nodded, incapable of unclenching her fists.

'The first is about Blast Management.'

She nodded again. His expression was infuriatingly neutral.

'I didn't tell you before, but, well . . . I've sold the company to Universal.'

Zoë's jaw dropped. She wasn't entirely sure what this meant, but she knew it was big. Universal had acquired Blast Management . . . So . . . So, now what? Was this Louis's way of saying he was walking out on them?

'Don't worry, I'll still be running the shop,' he said quickly, clearly sensing her concern. 'It's actually a part-sale. I get to keep fifty-one per cent and I'm contractually obliged to stay in charge – at least for five years.' He grinned smugly.

'Oh, good.' Zoë was still trying to work things out. He wasn't leaving the firm, but now Blast was part of Universal, which meant . . . what, exactly? Other than the fact that Louis Castle was probably a multimillionaire, if he hadn't been already.

'This is good news for you,' he affirmed. 'Don't look so worried.'

Zoë managed a smile, feeling ignorant and small. She reached for the juice that had appeared on the table.

'It means that Blast kinda has a permanent foot in the door of some of Universal's labels. *Island, Polydor, Vicinity* . . . I mean, it's not like we couldn't have gotten into conversation with them before, but, you know, their doors are kinda *propped* open now. And in return, they get first pick of the artists we manage.'

'Wow.' Zoë didn't understand exactly how the propped-open-door model worked, but she sensed that on balance, the acquisition was a good thing for Dirty Money.

'Which brings me onto—'

'Hold on,' said Zoë, spotting the potential pitfall in the arrange-ment. 'Does that mean that Blast can *only* sign artists to Universal labels now?'

'No, we can go elsewhere once Universal has had its pick. They just get first dibs. But . . .' A grin spread across Louis's face. 'As it happens, you don't need to worry about that. Not after my meeting with Vicinity last week.'

Zoë stared, holding her breath. She needed to hear it in plain English before she could allow herself to get excited.

'Do you mean . . . Vicinity want to sign Dirty Money?' She could barely control her voice.

'Well, not exactly,' he replied, looking briefly uncomfortable. 'I've had a few meetings now, with Edgar and Jenson and that . . . Basically, they really liked the band, but . . . well, it doesn't quite fit with what they're looking for right now.'

'Oh.' Zoë looked down at the table. She felt deflated. And confused. Louis had led her up this path – building her hopes, dropping hints, flashing that giant smile of his . . .

'See,' Louis swilled a sip of whisky around in his mouth and then finally swallowed. 'There's trends in the music industry. Hot things come and go. A few years ago, two lads from Manchester came down in their dirty T-shirts and suddenly indie was big – everyone wanted to sign hairy guys with guitars. The labels don't wanna miss the next "wave".'

Zoë nodded impatiently. She was no hairy guy, guitar or otherwise.

'This year, bands just ain't hot.'

'So . . .'

'Honey, they wanna sign you.'

Zoë frowned. It was the way he emphasised the last word that worried her.

'They're looking for a female solo act,' he explained, confirming her suspicions. 'A *real* singer. A Florence. An Amy. A Lady Gaga, you know? They're all about girls with big attitude as well as a big voice.' His piggy face poked out from inside all the chins, blinking and grinning at Zoë.

This was absurd. Zoë couldn't sign to a label without the others. She was part of a band. They came as a four. This was like trying to sell a car on the basis of only one of its cylinders. It just couldn't happen.

'Jeez, Zoë . . .' Louis swallowed a mouthful of whisky and planted the glass on the table. 'I was kinda expecting a bit more enthusiasm!'

'Sorry,' she mumbled, trying to fend off his indignation while she straightened her thoughts.

'This is *Vicinity* we're talking about. Universal. You know?'

Yes, Zoë knew. She knew exactly how big a deal this was, which was why she felt so low. It was a massive thing to turn down.

Zoë had never considered the idea of standing on a stage without the others. She didn't know whether she even could. In principle, perhaps it was possible. They were her songs; it was always Zoë on vocals. But in reality . . .

'How would I sing without them?'

It was a stupid question. She knew as soon as the words left her lips that she needn't have asked it.

'You've heard of session musicians?'

He was being sarcastic now – presumably miffed that Zoë hadn't jumped at the proposition.

'But what's wrong with Kate and Ellie and Shannon?' she pressed.

Louis raised his eyes heavenward and let out an exasperated sigh. 'Because Kate and Ellie and Shannon would make it a *band*, and a band is not what the label is looking for.'

It was Zoë's turn to sigh. This wasn't how things worked. At least, it wasn't how she'd imagined things worked. Based on everything she had read online, every story she'd heard on the grapevine, artists got signed on the basis of who they *were*. Louis was implying that the record companies just conjured up a series of typecast moulds and then asked the managers to fill them.

'What about other labels?'

'What about them?'

'Well, isn't there a chance one of the Sony labels might go for Dirty Money? Or Warner, or . . .' She trailed off under Louis's withering gaze.

'Honey,' he said, as though she were four years old. 'When you got a deal on the table, you don't go pissing around with the competition.'

Zoë nodded, feeling like a cornered animal. There *had* to be a way of making things work for the band. She tried one last tack.

'Don't you . . . I mean, Blast . . . Doesn't Blast represent Dirty Money?'

Louis nodded slowly, his face dipping in and out of his fatty neck. 'Of which Zoë Kidd is a part. I represent the interests of the band members. So when I hear that a label wants to sign one of those members, I kinda wanna make it work.'

His tone suggested that Louis was running out of patience.

'What happens if I say no?' she asked quietly.

He was shaking his head now, looking at her as though she was mad. 'Then they find someone else,' he replied, loudly and slowly.

Zoë gulped. She couldn't believe it was this mercenary, this . . . *premeditated.*

'So, are you in?'

Louis raised an eyebrow, trying to smile despite his evident frustration.

Inhaling deeply and letting out a slow, shaky breath, Zoë met his gaze. 'I don't know,' she said. 'I'll have to think about it.'

Suddenly, she had to get out of this dark, cosy place. She had to breathe. To think. She stood up and gave a brief, awkward wave goodbye. The sound of Louis's empty glass slamming down on the table echoed around the empty bar as she climbed the stairs.

'Don't think for too long!' yelled the manager. 'Plenny of wannabes out there!'

12

'We're Dirty Money, and you've been amazing!' yelled Zoë.

There was a whoop from the front of the hall, where Crazy Jeff could be seen bobbing around, arms waving. Then a deathly quiet fell on the room. Zoë stood, her features set in a broad smile, silently willing Shannon to bring them in for the final song.

The crowd had not been amazing. In fact, nothing about tonight had been amazing. In terms of reception, the gig ranked somewhere alongside the one they had played in the geriatric hospital five years ago. They had played well, but the audience, made up mainly of self-conscious art students and young fashionistas, just hadn't warmed to them. Perhaps the Hoxton crew never actually warmed to anything; they were just too cool.

She should have known that tonight would be a disaster. Not just because of the huge decision that hung over her like a black thundercloud, a cloud she was struggling to keep from the girls, but because the promoter was a renowned money-grabbing bastard. He had done exactly what money-grabbing bastards always do and put on a mixture of funk, electro-pop, rock and a trio of Ukrainian keyboard players in the hope that more genres would attract more punters. Zoë wished she had turned it down.

Ellie played them out with an impressive solo that was wasted on the pouting crowd and, to the sound of muted clapping, Zoë led the girls offstage.

'Fockin' hell, that was hard work.' Shannon barged her way into their dressing room – a cubicle no larger than a public toilet and not dissimilar in terms of smell. 'What's wrong with these people? It's like they've had broomsticks shoved up their arses or something.'

Ellie laughed quietly. 'I think one of them did actually have a broomstick.'

'There was definitely one dressed as a tree.' Kate nodded as she started quickly packing away her guitar.

'We should've thought,' muttered Shannon. 'We're playing in the most pretentious district in London. We should've planned it better.'

'What d'you mean?' Zoë frowned, not feeling like getting drawn in but unable to see how preparation would have helped.

'Well, look at us!' Shannon waved a dismissive hand over her body. 'We look like freaks!'

Even Zoë managed a laugh. Hoxton was the only place in the world where you felt like a freak for wearing jeans. One female member of the audience tonight had been dressed in a knee-length foil wrap, of the type that runners get given at the end of a marathon.

'No,' Kate said earnestly. 'We shouldn't change our image just because of who we're playing to.'

Zoë sensed that the bassist was looking to her for support. Ordinarily, she would have given it. She was, as ever, speaking sense. But today, Zoë kept her head bowed and started rummaging randomly in her guitar case. She couldn't bring herself to discuss what they should or shouldn't do to improve Dirty Money's chances of success – not when she knew that their manager was waiting for her to sign off on their demise.

'I didn't mean – ugh!' Shannon cried out as she stepped, mid-shoe-change, in a puddle of brown liquid on the floor. 'This place sucks.'

Shannon was right. The place sucked. As did most of the

venues they played. There was a reasonable probability, she knew, that Dirty Money would be forced to continue playing gigs like this, in clubs where the floors stank of piss, the promoters were short-sighted gits and the crowds didn't know your name. It was quite possible that the girls would never break free from the grubby London music scene, that they'd still be here with their zimmer frames in fifty years' time, still trying to make it onto the international circuit.

They never talked about it, but they all knew the truth: it was possible that their dreams would eventually fizzle. Yet despite the odds, they kept plugging away. And up until two days ago, Zoë had never stopped to doubt it. But now Louis's proposition was taunting her, goading her away from the path they were on.

'Quick drink?' asked Shannon, holding her sodden sock at arm's length and slipping her bare foot into the shoe.

'I said I'd meet Sam.' Ellie pulled an apologetic face.

'Sorry,' Kate mumbled sheepishly, pulling on her coat. 'Gotta go.'

'I can't.' Zoë dipped her head as the drummer's attention turned to her. She couldn't wait to get out of this place – away from the gig, away from the girls. Away from everything that reminded her of the decision she had to make.

'What?' Shannon threw her hands in the air. 'Why not?'

'I . . .' Zoë could feel the drummer's eyes upon her. She tried to think of a bullet-proof reason. 'James . . .'

'James can wait. So can Sam,' she said, glaring at Ellie. 'Lord knows, he makes people wait long enough.' Shannon stormed over and grabbed Ellie's jacket. 'Come on. We're going for a pint. I need to tell you about the Irish TV thing. Kate?'

Kate was pulling faces into a small makeup mirror. A smirk crept across Shannon's face.

'Hang on . . .' She peered at the bassist. 'D'you have a *date*?'

Kate swung her guitar onto her back and headed down the corridor, avoiding the question.

Shannon gave chase, leaving Zoë to lock the flimsy door.

By the time she caught up with them, Kate's cheeks were glowing and squeals were coming from both Ellie and Shannon.

'Your boss?!' shrieked Shannon. 'Oh my God!'

'Stop it!' Kate glared at the drummer as they slipped through the back entrance into the noisy club. 'He's here somewhere.'

'You shouldn't have a problem spotting him,' Ellie remarked, as a girl in a floor-length nightie and full Indian headdress walked past. 'Can't be many actuaries in here.'

It was true. Within seconds, they had identified the suave man in the pinstriped suit at the end of the bar. He was finishing a Corona and pretending to be busy on his BlackBerry.

Under strict instructions to leave them alone, Shannon, Ellie and Zoë hung back while the misfits left to find another late-night bar.

'Cute,' remarked Shannon, approvingly.

'Mmm.' Ellie nodded, with less conviction.

Shannon rounded on Zoë as they elbowed their way to the bar. 'What's up with you today?' she demanded. 'You've hardly said a word all night.'

Zoë shrugged. 'Headache,' she said, pointing up at the nearest speaker.

Shannon pulled her head back and squinted at her. 'You've not had a headache in six and a half years.'

Zoë managed a little smile. This was the problem; the girls knew her too well.

'Is everything okay with James now?' asked Ellie, presumably referring to a conversation they'd had the previous week about the missed Valentine's date.

'Well,' Zoë gnawed on her lip, wondering whether it was un-ethical to do this. It was, she decided, but she couldn't think of another option. 'It's still not great, no.'

Ellie tutted supportively. Shannon leaned over and yelled their drinks order at the barmaid, then turned to Zoë, eyebrows raised. It was apparent that more details were required.

'We're just . . . I dunno. It's partly my fault for spending so much time with the band.' She felt awful for doing this. 'He just doesn't seem to understand.'

Shannon pushed their drinks over. 'Men, eh.'

Ellie gave a wry smile. 'Poor you.'

Zoë sipped the head off her pint, relieved to see a lanky figure lollop through the crowds and appear at Ellie's side.

Zoë raised a hand as Sam caught her eye, watching with a mixture of adoration and envy as he slipped a hand around Ellie's waist, whispering something into her hair and kissing her on the forehead. Their relationship was as beautiful now as it had been six years ago. They still fitted perfectly together – physically, intellectually and spiritually. They wanted the same things from life – the same things they had always wanted. Zoë couldn't help wondering whether she and James still fitted perfectly together.

'So.' Shannon elbowed her in the ribs. 'Kate's seeing her boss, eh?' Zoë nodded half-heartedly, concerned for their bassist's relationship – which, based on track record, would be over in a fortnight – but quietly pleased to be back on neutral territory. Being a blue-eyed blonde, Kate had a habit of finding herself brash, chiselled men who, for the first few dates, were 'the perfect match'. Inevitably, as the charmer discovered that Kate wasn't trophy wife material, things turned sour and the city slicker would leave her for a six-foot Barbie, further crushing Kate's self-esteem.

'Why does she do it?' asked Shannon. 'Get with all those toss-pots, I mean.'

It wasn't a new question. The subject of Kate's doomed relationships had reared its head many times before.

'It's a confidence thing,' said Zoë, finding herself getting drawn in.

'Is it?'

Zoë sighed. 'I think so. She doesn't realise that she's pretty and funny and talented and all the rest of it, and she gets flattered into it because she doesn't realise she could do better. Then the tosspots use up all their flirtatious lines on the first few dates and the relationship fizzles. Obviously, they don't want to be the ones getting dumped, so they get in there first.'

Shannon looked at Zoë across the rim of her pint glass. 'You know,' she said slowly, 'I think you might be right.'

They sat for a while, thinking, drinking, immersed in the techno beat.

'Anyway!' cried Shannon, springing to life again and reaching for Ellie's sleeve. 'The TV thing!'

Zoë gulped her mouthful of beer, overwhelmed by a fresh wave of guilt.

'So, I was speaking to my cousin, Paddy.' Shannon leaned in, her eyes glinting with excitement. Sam's expression looked almost as rapt as Ellie's, Zoë noticed. 'He's a producer, and he's just got this late-night job on RTÉ. He reckons he could get us on. And if it all goes to plan, he'll get a minor celebrity on the show and then we can get them to rave about us!'

'Wow,' gasped Ellie, squeezing Sam's arm. 'That's amazing.'

Zoë managed to look suitably impressed as Shannon started to prepare for their performance, right down to the shoes they would wear. Ordinarily, they would have planned it together, discussing PR strategies, dreaming up ways of getting noticed. Today, though, she couldn't get excited. She wanted to believe that Dirty Money would get endorsement from a celebrity on Irish TV, but she knew what she had to do in order to make that happen.

'I guess Louis will want us to dress up a bit,' Shannon went on. 'He said something about getting us out of our hoodies . . .'

'Hey, look at *that* outfit,' Zoë pointed at a girl with asymmetrical hair and braces as she strutted past.

'Hasn't he called yet?' asked Ellie, oblivious to her attempted distraction. 'I thought he was seeing the label last week?'

Zoë could feel both sets of eyes on her. 'I guess he's busy,' she mumbled, shrugging.

'We'll show him!' Shannon held up her glass, waiting for the others to do the same. 'Even if Universal doesn't want us, somebody will. Here's to getting signed!'

'To getting signed!' they chimed.

Zoë tipped back her head and swallowed the last of her beer. She could feel the bile rising up in her throat to meet it.

13

'But you shouldn't take *every* opportunity, should you?' Zoë looked over at James.

'Well . . .' He ran his hands over his face and through his short, wet hair. 'Depends on your long-term plan, I guess.'

Zoë slid down so that her whole body was submerged in the hot, bubbly water. They were taking advantage of the gym membership that had seemed like such a good idea at the start of the year, by spending the morning in the jacuzzi. By Zoë's calculations, the trip was costing them forty pounds each.

She re-emerged, her head throbbing pleasantly with the heat. 'Exactly. Sometimes it's better to sit back in the short term and wait for something better to come along.'

They were, of course, talking about the decision she had to make about Vicinity – the unmade decision that had occupied most of her waking hours for the last five days, and some of her sleeping ones too. Louis had left two voicemails, both saying the same thing: Make up your mind.

Zoë realigned herself so that the jet of hot water hit her between her shoulder blades. She had distilled her dilemma down to one simple question – *What did she really want: success for the band, or success for herself?*

The problem was, even in its succinct form, Zoë couldn't answer the question. She had lived with the dream for so long – the dream of world tours, of Dirty Money songs being hummed across the nation, of fans stopping them in the street for auto-graphs – that she could no longer identify the different strands of the dream. Was it the idea of touring the world with her three closest friends? Or was it a vanity thing? Did she just want to see her own face splashed across the front page of *Q*?

'It depends on your risk level, I guess.' James blew upwards, sharply, clearing his forehead of water. 'You've gotta take a punt on what might happen in the future.'

Zoë nodded slowly. That, in essence, was the problem. She didn't know what was going to happen in the future. At least in the real world, you could take a stab. You could predict whether you would pass an exam, or save enough money to buy a house. In the music industry, anything could happen. Artists rose from nowhere. Often they'd return to nowhere. Some would shoot up so quickly that they'd burn out and fall into oblivion to join the others. All you could do was pick a plan for the future and hope.

'I usually just go with gut instinct,' Zoë admitted.

James nodded, looking into space.

The problem was, her gut instinct was letting her down. In fact, all of her usual mechanisms were letting her down. Weighing up the pros and cons didn't work; the items on either side were so immense, so substantial that the scales fell apart. She had tried drawing up the matrix in an Excel spreadsheet at work.

Benefits of signing with Vicinity: Potential for megastardom, escape from daily tedium and a meaningless existence.

Drawbacks of signing with Vicinity: Loss of three best friends, collapse of Dirty Money.

Benefits of turning them down: Possibility of future success with the band, loyalty to Ellie, Shannon and Kate.

Drawbacks of turning them down: Likelihood of obscurity, a lifetime of spreadsheets and pie charts.

It was like having to choose between your parents: you just couldn't. Many hours had been spent contemplating various scenarios. Often, she had veered towards the Vicinity option – probably because the alternative was staring her in the face: Auto-sums, circular references, decimal points – but then, seeing the girls at the gig had sent Zoë reeling the other way, almost reaching for her phone to call Louis and tell him where to go with his offer. *Almost.* She loved Ellie and Shannon and Kate, but she couldn't just ignore this opportunity. It deserved some contemplation.

Zoë sighed, dipping her head under the water again. James was looking at her when she surfaced.

'I guess,' he said, looking at her as though he'd given the matter some serious thought, 'you never really know whether you've made the right decision – even once it's been made. You could always look back and wonder, *what would I be doing if I'd . . .'* He gently splashed the surface of the water with his hand.

Zoë nodded, grateful for her boyfriend's support, even if it wasn't getting her much closer to a decision.

'And really, it's all hypothetical anyway,' he said. 'No point in trying to decide what to do when the options aren't all there.'

Zoë frowned. 'What d'you mean?'

'Well, they haven't offered me the promotion yet.' He shrugged. 'No point in tossing up between jobs when there's only one offer on the table.'

Zoë felt herself nodding automatically, dumbstruck. In her head, she replayed snatches of their conversation, slowly realising what had happened.

'Are you . . .' She felt silly, all of a sudden. 'Are you talking about that other role you were thinking about going for?'

James looked at her, cockeyed. 'What else would I be talking about?'

Zoë was lost for words. For the last twenty minutes, they had been talking at cross purposes.

'The consumer insight job?' he prompted. 'The one that would pay less but give me better career options?' He tilted his head at her, waiting for a sign of acknowledgement.

'Of course,' she said quickly.

Zoë studied her fingers, which were beginning to wrinkle. She wondered how this had happened. In their uni days, this situation could never have occurred. It just wasn't feasible. From waking up together, they would hang out, eat lunch, walk to occasional lectures, drink beer – all in each other's company. Conversations barely needed to happen; they each knew what the other was thinking. They'd see something – on TV, in the union – and a quick smirk was enough. A wary glance. A laugh. Now, here they were holding entire conversations about different things.

James's gaze was fixed on something distant outside the glass-walled leisure complex. Presumably he was thinking about his career. He had outlined to Zoë his predicament – although in her opinion, predicament was not quite the right word. His options were: take the more interesting job he'd been offered in another department where the career prospects were better, or hold out for a promotion in his current job, which would mean slightly more money but a continuation of his current routine, in which the most exciting thing to happen was the vending machine giving out an extra packet of crisps.

Shifting away from the jet-stream, Zoë lowered herself, leaned back and looked at her boyfriend through half-closed eyes. He had always been smart and ambitious. He wore smarter clothes now and drank more expensive beer, but material differences aside, he hadn't changed. Only his priorities had.

It was the workplace that did it, thought Zoë. It had taken her a while to adapt to the regimental nine-hour days, the corporate wallpaper and the unwritten rules about leaving your desk. It was a far cry from the laissez-faire world of Goldsmiths. James, on the other hand, had acclimatised instantly.

Thriving on competition, James had quickly worked out his

new priorities. Suddenly, he was being faced with bigger challenges than how to lever the traffic sign off its post without being caught on CCTV. He relished the long hours and the pressure. He slotted straight into the departmental team and, although he'd never admit it, Zoë knew he got a kick out of being asked to stay late for an important assignment. While James's focus was sharpening on his career, hers was doing the opposite; the longer she stayed in the corporate environment of Chase Waterman, the more she wanted to break free, to live the dream.

'What about you?' James said, suddenly. 'D'you know what *you're* gonna do?'

'Oh . . . me?'

That was the thing about James. Despite his new slick sheen, he was a sensitive guy. He really did care about her.

'I haven't decided yet.'

'Well,' he said, pushing himself up from the plunge pool and holding a hand out to her. 'I'd give you my advice, but I know you won't take it.'

Zoë allowed herself to be hauled upright and smiled, curiously. 'What advice?'

James smirked, reaching round to the bare flesh of her back. 'No, no point.'

She slapped his wet shoulder. 'Tell me!'

He shrugged and casually led her out of the pool. 'I'll tell you when you've made your decision.'

14

Zoë's mind kept wandering. More so than usual. A whole week had passed since Louis had told her about the offer from Vicinity. Time, she knew, was running out.

She flipped shut the annual report and looked at her screen, deleting an email from HR demanding to know why she'd failed to attend a 'stress busting' seminar. Life at Chase Waterman was full of small irritations: regulations, procedures, initiatives . . . Zoë couldn't be bothered with it all.

The familiar buzz of her phone could be felt against her foot.

'Hello?' she gasped, banging her head on the underside of her desk as she pulled it out of her bag.

The line was dead. As she looked at the display, she realised that fate had intervened kindly, for once. *1 missed call: Mum – home*, flashed up. Zoë waited for the inevitable beep and dialled the number to pick up her voicemail.

'Hello dear, only me. Good news! Tamsin just won her first jury case! I hope everything's all right with you. Don't forget to congratulate your sister, will you? I must go – so many people to call! I'll speak to you soon. Byee!'

Zoë lowered the handset and jabbed at the delete button. She couldn't work out how she felt. Of course, she was proud of her sister. Tamsin wasn't even fully qualified and already she was standing up in court, winning cases. But the pride was tinged with sadness. Yet again, Zoë's mother was rejoicing about her daughter's achievements, and yet again, that daughter wasn't her.

It wasn't envy, exactly; Zoë had never been jealous of her sister. It was more a sense of dejection. The last time she had provoked a reaction like the one she'd just heard had been years ago, when the whole family had trooped up to Buckingham Palace to watch her collect her Duke of Edinburgh's Award. She never impressed them any more.

It wasn't as though she couldn't impress them. She was as gifted as her sister – more so, in some ways. The problem was that Zoë didn't *want* to win trophies. She was done with passing exams and getting awards. She just wanted to realise her ambition. Sadly, though, her mother and father didn't share that ambition.

She hadn't told her parents about Louis's proposition. They wouldn't be interested. Or rather, they wouldn't approve. It was worse than not caring, thought Zoë. They actively condemned her determination to succeed on the stage.

Her father – whose father had been a barrister, and his father before that – was a firm believer in tradition, discipline and the job for life. The idea of leaving university without a firm plan for the next forty years was alien to Rupert Kidd, QC. The only thing more idiotic, in his book, was the idea of leaving university with the notion that you were going to become a rock star.

That said, her father's disapproval didn't upset her. She saw where it came from, she understood his principles and in a strange way, she felt comfortable being at constant loggerheads. No, she didn't feel hurt by her father's rejection of her philosophy. The person who *did* get under her skin was someone who had never achieved more than a D-grade in school, never been to university and never been promoted beyond the position of trainee legal secretary. Zoë's mother could move her to tears.

She probably didn't even know she was doing it, thought Zoë, pretending to hunt for a document as someone walked past her desk. It was just a subconscious thing, this pressure she exerted on her daughters to succeed. Psychologists would probably put it down to missed opportunities during childhood. She hadn't had the luxury of one-on-one music lessons, so she was determined that at least one of her daughters would become a virtuoso. There had been no extra French tuition in her childhood, so the onus was on Tamsin and Zoë to become multilingual. Zoë wondered whether . . .

A message alert appeared on the screen, interrupting her trail of thought.

Hey babe,
    I got the promotion! The pay rise is £5k . . . Can't turn that down!
    See you later.
    xx J

Zoë's mood jumped and then plummeted again as she realised what this meant. She reread the email to check that she hadn't misunderstood, then hit Reply.

Congratulations!
    But, er, didn't you decide that you were bored in that department and wanted a change? Thought you were going for the other role?
    Zx

Distractedly, Zoë flicked back to the electronic directory and tried to focus. She couldn't. Why wasn't James going for the interesting job in the other department? Was the money really that big a deal? What was wrong with him? Or rather, what was wrong with *her*? Was she the only person in the world who valued her sense of personal fulfilment more than her salary?

Nobody else seemed to feel like a hamster in a cage, trapped on an eternal treadmill. Her quest for something bigger, something more exciting, something – anything – that wasn't mundane, seemed frustratingly unique.

'Zoë?'

She looked up with a jolt, wondering how long Brian had been watching her daydream.

'Yes?' Zoë switched on her breezy, efficient tone.

Brian was rubbing his shiny forehead. 'It's about the course,' he said, looking down at her awkwardly.

'Oh.' The adrenaline dissipated. For a moment, she'd thought it was something serious.

'I'm aware of your correspondence with HR.'

'Right.' Zoë straightened up, ready to defend her position. She should have realised that Debbie and co. didn't back down that easily.

'As your line manager, it is my duty to ensure you attend the course.'

'I don't need to. I'm not stressed.'

'Everybody gets stressed from time to time,' he replied with a patronising smile.

'I only get stressed when I'm forced to take time out of my working day to attend courses.'

'I see your point, but the employee satisfaction survey indicated that sixty per cent of us feel stressed at work, and this course is designed to combat that.'

'I'm in the other forty per cent. I'm not stressed.'

Brian closed his eyes briefly, like a parent dealing with a diffi-cult child. 'Zoë, it would make everybody's life easier if you attended the seminar. It's only three and a half hours.'

'Three and a half hours?' she yelped. Several heads bobbed up from behind the pin-board dividers around the office. 'Where am I supposed to find three and a half hours?'

'You sound stressed,' said Brian, lifting an eyebrow knowingly.

Zoë let out a quiet groan of frustration and looked at her boss. She was beginning to realise that this wasn't a battle worth fighting.

'Fine,' she said eventually. 'I'll go.'

Brian smiled again, pointing his finger in her direction. 'That's the way. PMA. Positive Mental Attitude. Just make sure you let HR know, won't you?'

Zoë lifted the edges of her mouth and watched him strut off.

For several seconds, she stared at the Chase Waterman screen-saver, feeling morose. She wasn't the type to cry, but all of a sudden, she didn't know what else to do. Her job was meaningless, she had wasted precious time arguing over a stress busting seminar, her boyfriend was putting a five grand pay rise ahead of an interesting career and her parents saw her as a failure.

She wanted to pull herself together, to get on with things, but all she could see was the drab, grey landscape stretching out all the way to the horizon. Her feet were pounding on the treadmill, her legs aching, yet she was getting nowhere.

Her watery gaze settled on the free newspaper that Eric had left on the edge of his desk. It was open at an interview with an Olympic hurdler.

Your advice for young athletes? Focus. You can't half-want to win a gold medal. If you really want to achieve something, you have to throw everything you've got into it. It's about taking a risk.

Zoë wiped her eyes, picked up her mobile phone and marched into the lift lobby, pressing the Call button quickly before she could chicken out.

'Louis? It's Zoë. I've made up my mind. I'm going for the deal at Vicinity.'

15

It was a typical Friday night at The Mad Cow: Irish jigs blasting out of the speakers, all-day drinkers slouched at the bar and every inch of flowery, carpeted floor space taken up with jabbering revellers from around the world.

Zoë pushed onto her tiptoes and scanned the pub for a sign of her friends. Her legs felt weak beneath her. She'd barely eaten or slept in the past two days and it probably hadn't been wise to gulp down a large slug of vodka before coming out.

She was nearly an hour late – deliberately so. She wanted to make sure the others were already there, including Ellie, to minimise the amount of time she had to spend with them before breaking the news. A glossy, jet-black ponytail was dancing animatedly in the corner. With a sense of foreboding, Zoë pushed her way through the crowds, following the sound of Shannon's voice.

'Like what? What do you have in common?'

'Well . . .' Kate shrugged defiantly. 'We both like . . . The Charlatans.'

Shannon's hands flew up into the air. 'Oh, right! Well, that's fine then! It's okay to get involved with a married guy who—'

'Divorced,' Kate put in.

'A *divorced* guy who has a small child and – oh, who happens to be your boss – because you both like The Charlatans!'

Zoë stepped forward at this point, forcing a smile and checking the girls all had drinks. Having accepted the inevitable abuse from Shannon about arriving even later than Ellie, she headed off again towards the bar.

The feeling of dread was overwhelming now. It was the same nauseous sensation she'd got just before exams, when everybody started reeling off facts and theories she'd never heard before and she suddenly realised she hadn't done enough revision. She wanted to run out, to think again about what she was doing, to reconsider. But just as the invigilator had stood at the door of the examination hall, making sure everybody stayed inside, the towering barman was standing at the bar, pouring her a pint of Kinsale.

'Wondered where you'd got to,' Eamonn shouted as she edged her way to the bar. It was too late to tell him that today she only wanted a half. 'Call it two pounds, Zola.'

Zoë handed over the money and raised a hand in thanks. She took a circuitous route back to the table, trying to iron out her thoughts as she went. Tonight was, as far as the other girls knew, a planning session to decide what to do if the deal with Blast Management didn't come to anything. Zoë had pitched it as such in the hope that the girls might lower their expectations of Louis – or at least, not raise them any higher. It would have been hard enough to manage Shannon's fantasies with the band staying together, but now that Zoë was effectively breaking it up and taking their manager with her, it was going to be a hundred times harder.

'But listen,' Kate protested as Zoë started removing the coats from the stool they had managed to put by for her. 'You know how I hate standing up and presenting? Well, Mark says I don't need to do it. He's happy to put me on other things.'

'So your relationship is steering your career! Great!' Shannon raised her eyes heavenwards and took a swig of beer.

'No . . .' Kate looked like an injured animal. 'I know it looks as though I'm using Mark to get on in my career, but—'

'It looks like completely the opposite!' yelled Shannon.

'What d'you mean?'

Shannon just shook her head and took another swig.

Kate's eyes darted anxiously from face to face.

Eventually, Shannon explained. 'I mean, *he's* using *you*,' she said. 'Exerting his authority to get what he wants.'

Zoë perched on the stool, half-listening to the conversation, half-thinking about how she was going to break the news. What she dreaded most was the idea of bringing up the subject in the first place. The mere mention of Louis Castle would make them hysterical with excitement and misplaced hope and she knew that once they were screaming about world tours and platinum discs there would be no way she'd be able to break the news.

'It's not like that,' Kate pleaded. Unfortunately, it was all too obvious that it *was* like that. It was ironic; Kate didn't have the confidence to stand up and talk to a bunch of actuaries, so instead she was entering into a relationship with her boss to avoid the situation – a relationship that stood to dent her confidence more.

'You have thought about what might happen if . . .' Even Shannon was sensitive enough to consider her words here. 'If things don't work out?'

At this, Kate seemed to reassert herself. 'Shannon, I'm fine,' she said firmly. 'You don't need to worry.' She looked at Ellie, then Zoë, both of whom were eyeing her warily, although only one with her full attention. 'Stop it! Mark and I are very happy together. We're . . . It's hard to explain. We're just *really well suited*.'

There was a pause. They had all heard that line before.

'What about you?' asked Ellie. 'How's things with James this week?'

It took a couple of seconds for Zoë to register that Ellie was talking to her.

'Oh, er . . .' She looked up. 'Better now, thanks.'

'Oh, no!' Kate stared, her face taught with concern. 'I'm sorry!

Here I am going on about my blossoming romance . . . I had no idea you were having issues with James!'

'No,' Zoë shook her head quickly, the guilt intensifying. 'No, really. It's fine. We're, um . . . we're totally fine now.'

'I didn't realise . . .' Kate looked mortified.

'Seriously, it's fine.'

'Men!' cried Shannon, to Zoë's relief. 'Fuck the lot o' them! Who needs them anyway? Not us! Not Dirty Money, eh?'

Zoë's chest tightened again. She had to do it. Now, before they all got too excited.

'I, um . . . I heard back from Louis,' she said.

'Really?' chorused Shannon and Kate, sitting up instantly. Only Ellie seemed to have gauged from her tone that the news wasn't good.

'Yeah. So . . .' Zoë still hadn't worked out how this was going to come out. She'd set off now; there was no going back.

'What did he say? How did it go with Universal?'

'Well . . .' Zoë stammered and tried to let her hesitation speak for itself.

'Did they listen to the demo tracks?'

Shannon still wasn't getting it. Zoë forced herself to meet the girl's wild gaze and shook her head. 'They turned us down.'

The girls visibly crumpled. Zoë waited for the news to sink in, knowing that the hard part was yet to come.

'But . . .' Shannon's head was lifted again. 'There are other labels, right? It didn't have to be Universal. There are loads of other labels for Louis to call on.'

'Exactly!' cried Kate. 'Their loss, I say.'

Ellie nodded. 'Something else will come along.'

Zoë tried to swallow. She should have expected this. She should have remembered that the girls didn't take rejection easily. The one thing she could count on from the members of Dirty Money – and the one thing she could have done without today – was their resilience.

'Who's he going to next? Did—'

'No!' Zoë shook her head, silencing Shannon's comeback. 'That's just it. He can't go to another label.'

'Why not?' Kate frowned. 'There's no rules that say—'

'He can't put Dirty Money in front of another label, because . . .' This was it. The next sentence would be the most hurtful and damaging one that she would ever say. Like breathing underwater, it was against every instinct in her body to let the words out.

'Because what?' asked Ellie, gently.

Zoë looked at her best friend. Maybe these would be the last words they ever exchanged. In a moment of panic, she wondered whether it was too late to go back on her word, to tell Louis she'd changed her mind. He didn't have anything in writing from her, he couldn't hold her to the decision. Then she realised. This wasn't about Louis. It was about Zoë Kidd. It was about making something of herself and finally fulfilling her dreams.

'Because Universal want a solo artist and I've said I'll sign with them.'

Zoë looked down at her lap, expecting to feel relieved. Instead, all she felt was an overwhelming sense of self-loathing. Suddenly, tears were rolling down her cheeks and dropping onto her hands, her lower lip quivering uncontrollably.

Eventually, she forced herself to look up, then immediately wished she hadn't. Ellie looked distraught, her eyes filling up as she stared into space. Kate was frowning hard at her drink. Shannon was the only one looking right at her.

'How could you?' she snarled, as their eyes met. 'How the *fuck* could you?'

Zoë couldn't reply. Not just because of the tears that were choking her throat but because she didn't have an answer. There were too many elements in the equation to list; saying any one of them would just make her sound pathetic.

Slowly, Kate lifted her head. Then Ellie looked up, her olive complexion blotchy with the tears. There was nothing to say.

For several seconds, the girls stared at Zoë and Zoë stared back, the guilt and the shame building up exponentially.

Suddenly, she could bear it no more. Sniffing away a fresh batch of tears, she pushed back her stool and walked out, leaving her pint untouched on the table.

16

Zoë flipped over the page and groaned inwardly at the sight of the three empty boxes.

10. *Please give details of any achievements that you believe have furthered your career in the last 6 months.*
11. *Describe your career intentions in terms of promotion and direction.*
12. *Please list at least three objectives that you hope to meet in the next 6 months.*

Her computer flashed another reminder that she was due in Brian's office five minutes ago. Zoë dismissed it and stared again at the blank boxes. Appraisal forms annoyed her at the best of times, but today the idea of filling four pages with meaningless waffle pushed her into a state of despair.

The girls still weren't talking to her. Zoë had left voicemails with each of them over the weekend, but unsurprisingly, none of them had returned her calls. She had lost track of the number of times she'd picked up the phone to tell Louis the deal was off and then put it down again. The last three days had been spent in a state of morbid doubt. She wondered whether the feelings would ever abate.

As quickly as her sluggish limbs would allow, Zoë filled the boxes, scribbling 'promotion' and listing some vague points about 'adding value' and being more 'client-centric'. Her phone buzzed on the desk.

> Well I'm behind u
> whatever u do –
> don't beat yourself
> up about the band.
> Call if u need.
> Tam x

Zoë read the text quickly, feeling a surge of affection and wishing she had time to reply. It was good to know that someone was with her in all this. Ironically, she was only just realising that the people she really wanted to speak to, the ones she turned to when things weren't going so well, were the three people in the world whom she couldn't consult.

Her landline was ringing.

'Hello?'

'It's Brian.'

'Ah, right. I'm just . . .'

'You're late for your appraisal meeting.'

'I know, I was just—'

'Punctuality is one of the attributes we're evaluating.'

'I'll be—'

'PAP!'

'I'm sorry?'

'I said, *PAP*! Punctual And Polite – that's our motto, isn't it?'

'Er . . .'

Zoë scooped up the reams of paper that littered her desk and pushed back her chair.

'Sorry,' she muttered, bursting into her boss's office and handing over her form.

'Right . . .' He thumped the pages against his desk for a while until they were all aligned, then laid them flat on the surface. 'We'll start with your self-evaluation, shall we?'

Zoë nodded, trying to stay focused and not think about the look on Ellie's face as she'd broken the news – a look that was emblazoned in her memory forever.

'Okay . . .' Brian scanned the first page then flipped it over, nodding half-heartedly and rubbing his shiny head. 'Meeting client deadlines, yes . . . financial expertise, yes . . . time management, hmm.' The rubbing stopped for a second. 'We'll come onto that.' He turned the final page and squinted at her handwriting. 'OK,' he said, eventually. 'I think everything's fine on your self-appraisal.'

Zoë nodded, wondering what the girls had done after she'd left on Friday night and whether they'd met up over the weekend.

'Let's talk about what your colleagues have to say.'

Maybe they'd all gone to Shannon's and jammed without her. Maybe they were looking for another vocalist – maybe they'd already found one? The thought panicked her.

'It's not all good, I'm afraid.'

What if Dirty Money had re-formed and were currently working on a future hit single with some new frontwoman?

'Zoë? Are you listening?'

'Yes.' Zoë forced her mouth into a smile and tried to summon the echo of Brian's last words. Her smile disappeared in an instant. *Not all good.* This didn't bode well. She looked at the new set of papers in her boss's hand, suddenly realising what they represented. Within those pages were the comments that other members of Chase Waterman had made about her.

He flicked through the sheaf. 'A pleasure to work with, diligent and professional . . .'

A knowledgeable young accountant with good regard for time-keeping, she finished off in her head. Zoë had written the review herself and got a friend in another department to submit it for her. It was a form of self-preservation; everybody did it.

'But look,' Brian pulled out another page. 'Slapdash of late, missing deadlines . . .' Then another. 'Bright and switched-on but recently seems somewhat lacking in motivation.' He searched for another. 'Sweet temperament but variable performance.'

Zoë could feel her throat drying up. She hadn't expected this. Of course, she didn't care what any Chase Waterman employee thought of her, but this . . . this was a shock. She was letting people down. She was failing in her job. Her *career*. And she hadn't even noticed.

For the last six months, she'd been devoting less and less time to her day job: slipping off halfway through the day to write songs, sneaking out early for sound-checks, editing MySpace instead of company audits. Her attention had drifted. In meetings, she'd pretend to be considering a client's choice of accounting practice when in fact she was working out the set list for that night's gig.

Brian was looking at her expectantly. She wasn't sure what to say. This wasn't a situation she'd ever encountered. Usually, when she let people down, it was because she'd decided that something else took priority. She knew in advance that she'd disappointed them and she had an excuse lined up.

'I . . .' There was no excuse. Except to tell Brian that she was secretly planning to become a rock star and that the preparations were distracting her from the day job – which she didn't think would go down very well. 'I've been a bit off colour recently.'

She should have known that Brian wasn't the type to swallow an excuse like that without a detailed explanation. She decided against a full-blown lie, knowing that at some point HR and Occupational Health would want to get involved, summoning time-consuming things like personal statements and doctors' notes.

'Now, Zoë. I'm afraid we can't have comments like this sitting on your appraisal without some serious action.'

She nodded meekly.

Brian stabbed his finger at her self-appraisal that lay on the desk. 'You need to buck up your ideas, and the way to do that is to set yourself targets.'

Zoë nodded again.

'You need to get motivated, you need to improve your concentration and you need to *learn to tell the time*.' He jabbed again at the form, in time with his words.

With excruciating slowness, Brian proceeded to fill out her Objectives box, making suggestions such as 'observe PAP (Punctual And Polite) protocol' and 'ensure RAD (Rigorous Attention to Detail)', to which Zoë could only nod in mute agreement.

She returned to her desk feeling even more subdued than she had done before. The small plastic guitar-shaped calculator – a joke from Ellie – reminded her, yet again, of her betrayal, and now she was clutching a piece of paper that served as the first solid nail in her professional coffin. She had let everybody down: her friends, her colleagues, her family . . . and now herself.

'How was it?' chirped Eric, pushing his angular little face in front of her screen.

Zoë sighed. He clearly wanted to gloat about the success of his own appraisal, but she didn't have the energy for mind games right now.

'It was shit.'

Remarkably, Eric recoiled with little more than a grunt. Zoë leant forward, her head in her hands. The cloud wasn't so much looming as engulfing her. All of a sudden, it seemed quite possible that she would die a lonely death, having achieved nothing and impressed nobody.

It took a while for Zoë to notice the chocolate digestive. It must have been pushed between her planted elbows during her moment of despair.

'Looked like you needed it,' Eric said quietly, staring at a spreadsheet and munching his way through a biscuit of his own.

Zoë stared for a moment, trying to remember a time in the

last eighteen months that her nerdy desk buddy had showed an ounce of compassion. This was unprecedented. She found herself breaking into a weak smile.

'Thanks.'

Eric shrugged. 'Your mobile rang by the way,' he said, not taking his eyes off the screen.

Zoë reached for her phone, quickly navigating to the call register and feeling her spirits fall. It wasn't Ellie or Shannon or Kate.

'Hiiiiii!' began the voicemail. Zoë sat up and clamped the phone to her ear. 'Louis here. I have some good news! The A&R guys at Vicinity wanna meet up to talk about a development contract. They've suggested ten on Friday, their offices, High Street Ken. Hope that works for you. Gimme a call – and then let's get the Zoë Kidd show on the road!'

A shiver ran all the way down Zoë's body as she put down the phone. They were talking about contracts already, and they hadn't even met her.

With a burst of energy that nearly masked her despair, Zoë leapt to her feet and bounded off to the lobby to call Louis back. Then she'd call James, to share the news. And Tamsin. And anyone else she could think of. Suddenly, it didn't matter so much that her colleagues saw her as slapdash or 'somewhat lacking in motivation'. Fuck them, in fact. They were middle managers in an auditing firm. She was an artist. A rock star-to-be. She was about to be signed to Universal.

17

It looked, from the outside, like an ordinary glass-fronted office: an eighties monstrosity on concrete stilts, sealed off from the road with panels of Perspex. If it hadn't been for the small globe symbol painted onto one of the walls, Zoë might have walked on.

As soon as the revolving glass doors sucked her into the atrium, it became clear that the eighties theme was purely an external feature. Inside, the vast, tinted windows cast a futuristic blue glow on the whitewashed surfaces – surfaces across which very serious-looking people were strutting and sashaying. Zoë looked down at her ripped denim as the suited woman handed over her badge, wishing she'd dressed up a little. Her work clothes would have been a closer match to the Universal dress code than what she had on. In fact, if it hadn't been for the giant plasma-screen TV hanging in the centre of the room, blasting out the latest Kate Nash release, she might have thought she was back at Chase Waterman.

Zoë walked over to find her manager reclining on one of the leather couches in the reception area. He was wearing another tasteless shirt, this one black with little bursts of silver and gold.

A pasty young man was striding towards them, hand extended. Despite his young age – Zoë guessed mid-twenties – he had the beginnings of a paunch hanging over his suit trousers. His hair was sculpted into a quiff that resembled a Cadbury's Flake.

'I'm Ben,' said the guy, emerging from the manly handshake with the manager and turning to Zoë. 'A&R at Vicinity.'

'Nice to meet you.' She smiled, trying not to look at the greasy sheen on his forehead.

'Zoë Kidd,' Louis announced loudly. 'Top-selling artist of next year!'

Zoë looked at the floor as they gathered their belongings and headed towards the lifts, which were something of a feature in the middle of the atrium.

'Will Jenson be joining us?' asked Louis as they accelerated upwards.

Ben pulled a face. 'He sends his apologies.'

Louis nodded, slowly. 'And Harry?'

Ben pulled the same face again. 'He might make it along later.'

They arrived almost immediately at the fourth floor. Zoë waited for her stomach to catch up and stepped out in front of a large, disc-like sign saying Vicinity.

She followed in silence as they passed through the blue-tinted offices, wondering who Jenson and Harry were and trying not to stare too much. The Vicinity offices, it transpired, were nothing like those of Chase Waterman. Everything was made of either glass or chrome and there were discs everywhere: disc lamp-shades, disc desk tidies, disc wastepaper bins . . . Zoë gawped like a little girl on a school trip.

This was where all the magic happened, thought Zoë, still staring as they entered the meeting room. The table was suspended from the ceiling and even the conference phone looked like something out of *The Matrix*. She wanted to call someone up, just to describe it all to them. If only she could call the girls, if only Ellie could see her now, if only . . . Zoë felt wretched. None of the girls had called her back.

'So.' Ben was looking at her quite intensely, his red, sunken eyes roaming her body as though she'd forgotten to put her clothes on. 'Thanks for coming in.'

Zoë summoned her thoughts back to the meeting, which had clearly started, despite the lack of agendas or notes. She wondered what her boss would make of the situation.

'We love your music,' he said, his gaze flitting down to her cleavage. 'The DVD . . .' He looked across at Louis. 'Well, it gave us an idea.'

Zoë smiled meekly. If only she'd known, weeks ago, that the disc would end up in an office like this. Perhaps, if she'd known, she would have asked somebody other than Shannon's mate's mate to record the gig. Perhaps if the video had been of better quality, the other girls would have come across better and . . . no. She stopped herself there. She had spent too much time lately playing What if. They were here to talk about the future, not the past. It was Zoë Kidd they were interested in, not Dirty Money.

'I'm a signer for Vicinity,' said Ben. 'I work under Harry Poole, who reports directly into Jenson.'

Zoë nodded slowly. Jenson. Clearly this was a name she was supposed to know.

'Jenson Davies,' Ben clarified. 'Head of A&R at Vicinity.'

'Yeah, of course.' Zoë nodded, fooling nobody.

Ben started talking about the different departments within the label and how they all fitted together. 'The press guys work closely with the pluggers while they're trying to get you airplay and screen time . . .'

Zoë tried to listen, but the mention of words like 'publicist' and 'chain stores' sent her imagination into overdrive. She was seeing herself walking into HMV and finding blocks of CDs bearing her name piled up on the shelves, opening iTunes and finding her cover artwork plastered all over the homepage. That was all she'd ever dreamed of. She couldn't believe this was actually being discussed.

'Do you have a view on that?'

'Um . . .' Zoë blinked. She had lapsed into nodding mode.

'Courtney Love meets Lady Gaga,' Louis put in.

Before Zoë could ask about the supposed encounter, Ben was off again.

'It's very important to know where you sit on the shelf, so to speak. Too many artists fall by the wayside because they don't have a firm grasp of their genre. Their *market*.'

Zoë nodded, trying to work out the connection between Lady Gaga, Courtney Love, shelves and markets.

'It sounds mercenary,' Ben went on. 'But music has become commoditised. Artists are products, if you like, each one suiting the tastes of a different group – each one branded to reflect who they're aimed at.'

A quick glance at her manager told Zoë that the best thing to do was keep nodding. She was beginning to suspect that Louis had just compared her music to that of Lady Gaga and Courtney Love – which was absurd; she was nothing like either of them.

'We're one of the most commercial labels at Universal,' Ben explained. 'Jenson was one of the founders with Edgar, only three years ago, and already we're outselling all but one of the established labels. We're efficient, smart and we like to do things a little differently. We push our artists out quickly.'

'Right.' Zoë looked at him, not particularly liking the toothpaste analogy that sprang to mind. Still, if being 'pushed out' meant selling records and playing to millions of fans, it was a process she was willing to endure.

'I'm telling you this because it's important you know what you're letting yourself in for,' said Ben, smiling with one side of his mouth and then looking at Louis.

'To make sure you're ready for the *big time*,' the large man added.

Zoë forced a laugh. She wished he would stop using that phrase.

'Now, I know you've been with your band for—' Ben looked down at the blank page of his notebook.

'Six and a half years,' she put in, trying not to think about what she was saying.

'Okay,' he nodded. 'So we're going to have to think carefully about repertoire. I think Louis said you wrote most of the songs for . . .'

'Dirty Money. Yes, but it wasn't just me. Ellie, our rhythm guitarist, helped with most of them.'

'Helped?' Ben tilted his head to one side, his sunken eyes turning to little slits. 'Did she write any of the words?'

'N-no,' Zoë replied hesitantly, wondering what he was getting at.

'Did she write the tunes?'

'Well . . . no. She added harmonies. Brought the songs to life . . .' Zoë forced herself to stop reminiscing.

'Okay. So we might need to cut her in on some of the publishing rights.'

Zoë nodded, not sure whether this was a question or a state-ment. She hadn't considered this part of the transition from band member to solo artist. All those afternoons spent with Ellie in their cramped student bedrooms, strumming guitars, playing with words . . . she had never imagined that she'd have to think back and agree on exactly who wrote what.

'And you have other repertoire, besides what you played with the band?'

'Oh, I've got loads—'

'Not that you'll need to write *all* your own material,' he added, looking quickly at Louis. 'You're in safe hands when it comes to finding songwriters. We have a strong publishing arm.'

Zoë frowned. *Songwriters?* There had been no mention of that up until now.

'Now, fan base,' Ben went on quickly, as though ticking off points on his imaginary agenda.

It was clear that he'd had this conversation several times before. Zoë wondered how many artists they signed each month.

'I think Louis said you had quite an online following. Who ran the MySpace page for Dirty Money?'

'I do – did.'

If Ben noticed the slip in tense, he didn't show it. 'So you can easily transfer the fan base. Send out a message, make it read-only, that sort of thing?'

This was another thing Zoë hadn't thought about. She nodded, trying hard not to think about the implications. It was small things like this that hurt the most: the practical details like log ons and passwords made up of band member initials and birthdays. Old messages from fans that had been left after memorable gigs. It was like a form of bereavement following the death of a family member; you didn't cry when it happened, only when you picked up their favourite mug or found a shopping list in their handwriting.

'No problem,' she said, injecting some strength into her voice.

Ben went on to explain how a decent fan base was the key to a successful career in pop.

'We want artists who can stick around for ten, twenty years, selling a steady stream of records and – most importantly – working the live circuit. But to get there, you have to compete with the one-hit warblers. Which means . . .' He drew a breath. 'Which means building up a fan-base that compares with the Saturday night viewing figures for a certain televised talent contest.'

Zoë looked at him as it all began to sink in. Ben was young, but he knew his stuff. He may have been checking out her breasts as he said them, but his words made sense. It was going to be a tough slog getting Zoë Kidd out there. Her MySpace page – or rather, her ex-band's MySpace page, had twelve thousand friends. Talent Tout was watched by twelve *million* viewers.

'Don't worry,' Ben went on, perhaps seeing through her rigid smile. 'It's doable. Vicinity had forty-seven top tens last year.'

'Toadally doable,' Louis added, grinning. 'We just gotta get you up there on the stage!'

Ben nodded. They were like a double act: Mr Pallid and

Mr Round. 'We'll get some decent musicians behind you and you'll be up and running.'

Musicians. Zoë looked at him. She had almost forgotten the small matter of replacing the members of her band with a bunch of strangers.

'Once you've got a few solo gigs to your name, I'll bring the guys down to watch. Then we'll go from there,' said Ben, flipping shut his blank notepad. The meeting appeared to be over.

Zoë followed the men through the open-plan office, taking less notice of the disc-based furniture and thinking about some of the things that had just been said. The meeting had raised more questions than answers. Suddenly, the idea of getting signed had taken on a different form in her mind. It was still exciting, but it no longer felt like the final solution. Whereas before she had thought of Vicinity as some kind of catapult that would propel her to stardom, she now saw it as more of a mule – an aid that would do its best to take her up this enormous mountain she was trying to climb, but with no guarantees. It could easily drop her along the way.

Ben took a final glance down at Zoë's legs and leaned in to kiss her cheek – something else Zoë had never experienced in the auditing world. 'I'll see you on the stage.'

It was only when she had parted company with her manager that Zoë realised her phone was ringing.

'Hi, is that Zoë, of Dirty Money?'

She hesitated. 'Y-yes.' It was half correct.

'It's Roy Davison here, of Hot Rocks Records. You sent us a demo CD a few weeks ago? With a . . . a fiver enclosed?'

Zoë's heart started thumping.

'We really like the tracks and we're keen to hear more. Can you tell me when you're next playing live?'

18

'Charcoal grey?' James pulled the jacket off its hanger and slung it over one shoulder.

Zoë shook her head. 'Too shiny. You look like an estate agent.'

'Black?'

'Undertaker.'

'Pinstripes?'

'Tosser.'

'Cheers, Zoë.' He ran a hand along the line of padded shoulders, wandering into the next aisle.

James had decided that in light of his imminent promotion – which, as far as Zoë could make out, meant that he'd be doing the same job but in a different part of the office – he should buy some new clothes.

'Next shop?'

Zoë nodded, scanning the department store to check they had left no rack unscoured.

'They're like buses, eh.'

Zoë frowned. 'What, suits?'

'Record deals. I presume that's what you were thinking about.' He smiled.

Zoë's mind flipped back to their previous conversation and her hand went instinctively to the pocket containing Roy Davison's phone number. As it happened, for a couple of seconds, her mind had ventured away from the subject of record deals.

She had been comparing her career to that of her boyfriend's and wondering why she couldn't get excited about hers in the way that James did about his.

'I am now. Shall we try in here?'

They entered another characterless store and headed for the menswear department.

'More like rally cars than buses,' she said, having thought about it. 'They stick together on purpose.'

'What d'you mean?'

'A&R guys. They hunt in packs – they don't think for themselves.'

'So . . . you think the two offers are related?'

'They're not offers yet,' she reminded him. 'But yeah, I reckon they might be. As soon as there's a 'buzz' around an act, they all leap on the bandwagon. It's possible Hot Rocks got wind of Louis Castle's involvement and went diving into the bin for our demo CD.'

'Or the other way round,' he suggested. 'Vicinity heard about Hot Rocks' plans and tried to get in first.' James picked up the first suit they came to, a pale grey affair with a salmon-like sheen.

'No,' Zoë said firmly. 'To the jacket, I mean. And no . . . I don't think Hot Rocks would have sat on it for this long.'

James grunted, finally pulling out a reasonable-looking jacket and getting Zoë's nod of approval. Finding no other options within his price range that didn't look as though they'd been waxed, he went to try on his choice, leaving Zoë sitting on a small, fabric cube.

If, as Zoë suspected, Hot Rocks were bandwagon-jumpers, they probably didn't have any firm plans for Dirty Money other than to try and poach them from under the noses of whichever labels Louis was trying to sign them to. But if that was the case, it seemed odd that they hadn't approached their manager directly. The fact that they'd used the contact details on the CD sleeve implied that they might be genuinely interested in the band, which would mean . . .

'No.'

'No?' James turned a few times, trying to look over his shoulder at his own backside.

'You look like someone from Riverdance,' she said.

'Right. Okay.' James pulled a face and disappeared again.

It almost seemed plausible that Hot Rocks Records had plans for Dirty Money. If that was the case, she thought excitedly, then maybe they could follow their dream after all, get signed, make it as a band . . . She was, of course, ignoring the two big, white elephants in the room – the first one being that the girls were unlikely to talk to her ever again and the second one being that Hot Rocks Records was, in Louis's words, 'small fry'.

Earlier in the week, calling her manager on the premise of discussing their meeting with Universal, she had dropped the label's name in an attempt to elicit information. Louis's answer was delivered in the form of a short hoot of laughter and those two words.

'Onwards?' said James, forcing her out of her thought bubble.

Zoë was relieved to see the Riverdance outfit draped over the rejects rail. They returned to the escalators, both slowing as they passed the in-store café. With a quick, reciprocal grin, they changed their course and headed for the sticky bun counter.

'So.' James sat down first, reaching across and breaking a chunk off her muffin. 'Why d'you actually need a record label, anyway? I thought you said these days you could get your tracks onto iTunes without leaving your bedroom.'

Zoë thought for a second. It was true that record labels were becoming redundant; in theory, an artist could release their own material and become a success on their own. But examples of that actually happening were rare.

'It's the marketing budget, I guess. And distribution. Getting 'in' with HMV and Tesco and that.'

That was the reason 'small fry' labels like Hot Rocks couldn't compete with the likes of Universal. According to Louis, whom

131

Zoë had asked surreptitiously the previous week, HRR comprised just three men: Roy (A&R), Rupert (Legal) and Tim (everything else). It was Tim's job to ensure airplay for their artists on radio and TV, to get them covered in the national press, to spread the word on the web, to liaise with distributors . . . Unless Tim was superhuman, it was unlikely that Hot Rocks would be pushing out many chart-topping hits this year.

'As a marketing man,' said James, 'I'd say the bigger the better.'

Zoë nodded, already having come to the same conclusion.

James popped the last crumb into his mouth and put down his fork. 'So, decision made.'

Zoë said nothing. Everything seemed so simple in James's world. It was all black and white, never grey. In some ways she envied him for being so decisive. He took a stance and then stuck to it, while she dithered around, trying to see things from every possible viewpoint. Zoë ate all she could of the giant muffin, transferring what was left onto James's plate. Then she reached into her pocket and drew out the scrap of paper.

She closed her eyes, rubbing them with the heels of her hands. What it all boiled down to, she realised, was whether she could bear to see the girls go on and 'make it' without her. If her deal with Vicinity fell through, could she watch her old band mates reach number one? Did she want to see them perform live at Glastonbury? Did she relish the idea of hearing their songs on the radio, knowing that she'd made the decision to cut them loose?

'Right.' She pulled out her phone out of her bag. There was no question, all of a sudden. She couldn't deny her friends a shot at the big-time – especially after what she'd already done.

'Right,' echoed James, smiling as Zoë texted Roy Davison's details to Kate. 'Now let's go and buy me a suit.'

19

'Okay, so you keep playing that riff, no – yeah, that one, and then the bass comes in . . .'

Zoë closed her eyes briefly, trying to map out the parts in her head. It was harder than she had imagined, teaching other people how to play her songs.

The problem wasn't a lack of talent; the guys were spot on and very responsive. Ben had meant what he'd said about getting decent musicians to play for her. The problem was that they weren't Shannon, Ellie and Kate. Never, in all her years of playing in the band, had Zoë told the girls what to play. They'd just known. Or at least, they'd played something that worked, that had stuck.

Zoë realised now that what she'd told Ben was a lie. The Dirty Money tracks hadn't been written by her and Ellie; they were a group effort. She'd written the lyrics and come up with the outline, but the colours, the shading, the intricate little details . . . she couldn't take credit for them. In places, she could barely describe what Ellie was playing, let alone demonstrate for the sandy-haired rhythm guitarist.

'I'll make something up,' he said, as Zoë exasperatedly tried to explain how 'Ball and Chain' was supposed to sound. 'From the top?'

Zoë nodded gratefully. They had been in the studio for nearly an hour and the knot of tension in her stomach had yet to dissolve. It didn't help that every time Louis popped his head around the door of the studio, she was tripping over muddled descriptions of bass lines, trying to unravel the fabric of six and a half years' work.

'Cool,' said the guitarist, nodding as they came off the final note.

Zoë nodded. It sounded all right. Perhaps she would just have to get used to the idea that the songs would be played differently now. She knew that to replicate the exact sound of Dirty Money was an impossibility. A change of musicians meant a change of sound. She had to accept it, to embrace it.

'What do you sink for ze end?' barked Christophe, the drummer. 'Ziss?' He bashed out an impressive finale. 'Or ziss?'

Zoë listened as the Frenchman performed option two. They sounded exactly the same.

'Um . . . The second one?'

Christophe grunted. 'I prefer ze first.'

Zoë glanced at Tommy, who was clearly grinning behind his hair as though he'd seen this before. According to Ben, the musicians had all played together in the past.

'Oh, er, well . . . let's go with that then.'

The drummer seemed satisfied. 'Good.'

Playing with a new set of musicians would, Zoë realised, take a bit of getting used to. Shannon was the most blasé drummer on the circuit, while Christophe was like a click-track. And as for her new bassist, she had nothing to go on but long, greasy black hair and a frighteningly tight pair of jeans.

It felt awkward, instructing the guys on how to play. She was used to a world where all members were equal. Now, all of a sudden she was playing the lead role and she wasn't sure she liked it.

Louis had advised her to 'get through as much as you can', which, looking at the song list and the available rehearsal time, she had translated as meaning, *don't rehearse, just play*. They were on song four of sixteen; Zoë hoped the musicians had good memories.

'This one's called "Clap Now Turn Around". It's . . . it's a kind of piss-take on the teenybop music that fills the charts and we wrote it a couple of years ago, after we, er, did a gig supporting this girl-band type group . . .'

Tommy, the guitarist, met her eye as he picked out his part. Of the three musicians, he seemed the most responsive. His over-grown hair hid much of his face but his brown, smiling eyes were just visible behind the scruffy locks.

Zoë started to play. The explanation of the origin and senti-ment of each song was important, she felt, to let her new band members know what the hell she was singing about. The problem was, spelling it out brought it all flooding back. She could smell the white musk in the air, could hear the high-pitched jeering from the pubescent crowds as Dirty Money had left the stage, tails between legs, after that stupid gig.

The Girl Friday gig had been one of the band's lowest points. But, as ever, they'd bounced back, turning the experience into some-thing positive. After a few days of moping, Ellie and Zoë had written one of their most upbeat, ironic tracks to date. Zoë forced herself to focus, hoping the guys hadn't noticed the wobble in her voice.

Before long, the rhythm section had cottoned on and Tommy was improvising with his own harmonies. It was almost a relief to Zoë when the song started taking a form of its own – a form that was different to the one she remembered. The new sound was a good thing, she decided.

'How's it goin'?' It was Louis. Zoë wished he would just leave them to it; he was like a mother checking up on adolescent kids on their first date. 'I'm gonna shoot. You'll be okay without me?'

'I think we'll manage.'

Tommy nodded, catching her eye. 'Just about.'

'All right, you guys.' Louis winked, missing the sarcasm. 'Have a good 'un!'

The door swung shut. In the silence that followed, there was a frog-like croak from behind the bassist's greasy locks.

'Ciggy?' he croaked again. 'Ciggy?' It was the first thing he'd said all day. By common consent, they left their instruments and walked out into the corridor.

The building reminded Zoë of school: old and draughty with pipes running along the whitewashed walls and all the windows painted shut. The setup was basic, but Zoë couldn't complain; at least they didn't have Mrs Costello banging on the ceiling for them to stop.

Zoë bought a Coke from the vending machine and looked around. 'Anyone . . . want anything?'

'Get me a Sprite,' replied Christophe, pulling a cigarette out of its packet and ramming it behind his ear.

Biting her lip, Zoë did as she was told and handed the drummer his drink. She had a feeling he knew he was being rude; he was just on some sort of ego trip. Christophe was probably in his mid-twenties and good-looking, in an angular way. The arrogance suited his looks.

'Come,' he said, taking the can and indicating for the bassist to follow him outside.

'Coming, man,' Rod mumbled, perching on the tiny couch and rolling a Rizla on his knee.

Zoë watched as the unlikely pair headed off, relieved that of the three guys, the non-smoker was Tommy.

'So,' he said, slouching against the back of the couch, which they had subliminally agreed was too small for the two of them to share. 'What d'you think?'

Zoë hesitated, not quite sure what he was asking.

'Of Tweedledum and Tweedledee,' he clarified, nodding at the space where Christophe and Rod had been.

'Oh.' Zoë smiled, relieved. Tommy's eyes had a permanent, mischievous glint, as though he always saw the funny side. 'Well, they're very good musicians.'

Tommy nodded.

Zoë wanted to point out that all three of them were, including him, but couldn't think of a way to do so without sounding as though she was flirting. Tommy was probably used to having girls flirt with him. His dark, friendly eyes and tousled hair gave him a rugged charm.

'If a little eccentric,' he added. 'You get used to them.'

'Do you . . . Have you worked with them a lot?'

'Our paths cross now and then.'

Zoë felt suddenly intrigued by Tommy and Christophe and Rod and the whole world of jobbing musicians – a world she knew almost nothing about.

'Are you a full-time musician?' she asked.

Tommy's lips curled up at the edges. 'Is there such a thing?'

'Oh.' Zoë floundered. 'I mean—'

'I'm kidding. I guess I am – or as full as it's possible to be. I don't have to wait tables, if that's what you mean. I'm a song-writer, too. That's what pays my bills.'

Zoë wanted to ask what he wrote, who performed his songs and how much money he made, but it all seemed too soon.

'What about you?' he asked, pulling a packet of gum from his faded jeans pocket and offering her a piece. 'Are you full time on Project Zoë?'

'N-no,' she stammered, extracting the chewing gum and real-ising that she was probably the only person in the building who wasn't making money from music.

Tommy nodded. 'Holding onto the day job until the dream comes true?'

Zoë looked at him, relieved that he'd grasped it before she had to explain. 'Something like that.'

Zoë allowed herself to dwell on the sad truth: she didn't have the balls to break free entirely. How many successful artists were there who had held down 'proper' jobs until the moment they got signed? Most were living off the breadline, barely able to keep their guitars in strings. Her mind returned to the newspaper interview with the Olympic hurdler. *You can't half-want to win a gold medal. If you really want to achieve something, you have to throw everything you've got into it.* She blamed her parents; she wasn't brave enough to take the risk.

'Wish I'd done that,' he said quietly.

She looked up. Tommy was squinting at a spot on the wall opposite, chewing slowly. The glint in his eye had gone; he looked pensive, all of a sudden.

'What d'you mean?'

Tommy blinked and shook his head, as though drawing a line under his thoughts. 'Nothing. Oh, hey.' He turned and raised a hand to the other musicians as they trooped back in.

'Ziss wezzer is orrible,' Christophe spat. 'I ate ziss fucking country.'

Tommy grinned. 'Shall we . . . crack on?'

Zoë nodded and led them back into the studio.

20

'Alrighty,' Louis blew down the phone line as if limbering up for the conversation. 'So, the site's looking good, but we need some fresh shots.'

'Fresh shots?' Zoë pulled the kitchen chair closer to the table and looked again at the website. It did indeed look good, although she wasn't sure it needed quite so many photos of herself all over the homepage.

'Yeah. Like, *proper* ones. These look like prison mug shots, like you're in your pyjamas or something.'

Zoë looked at the images. She was wearing jeans in most of them, either with a T-shirt or a baggy top. They had been cropped from group photos taken by Tam's boyfriend, outside Ellie's caravan. She remembered the shoot vividly. The girls had agreed to go for the semi-clad, gypsy look – Shannon had seen the caravan as a prop too good to waste – but then it had rained all night and the mud had proved impossible in heels, so they'd decided to wear what they always wore on stage.

'We need an image for you, y'know?'

'Right.' Over the course of the last week, Louis had called with almost hourly updates on what needed to be done in the run-up to her first proper gig. Makeovers had been booked, exercise regimes laid out, special diets recommended. Holidays were out of the question for at least the next year. She wondered how much longer she'd be able to continue leading her double life.

'Certain images have already been taken,' he said. 'Kylie's done the "brave" thing, Lady Gaga's bagged "mad", Joss Stone is kinda "alternative", Lily Allen's got "rude" all sewn up . . . Florence, well, she's kinda ginger . . .'

'Ginger isn't an image,' Zoë objected, slightly appalled by the implication that every artist's attributes could be boiled down to a single word.

'Okay, whatever. Point is, we need to decide how you'll be seen. And I had a little word with Harry, who agrees with me.'

'So . . .'

'We think we should go with "bold".'

Zoë nodded into the handset, pleasantly surprised with the conclusion, if a little perturbed that it had been drawn in her absence. Bold seemed okay. It implied confidence, individuality, a bit of audacity, perhaps . . . Yes, bold could work for Zoë Kidd.

'It's important to get the label's buy-in at an early stage,' he explained. 'No point in going down one road and then having to repackage you later on.'

Zoë mumbled her agreement, the alarm bells getting louder. The production line analogy seemed suddenly very real.

'We're thinking bold songs, bold statements, bold hair, bold clothes, everything kinda . . .'

'Bold?' Zoë wondered what bold hair looked like.

'Yeah. Now, you say you wanna use your own photographer?'

'Yes,' Zoë replied firmly. She hadn't actually asked her sister's boyfriend to take the photos, but she felt sure he'd do it. She'd rather have Jonathan revelling in her attempts at boldness than some stranger.

'And clothes?'

'Well . . .'

'I'm thinking, like, jumpsuits. Lycra. That sorta thing.'

Zoë spluttered. 'I've got . . . leggings?'

'Shiny?'

'Er . . .'

'What colour?'

'Black.'

'Not bold enough. Sounds like you need to go shopping. I'll get Jenson to sort something out from the development budget.'

'But . . .' Zoë liked the idea of shopping at the label's expense, but not if it meant coming back with bagfuls of Spandex. 'Can't I base my image on my wardrobe, rather than the other way round?'

'What does your wardrobe look like?'

'It's . . .' Zoë refrained from describing the tall, wooden structure at the end of her bed. 'Bold, in a casual sort of way.'

'Uh-oh. You mean like those PJs?'

'N—' Zoë smiled reluctantly. 'Okay. I'll go shopping.'

'Great. You'll enjoy it! The bolder the better, yeah?'

'Yeah,' she replied, wishing for the millionth time that the other girls were with her on this. Shannon would have plenty to say about shopping for spray-on outfits.

'How quickly can you get the photos done?'

Zoë rubbed her eyes and pushed the laptop away. The photos of her outside Ellie's caravan were making her feel sad.

'The next week or two?'

'Okay. I've told the web guys to put things on hold until we have the full set. Don't leave it too long. Designers don't come cheap and I've told Jenson I'll stump up the cash while we're getting started.'

'Sure.' Zoë forced herself to sound positive. She hadn't realised Louis was putting his own money on the line. He and the Vicinity guys were expecting great things from her. They were making an investment. The musicians, the outfits, the website design – they would all be recouped, in the long run, from her record sales.

'Now, I have some good news. Neil's got you your first solo gig.'

'Really?' Zoë's heart started pounding. 'Where? When?'

Louis laughed. 'It's nothing big. Just a grubby little place in Denmark Street. Next Thursday, ten o'clock. Supporting a Scandi band called Toffeeheads or something.'

Zoë felt a flutter of nerves rise up from her stomach. 'Thanks!'

She was going to go on stage as Zoë Kidd. Without the girls.

'Actually,' he went on, 'it's a dive, to tell you the truth. But it'll be a good place to start.'

'Right,' she replied, less certainly.

'Don't worry, we'll get you some bigger deals later on. I've told Neil to hold fire a while. Get a few weeny gigs under your belt before we let you loose on the main circuit.'

Main circuit. Zoë swallowed anxiously as images of the Hammersmith Apollo and Shepherd's Bush Empire flashed through her mind.

'Ben will probably swing by, but we'll leave it a couple of gigs before we get the big guns down to watch. You'll be ready by next Thursday?'

She cleared her throat and made a concerted effort to sound bold. 'Of course.'

'You getting on okay with the guys?'

'Really well. They're great.'

Louis seemed pleased and spent a couple of minutes talking about various musicians he'd come across during his time and how Tommy and Christophe and Rod were among the best he'd seen. It was true, thought Zoë. The musicians were fantastic. Vicinity obviously had access to the crème de la crème of the talent pool. After only a couple of rehearsals, Zoë was beginning to feel at home in her new ensemble. But the fact remained, they weren't Dirty Money.

'Let me know about those photos,' he said, bringing the conversation to a close.

'Will do.'

'Remember, *bold*.'

'Bold,' echoed Zoë, shuddering slightly.

'And then we can think about getting you some new songs. Great! See you next Thursday.'

'Get—' Zoë stammered, but the line was already dead.

21

Zoë leapt up the steps two at a time and flung open the door, glancing around for her mother. A waitress shot her a look that implied this was not the sort of establishment in which doors were usually flung, and leaned over to press it shut. The clock on the wall told her she was fifteen minutes late.

The red silk blouse shone out like a beacon from the back of the café, guiding Zoë through the maze of chintzy tables and chairs. Her mother always liked to meet in places like this.

'There you are!' Mrs Kidd rose to her feet, revealing a floral, calf-length skirt. Two loops of pearls hung heavily on the gaudy red blouse.

Zoë emerged from their embrace, noting her mother's freshly coiffed hair. It was ironic; most of her mother's life – the married part – had been spent trying to cultivate this image of middle-class chic, with pearls and perms and floral attire. Meanwhile, Zoë had spent most of hers trying to shrug off her privileges, turning her back on the orchestra, tennis coaching and Latin.

'*Lovely* to see you.' She beamed at Zoë, who smiled back. 'I was beginning to wonder whether you'd make it. Are you working flat-out at the moment?'

Zoë shrugged. 'Pretty much, yeah.'

In truth, she was late because she'd been scouring the online boutiques for outfits that might qualify as 'bold'.

'How's it all going? Shall we order?'

Catching the eye of a passing waitress, Mrs Kidd started pointing at various items on the menu. Zoë ordered a jacket potato and wondered how long it would be until they got onto the subject her mother really liked to discuss: Tamsin's career.

'It's going really well,' she lied.

It was futile to be honest about the situation. If she told her parents the truth, they would only berate her and remind her of what she already knew – that she would do better to put more emphasis on her career.

'Oh, I am pleased.' Her mother was beaming. 'I was worried for a while that something might have been out of place at work – you know, when you had that little . . . outburst.'

Zoë forced her mouth into a placid smile, fighting the urge to scream. That was what they were calling it. First, they had given away her guitar, and now they were patronising her by referring to her reaction as a *little outburst*.

They had talked on the phone a few times since that night at the Royal Festival Hall. They had discussed Tamsin's pupillage, Zoë's job, the cold spell of weather they'd had during March . . . but not, of course, Zoë's *little outburst*. In true British style, they had tackled the situation by sweeping it under the carpet and pretending it wasn't there.

'I was upset about my guitar,' Zoë stated coldly. 'It was nothing to do with work.'

'Oh,' she nodded. 'The guitar. Of course.'

Zoë tried to maintain her exterior calm. She was seething. Her parents just couldn't help judging everybody according to *their* values. They resolutely failed to see anything from another person's point of view. When she'd agreed to meet up today, Zoë had fully intended to go with the flow, to nod and smile, to laugh at whatever bad jokes came along. But, just as it was impossible to prepare for the effect of nerves in a performance, it was impossible to plan for unexpected provocation.

'Don't say it like that.'

'Say it like what, dear?'

'Like, *oh, of course, I'd forgotten.*'

'Well, I had forgotten.'

'What, you'd forgotten about chucking out one of the most precious things I ever owned?'

'You never used it, darling.'

Zoë let out a growl of frustration just as their plates were set down. There was some mention of sauces, but Zoë's thunderous expression sent the waitress teetering off without an answer.

They ate in silence, Zoë hacking and sawing at the potato skin like a crazed murderer disposing of the evidence.

'I'm glad your job's going well, anyway,' said her mother, setting her cutlery neatly on the side of her plate.

Something inside Zoë snapped. Her mother's remark, which could well have been perfectly innocent, suddenly seemed laden with meaning.

'I hate my job, Mum.'

She knew it was childish, but Zoë took pleasure in the look of shock on her mother's face.

'And I'm going solo.'

The startled expression turned to one of confusion. 'You're . . . what?'

An overwhelming feeling of victory swept over her. 'I'm going solo. As an artist. Our manager's got me a deal with Universal.'

Okay, it wasn't quite true. But nearly. Vicinity was funding her musicians and studio time. It was only a matter of time before the proper record contract was signed.

Her mum didn't speak for a few seconds. She reached for the pearls around her neck and started working her fingertips along them.

'So, you've . . . left the band?'

Zoë's jubilation evaporated. Deliberately or not, her mother had brought up the one element of the plan that left her feeling wretched.

'Yes.' She forced aside her despondency. She couldn't fall apart in front of her mother.

'So . . . what does that mean?'

'It means I do a few gigs with the new musicians, then I write some new songs and get signed to the label, then I release a record.'

Deep down, Zoë knew what she was trying to do. It wasn't a question of shocking her mother. It was a matter of impressing her. She wanted her mother to be *happy* for her.

'Is that . . . the plan, then?' She still looked perplexed.

'That's the plan.'

'And your job?'

Zoë sighed. She should've guessed that this would be one of her mother's first concerns.

'Don't worry; I haven't quit or anything.'

'But . . .'

'I'm going to play it by ear.'

Zoë pushed her plate away, feeling irritable. It wasn't as if she hadn't thought this through. She knew that living a double life as rock star-cum-auditor might get tricky. She knew that at some point, one would have to give.

The waitress placed their bill on the table and scurried off. Zoë's mum looked at it, frowning in a way that suggested she had bigger things on her mind than the price of their potato and salad.

'Is it . . . Is there a salary?'

Zoë looked at her. 'Yeah, it's forty thousand a year with a pension scheme, health insurance and company car. No, Mum. You don't earn a salary as a musician.'

'Oh.' She blushed. 'So . . .'

'Royalties,' said Zoë. 'From album sales.'

'Right, yes, of course.'

Zoë placed a five-pound note on the table and watched as, inevitably, it was pushed away. Her mother looked suddenly . . .

vulnerable. Her face and neck had turned red and she was obviously cursing her ignorance. Zoë found herself relenting a little, feeling almost sorry for her.

'You know,' said Zoë as the fiver was rejected for the third time. 'Some parents would be proud of their daughter getting signed to a big label.'

Mrs Kidd let go of her pearl necklace and let her hand drop onto the table, reaching out for Zoë's. Slowly, a meek smile spread across her lips.

'I am proud,' she said, squeezing her daughter's hand. 'We both are.'

22

'Thank you! Thanks. That was called *Why not?* And now I'm gonna hand you over to the boys from Norway . . .' She glanced down at the beer-soaked set list. 'Tøffelhead! Enjoy your night!'

Zoë pushed the mike back into its stand and picked her way to the edge of the stage. Louis had been right about the venue. It was like a draughty railway station toilet with cables all over the floor.

Zoë rammed her guitar into its case and sighed. All things considered, the gig hadn't gone badly. Nothing had broken, none of the songs had fallen apart and the crowds, sloshing about in their damp-walled pit, had made all the right noises. Zoë couldn't think of a way in which it could have gone better; she just didn't feel high as she usually did at the end of a gig.

'What is ze problem?' asked Christophe, looking over and frowning, as though it was something that needed fixing, like a leaking tap.

'No problem.' Zoë waved a hand casually. 'It was great. Thanks guys. Really good gig.'

She stepped out of the stilt-like shoes that Louis had convinced her to wear and rummaged about for her hoodie. That was probably part of the problem, she thought: she'd spent the last half hour tottering about in pink heels and a matching plastic mini-dress in front of a roomful of indie fans.

'Nice look.' Tommy glanced down at her bare legs and trainers, swinging his guitar case onto one shoulder.

She glanced down. An inch of pink fabric peeped out from beneath the baggy top, giving the impression that she had forgotten to put on her trousers.

'I've gotta shoot. Big day tomorrow.' He raised a hand. 'See ya.'

Zoë reached for her jeans and returned the gesture. For some reason, she wanted to find out what was happening tomorrow. What made it a 'big day'? It felt wrong, knowing so little about her band members' lives. When Dirty Money had played a gig, the girls would all know exactly what each one was doing the following day. That was why, Zoë believed, they had made such great music. That was why . . . That was why she didn't feel high.

The door slammed and Zoë zipped up her case. She was beginning to wonder whether she'd ever get over the breakup. It was silly, really, especially as she'd been the cause of the separation – she was the adulterer here – but every time the new band played a song, took a break, made a joke, whatever . . . she couldn't help thinking about how it would have been with the girls instead of Tommy, Christophe and Rod.

'Con-grat-u-la-tions!' sang a voice, loudly, as the door crashed open again. Louis appeared, drink in hand, grinning. 'Nice going, guys! Not bad, for a first gig!'

Zoë gathered up her belongings, raising a hand just in time for the high-five.

'Happy?'

She nodded as enthusiastically as she could, her palm throbbing.

'Good! Let's all get a drink! Oh. We're missing one.'

'Tommy had to go,' she explained. 'Actually, I have to—'

'Ah well, his loss. C'mon, we're in the bar. You went down a treat with young Ben!'

Christophe pressed himself against the wall, escaping Louis's grasp. 'I am staying 'ere. Ze Norwegians 'ave my drerms.'

Rod nodded, picking a strand of tobacco out of his hair and inserting it into the Rizla on his knee, the implication being that he would wait to get a lift home with Christophe.

Perhaps if Zoë had been in a better frame of mind she might have demonstrated more willpower, but as it was, she found herself trailing the oversized American through the pub towards the exit.

'Zoë?'

She looked up, straight into the piercing blue eyes of her boyfriend.

'You came!' Extricating herself from Louis's armpit, Zoë flung herself at James. It had been touch and go whether he'd make it along tonight; he was working long hours in his new role. She squeezed his shoulder, feeling overwhelmingly pleased to see him. The gig had been stressful, not just because it was the band's first live performance or because Rod had turned up smelling like a cannabis bonfire, but because she'd been doing it alone. For the first time in years, she was singing without her best friends on the stage, without Crazy Jeff at the front, without all the usual faces in the crowd. But at least James was here.

'Er, Louis, this is James, my boyfriend. James, Louis.'

After a period of manly back-slapping and complimentary remarks about Zoë's performance, Louis scooped James into his entourage and continued to head through the bar.

James pulled a face. 'We should probably—'

'This way!' the manager yelled, leading them out. 'Drinks are on me!'

James shot Zoë a startled look. She nodded desperately, knowing he had an early start the next day.

'Where are we going?' she asked.

'It's a great little bar. Only opened last summer—'

Zoë wondered whether Louis and Ben had actually watched her performance. She tried to remember what she'd seen from the tiny stage. At one point she thought she had spotted a billowing, light-coloured shirt at the back, but now she wasn't so sure.

James nudged her gently, jabbing his thumb over his shoulder. Zoë shrugged helplessly.

'I'm sorry, mate,' he said, clearly taking the matter into his own hands. 'We've gotta head.'

'No!' Louis's hands flew into the air. 'Stay for a drink!'

Zoë was about to strengthen James's case when she noticed something. In the window of the bar was a pale, round face peeping out from beneath a giant quiff. Ben was grinning at her through the glass.

She suddenly saw how this would look from Universal's perspective. They wanted an artist who would strut her stuff, on and off the stage. They were after a shameless self-publicist, a girl who could get herself in the papers to sell records. And here she was turning down a drink at half-past eleven.

'We could . . . stay for *one*,' she suggested.

'That's the spirit!'

'*What?*' James hissed under his breath.

'Ha – spirit! Get it? Let's go for some spirits!' Louis sniggered at his joke and barged his way up the steps.

'You know, I think I'll leave you to it.' James stopped on the threshold, untangling his fingers from Zoë's and backing away.

She stood in the doorway, exactly halfway between her manager and her boyfriend, not knowing which way to go.

'Hey, Zoë.' Ben waved her inside. 'Great gig tonight!'

Zoë faltered, looking back at James's sleepy eyes. He'd made an effort to see her tonight; it was the least she could do to go back with him.

James smiled. 'Don't worry,' he said. 'You stay for one. I'll see you back home.'

Zoë hesitated a little while longer, then decided that his indifference was genuine. She hopped back down the steps and kissed him on the lips, squeezing his hand and whispering her thanks.

Ben rose to his feet as she entered the bar, beaming. 'Looking good, Zoë.'

Zoë congratulated herself on having changed into jeans before she'd come out. She didn't mind people staring at her on the stage – she welcomed it, in fact. Up there, she was Zoë Kidd, an act. But offstage, she was Zoë, a person. She couldn't help finding people like Ben a little creepy.

'Looking *great*,' Louis added, sliding the bottles and glasses around. There appeared to be twice the necessary number of drinks for the three of them. 'I gat double. It's happy hour.'

'Happy days!'

Louis raised one of his glasses and waited for the others to do the same.

'I wasn't sure about the vocals on that PA system,' she said, sipping her wine. She wanted to know which songs, if any, the men had heard.

'Always the way with the crummy gigs, eh.'

Ben winked at her. 'You sounded fine, honestly.'

'Right.' Zoë nodded, not sure whether to believe him. Perhaps she was being paranoid. Of course they had heard her sing. What A&R guy *wouldn't* go and see the act he was about to sign? She took another sip, feeling herself begin to relax as they moved onto the subject of her new 'bold' look.

'It toadally works,' agreed Louis.

'Are you sure the whole tight, bright thing suits the music?' she asked, open to suggestions.

'Oh, toadally.'

'It's a contrast. An antithesis. Like bitter-sweet,' Ben explained. 'So, how's the new material coming on?'

Zoë was about to reply that she had hundreds of ideas floating around in her head and was just waiting to find the time to sit down with her guitar, but Louis had already answered.

'We're gettin' there, don't worry.'

Zoë looked at her manager. Surely, songwriting was a solitary

153

activity – except, of course, when you had someone like Ellie to help with the harmonies. But Ellie was special. Zoë wasn't sure she could say the same about Louis.

'I'll be writing some in the next few weeks – is that what you were thinking?'

'Great,' said Louis. 'If you get the *muse*, go for it!'

Ben nodded. 'Absolutely. Keep writing, that's the best way. Then when it comes to pulling together an album we'll have various sources to draw on.'

Zoë frowned. 'Sources?'

Louis leaned forward. 'You'll wanna put a couple of song-writers' gems on there, eh?'

The wine glass froze on its way to Zoë's lips.

'Don't look so shocked,' Ben chuckled. 'It's perfectly normal. Check out any album, you'll see it's the same. You don't wanna put all your eggs in one basket, so to speak.'

Zoë lowered the wine glass without taking a sip. The eggs, she was beginning to realise, did not belong to her. It was Universal who was risking its money, time and reputation on Zoë Kidd. This was Ben's way of telling her that he and his colleagues dictated what went on her album.

'So, *most* of them . . .' She trailed off, hearing the desperation in her voice. She sounded like a girl coming to terms with the truth about Santa Claus.

Ben smiled. 'Most of the tracks will be your own.'

Zoë took her deferred sip of wine, feeling mildly reassured. Ben worked for a reputable label. He wouldn't tell an outright lie.

'Zoë Kidd, rock star!' cried Louis, unnecessarily loudly. 'Ha – Kidd rock! Get it? Kid Rock – like the band . . .'

Louis's jokes continued as they went on to discuss promotional tours, rights deals and festival season. Zoë slowly shrugged off her anxiety. It was impossible to feel down when people were talking about dedicated publicists and album cover artwork.

'More drinks,' Louis declared.

'I should—'

'Stay,' said Ben, smiling with heavy-lidded eyes. His forehead was shining in the glow of a spotlight.

Zoë glanced over her shoulder. Louis was thundering towards the bar, parting the crowds as he went. It would seem rude to walk out now.

'You're a cool customer, aren't you?' Ben raised an eyebrow.

'What d'you mean?'

'Well, most artists are blown away by the whole idea of getting signed, hitting the global circuit and that. You seem kinda . . . blasé.'

Zoë laughed quietly. If only he knew what had been going on in her head for the past ten minutes.

'Seriously,' he went on, 'it took about two weeks for you to get back to us on the idea of going solo . . . and now when we talk about plans for the future you just seem, like, *yeah, whatever.*'

'I . . .' It was hard to explain how she felt – especially to the young man responsible for her imminent record deal. Of course she was excited. She was thrilled. She could barely sleep at night when she thought about everything they'd told her. But at the same time, she felt this overwhelming sense of guilt. 'I . . . keep thinking about the other members of my old band.

'It's as though, all this stuff that's happening to me . . . it should be happening to all of us. We've been together for so long, all going for the same thing, all doing our best to make it happen . . . And now it's just me who gets the reward.'

Ben was shaking his head, smiling. 'Unbelievable.'

She frowned. 'What is?'

'You! You're so . . . I dunno, modest or something, you can't see it for what it is.'

'What *what* is?'

'The situation. *You* used to sort out the gigs. You wrote the

155

songs. You got the band together for rehearsals and recordings. You were the one who tirelessly PR'd the band . . . Who's responsible for your twelve thousand fans on MySpace?'

Zoë looked at him. She had never thought about it like that. Put in those words, it seemed almost fair that she was the one taking the prize. But then, you could spin any situation to justify your actions if you tried hard enough. The fact was, they'd been a team. You couldn't say a team was only good because of its strikers. You needed the whole squad.

'I couldn't have got here without them.'

Ben looked at her incredulously. 'You could, and you did. If there's—'

'Happy days!' Louis reappeared with another well-stacked tray. 'I got chasers too. Absinthe.' He raised his hand in a toast. 'To Zoë Kidd!'

After that, Zoë became dimly aware that she was mixing her drinks and that she had work in the morning and that the buses had stopped running and that James would probably be wondering where she was, but there were more important things to worry about. Like, for example, how to balance a box of matches on her forehead whilst downing her glass of wine.

'Hey, good going!' Louis clapped as she slammed the empty glass on the table.

'I shouldgo,' she slurred, standing up and immediately tripping over the strap of her handbag.

Ben reached out as she crashed into his lap. 'Ooh, easy.'

Zoë looked around for a moment, half-sitting, half-lying across her potential employer's legs, disorientated. Then she pushed herself up and stumbled to retrieve the bag.

'Sorry. Very tired . . .'

'You okay to get a cab?' Louis looked at her with an expression that managed to combine concern with embarrassment.

Zoë nodded and promptly walked into a pillar.

'I'll get you one.' Ben rose to his feet, putting a pasty arm around her whilst pulling what looked like a wad of forms from under his chair. He looked sober, Zoë suddenly realised. 'I meant to ask. Can you sign this?'

She squinted, clinging to the pillar. 'What is it?'

'Just a . . . like, an agreement. A thing that says you won't sign with another label while we're in talks.'

She reached out, still clutching the pillar with one hand. Everything else in the bar was rocking but the pillar felt reassuringly sturdy.

'It's . . . long.'

What she wanted to do was to flip through the document, although it was impossible with only one free hand.

'Here's a pen.'

Zoë took it and pressed the agreement against the pillar. At the back of her mind, a little bell was ringing. It was the sort of bell that rings when you know you're doing something a little bit risky but you decide to do it anyway. Like bunking off school for an afternoon or taking a drag on a friend's mate's spliff. It was ringing as she scribbled her signature on the dotted line.

'Oh,' she said, looking at the page. 'The pen doesn't work.'

'Try on the table,' Ben suggested, guiding her over.

Zoë glanced at Louis, who was looking on happily. She took this as a good sign and the alarm bell faded a little. Then, just as she put pen to paper for a second time, her phone started buzzing in her bag and all sorts of thoughts started flashing through her mind. She knew that it would be James calling, and she knew that he'd want to know where she was. And she knew that if she told him precisely what she was doing, i.e. signing a piece of paper that she hadn't actually looked at, he would tell her she was being an idiot, and all of a sudden it became clear to Zoë that she *was* being an idiot.

'Can I take it t'lookat at home?'

Ben looked briefly at Louis, then turned back to her and smiled.

157

'Yeah, of course.' He was still holding her around the waist. 'Just get it back to us as soon as possible, yeah?'

With a little help, Zoë stumbled out of the bar and onto Tottenham Court Road, where Ben deposited her in a taxi with a handful of ten-pound notes.

'Good gig tonight,' he called, patting the roof of the cab.

'Good gig,' she mumbled happily, her head falling sideways against the window.

23

Zoë stared into the distance, stifling a yawn as Brian's monologue washed over her.

'We tend to find that our clients stay with us for a number of years . . .'

She tuned in for a second in an effort to stop herself from falling asleep. Her boss was lying. Clients didn't stay with Chase Waterman for years. Most of them spotted within the first audit that they were paying double for a service that was no better than they'd get elsewhere. Auditing wasn't complicated; it was still essentially adding up. Paying the rates Chase Waterman charged was like forking out for fancy bottled water in a posh restaurant: you got the quality stamp, but you couldn't honestly notice the difference.

'Turnaround time?' Brian looked up. Someone had asked a question. 'Oh, we work very quickly. It's a matter of weeks, if not days . . .'

Another lie. Zoë sighed and zoned out. She was becoming proficient at the art of spinning her pen around her thumb.

'Zoë?'

The pen skittered across the table.

'The British Trust audit – how long, would you say?'

'Oh, um . . .' Zoë shrugged. The truth was, that project had been doomed from day one. The clients were a bunch of old biddies who couldn't use email and couldn't hear properly on the phone. 'It probably took a couple of months, all in all.'

Brian shot her a furious look and then turned to the women with a smile. 'Yes, well . . . I suppose that was an exception. In general . . .'

Zoë reached for her pen and gave it another spin. She knew she had riled her boss, but in a perverted, slightly malicious way, she had enjoyed embarrassing him in front of prospective clients.

The tiredness was making her grouchy. She'd never been good at surviving on reduced sleep and for the last few weeks she had averaged no more than five or six hours a night. Rehearsals invariably overran, often going on until eleven or whenever the studio shut, and despite having a manager, she seemed to spend an inordinate amount of time 'managing': sorting out photo shoots, agreeing gig dates and vetoing ludicrous outfits put forward by Ben and Louis. Zoë was beginning to see how being an artist was a full-time job.

'Tell you what,' Brian was saying. 'We'll pull together a list. Zoë – you can pull together a list of our non-profit clients, can't you?'

'Won't take long,' she replied, smiling beatifically.

Brian changed the subject very quickly and brought the meeting to a close. Ten minutes later, Zoë was sitting in his office, staring blankly at his mouth as it opened and closed on a string of negative words.

'. . . not clever, and not helpful. In sales meetings it's important to show a united front.'

'I was just answering your questions.'

'You answered them negatively.'

'I answered them truthfully.'

Brian grunted.

'We only have one non-profit client,' Zoë pointed out. 'What can I say?'

He scowled. 'I think we need to have a little chat about your attitude, Zoë.'

She sighed. Had she not been rehearsing until nearly midnight the previous night, had she not hung around in the studio car park for twenty further minutes talking to Tommy about guitars, she might not have been so insolent. But when Brian started talking about her attitude as though it was something Zoë had picked up on a dirty bus or a swimming pool floor, something inside her snapped.

'What's wrong with it?' she challenged.

Brian looked at her in a way that suggested she had answered her own question, which infuriated her more.

'What's wrong with my attitude?' she asked again.

He drew a breath and sighed.

'I didn't do anything wrong in the meeting,' she said. 'I just told the truth.'

'I didn't say you had done anything wrong.'

Zoë shrugged. He hadn't needed to say it.

'I was referring to an attitude *suggestion*: PMA. Positive Mental—'

She couldn't bear for him to spell it out. Emitting a noise that was half-scream, half-growl, Zoë drowned out her boss. 'Don't say it! Don't say any more of your stupid acronyms. If you called me in here to talk about PMAs and RAPs then you might as well save your breath.'

Brian looked at her for a couple of seconds, realising something. This was the first time, since stepping into the glass-walled offices of Chase Waterman three years ago, that she had spoken her mind. Feeling overwhelmingly liberated, it occurred to Zoë that she no longer gave a shit. She could no longer be bothered to keep up the pretence.

Brian was staring at her with a look of incredulous disapproval. Zoë hesitated. Her fingers were wrapped around the handle of a door that led to freedom, ready to fling it wide open. She knew there were advantages to staying put: familiarity, financial stability, acceptance and approval of her family and friends, but

161

there was also a downside. Her life as an auditor was wearing away at her soul. It was stifling her creativity and compressing her personality. She looked at her boss.

'I quit,' she said.

'I beg your pardon?'

Zoë straightened up, enjoying the look of bemusement on her boss's face. 'I quit,' she repeated, loudly. 'I'm handing in my notice.'

With impressive speed, Brian collected himself together. 'Now, there's no need to react in haste. You're obviously under a lot of pressure at the moment and with a bit of TL—'

Zoë stood up. She thought about making a parting comment; she'd been through so many variations of this moment in her head that she wasn't short on ideas, but in the event she just walked serenely through the door of his office.

The feeling of pure, untainted joy stayed with Zoë as she crossed the seventh floor, said goodbye to the automatons blinking up at her from the surrounding desks and took the lift down to the atrium. She was still smiling as she pushed her way into the warm, spring sunshine and decided to walk all the way home. The brilliant thing about not having taken a holiday in the last nine months was that she had four weeks' annual leave to use up: exactly enough to cover her notice period. She would never, ever have to enter the Chase Waterman offices again.

Her mood was pushed higher still by the long walk home; it was as though every step helped to shake off a few more scales, shed a layer of dead skin. The opportunities seemed endless. Finally, she could focus on what she wanted to do. She could write songs and rehearse in the daytime, take calls from Louis without having to hide underneath her desk. She could lead the life she had always wanted to lead. By the time she climbed the steps to the flat, Zoë felt almost weightless.

A shot of adrenaline rushed through her bloodstream as she

let herself in and heard a grunting noise emanating from the kitchen. She grabbed James's old hockey stick from the hallway and crept through the flat. Then, on seeing his body hunched over the kitchen unit, she let it clatter to the floor.

'Jesus, James! You nearly gave me a heart attack.'

He grunted again, grabbing a beer and slamming the fridge door shut.

'What are you doing at home?'

'Not needed at work any more, evidently.' He shrugged.

'Oh.' Zoë stepped over and re-opened the fridge. Three o'clock in the afternoon wasn't usually the time to start drinking, but today was different. Today, they had something to celebrate.

'I've got some news,' she said, opening her bottle and skipping over to join him. 'I quit my job.'

James's response was not as immediate or joyful as she had hoped. He frowned for a moment, then looked around the kitchen, rubbing his forehead.

'Well, that's bloody great,' he said eventually.

'What? What d'you mean? It was gonna happen at some point, and now that I'm practically signed I need to devote more of my—'

'I mean, *great; now neither of us have jobs.*'

Zoë drew her head back and looked at him, trying to work out what he meant.

'You weren't listening, were you?' He glared at her. 'I got made redundant,' he said, slowly and loudly. 'The whole team's been bulleted. They've rolled Marketing into the Consumer division and now we're all out of jobs. So, unless you make it to number one in the next four weeks, I think I'm correct in saying that we'll have *no income between us*. We're shafted.'

Zoë stumbled backwards into the kitchen unit. Her mood had suddenly plummeted.

'Happy now?' James brushed past her and threw himself

onto the couch. 'Is this the anti-establishment lifestyle you were after?'

Zoë let out a shaky sigh. Things no longer seemed so rosy after all.

24

'Try holding it as though you're playing it.'

Zoë looked left and right, then struck a tentative pose. She always felt nervous getting her guitar out in public in case someone knocked it or spilled something down it – and that was just at gigs. Here she was, waving it about on one of the busiest shopping streets in Europe on a Saturday afternoon.

'That's it. Now stand *really* still. I'm going to use a long exposure to get the crowds blurred.'

Zoë obliged, contorting her face into what she believed was a smile, although it was difficult to tell after so many hours. She was beginning to understand why supermodels pouted; it was far less tiring on the cheek muscles.

'Okay, this isn't working.' Jonathan scratched his head, looking down at the camera. 'There's a massive gap all around you. I think people are a bit put-off by the tutu.'

She glanced over her shoulder. A vast expanse of pavement had opened up, bordered by tourists and ogling men, some of them shamelessly clicking on cameras and phones as though she were some sort of public exhibit.

Louis had been quite insistent on the outfit front. It was beginning to look as though 'bold' was his code word for 'semi-pornographic'. The figure-hugging ballerina get-up was one of a small selection of possibilities that fell within his acceptable bounds of boldness. Earlier in the day, they had shot her in hot pants on Primrose Hill, leopard print underneath the London Eye and a bizarre combination of leather and tassels as she posed outside the entrance to the Houses of Parliament. Zoë sensed that her sister's boyfriend was more than a little uncomfortable with his involvement – as was she – but neither had said anything. Even when the guard at St James's Palace had tried to walk them off the premises, Jonathan had simply put on his best Russian accent and explained that they just wanted some holiday snaps.

'Put this on, while I think.' Jonathan shrugged off his jacket and held it out to her.

Zoë gratefully retreated into the dark brown folds of fabric and the onlookers gradually dispersed.

'Hey.'

Zoë jumped as someone tapped her on the shoulder.

'All done?' It was Tamsin.

'Just about. Last few shots.' Zoë opened the coat for just long enough to give her sister a glimpse of the leotard.

'Oh my God.'

Zoë pulled a face. 'I know. Don't say it.'

'Hey, Tam?' Jonathan was waving. 'Can you do us a favour? We need people to keep moving around her. Can you stand there so they don't see what's coming? Yep, great. Maybe stoop down a bit so you're out of shot . . . Yeah. Perfect. And now quickly take her jacket off . . .'

Eventually, the ordeal was over and the three of them retreated to a side street, Zoë pulling on layers of clothes.

'Thank you so much.'

Jonathan shook his head, squatting in the gutter to pack away his various lenses. 'My pleasure.'

Tam nudged him with her knee. 'Oi. I'll be censoring those photos.'

'Don't,' said Zoë. 'There won't be any left.'

Tam laughed. 'Coffee?'

Jonathan rose to his feet. 'I'll leave you to it. I'll send you the link to the photos once they've been through Photoshop.'

Zoë danced over and kissed him on the cheek. 'You're a star, Jonathan.'

The girls wandered into Soho, away from the bustle and blare of Oxford Street and into the first café they came to.

Zoë glanced down at the suitcase that was hampering her sister's progress. 'Planning to flee the country?'

'It's case notes.' Tam pulled a face as they sat down. 'Just a bit of light weekend reading.'

'Wow. That's all one case?'

Tam gave a long-suffering nod.

'Now I'm *really* glad I didn't get into law.'

Tamsin didn't reply; she never liked talking about other people's failures – especially her sister's. That was the thing about Tam. She was so modest. It was almost as though she was ashamed of her own achievements.

'How's *your* work?' asked Tam, once the waitress had taken their order.

Zoë hesitated. Inadvertently, her sister had led them straight to the point. Her work – or lack of – was the reason she'd summoned Tam for a coffee today. In the last four days, the only conversations she'd had about her precarious situation had been inside her own head. James wouldn't talk about it – preferring instead to sulk on the sofa in front of farming documentaries and old westerns – and nobody else knew. She was desperate to talk to someone, but now that the moment had come, she suddenly felt nervous.

'Not . . . Not so good, actually.'

'Oh?'

Zoë took a deep breath and held it for a couple of seconds. Then she let it out.

'I handed in my notice.'

'You what?'

'I han—'

'I heard what you said. I just . . . I mean . . .' Tam looked around the café.

Zoë nodded, watching and waiting for a reaction.

'Does Mum know?'

Zoë hesitated. '*Mum*?'

'Sorry – I didn't mean – oh, Zoë, don't look at me like that. I just wondered whether—'

'No. She doesn't know.'

Her snappy retort hung in the air for a few seconds while the waitress brought over their coffees. Zoë should have known. Her sister had always worried about other people's opinions – most of all, their mother's. Tam seemed to live in constant fear of displeasing their mother, who, in turn, lived in fear of incurring the wrath of their father. Of course, their mother's opinion would figure in today's conversation. Zoë just hadn't expected it to figure so soon.

'She'll go mental,' Tam said quietly, scooping the froth off her cappuccino.

Zoë nodded mechanically, half wishing she hadn't bothered to share the news. If Tamsin was just going to bang on about their mother's disapproval, she could have saved herself the trouble and just called her parents straight-up for an earful.

All she wanted was for her sister to ask *why*. It was the obvious question, surely? Then Zoë would explain about the hamster wheel and the claustrophobia and the overwhelming desire to escape, to do what she had dreamed of doing for years . . . That was what she wanted. Reassurance from Tamsin that she'd made the right decision.

'D'you want me to tell her?'

Zoë snarled. 'Tam, will you stop going on about Mum? This has nothing to do with her.'

'Sorry,' mumbled Tamsin. 'Just trying to help.'

'Yeah, well . . .' Zoë stirred her coffee ferociously, increasingly aware that she sounded like a stroppy teenager. 'Sorry.'

'So . . . What are you gonna do?'

Zoë sighed. Clearly she had been naïve to expect unconditional support. Her sister wouldn't just ask the questions and then shout, 'You go, girlfriend'. She was more sincere than that.

'I'm gonna focus on my solo career.'

'So you're signed then? Wow. Universal, that's—'

'No, not quite.'

'Oh.' Tamsin looked perplexed. 'So . . .'

'I'm as good as signed,' Zoë explained. 'Which reminds me . . .' She reached down into her handbag and brought out the wad of papers. 'Can you do me a favour? They asked me to sign this thing, and I just wanted your opinion on it before I do.'

She was sounding a lot more confident than she felt. The truth was, since hearing the news about James's redundancy, she had started having serious doubts about whether she'd jumped too soon. Vicinity was offering no guarantee for the future and for all she knew, they might have been talking to hundreds of prospective signings, stringing them all along while they made up their minds about which horse to back.

'Okay.' Tamsin sipped her coffee, looking over the document on the table. 'Looks like a kind of non-compete contract.'

'Yeah,' Zoë agreed, trying to sound knowledgeable. 'That's what they said. To stop me signing with Warner or whatever.'

Tam nodded. 'Can I take it away?'

'Yeah. Add it to your pile.' Zoë smiled, looking at the strained zips on the suitcase.

'It's a bit . . . weird, don't you think?' Tamsin rammed the document into a side pocket. 'Them wanting to sign you after only hearing you, like, once or twice?'

Zoë's smile faded. 'Not really,' she said, with as much conviction as she could muster. 'My manager has a good reputation. They've talked a lot. They trust him.'

'Oh, right.' Tam nodded uncertainly.

'Louis is known across the industry. The A&R guys know he wouldn't peddle any old shit.'

Zoë had more that she wanted to say but she stopped there. She could hear the defiance in her voice. She sounded like a kid trying to prove he had the best BMX.

Tamsin tipped back her head, waiting for the frothy milk to slide down the cup.

'Well,' she said, re-emerging with a smile. 'Good for you, Zoë. I'm really pleased for you. You'll be raking it in before you know it, and then you'll wonder why you ever had the dull job in auditing.'

Zoë hid her face behind her own cup. She couldn't quite muster a smile to match her sister's.

'And you've got savings, haven't you? A few months' worth, to tide you over?'

It was so typical of Tam, thought Zoë. She pretended to be all blasé and pleased about the whole thing, but then she gave herself away with a comment like that. She just couldn't hide the conformist in her.

'I'll manage.'

A nasty feeling crept over her as she stopped to think about the question. She did have a few months' savings, but no more than that. When she had resigned, in the back of her mind she had known that there was a safety net: if the money ran out and her Vicinity sign-on advance didn't amount to much, James could step in to tide her over. Now the safety net was gone. James had no monthly income and they'd both be eating into whatever they'd managed to squirrel away in their short careers.

'You've always got James,' said Tam, right on cue.

Zoë squirmed. 'Actually . . .'

'Oh, Zoë.' Tamsin laughed softly. 'Don't say you're too proud to be a kept woman.'

'No. It's—'

'Is he being tight? Won't he—'

170

'No.' Zoë swallowed. 'He lost his job.'

'What? Oh my God.'

Zoë shrugged, as though she was taking it in her stride. 'The whole department went tits-up. It's ironic, really, because James had just turned down a position in the team that's just taken over. He'd be okay if he'd gone for it. Oh well.'

Tamsin stared at her. '*Oh well?*'

'Look . . . stop worrying.' Zoë pulled out her purse and put down enough change to cover the bill.

'Well, you're not paying that, for a start,' said Tam, replacing Zoë's money with her own. 'I can't believe it. Poor James. Poor you!'

Zoë suddenly felt a sense of relief. Tamsin was clearly appalled, but that was because Tamsin's priorities were different to hers. Zoë and James would be okay. Their situation wasn't life-threatening. Zoë could see – even though her sister might not agree – that she *had* done the right thing. 'We'll manage.'

Tam's smile reminded Zoë of the sort newsreaders use when moving from a tragic story to a happy one: stoic. Zoë didn't mind. She was smiling for real. They left the café and wandered towards Leicester Square.

Zoë guided her sister across the road, slowing to a halt outside the dirty shop window.

'Look.'

It wasn't the first time she'd gazed at this particular display. Guitars were her equivalent to porn; she could spend hours admiring their curves, their sheen, their intricate features.

'They all look the same,' Tam said, apologetically.

Zoë cast a lustful eye over the white Fender in the centre of the display, ignoring her sister. 'That one,' she said. 'That's the one I'll get when I'm rich.'

'What is it?'

'A '65 Mustang. Like Kurt Cobain's.'

Tamsin nodded mutely, waiting as Zoë drooled over the

flawless bodywork and fantasised about how it might sound. She had only ever held one before, in Ellie's shop, but never plugged one in.

'You'll own one, one day,' said Tamsin, slinging an arm around Zoë's neck and guiding her away.

'Yeah.' Zoë nodded, smiling ruefully. 'One day.'

25

'Fucking hell,' James groaned at the television, flicking channels again.

Zoë scrolled down the new Zoë Kidd homepage, not bothering to turn around. She knew what was troubling her boyfriend, and it wasn't the quality of daytime TV. James was annoyed at himself because he had lost his job.

It was a pride thing, she suspected. If James had left of his own free will, he would probably have spent the last week enjoying his newfound spare time, spending hours at the gym, catching up with old friends and messing about online. As it was, his daily routine entailed waking up, wandering into the lounge via whatever food was lying about in the kitchen, switching on the TV and then swearing at it until about five o'clock in the afternoon, at which point he'd forage about for a beer and something to put in the microwave and then return to the couch.

At first, Zoë had assumed it was a form of shock. She had tolerated his moods, even indulged them by cooking proper food and carrying it over to him on trays. Early attempts at conversation had floundered, however, so she had taken to working in silence in whichever part of the flat James was not inhabiting. They were living separate lives within the space of about ten square metres.

Zoë looked again at the website. Her eyes stared back at her from every page, each photo tinted a different colour, cropped and resized so that you couldn't help but stare back. It wasn't just her eyes on display, either. Her teeth, lips, thighs, belly-button . . . almost every part of her body shone out from different parts of the site, dressed in the full range of absurdities. The designer had clearly touched up Jonathan's already-touched up images, rendering her legs even longer than they already were, her hair thicker, her teeth whiter. Zoë looked at the skin-tight leopard print and tried not to think about what her parents would say.

She returned to the email from Louis and tried to pick out the action points. His writing style was like his speech: Enthusiastic but utterly random. There was reference to a summer tour – something about university towns – and a reminder about getting the signed agreement back to him. The last line of the message was clear enough. *Have you written any new material?*

No, she thought. There had been too much going on; she hadn't had time. Or at least, that had been her excuse until a week ago.

The luxury of time, she was beginning to realise, was a misnomer. In the blissful absence of financial audits, irritating colleagues and the unpleasant commute to work, Zoë had had enough time to write a symphony but she hadn't penned a jot. The guitar had been lifted from its case more times than she could remember: lifted, strummed, abandoned in favour of some urgent assignment like cleaning a cupboard or making a cup of tea. The minutes stretched into hours, which stretched into days . . . and still the notebook was blank.

Louis might have thought otherwise, but songs couldn't be written on demand. Not Zoë's songs, anyway. They needed a spark. You couldn't just clear a space in your diary and say, *I'll write something now*. You had to feel so deliriously happy or so despondent or so petrified or so fucking pissed off that you wanted to shout it out to the world. It wasn't about having time. It was about having emotions.

Some of her best songs had been scribbled on chewing gum

wrappers whilst jerking along on the way to work, full of pent-up aggression as she got squeezed between somebody's armpit and the train door. One had been typed into her BlackBerry during a meeting. It was therapy; writing songs was a way of lashing out or wallowing or calming down. This week, the spark just hadn't been there.

James's groan almost drowned out the sound of the *Neighbours* theme tune.

Zoë turned round. 'You okay?'

'Oh, yeah. I'm fucking great.' James rolled his eyes and sunk a little lower into the couch.

'Why don't you . . .'

She knew, as soon as she'd started the sentence, that she should have kept quiet. She'd been about to suggest that he went for a walk or did something – *anything* – that didn't involve lying in front of the TV looking morose, but James's expression silenced her.

'What? Why don't I what? Get a job?' He seemed to perk up as he said this, as though he'd been waiting for the confrontation – a bad sign, Zoë thought, as James was usually against conflict.

'No, I was just—'

'Or don't we need to do that?'

'James,' Zoë pleaded, although the wheels were clearly already in motion.

'Jobs are overrated, aren't they? I mean, who'd want one of them?'

Zoë sighed as her boyfriend stormed over to the fridge. She knew exactly what he was getting at. She had left a perfectly good job with a decent salary in order to follow a dream that could potentially earn her no money at all. He, meanwhile, had been forced out from a position he had taken purely to improve his (i.e. their) income and he didn't see why the onus was on him to find another one.

175

Zoë hadn't actually brought up the subject of job-hunting; she hadn't dared. But if, inadvertently, she had implied that James should look for another role, it would have been for his sanity, not for the household income. Watching two episodes of *Neighbours* a day was not good for anyone's mental health.

'Look, I'll get a job if I—'

'Oh, don't worry about it,' he said, slamming the fridge door in disgust at the lack of beers. 'I'm sure the royalties will start rolling in before we know it.'

Zoë watched mutely as he picked up his keys and marched out. The door slammed and she sat there, hearing the echo of his words in her head, over and over again, feeling the pressure build up behind her eyes.

The money wasn't the problem; she had come to terms with the likelihood that her royalties wouldn't compensate for her lack of salary. She thought James had too, but clearly that wasn't the case. That was the crux of it: she had assumed James understood, but he didn't.

Zoë stared, unblinking, at the stark self portraits on the screen. Slowly, the images started to blur and she felt the warm, weighty droplets run down her cheeks, hang from her chin and then drop, seeping into her jeans. More than ever, she wished she could talk to the girls. *They* understood. They knew about the risks involved, they would reassure her that she'd made the right decision. But of course, she couldn't talk to them. She'd cut herself off from the girls in the same way that she was in danger of cutting herself off from James.

She pressed her fingers into her eyes and wiped away the moisture, pulling the laptop towards her. The thoughts of Shannon and Ellie and Kate had stirred something inside her. All of a sudden, she needed to know what they were doing.

The first few hits on Google were links to old Dirty Money reviews, their old website, their defunct MySpace page. Zoë filtered the search by 'last month' and saw, with some surprise, that there were over two thousand hits. She glanced down the page and then stopped. There was a YouTube link entitled 'Dirty Money on RTÉ'. The girls had gone and played on Irish TV.

The video quality was poor – presumably another one of Shannon's mate's efforts – but it was good enough to make out what was going on. The presenter, a middle-aged man with a black toupee and overly white teeth, was perched on a purple couch, talking to the blond member of Westlife. Before the girls started to play, the presenter asked Kian what he thought of this 'sassy new outfit from London' and he said – Zoë could hardly believe it; she had to replay this twice – 'These girls are heading for the top of the charts, make no mistake.'

Zoë watched as Shannon brought the trio in. Her incredulity turned to pride and then to an overwhelming, heart-wrenching sadness. She had missed being a part of it all. She could have calmed Kate's nerves before they went on. She could have helped Shannon plan the set. She could have made sure Ellie got to the airport on time.

She stared at the screen, waiting for the song to get going. It was a new one – written, she guessed, by Shannon, with Ellie's help. Full credit to the drummer, thought Zoë. She had done exactly what she'd set out to do: she had put Dirty Money on TV and come away with a celebrity endorsement. Having lost their lead singer and songwriter, instead of sinking without a trace, the girls had made a serious comeback.

The performance wasn't exactly slick, it had to be said. Even watching on the wobbly recording, it was clear that the girls had needed more rehearsal: Shannon was trying to sing while she played, which didn't really work, and Ellie had obviously smoked something before the show and kept wandering away from the mike mid-verse.

It was an angry song, with a catchy tune and a solid beat that almost eclipsed the vocals. Zoë closed her eyes, straining to pick out the words. Then the chorus came round again and she could feel the moisture starting to creep out from between her fingers. There was a phrase that kept coming round, again and again. 'Better Off Without You'. That was what they were singing. It was a song about her.

She slammed the laptop shut, stopping them mid-track and leaving the flat enveloped in a blanket of silence, punctuated only by the sound of her sniffs and sobs. The tears were streaming down her cheeks now. It wasn't just the pain of rejection, or the sense of loneliness that came from knowing that nobody, not even her three closest allies, were on her side; it was the remorse. *This was all her own fault.* If she'd made different choices, it wouldn't have come to this.

She reached for her phone, taking a long, shaky breath and dialling her friend's number. She knew Ellie wouldn't pick up. She knew it was too late to make amends, but she had to do something.

'Ellie,' she sobbed, the sound of her friend's greeting bringing on a fresh stream of tears. 'I'm sorry. I know it's too late, but I'm sorry.'

Too late. The words hung in the air as she put the phone down. She had thought that leaving the message would help, somehow – maybe lessen the guilt. But nothing had changed. She still felt worthless and wretched, she still wanted to scream.

Too late. Zoë pushed back her chair and flew through the flat, suddenly seeing the one thing that could make things better. Not better, exactly, but manageable. She pulled out her guitar and started hammering out the chords that had been circling in her head along with the despair and the regret and everything else.

At last, she had an outlet for the angst. For a week, she had tried to force something out, but the vessel had been empty. Now, all of a sudden it was overflowing. The words and the chords were surging out of her so fast that her fingers could barely keep up.

Things hadn't changed; she had still turned against her friends and her family in the name of her own ego. But something good had come out of it all. Something small, but incredibly good: her first solo track.

26

Christophe was high on something. His eyes had seemed inky and wild before they'd come on, but Zoë had convinced herself that it was the poor lighting in the dressing room. Now, she was in no doubt. He was grinning madly, whacking his drums and jumping around as though his seat was on fire. Rod, by contrast, was stoned. Zoë pressed her mouth up against the microphone and tried to drown out the offbeat cacophony.

She needn't have worried. Nobody was looking at the stage. The audience, consisting of preppy lads with upturned collars and long-haired princesses with bows in their hair, had formed clusters around the room and were chatting, flirting, admiring themselves in the mirrors . . . They might as well have just plugged in somebody's iPod.

The venue was a large, mirrored concert hall in West London with art-deco chandeliers and fake leather upholstery that nobody seemed to want to sit on. Zoë remembered it from the early days of Dirty Money; they had vowed never to return to the place after Ellie had been refused a last-minute sound-check by the botoxed manageress and consequently played in the wrong key for the whole of the first song.

With a sense of anticlimax, she ended the set and shouted her hollow thanks to the preening masses. Barely a head turned. Having spent most of her final song scouring the audience for large, garish shirts and pale faces, Zoë concluded that neither

Louis nor Ben was present. Had the gig gone better, she might have been disappointed. As it was, she felt enormously relieved.

Christophe and Rod, thanks to whatever they'd pumped into their systems, didn't find their way back to the dressing room straight away – which was good, in a way. Zoë knew it was her duty to berate them for their performance tonight, but she didn't feel she knew them well enough for a showdown. And besides, she wanted to let off steam without their bizarre interjections.

'Bollocks!' she shouted, slinging her guitar in its case and sighing loudly.

Tommy raised an eyebrow. 'Better now?'

Zoë didn't even bother to smile.

'I probably should've warned you about Christophe,' said Tommy, pulling off his T-shirt.

Zoë grunted, glancing at Tommy's ripped stomach while his head was behind the fabric.

'He likes to pop a few Es.' Tommy rummaged in his bag for a clean top, glancing over and catching her eye. Zoë looked away.

'A few?' she echoed, peevishly. 'What, like, several? That's normal is it, before a gig?'

'Not . . . normal.' Tommy pulled on a fresh T-shirt. 'There's no routine. He just does it from time to time.'

'Right. Great.' Zoë kicked a chair out of the way and yanked her jeans up over the horrible white miniskirt.

'Not like Rod, who's reliably caned.' He zipped up his case, looking over again. 'Hey,' he said, smiling. 'Loosen up.'

Zoë maintained her moody expression. She didn't feel like loosening up.

'You need a drink,' he said.

Zoë grunted. She couldn't tell whether Tommy was stating a fact or suggesting they go for a drink together. He was probably right; she needed something to help her shrug off this rage, but she had to get home. Part of the reason for her angry demeanour was the fact that James was still sulking, still not making any effort to find a job, presumably making a point by waiting for her to find one first. She could picture him now, spreadeagled on the couch, can of lager in hand, eyes lazily following the movements of some trashy late-night chat-show host.

Tommy was still looking at her. Zoë averted her gaze, still not sure whether it was an offer or not. Deep down, she was hoping it might be. She didn't really want to go back to the flat. She knew it was disloyal to think like this, but the idea of Tommy's good-natured company appealed more than that of her sloth of a boyfriend right now.

'Cheeky pint?' he said, grabbing his bag and slinging it over his shoulder.

Zoë relented quickly, convincing herself that James wouldn't be missing her anyway.

'I'm buying.' He yanked open the door, through which tumbled their bassist and drummer, both giggling like naughty children.

Zoë stepped over them. She was too exhausted to comment.

Sliding the bottles across the shiny surface, Tommy pulled up a second stool for Zoë. 'It's not just the gig you're pissed off about, is it?'

Reluctantly, Zoë shook her head. She wondered whether he could tell, or whether it was just a lucky guess.

Tommy took a long swig of beer. His hair fell away from his eyes and she saw, in the mirror, that he was smiling at her reflection. She looked at the floor, embarrassed to keep catching his eye. Inside, she wanted to tell him everything. It was a rare treat, having someone impartial and intelligent who was willing to listen, but the fact was, they barely knew one another. It seemed too soon to open up.

Eventually, the presence of his gaze on her face became too much to bear.

'Before I went solo I was in a band,' she said, briefly meeting his eye.

182

Tommy nodded, laughing softly. 'Weren't we all.'

Zoë faltered. 'Y-were you?'

'Long story.' He dipped his head for her to go on.

'Right. Well . . .' Zoë hesitated, intrigued by Tommy's previous life. At some point, she was going to have to hear it in full. 'I . . . It was called Dirty Money, and we were kind of close. Like, really close. Best friends. For years, it was all we ever dreamed of – making it big with the band, you know?'

'Oh yeah,' Tommy nodded wryly. 'I know.'

'And then Louis came along and—'

'Let me guess.' Tommy held up a hand. 'He couldn't get a deal for Dirty Money but he sold the idea of Zoë Kidd, because female solo artists are hot at the moment.'

'Did he tell you that?'

Tommy laughed, taking a swig of beer. 'He didn't need to.'

'Oh.' Zoë looked down at her hands, wondering whether she sounded naïve. Tommy had obviously worked in the music industry for a while. 'Well, basically, we went our separate ways. The band stayed together without me, just the three of them. I saw them on YouTube the other day. On Irish TV.'

'Wow.' Tommy nodded. 'That's good going. Someone pulling some strings for them?'

'They're pulling their own strings.'

His eyebrows lifted. 'Impressive. Every band needs a good string puller.'

'Mmm.' Zoë poured some beer down her throat, hoping it might numb the despondency.

'Jeez, Zoë. Is that what's getting you down? You think they'll make it without you?'

She shrugged. 'Partly.' She wasn't going to discuss all her issues with Tommy.

'Cheer up.' He looked at her. 'I was only kidding about the string pulling.'

'What d'you mean?'

'Well, I mean, a band can get so far on their own, but it's still nowhere compared to where you'll be going with Vicinity.'

'*If* I go anywhere with Vicinity,' she reminded him. 'And they might be going places, anyway. They had interest from Hot Rocks Records.'

He laughed – not in a nasty way, but in a way that suggested there was something amusing about the idea of Hot Rocks turning the girls into stars. Zoë rushed to their defence.

'They're a good band,' she said. 'You have to hear them. They're really talented.'

Tommy stopped laughing and looked at her. 'Yeah. Sorry. I didn't mean they weren't. I just meant . . . Well, let's face it, that's not really what it's about, is it?'

Zoë drank some beer to buy herself time. She wasn't sure what Tommy was getting at.

'I guess not,' she said eventually, unwilling to reveal her ignorance. 'Anyway. That's me. What about you? What happened to your band?'

Tommy rattled his empty bottle and looked at it, as though contemplating buying another and rejecting the idea.

'Nah. That's one for a night when we've got the early slot.'

'Didn't you . . . did you ever think about going solo?'

Zoë couldn't help herself. It didn't make sense that Tommy was plugging away as a session musician. His voice was sexy and powerful and he played the guitar to a standard that rivalled Ellie's. He was good-looking, in a rugged sort of way, and if Christophe and Rod were to be believed, he had written songs for some very well-known bands. He had everything it took.

'Me? In the spotlight?' He laughed.

Zoë looked at him, puzzled. 'Why not?'

'Why *not*? Surely the question should be *why would I*? Why would anyone? You tell me, in fact. Why do you—'

'There you are!'

They turned in their seats. Tommy looked confused for a

184

moment. Zoë opened and closed her mouth like a goldfish. James was the last person she'd expected to see in here tonight.

'I've been calling you since you came off,' James said, with a demeanour that seemed almost . . . jolly. 'Thought you must've disappeared through a stage door or something.'

'Tommy,' Zoë muttered weakly, 'this is my boyfriend, James.' She hopped awkwardly off the stool, preparing for explanations. 'James, Tommy.'

They exchanged a solid handshake.

Zoë stared, speechless. If someone had told her that her guitarist and her boyfriend – in his current state of mind – were to meet like this, she would have predicted fireworks. James, almost undoubtedly, would have got the wrong end of the stick and either stormed off in a huff or picked a fight with Tommy. She certainly wouldn't have envisaged a cordial handshake.

'I went backstage, looking for you,' James explained, pulling up a stool. 'Saw your other musicians, I think. One with long, black hair and the other one like an Action Man?'

'That's them.'

'I wasn't sure; they were sort of . . . the wrong way up.'

'What d'you mean?'

'Well, they were lying across the corridor. Making a kind of wailing noise.'

Zoë and Tommy exchanged a look.

'Anyway. Mind if I join you?'

James tucked his stool in just as Tommy hopped off his. 'I've gotta go,' he said, extracting his guitar and backing out. 'Gotta . . . walk the dog.'

Zoë felt a mild sense of relief as the guitarist beat a hasty retreat, raising his hand in a farewell salute. She watched in the mirror until Tommy's reflection had disappeared, then turned to her boyfriend. 'Okay,' she said. 'I'm baffled.'

'What d'you mean?'

She shrugged helplessly. 'Well, the guy I left in the flat wouldn't even say goodbye to me and he *certainly* wouldn't come along to my gig. To tell the truth, I don't think he even likes the idea of my solo career. So . . . I guess . . . I'm wondering who you are.'

James rolled his eyes and let out a theatrical sigh. 'Well, *that's* gratitude.'

Zoë smiled, still looking at him expectantly.

'Okay.' He held up his hands. 'I'll come clean. I'm sorry. I've been a dork.'

She spluttered. 'A *dork*? James, you've been watching too many Australian soaps.'

'Ah, yes. That's true. I have. And I apologise for that too. I was so wrapped up in my own self-pity I couldn't see anything else. So, I've kinda . . . *emerged*, and realised that it's not the end of the world, losing my job. And it's not so bad that you quit yours, either, because you hated it.'

'We both hated our jobs.'

'Well, yeah. So this is like . . . an opportunity. Not a set-back. You can give your music a go, and I . . . well, I've had a look around and seen a couple of roles I might like. I'm sure something will come up.'

Zoë knew that this wasn't the sort of bar where public displays of affection were generally accepted, but she didn't care. She reached over and squeezed him, kissing him long and hard on the lips.

'You're back,' she said, pulling away, beaming. 'I'm so happy.'

'Me too. Daytime TV sucks.'

She laughed. 'What, um, what made you *emerge*?'

'Oh. Well. I was watching this thing about a brain surgeon guy who tried to do his own lobotomy and – well, anyway. I went to change the channel and I must've pressed the wrong thing because your CD came on. You know, the demo you did with the girls? It was still in the machine. So I listened to it, and I realised, well . . . It sounds silly, but I could hear it in your voice, how much you wanted it. You couldn't have stayed in that dead-end job. You *love* the stage, and the music, and . . .' He shrugged, his inhibitions beginning to catch up.

Zoë leaned forward and kissed him again. 'You got it,' she whispered in his ear. 'Thank you.'

27

'So, is that the plan, then?' She looked scathingly at her daughter.

Zoë nodded as calmly as she could. 'That's the plan.'

'Well . . .' Zoë's mother looked around the room, her eyes settling expectantly on her husband.

'You can't have Valice' he grunted. 'It's a proper noun.'

Zoë set about removing her letters from the board, secretly pleased that her dad wasn't getting involved. She had deliberately broken the news early on in the day in the hope that her parents might have run out of things to say on the matter by mid-afternoon. She had been overly optimistic.

Her father had taken it quite well, she thought. After turning a shade of mauve, he had taken some deep breaths and told Zoë that he despaired of her intentions and couldn't bear to hear any more of her nonsense. In truth, she'd been quite surprised by the measured tone of his response. She had initially wondered whether her sister might have dropped a few hints, to soften the blow, but her mother's reaction knocked that theory out the window.

After yelping loudly, Zoë's mum had gone very quiet, indicating that she might be in shock. After a few minutes, she had pulled herself together and gone back to doing what she did best: nagging.

'Why, darling?' she asked for about the eighth time that day.

'Mum, please. I hated my job. You have no idea how I felt

every Sunday night, knowing I'd have to walk through those doors the next day. I loathed it. Chase bloody Waterman was sapping the life out of me.'

'Language, darling. It was paying good money. Perhaps you don't understand the value of money?'

Zoë could feel herself getting agitated, but managed to rein it in. It was an easy dig for her mother to make. She of all people knew the value of money. She was the one who had grown up in the shadow of the Croydon flyover.

'Is vacil a word?'

Her father cleared his throat. 'An anagram thereof would be feasible, would it not?'

She frowned at the plastic letters while her mother fumed beside her.

'Cavil,' he said eventually. 'Now hurry up and put it down.'

'Cavil?' Zoë glanced at James, who responded with a look that said, *no idea either.*

'To raise trivial and frivolous objection,' her father said pointedly. 'I would have thought you of all people should know the meaning of that.'

'Oh.' Zoë laid down the letters, avoiding eye contact with both of her parents. 'Your go, James.'

'I thought you said they hadn't contracted you yet, or whatever it's called.'

'Signed,' she said, wincing as her boyfriend laid down the word VINYL for a whopping forty-five points. He couldn't have picked a less appropriate word. 'No, they haven't yet. But it's practically a done deal.'

'Practically,' she echoed disdainfully.

'It's your go,' urged Zoë, determined to push them away from the subject of her record deal.

'I just don't understand your thinking, Zoë. You left a perfectly decent position in a firm—'

'Which I hated.'

'. . . which paid good money, for a non-existent contract in an industry that is riddled with uncertainty.'

'Maybe I don't want certainty,' she said, quietly.

'I'm sorry?'

James leaned forward. 'Your turn, Mrs Kidd? I'm afraid to say, I think I just overtook you on the scoreboard.' He tapped the notepad and smiled.

Zoë let her hair fall over her face and mouthed her thanks to James. He was a genius when it came to dealing with her family. Just as cats and dogs could sense storms brewing, James could foresee a Kidd family row.

Her mother huffed for a bit, then came up with the rather uninspired HALL for seven points.

'At least *one* of you has your feet on the ground,' she said, taking the bag from James.

Zoë shot her boyfriend a look. The fact that both Zoë and James were out of work seemed like too much trauma for her parents to deal with in one day, so, as they'd discussed, James would keep quiet about his redundancy until another time, unless the moment seemed right – which it didn't.

'I wouldn't say they were *on the ground,* exactly.' James's head danced genially from side to side.

'Well, at least you have a proper job.'

Zoë widened her eyes warily in his direction.

'There.' Her father dusted his hands against one another, admiring his handiwork on the board. He seemed to be studiously ignoring the conversation around him, which suggested to Zoë that his feelings might be – rather ominously – beyond words.

'What's . . .' James twisted his head and squinted. '*Gadoid*?'

Zoë's dad sighed and shook his head. 'You are aware of the sea-dwelling vertebrate known as the *fish*?'

Yes, he was really pissed off; Zoë could tell. He always got like this when he was angry – all aloof and superior.

'I am, yes.' James was playing along, which was the best thing to do. Trying to outsmart Rupert Kidd wasn't something anyone tried more than once.

'Then you will be aware of species such as cod, and hake?'

'Indeed.'

'Which are members of the family known as, to give it its Latin name, Gadidae. Hence the adjective, gadoid.'

'Ah.' James nodded as though enlightened. 'I see. Oh look – we're out of letters. Your go, Zoë.'

She smiled, setting down a rather lame DOSH and wondering how she would have got through the day without her boyfriend. She wasn't the type to stand by as people insulted her way of life or attacked her opinions. If it were anybody else casting aspersions on her decisions, she would have stood up and fought. But in the face of her father's animosity and her mother's anguish, she found herself retreating inside her shell. It was pathetic. She wanted their approval more than she liked to think.

'Oh, *that's* appropriate,' her mother spat. 'You're spelling it out, are you, instead of earning it?'

Zoë looked at the board and saw what she'd done.

'It's a pity you don't have an L and an E; you'd be able to make DOLE. Because that's what you'll be on, soon enough.'

'Mum . . .'

'What do *you* think?' She rounded on James in a way that was somehow aggressive and sympathetic at once. 'Have you had any say in all this? Given that you're likely to be the one supporting our daughter – God help you – when all her brilliantly laid plans go to pot.'

'Well, actually, the truth is—'

'Actually,' Zoë butted in, realising what he was about to say.

Her parents both looked at her, perplexed by the volume of her voice.

'James won't be supporting me,' she said, glaring at him. 'I've made that quite clear. I'll earn my own living, whether it's from singing or flipping burgers.'

'Flipping burgers.' Her mother recoiled. 'Well that's marvellous, Zoë. Fifteen years' education well spent.'

'My go!' cried James, zealously rubbing his hands together. 'There!' He pressed down the S of TRELLIS and made a fanfare noise, to the sound of stunned silence.

'Well,' said Zoë, when it became clear neither of her parents would speak. 'Anyone else? Or are we done? I can't go.'

'I'm done,' her dad replied, sombrely. He might equally have been referring to his parenthood, thought Zoë, watching his mouth return to its grim pout.

'Me too.'

'Well! Let's tot up the scores . . . Ooh. Well, looks like I won! I got two hundred and three points, Mr Kidd was a close second with a hundred and—'

'Well played, all,' said Zoë's father, pouring the letters into the bag and snapping the board shut. 'Very good.'

James looked at his watch and gave a cry of surprise that Zoë suspected wasn't entirely genuine. 'Five o'clock! Time runs away, doesn't it, with these light evenings?'

Zoë felt obliged to reply when nobody else did. It felt as though they were practising a foreign language role play. 'It does,' she nodded. 'We should probably get going.'

There wasn't any objection to the suggestion – in fact, there wasn't any reaction at all. By common consent, they all trooped through the house to the porch, where James, bless him, continued to fill the awkward silence.

'. . . and I suppose you'll be starting to think about the garden party soon?'

Zoë pulled on her boots, baulking at the thought of the annual ordeal. Each year, on the first weekend of June, the Kidd family hosted a lavish summer 'do' to celebrate the consecutive birthdays of her father, her grandmother and herself – complete with hog roast, marquee, obnoxious long-distance relatives and puff pastry vol-au-vents. It was a date that was inscribed in the calendar at the start of each year – a date which, under no circumstances, could be used for anything else.

'Already thinking about it,' replied her mother, visibly brightening. 'We sent the invitations out last weekend.'

'Excellent.' James forced an admirable smile.

'It was lovely to see you both.'

Despite her penultimate word, Zoë noticed, the phrase was very much directed at James. She often wondered whether, given the choice, her parents would have preferred James as their offspring rather than her.

'See you soon.' Zoë's mum kissed the air either side of her daughter's face.

They were about to leave when a new conversation started up about whether the tulips outside the house detracted from the Virginia creeper and Zoë realised her phone was ringing.

'Hiiiiii,' drawled Louis. Zoë wished she had taken the time to check the caller before picking up. 'How's it goin'?'

'Fine, thanks.'

She shimmied sideways, angling her face away from her parents. Weekends, she was beginning to realise, meant nothing to people like Louis. There was no such thing as out-of-hours in his world. Business and pleasure just blended into one, giving him the liberty to drink whisky at midday on a Wednesday, but also to pick up the phone to an artist on a Sunday afternoon.

'Great. Well, I got some news.'

'Oh?'

'Edgar and Jenson and Harry are gonna be at your gig on Thursday.'

Zoë's heart started thumping. This was Edgar Hutchinson, President of Vicinity, Jenson Davies, Head of A&R and Harry Poole, the much talked-of A&R manager. 'Oh my God.'

'Yeah, so make it a good 'un, eh?'

'I will.'

'This is the real thing, sweet-cheeks. You impress them, you come away with a record deal.'

'Cool. Okay.' Zoë tried to sound confident, aware that the Virginia creepers conversation had fizzled.

'You excited?'

'Y-yeah!' Zoë wished she could tell her manager how excited she really felt, how her hands were shaking at the prospect of seeing her name on that contract. But she couldn't. Not in front of her parents. For some reason, in front of them she felt stupid and small, getting all worked up over something that came with no guarantees.

'You don't sound very sure.'

'No, I am!' Zoë tried to convey as much enthusiasm as was possible in the circumstances. Even James had run out of small-talk.

'The reason I ask, Zoë, is this. I've seen you perform and I've met you enough times to know what kinda girl you are. And I'm impressed with what I've seen. We all are. But every once in a while, Zoë, I hear this wobble in ya voice that tells me you're not one hundred per cent. You know what I'm talkin' about?'

'No!' Zoë objected, wishing more than ever she was some-where else. 'No, that's not true . . .'

'I'm not sayin' you gotta be a self-righteous diva,' Louis went on, 'but you gotta *want* it. Real bad. And if we're gonna go ahead with this deal, I need to know you want it.'

'I do!'

'You do?'

'I do.'

'So say it.'

'Say what?'

'Say that you want it. Tell me.'

She hesitated, willing the porch floor tiles to swallow her up. Her parents would think she was mad.

'*I want it.*'

There was a brief pause, then Louis replied. 'Good,' he said. 'I thought so.'

Zoë breathed a little sigh, unable to resist a quick glance over her shoulder. James was looking at his shoes while her parents were staring at her, both wearing bemused frowns. She made a winding gesture with her hand and pulled a face. The furrows in their brows deepened.

'You look damned good on that stage,' Louis went on. Zoë wondered where this was all going. She'd told him she wanted it. Wasn't that enough? 'And you sound good, too. You're a natural performer.'

'Thanks.'

'But you gotta work on that presence. You gotta . . .' He cleared his throat. 'At the risk of sounding like Simon Cowell . . . You gotta *own* that stage, baby.'

'Right,' she said warily. She had always felt proud of her stage presence. Standing up in front of a crowd was what turned her on – what gave her the edge over other singer-songwriters.

'You need to take some tips from the pros,' he said. 'To put you in the next league.'

'Okay . . .'

'The premier league. I'm gonna get you some tickets. Leave it with me.'

Zoë didn't know quite what Louis had in mind but thanked him anyway.

'No problem. I'll see you Thursday. Like I said, make it a good 'un.'

Zoë nodded, hearing the line go dead and leaving it a few moments before turning round. She thought about Louis's advice. *Own* that stage. *Want it.* She would, and she did. The stage was her home. It was the one place she could go where her inhibitions and frustrations didn't follow. If Louis had any doubts, it was because he was speaking to her offstage persona. She'd show him. She'd show them all.

'Everything okay, dear?'

'Yeah, fine. Sorry about that,' she rolled her eyes, smiling. 'My manager. He likes to go on.'

'You seemed to be having some sort of argument,' her mother said pointedly.

'Oh . . . no. That was just . . . him being silly. He's a bit of a clown, you know . .' Zoë led the way onto the driveway and waved goodbye. 'See you soon!'

'A clown,' her father said gravely, shaking his head. 'Well, it's good to know your career is in safe hands.'

Zoë nearly replied, but caught herself just in time. The words she had nearly uttered were still going round and round in her head as they headed off down the gravel driveway, but soon they had a tune, and a beat. 'Why Do I Bother', her second solo song, was already underway.

28

'Honey, that was incredible.' Louis reached out and grabbed her by the shoulders, squeezing rather harder than Zoë would have liked. 'In . . . *credible*.'

She beamed back at him, too exhausted and too overwhelmed to speak. The adrenaline was still rushing round in her bloodstream, her head still light from the performance.

For once, Louis wasn't exaggerating. The gig *had* been incredible – and not just because she'd been headlining in one of London's most popular live music venues or because it was the start of a bank holiday weekend. Zoë had taken her manager's advice to heart and spent the last three days perfecting her act. Her set had been honed and refined, her songs, her stance and her on-stage banter rehearsed in front of James until he begged her to stop. And it had all paid off. She'd felt great up there in the spotlight. Her musicians – on narcotics ban – had done her proud and the crowds had gone justifiably wild. Tonight, nobody could have denied that Zoë Kidd owned that stage.

'Come on, let's go next door. You've *toadally* won the guys over.'

Zoë followed in her manager's wake as he ploughed through the crowds, wondering where 'next door' was and who exactly he meant by 'the guys'. Louis seemed to forget that whilst he'd been here a hundred times with his fledgling acts, she was new to this game. A few pointers every now and then wouldn't go amiss.

Pushing past the doorman, Louis turned left down a side street. Zoë hurried after him as quickly as her tall, plastic shoes would allow. A gold catsuit – another of her manager's fantasies – was all she had on beneath the long coat and it wasn't ideal for long-distance running.

They drew to a halt, Louis knocking on the unmarked black door of a Georgian terrace that looked, in the darkness, rather like 10 Downing Street. A man in a bowler hat stepped back to allow them to pass.

'Good evening.'

Zoë stared. It was like a scene from *Alice in Wonderland*. The doorman led them through an arched corridor lined with portraits of important-looking men and dusty bowls of pot pourri. It was one of those private clubs that rich people joined to get away from the riffraff, Zoë deduced.

'Edgar! Jenson! Harry! Meet Zoë!' Louis opened his flabby arms and drew her into the fold as the men rose from the soft leather seats. Ben was there too, in the background, smiling mutely at her cleavage through the gap in her raincoat.

'Hi!' Zoë shook the men's hands as Louis started enthusing about the cocktails and the 'arm-biance'.

Edgar Hutchinson was not how she had imagined him. For some reason, she had expected him to be stockily built, with long hair – maybe even a ponytail. She had pictured a swaggering, cocksure eighties throwback; a man who had smoked and snorted his way through the last two decades in order to reach his esteemed position in the industry. Instead, what she saw was a lean, clean-shaven forty-something with pitted skin and tired, hollow eyes that seemed more focused on his BlackBerry than his potential signing.

'Great show tonight,' said Jenson, who looked a lot like his boss but with slightly more hair. Again, no eighties throwback. Zoë smiled. She should have known better. The music industry was growing out of its stereotypes; it was run by accountants and lawyers now.

'We were really impressed,' added Harry, who seemed more old-school, more mellow than his superiors. Dressed in a wrinkled suit jacket and jeans, his overgrown hair and greying sideburns combined to give the impression of a man who had long since abandoned self-discipline – an impression confirmed by the large glass of wine on the table.

'Thanks.' Zoë sat down and allowed Louis to pick her a drink from the impossibly sophisticated menu. She hadn't noticed it until now, but she felt nervous. It wasn't just residual adrenaline; it was fear. Tonight, if he hadn't already, Edgar Hutchinson, the President of Vicinity, would make up his mind about whether to sign Zoë Kidd. She had made so many sacrifices to be here; she had nothing to fall back on. If she didn't come away with the promise of a contract tonight, she didn't know what she would do.

Edgar, on the other hand, clearly didn't see tonight as anything special.

'Can't stay for long I'm afraid,' he muttered, pulling up his sleeve to reveal a chunky gold watch. 'Gotta be somewhere else.'

'Hey, no worries,' Louis replied sycophantically. 'Just glad you made it down.'

Jenson grunted and turned to Zoë. 'You've got a good voice, good presence. Where do you see yourself in a few years' time?'

She blinked back at him. It felt, all of a sudden, as though she were back at Chase Waterman.

'I . . . I see myself writing songs and making records,' she stammered. Then, recognising that this was a test of her confidence as an artist, she looked him in the eye. 'I see myself on the stage.'

'On the *big* stage,' Louis put in unnecessarily.

Edgar nodded and sipped his drink, glancing down as his BlackBerry started flashing.

'How long have you been performing?' he asked, squinting at the display.

'Six or seven years,' she replied.

Edgar finally put down the gadget and exchanged a look with his head of A&R.

'Six or seven years . . . properly,' she went on, unable to bear the silence. 'Before that I used to perform . . . you know, just, kind of . . . for fun.'

Edgar's eyebrow arched, slowly and magnificently. '*For fun*?'

Zoë immediately wished she could redo the last ten seconds of her life. The truth was, she had never been on a stage before she'd got together with the girls – apart from the time she'd played the donkey's minder in the school nativity play. She'd never been to drama school or music college. The only singing she'd done before her Dirty Money days had been in front of the bathroom mirror.

'Oh, you know . . .' Zoë shrugged helplessly. She didn't want to lie, but she didn't want to admit the truth either.

'Great! Thank you!' cried Louis as the waiter brought over their drinks. 'Here you go . . .' He made a great show of presenting Zoë with her cocktail – a green paste containing rust-coloured streaks. 'That's called a Show-Stopper – appropriate, huh? Oh, that reminds me. I can *toadally* see Zoë's music working on a major TV drama – or a commercial, dontcha think?'

Zoë sank into the green drink, grateful to her manager for his effective, if heavy-handed, diversion. *TV drama*? Yes, please.

'I can see that,' Harry nodded.

Jenson grunted again. 'Who produced the demo CD for the band?'

Louis released the straw from his syrupy cocktail and made a guttural noise. 'Ah! I had Clive do it. Not bad for a first stab, huh?'

Zoë watched as Jenson took in the information, his head barely moving. Clearly surnames were not required in these circles.

'I'm . . . I'm thinking red one might work . . .' Jenson took a sip of whisky and swilled it around in his mouth.

200

Zoë looked at Louis for a clue. *Red one?* It was great that the head of A&R was already thinking about producers, but it felt very much as though the conversation was going on over her head.

'Red one, yeah,' Louis nodded. '*Yeah.*'

Zoë managed to catch his eye.

'RedOne?' he prompted, as though saying it a third time might suddenly spark recognition. 'One of the most successful producers of the century, baby. New Kids on the Block? Michael Jackson? Lady Gaga?'

'Oh,' Zoë looked down at the floor, feeling ashamed and excited at once. '*Red* One. Yeah, maybe.'

Jenson sucked on his front teeth, looking into the middle distance. 'Positioning,' he said.

Zoë waited for him to elaborate. Louis was nodding away as though he'd just made a very wise remark.

'Positioning,' echoed Harry.

Zoë looked around at the faces, wondering whether this was some sort of word game they were playing.

'Where do you *sit*, on the shelf?'

It took her a couple of seconds to realise that Jenson was talking figuratively. She remembered the words from her first meeting with Ben. He meant, she assumed, where did her music sit in the spectrum of popular music? Was it pure pop, or ska, or punk? These were questions she'd been asked a lot over the course of the last few years. Fans, promoters, managers, artists – they'd all quizzed her, they'd all presented their own analyses of her sound. Some had put Dirty Money in the post-Britpop punk box, one even deemed them to be electro-pop, despite their complete lack of electronic instruments.

The fact was, Zoë Kidd didn't sit on the shelf. Baked beans sat on the shelf, getting compared to all the other baked beans in terms of colour, weight, taste and style – but not Zoë. She was sick of being compartmentalised.

'I've been likened to lots of artists,' she said. 'But I'm not quite like—'

'Such as?'

'Um . . .' Zoë's self-belief faltered as she clocked Louis's wary glance. 'Well, Katy Perry – I get that, quite a lot. And Christina Aguilera, but I don't think I'm—'

'I'm not convinced,' said Jenson, narrowing his eyes and casting an eye over her body, which was still cocooned safely in the raincoat.

'Nor am I,' Zoë replied, smiling. 'For a start—'

'Ah. I know.' Jenson waggled a finger. 'You're a Florence Welch, only brunette.'

'I . . .' Zoë's protest fizzled. She couldn't quite believe he was serious. *Florence, as in, Florence and the Machine*? Florence was an exceptionally talented artist, but she didn't sound anything like Zoë. Their voices were different, their songs, their personalities . . .

'It's important to know where you fit,' Jenson went on. Zoë sensed that Ben had picked up a lot of his spiel from the master himself. 'It's not just other music that's vying for our listeners' time now; it's the playstation, the Wii, the social networks, the Sky channels . . . To make sure your records sell, you've got to know exactly who you're targeting and what they're into.'

Zoë nodded, too stunned to speak. It was as though they had a preconceived idea about what they were after and they simply wanted her to step into the shoes.

'So.' Edgar Hutchinson pocketed his BlackBerry, knocked back the last of his drink and turned to Louis. 'We're looking at a three-sixty, as you know.'

Zoë's head flicked round in time to see Louis's face fall.

'Uh . . . We can talk about—'

'I'm afraid not. You know how things are. It's three-sixty or nothing.' He swivelled to Zoë. 'You have a lawyer?'

'She does,' Louis replied.

'Excellent.' Hutchinson reached for his coat and paused on his haunches. 'Nice meeting you, Zoë. Great stuff. I look forward to having you on our books – oh. That reminds me. Have you signed the prelim agreement?'

'Oh . . . um . . .' Zoë waited for her thoughts to catch up. The agreement was still with her sister. 'Not yet.'

'Here,' Ben spoke for the first time all evening. 'I've got another copy.'

'Splendid,' muttered Jenson, also rising to his feet as Ben slid the document onto the table and slipped a pen into her hand.

There weren't many alternatives, thought Zoë, in a situation like this. With five sets of eyes, including those of the President of Vicinity, bearing down on her, there was only one thing to do. After a cursory glance at a couple of the pages, she signed the agreement.

'Lovely.' Jenson shrugged on his coat and followed his boss out. 'Ben, can I leave it with you to get the ball rolling on the contract next week?'

Ben nodded as assertively as was possible in the face of someone so imposing.

'Great meeting you, Zoë.' He thrust his hand in her face. 'And Louis, pleasure as always . . .'

Louis replied with one of his broad, American smiles. 'Well, you know . . . I'm part of the team now, huh? What's mine is yours.'

With a brief raise of the hand, Edgar Hutchinson marched out of the room with Jenson in tow.

Zoë was itching to make sense of what had just happened. Unless she'd got hold of the wrong end of the stick, it seemed very much as though she'd just been offered a contract with Universal's largest commercial label.

'I'd better head, too,' said Harry, draining his bowl-like glass of wine. 'Great gig tonight, Zoë. Ben, will you settle up?'

Seconds later, Zoë was following her manager into the balmy night air, practically exploding with unanswered questions.

'So . . .' Her heart started thumping at the prospect. 'Am I signed?'

He chuckled. 'Not quite, sweet-cheeks. The legals will take a while. The first draft is always written somewhat in the label's favour.'

'Oh.' Her spirits fell. 'And this . . . three-sixty . . .?'

'Mmm.' Louis's smile vanished. 'Yeah. It's short for three hundred and sixty degrees.'

Zoë frowned. She had already worked that much out.

'Listen,' Louis sucked on his teeth. 'It's probably best if your lawyer explains the details, huh?'

'Right . . . And . . . Do I have a lawyer?'

'You will do next week. I'll get you a guy from Coopers – one of the best.'

'Oh, right. Cool.' Zoë nodded gratefully. 'Thanks.'

Louis beamed back at her. 'Don't thank me. You did the hard work. Fantastic gig tonight – oh, that reminds me.' He reached into one of his sizeable back pockets and brought out a white envelope. 'One ticket to see The Cheats at Wembley Arena next month.'

Zoë stared at him. 'Seriously?'

'I tried to wangle you two, but my favours only stretch so far. You'll be looked after though; it's a VIP ticket. Take some tips from the top, eh?'

With a jovial wave, Louis disappeared into the darkness.

Zoë ripped open the envelope, just to see it with her own eyes. She fingered the thick, perforated card, reading every word on the ticket. Its face value was a hundred and twenty pounds. She peered closer. The seats were practically *touching the stage*.

She walked off with a spring in her step and a broad smile on her lips that only faded when she remembered that she wouldn't be able to share her excitement with the one person who loved The Cheats as much as she did: Shannon O'Leary. Shannon was infatuated with the lead singer, Niall King. Zoë forced the negative thoughts from her mind and pulled out her phone. She had to tell someone her news. She had just earned herself a contract with Vicinity.

Four missed calls flashed up at her, all from Tamsin. Zoë dialled her voicemail.

'Hey, Zoë. It's me. Just getting back to you on this agreement thing. Sorry it took me so long. Call me for a full rundown, but I just wanted to say, *don't sign that thing*. If you do, anything you sing or write from now on will belong to them, not you – even if you don't end up getting a record deal with them. Call me back. And *don't sign anything!*'

29

Zoë crouched down and pushed, with all her might, against the percussion-laden platform. Christophe had gone home, of course, either too lazy or too arrogant to put the furniture back how they'd found it. He had no motivation to remain on speaking terms with the rehearsal studio manager.

She strained for a second time, wondering how they'd moved the damn thing in the first place. Then she realised she was being watched.

'You're not one to ask for help, are you?'

Tommy smiled, kneeling down next to her and pushing the unit across the floor with apparent ease.

'Thanks.'

'Like the new songs, by the way.'

Zoë brightened. 'Really?'

'Yeah.' He dusted off his hands and dragged a mike stand back into its corner. 'Full of anguish. Great first album fodder.'

'Fodder?' She feigned offence. 'You sound like the guys from the label.'

He laughed. 'How did it go, meeting Edgar and co.?'

Zoë frowned. 'Good, I think.' She grabbed her guitar case and lifted it onto her shoulder as Tommy hauled open the sound-proof door.

'You think? Are they signing you or not?'

'They've sent a contract to my lawyer, apparently.'

Tommy waved to the security guard on reception and then stopped and looked at her. 'But . . . that's great, isn't it?'

'Mmm.'

She wasn't being deliberately coy; she just felt uncertain, and, if she was being honest, a little embarrassed about what she had done. Having called her sister for a full rundown on the terms of the agreement, Zoë was beginning to feel as though she might have been duped.

She could feel Tommy's eyes on her as they slowed to a halt next to his old VW. Everyone in her world, it seemed, had an incomplete picture of what was going on – not to mention ulterior motives. Her boyfriend knew what she was striving for but didn't understand the industry. Her sister understood the implications of being signed but didn't share Zoë's vision. Louis knew the industry inside out, but he was just looking out for his twenty per cent.

'I think . . .' Zoë stopped herself, suddenly losing faith in what she was about to say. Tommy wouldn't want to be burdened with her dilemmas. 'I should go. See ya.'

'Hey.' Tommy grabbed her wrist as she turned. 'You think what?'

She could just about make out his cautious smile in the half-light. The thought crossed her mind that perhaps he had been here himself. He seemed to know a lot about the industry.

'I think I've been a bit naïve,' she said, eventually. 'I signed this agreement with Vicinity and now my sister, who's a lawyer, has told me what it all means, and . . .'

'Uh-oh.' Tommy's smile vanished. 'I think I know where you're going with this.'

Suddenly, Zoë couldn't get the words out quickly enough. Here, finally, was someone who understood her situation and didn't want to say *I told you so*.

'I've signed away my rights to make music – even for myself, apparently. Vicinity own everything I do. It's like . . . I'm basically working for them. And I've got this feeling they just want to turn me into the next Britney or something – you know, put me up on a pedestal, churn out a couple of big hits and then drop me when someone else catches their eye. I'm not even sure they like my music – they barely even *talk* about the music. It's all about image – the *packaging*.'

Tommy's sigh wasn't exasperated, in the way that Tamsin's and James's had been; it was more just resigned – sympathetic, even.

'That's the majors for you,' he said. 'Not content to just screw over their customers, they have to screw over their artists too.'

Zoë nodded, her relief quickly turning to panic. Tommy's words weren't reassuring in the least.

'I'm screwed, aren't I?'

Tommy shrugged. 'Only as screwed as every other bugger trying to make it in the industry. That's the thing about trying to do something different. You want to define your own sound . . . but they don't want to take the risk. They'd rather launch you as the next Britney because they know you'll at least break even.'

A fresh wave of frustration passed over her as the problem began to crystallise. Tommy was exactly right. Zoë Kidd – the act that she wanted to put out there – was too new, too different, too edgy.

'You might've done better with an indie label,' he mused.

'You reckon?' Zoë closed her eyes, thinking back to the call from Hot Rocks. The independents may not have been held in very high regard by the likes of Louis Castle, but maybe they offered the artist more control. She couldn't help feeling that she'd made an enormous mistake.

'Not that there are many left now . . . But hey, look on the bright side.'

Zoë looked at him. Was there one? It felt as though she was languishing in the bottomless pit of the world's most obvious elephant trap.

'At least if you're the next Britney, they'll make you a priority act.'

'A what?'

Tommy rolled his eyes in the near darkness and smiled. 'Oh dear. Tell me you've heard the stories of artists who get signed and then sat on for years by the label?'

'*Sat on*?' Zoë squinted at Tommy, feeling stupid.

Tommy hoisted his guitar onto the other shoulder and took a deep breath. 'Okay. So say you're a run-of-the-mill singer-songwriter, and you get signed by one of the majors. They spend lots of money on your recordings, your musicians, your producer and that. Then the record's made and the promo guys start plugging it, but the radio stations and the retailers aren't feeling it. Instead of ploughing more money into the plugging and marketing, the label decides to cut its losses and pull the album.

'Some records go unreleased for years. Most of the time, there's some departmental reshuffle and they look at their books, decide the album has missed its "window" and just bin the whole thing forever.'

'And the artist . . .' Zoë didn't need to complete her sentence. She now saw the significance of the document she had signed. *The artist couldn't go anywhere else.*

'Yup. Then they're *really* screwed,' Tommy nodded. 'Unless, by some miracle, they can persuade the label to release them from their contract. That does happen, but not very often. Usually they just keep you on their books, hands tied, so the other labels can't pilfer you.'

Zoë closed her eyes. She felt sick. The situation was worse than she had realised. Not only did the agreement take away her creative control; it put her entirely at the mercy of a bunch of record label executives she might never even meet.

'Cheer up.' Tommy punched her gently in the arm. 'You're not there yet. You've got the blessing of Edgar Hutchinson, haven't you? They'll throw everything they've got at your first release.'

She smiled. 'You reckon?'

He shook his head, bending down to unlock his car. 'Jesus, Zoë. You need to have a bit of faith in yourself.'

Tommy wound down his window and turned the key in the ignition. On its third attempt, the Beetle spluttered into life. Zoë watched as he jerkily pulled away, one hand waving through the open window.

She was still thinking about the priority act thing when she reached the bus stop and realised that a buzzing noise was coming from inside her bag.

'Hello?'

'Zoë, it's me.'

She recognised the voice instantly, but there was something different about it: It sounded muffled and unsteady.

'Ellie?'

'Yeah. Can you come over? Please?'

'What . . .' Zoë's mind filled with questions. 'Are you okay?'

'I got your message.' There was a protracted sniffling noise. 'I'm . . . It's . . . Oh, Zoë, it's awful!'

'What's awful?'

'Just . . . everything. It's such a mess.' She groaned weakly. 'Come over, will you?'

Zoë looked up at the indicator above her head. The next bus was going to Old Street where she could pick up another to Hackney.

'I'll be there in half an hour.'

30

Even in the dim orange glow of the caravan, Zoë could see that Ellie looked different. Her cheeks were gaunt and blotchy and her long, glossy mane looked like pieces of frayed rope. For a moment, she just stood there, swaying gently and squinting at Zoë through half-closed eyes.

'Ellie?'

Stumbling backwards, she gave a confused nod, clutching the door as though it was all she had left in the world.

Zoë mounted the steps and made a tentative attempt at a hug. It was like squeezing a skeleton; Ellie seemed to have lost all the strength in her arms. A sickly smell filled the caravan and a blue fug hung in the air.

'I'msogladyoucame,' Ellie slurred, slowly pulling away and falling back into a plastic cabinet.

Zoë reached out to shield her head, guiding Ellie inside and pressing the flimsy door shut. She was used to her friend looking stoned, but she'd never seen her like this.

'Let's sit down.' She looked around, trying to ascertain where, underneath the layers of clothes, magazines, microwave meal containers, musical instruments, food-encrusted plates and books, the couch resided. 'Where's Sam?'

'He'sout.' Ellie dropped into the hole that Zoë had cleared in the debris and collapsed against the window.

'Whereabouts?' Zoë rooted around for a cushion and slipped

it behind Ellie's head. Her assumption, based on the state of the caravan and its owner, was that Sam had walked out – or been thrown out. Rows between Ellie and Sam were rare – neither was the type to get irate – but they happened from time to time.

'SeeingmatesinEdinburgh,' she said, weakening Zoë's theory.

Zoë rummaged for the kettle. She had no idea what the correct procedure was in situations like this, but it seemed appropriate to make a cup of tea. The idea of calling for an ambulance had crossed her mind, but for the moment it seemed unnecessary. Ellie was lucid, if a little confused.

Three out of four rings on the stove were buried beneath mounds of unopened mail, but the fourth remained clear – except for a small, crumpled piece of foil that had slipped down under the guard. Zoë extracted it and peeled away the edges. Warily, she looked over at Ellie, then back at the brown residue.

For a while, she said nothing, clearing the mail from the stove and lighting the gas, scouring the place for a mug that didn't contain mould and waiting for the kettle to boil. Ellie had always smoked joints. She got caned all the time, after gigs, at parties, in the caravan with Sam . . . She fell over, she giggled at things that weren't funny, she told the same stories over and over again. But she never ended up like this. As far as she knew, Ellie had never touched anything harder than cannabis.

Zoë made the tea and carried it over, clearing another patch in the clutter and squeezing in next to Ellie.

'Here. Drink this.'

Ellie jolted upright. The whites of her eyes – what little was visible around the heavily dilated pupils – were bloodshot. She turned to face Zoë, unable to focus.

'I . . . wantedtocheerup.'

Zoë held Ellie's bony shoulders, steadying her as she sipped the hot tea.

'You took something to cheer yourself up?'

Ellie nodded. The task of holding the mug seemed to be

focusing her mind. 'Yeah. Then I felt all . . . horrible – panicky, so I took some valium and had a joint, then I wanted to cheer up again so I found this coke Sam had left behind, then – oops.'

Zoë used her sleeve to mop the tea from Ellie's lap and waited in stunned silence for the explanation to conclude. Since when had Sam started keeping wraps of coke in the caravan?

'Then I . . . Then I was all jumpy . . . so I took some . . . some . . .' Ellie lost her train of thought.

'Here,' Zoë pushed the tea towards her. No wonder she looked such a mess. The cocktail of uppers and downers was enough to addle even the most hardened addict's brain. Zoë thought about Ellie's boyfriend, wondering whether things had changed in the last few months. The Sam she knew was a cool, laid-back type of guy. He liked art, he smoked grass and his favourite pastime was to sit outside the caravan, sketching Ellie while she played the guitar. He wasn't the type to take coke. Was he?

Ellie gulped down the tea and passed the mug back, letting out a quiet belch. She seemed a little more alert now – able to hold her head up, eyes staying open for longer.

The questions were mushrooming in Zoë's head: What had caused Ellie's frenzied behaviour? Had she done this before? Why had she chosen to call her in preference to Shannon or Kate? Perhaps she'd forgotten, in her stupor, that she and Zoë were no longer best friends.

'Why did you need to cheer up?' she asked.

'Uh . . .' Ellie crumpled again. 'It's just . . . I just . . . I'm not *good* enough, and everyone expects me to be really amazing and I just can't cope with all the pressure . . .'

'Better at what?'

She frowned. 'Singing.'

'Singing?'

'Yeah.' Ellie blinked back at her, as though Zoë was the one on drugs.

'So . . .' She let go of her previous theories. 'Sorry, are we talking about the band?'

'Yes!' Ellie stared at her. 'They make me get up there and sing and I'm not a lead singer, I'm not . . . I can't do it. I can't do it!'

'Calm down,' Zoë reached for her arm. 'It's okay.'

Ellie's eyes were darting frantically around the caravan. 'I'm hungry,' she said. 'I need to eat.'

Zoë leaned over and opened the fridge. There was a lump of parmesan, a chocolate mousse that was three days past its sell-by date and a furry courgette.

'The cupboard,' Ellie muttered, leaning back on the pillow again. 'God, I'm *starving*.'

Zoë stood up and rummaged through the motley selection: Furry bread, shrivelled fruit, a hardened hot cross bun.

'You're not exactly looking after yourself, are you?' Zoë looked at Ellie and was relieved to see a glimmer of a smile. She pulled out a packet of Hobnobs and some rice cakes. 'Here.'

Ellie attacked the biscuits as though she hadn't eaten in weeks.

'So, you don't like doing the vocals.'

'Mm-mmm.' Ellie shook her head, crumbs falling out of both sides of her mouth. 'I hayhit.'

'Why don't you just say that? Tell them.'

Ellie made a winding gesture to imply she had more to say. 'It's Shannon,' she grunted. 'She's gone mad.' Two biscuits and a rice cake later, Ellie was able to speak again. 'She wants me to sing like you did, Zoë, and I can't! I'm not like you – I hate being the centre of attention. And Kate says I have to, too, because she wants us to sign with this label, which Shannon doesn't want to do because she says we should audition for Talent Tout and the rules say you can't if you've got a record deal . . . But Shannon insists! I don't wanna go and audition. I *can't* be lead singer! I just can't do it!'

'Shhh.'

Zoë squeezed Ellie across the shoulders as she dived for another rice cake, tears running down her cheeks. She was beginning to understand the problem. Shannon and Kate were pulling Dirty Money in different directions and they were tearing Ellie apart in the process. A small part of Zoë felt impressed by their dogged determination, but mainly she just felt sad. Sad that things had changed so much.

'Can't you come back?' Ellie asked, rubbing her raw-looking eyes and sniffing. 'I can try and persuade Shannon and Kate—'

Zoë shook her head sadly. She wished, more than ever, that she *could* go back to the way things were, but after her conversation with Tommy she knew for sure that it could never happen. 'I . . . I signed something with Vicinity. I'm not allowed to come back.'

Ellie turned, her eyes watery and pink. 'Not allowed?'

Zoë held her gaze. It was all she could do to stop herself from crying. Sitting here next to Ellie with the biscuit crumbs and the mess and the guitars brought it all back. Their jamming sessions at Goldsmiths seemed like only weeks ago.

'They made me sign it. I'm sorry.'

A tear trickled down Ellie's face. She was calmer now – less hysterical, just miserable.

'That's it, then, isn't it?'

Zoë nodded grimly.

They sat in silence for a while, staring at their reflections in the caravan window. Zoë didn't know what to say. She had let them down once, and now she was letting them down again – cementing her rejection of them once and for all. Ironically, this time she knew exactly what she wanted to do, but this time she wasn't able to choose.

'Why don't you want to sing?' she asked, eventually.

Ellie shrugged. She looked exhausted. 'It's not the singing, exactly; it's the spotlight thing. I don't wanna be the one that everyone looks at. I can't do that chatty thing you do with the audience. I just . . . I hate it.'

215

Zoë nodded. She understood entirely. Ellie looked great behind her guitar and she was a talented musician, but she wasn't a natural front woman. 'Maybe . . .' She couldn't believe what she was about to suggest. 'Maybe you could get someone in. A new lead singer.'

Ellie shook her head. 'Shannon won't have it. Says it would spoil the dynamic.'

'But . . .' Zoë tried not to think about the fact that the girls had discussed getting in a replacement lead singer. 'You getting all upset like this isn't exactly good for the dynamic!'

'They don't know how much I hate it.'

'So tell them!'

Ellie shook her head again. A biscuit crumb fell from her hair. 'It would ruin everything.'

Zoë couldn't bring herself to say that things were already ruined.

'*I'll* tell them,' she offered.

'No! You can't.'

'You're being a martyr.'

Ellie turned to face her. 'No, I mean, you can't tell them because they won't listen. They won't talk to you.'

'Oh.' Zoë looked at her lap. 'Right.' She finally grasped what her friend was saying. All that talk earlier of bringing her back into the band was just Ellie's fantasy, she realised. Shannon and Kate still despised her.

They sat, shoulders to shoulder, for a while. Zoë kept trying to come up with a solution but all she could think about was how it was all her fault. If she hadn't been so self-centred, she wouldn't have gone solo and if she'd been less impatient, she would have waited before signing that agreement, and maybe she would have changed her mind in time to stop her friend from getting into this state.

At least, in a screwed-up sort of way, there was some comfort to be taken from the fact that Dirty Money lived on. Shannon and Kate seemed determined to drive the band forward – albeit via different routes. Zoë thought about the lead from Hot Rocks Records and wondered whether that was the label Ellie had mentioned. Before she could ask, there was a scratching noise at the door and a blast of cool air swept into the caravan.

Ellie jolted upright. 'Sam?' Suddenly energized, she launched herself across the cluttered space and threw herself at his gangly frame. Frowning, Sam drew her towards him, glancing over at Zoë, then down at his girlfriend's face, taking everything in along the way: the mess, the smell, the tears and the charred foil on the stove.

Zoë rose to her feet, quietly balancing the teacup in the over-stacked sink and catching Sam's eye over Ellie's head. Holding her close and stroking her hair, he returned Zoë's look with a nod. *It's okay*, he seemed to be saying.

Ellie sniffed into Sam's chest, letting out a quiet whimper of relief. Zoë smiled, easing past them and heading for the door. Pausing briefly to whisper goodbye, she crept out into the darkness. Sam was right, she thought. It was okay. If there was anyone qualified to take care of Ellie, then it was Sam. She just had to hope that tonight was a one-off occurrence and not the start of something more serious.

31

'Page eight, clause two, point one,' the lawyer went on, flipping the page and waiting for Zoë to do the same on her photocopy.

Charles McCarthy-Smith looked vaguely familiar, in the manner of an ageing rock star or TV personality. His thinning, auburn hair had been combed into a bouffant and beneath the open-necked shirt it was just possible to make out the black cord of a jewel-encrusted crucifix. He spoke in a tone that implied he would rather be somewhere else.

'. . . make sense?'

Zoë nodded. She hadn't actually read the paragraph to which he was referring, partly because it had been crossed out and annotated in some sort of madman's scrawl but also because, even if the words had been legible, they were in another language – some derivation of Latin involving phrases like 'all monies furnished' and 'embodiment of compositions theretofore approved'.

'I presume you understand the general principles of a multiple rights agreement?'

Zoë's hesitation clearly sufficed as a response. She had Googled '360 deal' but the search had simply thrown up a bunch of articles about Madonna and the Pussycat Dolls and some complicated forum debates about the future of the music industry.

'Okay.' He drew a deep breath and exhaled, slowly and noisily, through his nose. 'Traditionally, a record deal was an agreement that said you would record your songs and the label would press them onto vinyl. The company would finance the manufacture, the marketing, the promotion and so on, and then they'd take a cut of the sales.'

Zoë nodded wearily. She understood *something* about the way things worked; she wasn't completely naïve.

'In a multiple rights deal, the label gets involved in more than just the record. Contracts such as this,' he waved the thick wad of paper, 'stipulate that every time the artist performs, or earns royalties from somebody covering their song, or gets their music put on a soundtrack, or has a load of Barbie dolls made in their name . . . Every time you earn money, basically, the label takes a cut in some way, shape or form.'

Tours. Soundtracks. Dolls. These were things Zoë hadn't even dared contemplate. She wondered how she would feel, seeing a plastic Zoë Kidd replica in HMV. The lawyer was trying to imply that this 'three-sixty' contract was a bad thing – that the label was trying to exploit her celebrity status – but he didn't get it. The point was, if things reached a point where she *had* celebrity status then she would have achieved her goal. That was all she wanted. She didn't care if somebody shaved off a sliver of her income along the way.

Charles waffled on about shrinking fan bases, illegal downloads and declining profit margins, lamenting the days of old when artists were free to be artists and record deals were exactly that. His aggrieved tone was odd, thought Zoë, considering that music lawyers were probably doing a whole lot better now that there were all these complicated new contracts floating about.

'. . . to get on the road, get touring,' she heard, feeling a rush of adrenaline at the thought of a trip to America, or Scandinavia, or the Far East with roadies and groupies and truckloads of equipment. Charles had it all wrong. He assumed that her motivation for success had something to do with making money. In fact, money was a long way down on her priority list. If the label wanted to take a cut of all her revenue streams, then that in itself was an assurance that they would do all they could to make Zoë Kidd a sensation. They were incentivised to use their clout and their marketing muscle; if she didn't make money, nor did they.

'. . . these contracts tend to command sizeable advance payments.'

Zoë looked up. This was a subject on which she had tried to quiz Louis a couple of times, never receiving more than a vague hand-wave for an answer. Whilst it was true that she didn't care about becoming insatiably wealthy, she was very aware that she couldn't survive for long without an income.

'What sort of . . .' she trailed off, suddenly embarrassed to ask about her own worth.

'Your advance?' He glanced down and whipped over a few pages. 'It's on page thirty-seven. We're looking at twelve.'

Twelve. For a second, Zoë thought he meant twelve million. Then she looked down and saw the figure on the page. Twelve thousand.

Zoë was already playing with the numbers in her head. Twelve thousand was a third of her previous salary. Assuming it needed to last her a year, it would just about cover her rent, tax and bills. Based on a standard number of working days in the year and an eight hour day, that amounted to something akin to the minimum wage. Her parents would be horrified.

'That's split across the three albums, of course.'

The lawyer's words washed over her as she continued to divide, multiply, compare and forecast. Then she tuned in.

'I'm sorry?'

'You are aware that this is a three-album deal?' He smiled at her patronisingly.

'Y-yes,' she stammered. That much she had taken in during

the first tedious hour of page-turning. The concept that she would release three albums with Vicinity was not a concern; what *was* worrying her was the implication that the twelve thousand pounds would have to last her for the duration of three record releases.

'So, it's four K up-front, then the payment schedule as per . . .'

Zoë finally realised what he meant. She wouldn't receive the twelve thousand pounds up-front; she would get four. Four thousand. That was two months' income, by her old standards. It was equivalent to her father's annual expenditure on golf, or her mother's beauty regime. It was four days in a half-decent recording studio in Camden.

'Then there's tax, of course, and your manager's twenty percent . . .'

Zoë wondered whether Charles was secretly enjoying his role as bearer of bad news. He probably found the look on her face quite amusing, like that of a greedy child lured to a cookie jar that turned out to be empty.

'So in reality, you'll see about two thousand pounds.'

Zoë looked down at the final page, feeling ill. She couldn't believe she had been so naïve. Sitting in her fairytale world wearing her wraparound, rose-tinted glasses, she had imagined that the record deal would somehow solve all her problems. Getting signed was all she had dreamed about for so long that she had forgotten about the mountain that existed behind the hallowed gates of the label.

It wasn't that she didn't know the facts; she had read enough interviews in the music press to understand that not everything turned to gold once you were inside, but she had blotted it out. She didn't want to think about the ugly truths: the fact that ninety percent of *signed* artists never make a penny in their music career, the fact that most records that get released just sink without a trace, pulling their creators down too, the fact that those musicians she idolised, the ones that made it onto the front page of iTunes, were just a tiny, tiny tip of a very large iceberg – an iceberg that was sinking.

'. . . fairly standard for the label to take thirty per cent,' he was saying. 'And another thirty goes to the retailer, nine or ten to the distributor . . .'

Zoë tried to stand firm as another wave crashed over her head. Some quick mental arithmetic was telling her that for a 79p track download, she would make about five pence. *Five pence.* She still clung to the belief that her music and eminence were more important to her than the money, but this . . . this was a revelation.

'. . . fees and expenses, which are recoupable against your royalties. So you'll only start to see an income when your debt's been paid off, so to speak.'

She half-listened as Charles McCarthy-Smith started haughtily talking about superstars giving away their music in order to boost their fan base.

'. . . a three-week tour of the States can make you twenty-five million.'

Suddenly, it all crystallised in Zoë's mind. A&R guys signed thousands of acts each year but only a pathetically small number made it to the top. If you were talented enough, diligent enough and patient enough to make it up there, then the rewards were disproportionately large. *If.* For the others, even those who got within spitting distance of the top – it didn't matter how close you came – you still failed. There was no spectrum of success in this world; it was sink or swim.

Zoë shook her lawyer's hand and rose from her seat, feeling strangely elated. It was true, she was new to all this and she had underestimated the scale of the task, but she wasn't deterred – quite the opposite, in fact. Armed with this new insight, Zoë felt ready to embrace the challenge.

First things first, though. If she was going for the big time, she had to play the part. Take some tips from the top, as Louis put it. She had to look good in front of the Vicinity guys so they sat up and took notice. Zoë Kidd, she decided as she burst out into the warm May sunshine, was going to become a priority act.

32

'Madam?' The waiter swooped over with another tray of champagne flutes filled with sparkling cocktails.

Zoë hesitated. She hadn't intended to drink tonight. All through the gig she'd stuck to mineral water in the knowledge that around her were record label executives, producers and music journalists who, at some point, might have some influence over her career. But it was easier to remain sober when you were sitting in a private booth, watching one of the UK's biggest acts blast their way through a mind-blowing set in front of twelve thousand crazed fans than it was to stand on your own in the middle of the hospitality area, surrounded by strangers who all seemed to know one another. She had accepted drink number one to take the edge off her nerves, then a second to stop her from looking awkward, then another, then maybe two or three more.

Zoë wandered across the lounge with her cocktail, pretending to admire the oil paintings as she checked out her fellow guests. She had already completed several laps of the room, taking care to pick a different route each time. There were, she ascertained, three types of people here tonight: celebrities, suits and liggers.

The celebrities, alongside Niall King and the other members of The Cheats, included Kate Moss, Ricky Hatton, Russell Brand, Kanye West, Sienna Miller, a guy who looked like David Beckham although it was difficult to see with the floppy cap and giant sunglasses, a woman wearing a jewel-encrusted fur cape (fashion designer?) and a plain-looking young lady guarded by burly henchmen whom Zoë could only imagine was a distant member of the royal family. Each celeb was surrounded by an entourage consisting of at least one loud, bossy woman and several beefcakes.

The suits weren't actually wearing suits; they seemed to have their own special dress code consisting of jeans, cotton top (lurid colours optional) and suit jacket. They were the men who made it all happen – and they *were* all men: A&R reps, promo guys, marketing managers . . . She'd spotted Harry Poole loitering on the fringes of one of the groups but hadn't had the nerve to say hi. The Cheats were on another label within Universal, not Vicinity, so she guessed that Harry was something of a tag-along himself – as was Ben, who had clearly come for the free booze and whatever was being doled out in the gents'.

The liggers were the PAs, the interns, the marketing assistants, the friends of friends of the band's manager, the competition winners and, she supposed, others like her, who for one reason or another had blagged a VIP ticket to the show. They were as easy to identify as the celebs and the suits. It wasn't just the high street fashion or the self-coiffed hair that gave them away; it was their expressions. You could tell from their faces that they were savouring their free champagne cocktails, noting every last detail of the designer outfits so that they could regale friends and relatives with full-blown accounts of their night with the stars.

Zoë slammed the empty cocktail glass onto the marble top, suddenly realising what she wanted more than anything else in the world: to call her best friend. She nipped past the two bouncers on the door, making her way to the carpeted foyer that over-looked the enormous glass-fronted entrance of the arena and dialled Ellie's number.

'Hey! It's me! You'll never guess where I am!'

'Er . . . the after-party for The Cheats gig?'

Zoë faltered. 'How did you know that?'

Ellie's laughter crackled softly down the phone. 'Are you drunk, Zo?'

'Um . . . well,' Zoë stepped back from the railings overlooking the atrium below. All the walls seemed to be billowing outwards, then in, then out again. 'Maybe. A bit.'

'You called me about half an hour ago. Told me about the fake lion and the fireworks on stage . . .?'

'Oh. Oh yeah.' Zoë nodded sheepishly into the phone. It was a distant memory, like that of a dream. Maybe she was more drunk than she realised. The show tonight had been incredible. She was still buzzing from it now – from the way Niall King had roused the fans, the way he'd conversed with them, got them singing . . . he was the most natural performer Zoë had ever seen and she could see now why Louis had given her the ticket.

Initially, she had been sceptical of what she might learn from watching The Cheats. She'd been going to gigs for years; she knew how the pros worked the crowd. She'd seen their swagger, heard their big talk. The Cheats, though, and Niall King in particular, did more than just work the crowd. They were in another league.

'Ellie, I *have* to tell you about their last song – you know *Heads Up* from their latest album? They played that and they kinda disappeared into the video backdrop and—'

'Niall King flew off above the crowds?'

'Yeah!' Zoë frowned. 'How did you . . .'

'You told me that too. And how he got the audience to sing the harmonies on *Flying Half Mast* and how he swapped places with the drummer for two songs and how there was a crowd-surfer that got all the way to the back of the arena during *Hot Blood*.'

'Oh.' Zoë dredged her memory for a recollection of the previous phone call, aware that the bouncers were watching her from the doorway.

'You are funny, Zoë.' Ellie was laughing again. 'I've missed your drunken calls.'

Zoë smiled. 'I've missed you too. I love you, Ellie.' She could hear the slur in her own voice but didn't care. 'Not in that way, obviously,' she clarified, as the bouncers exchanged a look.

'You should go, Zoë. Go and enjoy the party and call me in the morning. You can tell me about the fireworks and the flying lead singer all over again.'

Zoë giggled and put the phone down, flashing her VIP pass at the bouncers and promptly falling back into the room.

'Easy,' said a voice above her head as she clambered to her feet. Flat shoes would have proved easier tonight, but Ellie had insisted on heels to go with the cocktail dress. She looked up. Ben's pallid face was bearing down at her. He held out a hand, which, reluctantly, she took. His eyes seemed brighter than usual.

'You gotta come and meet some people,' he said enthusiastically, drawing her by the waist towards a group of young men all conforming to the executive dress code. 'Rob, Jase, Tony, Mark, Dave . . .' Ben reeled off the names although nobody seemed to be taking much notice.

'U2,' said one.

'KFC?' said another. 'Could murder a chicken drumstick.'

'Karen in Accounts.'

'Nickelback?'

'I'm hungry.'

'Apparently she gives good head.'

Zoë looked around at the faces, feeling slightly wobbly and almost grateful for the arm around her waist. Then, in a moment of clarity, she realised that the arm belonged to her A&R scout at Vicinity and that everyone here was off their heads.

She slipped out of Ben's grasp and caught the eye of a passing waiter. She would have one more drink and then leave. Maybe she'd do another circuit of the room.

'Getting stuck in?'

227

Zoë turned, mid-sip, to see Harry Poole smiling at her across the rim of a smeary wine glass.

'Hi!' She straightened up and tried to think of something intelligent to say. 'It's . . . pretty warm tonight, isn't it?'

He looked at her strangely for a moment and then nodded. 'A little. Hope you're enjoying it, anyway.'

'Oh, I am.' She nodded fervently, steadying herself on the flower decoration by her elbow. 'It was such a great gig.'

'Excellent, excellent. Speaking of which, I heard about the Greenfly thing.' He gave her a meaningful smile.

Zoë racked her drunken brain to try and work out what he was talking about. Greenfly was a relatively new band on the scene, recently signed to one of the big labels at Universal, or maybe Sony. Zoë couldn't remember. She tried to recall what she'd read about them in the press.

'Aren't you . . . excited?' Harry looked at her. It was as though he had expected a different response.

'Um, I suppose . . .'

'Well, Zoë, I'm impressed with your level of cool,' he chuckled. 'Most artists, I have to say, would give their right arm to play at Brixton Academy at such an early stage in their career.'

'Brixton . . .' None of Harry's words were making sense. Zoë wondered whether he'd had too much to drink and got her confused with some other act.

'You have spoken to Louis today, haven't you?'

Zoë looked at him, her brow furrowed, trying to remember when she'd last spoken to her manager. 'He called on . . . Tuesday,' she said.

Harry started nodding slowly, as if things were starting to slot into place – which they weren't at all.

'Perhaps you should check your messages,' he said, still wearing a smirk that stretched from sideburn to sideburn.

Zoë started rummaging in her bag, still not convinced Harry had got the right girl. As she rummaged, she spotted the letter that

228

James had asked her to post the previous week. It was something to do with a job application. She pulled out her phone and checked the call register.

Interestingly, Louis had called twice that evening and left a voicemail – presumably while she'd been at the gig. James had also called, three times, but left no message. She must have been too drunk to notice the missed calls just now.

'You've been offered a slot to support Greenfly at Brixton Academy,' Harry said, as though he couldn't wait any longer. 'Fantastic, eh?'

Zoë looked at him for a moment, then looked at the phone. Then back at Harry. She couldn't let herself get excited until she knew for sure.

'You serious?'

He nodded. 'Something to do with a drop-out and the booking agent being Louis's mate.'

Zoë could feel every cell in her body coming alive. It was like an electric current running through her. She wanted to leap in the air, throw her arms around someone, run the length of the room, scream. In the event, she settled for a little jump on the spot (it was hard to do more in the shoes) and a yelp.

Brixton Academy was one of the ultimate live music venues before you got onto the arena circuit. It was part of the fabric of the British music scene. It was *big*. Not just in capacity, but in status. Zoë had seen some top acts play at Brixton. And now *she* was going to grace its stage.

In her excitement, she stumbled, but thankfully not far. As she reached out to stabilise herself, she felt a hand catch her arm.

'You seem a little pleased wid yaself.' His voice was smooth. Lyrical. Irish.

'Sorry. Thanks.' She brushed herself off and allowed the rescuer to steady her. As they drew apart it was possible to make out his features – thanks, in part, to the numerous flashes of light suddenly illuminating the scene. Brown hair, blue eyes, freckles . . .

'Good news, is it?' asked Niall King, one of the biggest living rock legends.

'Um . . . yeah.' Zoë felt all flustered, suddenly finding herself in the middle of a large group of people. Niall King's entourage had descended upon them like a swarm of bees to honey. 'I'm gonna be supporting Greenfly at Brixton Academy.'

Niall lifted his brow. 'Are you now? You're in a band?'

She hesitated, unable to stop the image of Dirty Money from flitting across her mind. 'No,' she said. 'Solo.'

He nodded. 'Nice one. Well. Good luck . . .'

'Zoë,' she said, thrusting out her hand with renewed confidence. The photographers were snapping away, but she ignored them and looked straight back at Niall. 'Zoë Kidd.'

'Niall King,' he said unnecessarily, grasping her hand and kissing her on the cheek. 'Maybe I'll see you around.'

Before she could reply, a prim woman with a clipboard started shouting and she found herself being ejected from the side of the group.

Zoë felt flushed with contentment. She had seen Britain's biggest band play live tonight, she had fallen over on the band's lead singer and she had discovered that in a few weeks' time, she would be performing in one of London's most prestigious concert venues. It was time to go home.

'James?' she whispered, one hour and three night buses later. 'Are you awake?'

There was a rustle of bedclothes and a quiet groan. 'Where were you?'

Zoë pulled off her clothes and slipped in next to him. 'The Cheats gig!'

Another groan – this one with an upward inflection as if he didn't know what she was talking about.

'I told you . . . didn't I?' Zoë was fairly sure she'd told him. He probably just hadn't listened. Either way, she had bigger news to share.

He rolled over so he was no longer facing her. 'Kate came round,' he mumbled. 'Picked up her amp.'

'James, I've got some news!' she hissed, trying not to think about Kate and wishing her boyfriend would turn round. 'I'm gonna be supporting Greenfly at Brixton Academy!'

'What's Greenfly?' he mumbled.

Zoë sighed, considered replying, then closed her eyes and fell into a deep, drunken sleep.

33

Zoë's eyes fluttered open, then closed again in protest. A shaft of light was searing through the gap in the curtains, burning a hole in the back of her retina. She turned onto her side and cautiously gave it another go.

The movement set something off inside her head: an audible, pulsating throb that seemed to be sending pressure waves through her skull. Her mouth felt furry.

It took a while to ascertain what time it actually was, as one hand of the clock seemed to have disappeared and her sense of perspective was all skewwhiff. It was either ten to ten or five to eleven; either way, it was late. Zoë rarely slept past eight. James's side of the bed was empty and the flat seemed quiet; presumably he was out at another job interview.

She tentatively swung her legs onto the floor and eased herself up, trying to piece together the previous night from her snatches of memory: *suits, oil paintings, shag-pile carpets, waiters, pink cocktails* . . . She half-ran, half-crawled to the bathroom and retched into the toilet.

Zoë hauled herself up via the sink, catching a glimpse of her gaunt, grey face in the mirror. She remembered now. She'd been scooped off the floor by Niall King. *Niall King.* A flush of shame mingled with the nausea. And then . . . Everything was muddled up in her head and her concentration span had shrunk to a millisecond.

She turned the shower to maximum heat and forced herself

to stand in its scalding blast, in the vain hope that her body would be shocked into recovery. Then it came to her. *Harry Poole. Greenfly. She had been offered a support slot for the Greenfly gig at Brixton Academy.* It seemed hazy now, as though she'd seen it in a film, but at the same time she knew it had happened to her, last night. A rush of excitement ran through her, despite the nausea. She'd have to call Louis.

Sitting at the kitchen table, wrapped in a bathrobe and clutching a mug of tea, Zoë allowed herself a few precious moments to bask in the glory of her revelation. She thought about what she would play on the night. She wondered what Ellie would say. Had she called Ellie last night? She kept losing her train of thought. How long would the slot be? Six songs? Eight? Ten? She only had nine new ones – enough to fill a short album, but not enough for a full set.

There was something different about the living room. Was the TV in a different place? Maybe she could slip in some Dirty Money tracks, or covers. Louis was always banging on about her doing some covers of old gospel numbers or something.

The sound of a text message rang out from somewhere in the kitchen. Zoë took another sip of tea and braced herself for movement. Despite the painkillers, her head felt as though it had been pressure-cooked overnight and all the strength seemed to have been drained from her limbs.

Kate's amplifier was missing. That was it. Her phone bleeped again. Maybe someone was trying to get hold of her. She really needed to call Louis. It was just a question of summoning the energy.

Her phone, when she did eventually make it across the room, was buried beneath the upturned contents of her handbag next to the kettle: wallet (open, devoid of coins and notes), lip gloss (cracked – had she fallen over?), umbrella (half-open – surely it hadn't rained?), compact mirror (also cracked), iPod (wet) and letter (also damp; James had asked her to post it a week ago). She wiped the envelope and laid it out on the worktop to dry.

Twenty-two missed calls, she noted, bringing the phone right up to her eyes to check she wasn't seeing double. Nope. And there were eighteen voicemails and thirty-one text messages. Zoë sat herself down as a fresh bout of queasiness swept over her. She tackled the text messages first, wondering anxiously whether something had happened. This volume of correspondence was unprecedented.

From: Ellie
PS Shannon is SO jealous!
I had to tell her :-)

From: Mum
ZOË WE ARE NOT AMUSED.
PRESUMABLY THERE IS
METHOD IN YOUR MADNESS.
DOES JAMES KNOW? PLEASE
CALL YOUR FATHER TO EXPLAIN.

From: Louis
How's the head? Nice one, girl!
U R a wanted lady. Call me! Vicinity
keen to progress contract ASAP. LC

From: Jake
So U went solo? If U need a mgr
let me kno, yeah? I always thought
Ud go far. Jake

From: Ben, Vicinity
Smart move, Zoë. Like ur style.
Let's get that contract signed!

From: Tommy
Has shit hit proverbial fan?
Call if U wanna chat.

From: Tamsin
Can't believe it, Zoë. Tell me
it's not true? Call me x
PS mum & dad v angry

She scrolled through the mysterious messages. Some of them were from people she barely knew – people like Eric, her ex-colleague, and Sara, the violinist who'd led the school orchestra with her about ten years ago.

With a mounting sense of unease, Zoë tried to decipher the comments. Finally, she found the clue that she needed. It was in Ellie's first message, sent after repeated unanswered calls:

From: Ellie
WAKE UP! Call me back!
You didn't tell me you'd
SNOGGED Niall King . . .?

Zoë gripped the phone, staring at the words as her heartbeat picked up pace. Trying to fend off the swelling, churning sensation in her gut, she reached out and drew James's laptop towards her.

She didn't need to refine the search; the story was all over the first page of results. *The Cheats and the Cheaters*, read the first tabloid headline, accompanied by a close-up picture of what looked like lip contact between Zoë and Niall. *Niall King . . . with New Queen?* said another – this one with a picture that focussed on Niall's guiding arm, taken at exactly the moment Zoë looked up to thank him for breaking her fall. Her legs were all over the place. *Who is Cheats Frontman's New Squeeze?* asked the *London Standard*. It actually looked as though the pair were locked in a passionate embrace, which, from her hazy recollections, hadn't been the case at all.

Zoë closed her eyes for a second, waiting for the sickness to pass, then forced herself to read some of the articles. *Niall King,*

235

partying the night away after the final night of the band's six-week tour of the UK . . . Seen here with a mystery woman rumoured to be Niall's secret girlfriend . . . relationship with long-term partner Jennifer Budd said to be on the rocks . . . Sources close to the band say that the leggy brunette is the lead singer's next . . . Rumoured to be a musician herself . . . goes by the name of Zoë Kidd . . . Zoë couldn't read any more.

How could these fabrications be all over the nation's newspapers and websites? She felt lost. Out of control. It was out there, this so-called news, and there was nothing she could do to rein it in or block it out. She grabbed her phone and called James, suddenly desperate to reach him before someone else did.

It rang and rang. Zoë left a voicemail, then realised it sounded too panicky, like an excuse and recorded it again, then decided that it all sounded pathetic so deleted the message and hung up. She *had* to talk to him. Face to face. This was crazy; she felt anxious and paranoid even though she hadn't done anything wrong.

She started to call Ellie, but stopped herself in case James couldn't get through while they talked. The laptop was still open in front of her, the image of the supposed encounter staring out at her in full colour. There were comments from members of the public, berating their 'inappropriate behaviour' and discussing the singer's apparently turbulent love life. Zoë snapped the lid shut, trying to decide how to explain things to James.

She was still grappling with the problem five minutes later when the front door slammed. Zoë could hear the sound of heavy footsteps. She knew, even before he entered the room, what James's face would look like.

'Big night last night, then?' He dumped his bag on the floor and stood, staring at her accusingly.

Zoë stumbled backwards against the kitchen cabinet. She had never seen James like this before. His eyes, usually so docile, were narrowed to angry slits and his chin was set forward for combat.

'Look—'

He sighed, loudly. 'We need to talk, Zoë.'

'I know.' She tried to spur her brain into action, to think about how best to explain the situation.

'Do you?' he challenged. '*Do* you know? Have you any idea how fucking pissed off I've been today because of you?'

Zoë nodded. She had to tell him. 'I do, and I'm sorry. The thing is, it's not what you think. The reports are complete bullshit, and the photos, well, I think the paps must've done something clever with their lenses or something . . . All that happened was that I fell over and he happened to be there and helped me up, then we had a really short conversation about music, but that was it, and now they're making out there's some sort of . . . *thing* going on. Which there isn't, obviously.'

James looked at her, frowning, for several seconds. Eventually, he spoke.

'What are you talking about?'

Zoë froze. Her eyes darted sideways to where his laptop sat, closed but conspicuously powered up. James didn't know. He hadn't read the papers. For a brief moment, Zoë wondered whether it might be possible to keep it from him – to hope that he never saw the articles. But already, she could see flaws in the plan. He would stumble across a reference to it at some point, maybe years down the line, and wonder why she hadn't told him at the time. Or, worse, this whole thing might blow up into something bigger and then there'd be no way of hiding it.

'Paps?' he said, moving over to the laptop.

'Yeah, they—'

It was too late. He was already prising open the jaws of the machine.

'What the . . .'

Zoë gave him time to read a couple of lines, then moved in to explain.

'James, you have to believe me, it's bullshit what they're—'

'Is it?' He slammed shut the laptop so hard that something

snapped inside. 'Is it bullshit, what they're saying? Or is it *you* bullshitting?'

'No!' Zoë shook her head, willing him to understand. 'They took the pho—'

'I'm not talking about the fucking photos!'

She fell silent, not quite sure what he meant.

'I'm talking about this,' he said, in a frighteningly measured tone, picking up the damp envelope that Zoë had removed from her handbag.

Zoë frowned. Surely this wasn't about her forgetting to post his letter?

'I lost a fucking job prospect today because of this.' He slammed it back down on the counter.

'Oh, shit.' Zoë swallowed. 'I'm so sorry, I didn't realise—'

'No, you never do, do you?' He shook his head angrily. 'That's just it. You never realise. You've got your head so far up your own fucking rock star arse that you can't even do the simplest things for anyone else any more. I didn't even know about this fucking Niall King shit, but . . .' He was still shaking his head, but despondently now. 'I dunno, Zoë. I just . . .'

She stared at him, desperate for it to all stop but sensing that James hadn't finished.

'Things have changed, haven't they?' he asked quietly. '*You've* changed.'

Zoë couldn't speak. She felt paralysed. His words hung in the air between them. She could feel her lower lip starting to quiver.

'Are you saying . . .' Her voice broke before she could finish the question.

He nodded. 'Yeah. Sorry, Zoë. I've had enough. It's over between us.'

34

'. . . and the lawyers are nearly there on the contract. You wouldn't believe how the Vicinity boys have stepped up the pressure since your little stunt . . .'

Louis rambled on. Zoë didn't bother to remind him that it had been a mistake, not a stunt. He could believe what he wanted; she didn't care.

'. . . perfect timing, what with the gig next week. You're gonna be okay for a ten-song set?' He didn't wait for a reply. 'They've said eight, but you know what Greenfly are like; they'll be late, and frankly the more stage time you get, the better. Are you handling the press all right?'

Zoë grunted, nibbling on another one of Tamsin's flapjacks. If 'handling' meant not picking up the phone, then she was doing pretty well. Perhaps in different circumstances, she might have taken the calls and given the journalists an earful – told them *her* side of the Niall-and-Zoë story, but as it was, she couldn't muster the energy.

It wasn't like her to be so apathetic, but since the breakup she had been unable to feel anything, except a dull, heavy ache. The exhaustion hung over her like a leaden blanket pulling down on her shoulders. There was no stabbing pain, no anger, no sense of remorse or despair – those would have been easier to deal with. She just felt numb. Her zeal had gone and she couldn't think of a single reason to be cheerful – even with a gig at Brixton Academy on the horizon.

Everything – sights, sounds, smells – seemed to remind her of James. Louis had mentioned the outfit he had in mind for the Greenfly gig, a sequinned affair with matching boots, and she could only think about the look on her boyfriend's face when she had first tried it on in the bedroom. Earlier, Tamsin's kettle had clicked as it boiled, taking her straight back to the time he'd tried to help her write a song using kitchen utensils. The hint of cinnamon in the flapjacks reminded her of how he liked his Starbucks lattes. She couldn't get him out of her mind.

'. . . really *milk* it, honey. Feed the press what you like, just as long as they keep talking about you. Oh, and are you blogging?' He bulldozed on without waiting for a response. 'It's really important to keep up your *presence*.' Zoë tuned out as he launched into his artists-are-brands speech that she'd heard several times before.

Louis was always going on about blogging, as if the secret to her success lay in her ability to spew out the contents of her lunch in verbal format online. In fact, she had logged on to the Zoë Kidd blog only once, and that had been to change the password on the account.

'You wanna get noticed? Tell your life story online. Do a Lily Allen. You wanna get your music noticed? Wander around Camden in your nightie when your album comes out. Amy Winehouse-style. That's the way to play it.'

Zoë mumbled her agreement.

'Oh, and Zoë?'

'Yeah?'

'Happy birthday.'

Zoë smiled wryly. She hadn't realised he even knew. He must have looked it up on the contract or something. 'Thanks.'

'I'll catchya next week. We can celebrate in style.'

For a few seconds, Zoë sat there, clutching the phone and staring blankly at Tamsin's kitchen table. Only four people had wished her a happy birthday today, and one of them was her Svengali manager. One was her sister, and one was her sister's boyfriend, who didn't really count, so that left just Ellie. Ellie was her only friend in the world.

Birthdays were supposed to be celebrations, she thought, miserably. But what was there to celebrate? Zoë's mind flipped back to previous years, when James had taken the day off work, surprised her with gig tickets or treated her to a new piece of kit for the band. Shannon would have forced her to down flammable shots and Kate would have made a rare foray onto a sweaty dance floor. That was then. Maybe birthdays would be different from now on.

Zoë blinked, suddenly realising her eyes were filling with moisture. A droplet trickled down the side of her nose and suddenly, the tears were flowing freely. It was as if someone had pulled a plug somewhere inside her head. The anaesthetic had worn off and she was hurting, thinking about James and how things had been and how they'd never be the same again.

When she'd arrived at her sister's place, bag in hand, Tamsin had convinced her that this was a temporary glitch – that James would come round and they'd patch things up. Now, after three days of thinking and countless unreturned phone calls, Zoë could see that her sister was just being naïve. James was right; things *had* changed.

She thought about his words, the tears forming rivulets down her face. *You never realise. You can't even do the simplest things for anyone else any more.* Was that true? Zoë tried to see herself from James's perspective. She had become more committed to her singing career than ever before, that was true. But was she really that preoccupied? Had she seriously lost all sense of perspective? She considered their recent conversations. They discussed his job hunt from time to time, and Zoë's gigs . . . and her songs, her contract, her royalties . . . Shit. He was right. She had become completely self-obsessed.

Suddenly, the emotions were pouring out of her: anguish, grief, angst, remorse. She hated herself for not spotting things sooner, not stopping to reflect on the damage she was doing. Because if she *had* noticed what she was doing to their relationship . . . well . . . that was the question. Would she have gone about things differently? Zoë wasn't sure. She loved James. But she loved her music, too. It had never occurred to her that she might have to choose between the two.

It was like watching a sad film and hoping, right up until the credits started rolling, that the lovers would get back together after all. Surely it couldn't end like this?

You never realise. The words had a ring to them. She played with them in her head, fitting them to notes and torturing herself by thinking about all the things she had failed to realise in the last few months: that James needed reassurance too, that she wasn't the only one trying to find her feet, that there were more important things in life than MySpace fans and Facebook friends. Blurry-eyed, Zoë hurried into Tamsin's spare room and unzipped her guitar. *You never realise who you actually are / You got ideas that you're some fucking star* . . . Louis would get his tenth song all right; he'd get a song so raw that it was like an open wound.

Zoë's voice echoed off the bare walls as she struck the metal strings, throwing all she had into the song. It felt incredible – like suddenly being untied after days in captivity.

The chorus came round for a final time and she was so far away that she must have missed the click of the door as it opened. It was only when she heard the gentle patter of applause at the end of the song that she looked round.

'That was amazing! Which . . . Oh my God.' Tamsin swept across the room and threw herself onto the bed next to Zoë. 'What's wrong?'

Zoë shook her head, swallowing a fresh batch of tears and wiping a hand across her face. 'Sorry. It's just . . .'

Tamsin opened her arms and smothered Zoë in a giant hug. 'Shhh.'

They stayed like that until Zoë's sobs relented and she could finally speak. She drew back her head and attempted a smile.

'Thanks.'

'Don't be silly. I'm your sister.'

'You're back early,' Zoë commented, trying to restore some normality to the situation.

'I had no cases this afternoon. Couldn't leave you alone on your birthday.'

The word 'alone' brought on another wave of tears.

'Sorry,' she sniffed, trying desperately to pull herself together. 'I'm fine, really.'

'Hey.' Tamsin rose to her feet and squeezed her sister's shoulder. 'I've got something for you.'

Zoë forced herself to stop sniffling. She hadn't cried this much since the night she'd left Dirty Money.

Tamsin hopped out of the room and returned with two parcels, one slim, almost like a wrapped-up piece of card, the other gold-wrapped and bulky, half-concealed behind Tamsin's legs.

'This is from Mum and Dad,' said Tam, holding out the smaller one.

Zoë reached tentatively for the package, wondering whether it had been passed to her sister before or after the paparazzi fiasco. Zoë had called to explain the situation, but her mother had shown no sign of understanding.

Happy Birthday, Zoë, she read in the card, as something fluttered out onto the floor. *We thought you might prefer your own taste in music to ours.* She crouched down and retrieved the slip of paper. It was a music download token for a hundred pounds. She let out a quiet gasp.

'I spoke to Mum yesterday,' said Tamsin, smiling. 'She said please don't turn up in any more tabloids; you nearly gave Dad a heart attack.'

Zoë managed a smile, still staring at the insanely generous gift. 'So they believe me, then? About the photos?'

'I think so. They just don't like seeing you in that . . . light.'

Zoë nodded. They weren't the only ones.

'Here.' Tamsin reached round for the shiny gold parcel. The giant bow around the middle did nothing to disguise its shape.

'It's . . .' Zoë dried her eyes and tore zealously at the paper. Then she saw the label attached to the guitar case strap and stopped. 'Oh my God.'

'Go on, then.' Tamsin smiled.

Zoë flung open the case and stared, open-mouthed, at the gleaming white Fender '65 Mustang. She couldn't believe it.

'Just like Kurt Cobain's,' said Tamsin.

Through the misery, Zoë felt a rush of something she hadn't felt in a long time. 'It's . . .'

The tears were flowing again, but they were no longer tears of anguish. Zoë threw herself at her sister and hugged her, smiling as she cried.

'Did I get it right?' asked Tam, wiping Zoë's cheek with her cuff.

Zoë nodded, staring at the beautiful instrument. 'It's the best present I've ever been given.'

35

Zoë cracked her knuckles, one by one, then walked over to her guitar case and checked – for the seventh or eighth time – that the plectrum was still lodged between the instrument's strings.

'You're pacing,' said Tommy, following her across the room with his eyes.

'I'm nervous.'

He smiled. 'Don't be. You've done this loads of times before.'

'Not in front of five thousand people.'

'They're fans. Think of them as your friends.'

'They're not *my* fans,' she pointed out, testing the steadiness of her hand. 'They're Greenfly's fans.' Her whole arm was quivering.

'They'll be yours after tonight.'

Zoë sank back into the leather chair, her knee bouncing nervously inside the semi-transparent chiffon dress. The problem was, she thought too much. Sometimes it was a blessing, but in moments like this, her inquisitive mind was a curse. Did Greenfly fans really want to hear her? Were the sounds alike enough? Would anyone bother arriving in time for the support act anyway?

'Can you watch the stuff for a minute?' She hopped out of the chair, gathering up the layers of fabric and swooping towards the door.

Tommy laughed. 'We're not in the ghetto now, Zoë.'

'I know,' she said, feeling sheepish. 'But . . .'

'Yes, of course I'll watch your beloved Mustang.'

'Thanks.'

Zoë left the room and turned right, heading for the stage. Tommy was right. This was no ghetto. Backstage at Brixton Academy was like nothing she'd ever seen before. The rooms were large and airy, the corridors subtly lit. Along the walls were black-framed photographs featuring Bob Dylan, New Order, The Prodigy, Chemical Brothers, Blur, Primal Scream . . . She had to stop looking at them; the nerves were getting too much.

When the woman had shown her into the dressing room, she'd had to stop for a second and check that the sign on the door really did say 'ZOË KIDD CREW ONLY'. There were mirrors all over the walls, coffee tables, sofas, towels and hairdryers . . . there was even a minibar. If she hadn't felt so nervous she might have gone round taking pictures of everything on her phone to show Ellie.

She peeped out from behind the curtain. Music was pumping from the sound system and a few keen fans were already milling about at the front, spilling beer from their plastic cups. Closing her eyes, she tried to visualise herself standing at the edge of the stage behind those giant amps, talking to the crowd, having fun.

''Scuse us, love.'

She opened her eyes just in time to duck as a roadie staggered past bearing a stage block on one shoulder. She watched as he deposited his load and set about raising keyboards, tweaking mike stands and making cryptic hand gestures to the sound technicians. Roadies often got overlooked. Their hairy faces and black T-shirts made them invisible to the fans but actually, they were the ones that made the night. Some were gifted musicians – often more gifted than the performers themselves. Rumour had it that in the good ol' days, when artists got properly tanked up before a show, it had been commonplace for the guitar tech to replace a stoned band member on the stage.

Zoë glanced one last time at the sloping auditorium floor, then retraced her steps.

'We thought you might've done a runner.' Tommy smiled.

Zoë took a deep breath and moved instinctively towards her guitar, relieved to see that her bassist and drummer had returned from their extended cigarette break smelling of nothing more sinister than tobacco. She fingered the corner of the flimsy card that was poking out from beneath the white belly of the instrument: Ellie's good luck card.

Other than the random internet fans, Ellie and Sam would be the only Zoë Kidd fans in the audience tonight – other than the guys from Vicinity, who didn't really count. Tamsin and Jonathan had some law society dinner and although she'd considered inviting her parents, the idea of her mum and dad moshing with five thousand jostling revellers had seemed too absurd to contemplate – not that they would have accepted the offer, anyway.

'From the boyfriend?' asked Tommy, nodding at the card.

Zoë looked down, embarrassed. She still hadn't told people about the breakup.

'No.' She pressed the card shut again and met his eye. 'We, um . . . actually, we're not together any more.'

Tommy stared at her. 'Shit, Zoë. I'm sorry. When . . .?'

'You 'ave not listened to ze words of ze latest song?' challenged Christophe, looking at the guitarist.

'I . . . oh, right. Yeah, that makes sense . . .'

'It's fine,' she lied. 'Happened just over a week ago. I'm over it now. The card's from my mate. My old guitarist.'

'Ah, right.'

Zoë felt suddenly desperate to get away from the subject of James. Tonight, she needed to focus. She couldn't afford to get emotional before going on stage.

'They're applying for Talent Tout,' she explained. 'It all sounds a bit ridiculous.'

247

Ridiculous, thought Zoë, was the wrong word. Disastrous was more appropriate. According to Ellie's note, Shannon had sent off the band's entry form without consulting the others and Kate had blown her top, claiming that an appearance on the show would scupper their chances with Hot Rocks Records. Ellie, still caught in the middle, had tried to explain that she wasn't happy as lead vocalist, but they hadn't listened. Zoë wondered whether an anonymous email to Shannon and Kate was in order.

'Bad move,' said Tommy, shaking his head. 'They'll sign away all their rights before they get a second's airplay.'

Zoë looked at him. 'How do you *know* all th—'

There was a loud knock on the dressing room door. Zoë's stomach tightened.

The door sprang open and a head of frizzy, greying hair appeared. 'All set?' asked the man, motioning for them to follow him down the corridor.

They walked in silence towards the stage, Zoë keeping her eyes straight ahead to avoid the daunting pictures on the wall. She felt sick.

'Hey,' whispered Tommy, squeezing her arm. 'You're gonna be great. Remember: just play to the back three rows. Forget about the rest.'

Before she could reply, the music stopped, the fuzzy-haired man gave them the all clear and she found herself marching towards the spot on the stage where she'd visualised herself earlier. The spotlights blinded her instantly, the heat so strong she could feel her makeup starting to melt. Through the fear, she could hear people clapping.

There were copies of the set list – typed, not scrawled – strategically taped to bits of equipment and out of the corner of her eye Zoë could see roadies loitering in the wings. She greeted the crowd. The response was better than she had expected: more clapping, some shouting and whistling.

She held up her hands, goading them to make more noise.

They obliged. As the noise level rose, Zoë felt something swell inside her. It was more than the usual excitement she felt when she stepped onto the stage; it was a pure, overwhelming joy. Sod the nerves. This was the opportunity of a lifetime. She and the audience were going to have a fucking great time tonight.

She turned and gave the rhythm section the nod. They came in, clean, precise and loud. Jesus, those amps were powerful. The speakers took up nearly all of the wall space on either side of the stage and the hall was literally throbbing. Zoë drew a breath and came in, her voice hurtling back at her a hundred times louder. She focused on the back three rows, or rather, the line in the darkness where she expected the back three rows might be, and within seconds, the anxiety had turned to something else. She felt alive again.

The adrenaline was like a drug, powering her through the set. It was passing too quickly; she wanted to hold onto it, savour the moment, take time to see the looks on people's faces. But the lights were too bright and the songs were just flashing by, punctuated only by her brief interactions with the manic fans – who were loving it. Tommy had been right. They were screaming and waving as though every last one of them had come to see Zoë Kidd.

She had saved 'You Never Realise' until last, keeping it up her sleeve as a spare even though, as a support act, she wasn't really supposed to do an encore. Leading the band off the stage, she looked around for the curly-haired guy, who dipped his head reluctantly, authorising her to return to the stage.

She poured out the words, purging herself of the conflicting emotions, forcing them out and into the microphone. It was like a release. She might have lost James forever, but at least she could hold onto this one thing, this special song.

'Fuck me,' said Tommy, wiping his brow with the back of his hand as they collapsed in their dressing room after the show. 'That was good, Zoë.'

'Yah.' Christophe nodded, lying back on the enormous leather chair. 'Zat was good.'

Zoë couldn't speak; she still felt high.

There was a knock on the door.

'Good set, guys. Thanks,' said the man with frizzy hair. 'Zoë, you've got an autograph queue. Are you signing? They're waiting by door two – that's left out of here, then second on the left.'

Zoë waited a few seconds and then looked at Tommy.

'An autograph queue?'

He raised an eyebrow. 'Well go on, then.'

The queue, when she reached it, was not as orderly as the word implied; it was more of a rabble: girls in their late teens and gangly young men jostling for elbow space by the door. One or two were bold enough to shout out her name, but most of them simply stood, vying for space, arms outstretched with tickets and scraps of paper for her to sign.

One by one, the fans tottered off, mumbling their thanks and clutching their makeshift memorabilia with huge grins on their faces. Zoë was about to slip back through the door when a girl stepped out of the crowd towards her. She was tall, with cropped white-blonde hair and a confident strut that belied her youthful looks.

'Hi,' she said, smiling. Her teeth were as white as her hair. 'I just wanted to say . . . I'm such a fan. I saw you in The Westbourne a few weeks ago and thought you were great then, but tonight was just . . . amazing.'

Zoë thanked her, feeling suddenly bashful in the face of such frankness.

'I'm Hazel,' the girl said, thrusting her hand out. 'I sing too, but not at your level.'

'Really? Well, um . . .' Zoë didn't know what to say. What was her level? A few weeks ago, it had been cramped pub gigs with toilets for changing rooms. 'Nice to meet you. Maybe I'll see you around . . . at another gig.'

Hazel beamed back at her. 'Your next one. I'll be there.'

Zoë watched as the girl spun back into the crowd, her hair splaying out as she turned.

Retreating to the muted backstage passageways, she let out a short hoot of excitement. Word seemed to be spreading. Zoë Kidd was building some kind of a fan-base.

36

Zoë looked around the glass-walled corner office, trying to maintain an air of indifference as she counted the people around her. Sixteen, excluding her manager. Sixteen record label executives – all here to celebrate the imminent career of Zoë Kidd. *They were here because of her.*

Harry Poole was standing at the head of the table, filling glasses and making jokes like the jolly uncle at Christmas, Ben was flirting with the spiky-haired girl from Promo, Charles McCarthy-Smith and the Universal lawyer were chortling in the corner and the PR girls were flicking their hair in the direction of Christian Marsh, the man who apparently headed up Marketing at Vicinity.

'Attention, please,' Harry called quietly, tapping an empty champagne flute against his full one. As the noise level fell, he gave one final, awkward glance in the direction of the door. Zoë knew why. The one person missing was the man who was supposed to be making the speech today: Edgar Hutchinson, President of Vicinity.

'A few words, if I may.' Harry cleared his throat and took a deep breath, the smile still wedged between his sideburns as he looked around the room. 'We are extremely fortunate to have just this minute signed a new artist to our books. She has a proven track record, an enviable fan-base and a very bright future ahead of her – not to mention her PR-able qualities . . .'

He paused for the inevitable wave of laughter to travel across the room. Zoë forced herself not to think about her inadvertent PR activities. In her mind, the Niall King episode was inextricably linked to the breakup with James, even though she knew it wasn't cause and effect. The photo fiasco was simply one more illustration in a long line of examples that highlighted the cracks that had been forming in their relationship for a long time. Zoë looked up in time to see the door swing open.

'Apologies,' muttered Hutchinson as he strode across the room.

Harry stepped backwards, one arm outstretched as though passing over an imaginary microphone. 'All yours.'

'Sorry, everyone. Sorry, Zoë.' He dipped a head briefly in her direction as Harry pressed a glass of champagne into his hand. 'Thanks. So, a few words, if I may.' He glanced at the Universal lawyer, who nodded, patting his bundle of papers meaningfully. 'I'm pleased to say that we have a new signing! She's a talented artist with an impressive track record and a *dazzling* future ahead of her . . .'

Zoë couldn't help glancing up to see whether Edgar was reading from some sort of autocue – the same one that his colleague had been using moments before. There was nothing in evidence. The only conclusion that she could draw was that this speech – and presumably the champagne and cheese straws – were a regular occurrence at Vicinity.

'. . . I am talking, of course, about Zoë Kidd. To Zoë!' cried Edgar, looking over at her and raising the flute high above his head.

Glasses were lifted and drained. There followed a polite silence, in which several flushed faces turned towards Zoë. A rush of adrenaline hit her as she realised that they were expecting her to speak.

It was ridiculous. Last week she had performed in front of five thousand strangers. Today, her audience comprised a dozen suited execs. Mathematically, her anxiety should have felt like a tiny pinprick, yet here she was breaking into a sweat and feeling her throat turn to sandpaper.

'Thanks,' she croaked, forcing a smile. 'Thanks, everyone. I'm looking forward to . . . to big things.'

She tipped back her empty glass and waited for the tiny drop of champagne to reach the back of her mouth. *Jesus*. Was that the best she could do? She'd just signed to one of the most commercial labels in pop and her opening line referred to 'big things'.

'Nice one,' muttered one of the freeloaders, sidling past her with a freshly filled glass and a fistful of cashew nuts.

'Yeah, congrats,' added another, motioning for one of the other guys to grab the spare flute of champagne on their way back to the office.

Zoë exchanged her glass for a full one and started to mingle. She couldn't help feeling subdued. It wasn't just the poor speech; it was something else.

This should have been the happiest moment of her life. It was one she'd been dreaming about for years. She had just put her signature on a contract with Universal. But what was the point in spending the afternoon schmoozing with publicists and marketing analysts?

She didn't want to be drinking with these strangers; she wanted to go to the pub with her boyfriend. She wanted to squeal in excitement with the girls. She wanted to make her parents proud. But none of that was going to happen. Nobody would drop what they were doing in order to celebrate tonight, because nobody cared for her any more. Tamsin was away on a long weekend with Jonathan and even Ellie had politely suggested a deferred celebration due to a last-minute rehearsal for the girls' Talent Tout audition. Zoë gulped down some more champagne, suddenly feeling very alone.

'Top-up?' Harry poured a foamy splash into her glass before she could reply. 'Oh. Here.' He reached into a back pocket and produced a small white envelope. 'We would be honoured if you made it along.'

Zoë frowned, half-smiling, and tore at the paper, grateful for the distraction from her unhealthy self-reflection. It was some kind of invitation.

'The annual summer ball,' Harry explained as she skimmed through the text on the gold-edged card. 'Should be a cracking night.'

'Thanks,' exclaimed Zoë, starting to feel a little more buoyant.

'We don't invite all our artists,' Harry confided. 'Only a select few. We're truly excited to have you on board. We all are.' He swept a hand across the room, just as Ben walked over, swerving to avoid an eye injury. 'Ah, sorry, Dover.'

Zoë smiled, clutching the invitation and trying not to show her excitement. 'Dover?' she echoed.

Harry chuckled while Ben looked at the floor, his pale face turning blotchy and pink. 'Pet name, eh. Ben Dover. A hangover from his days as office gofer.' He elbowed the younger man in the ribs.

'Rarely used now,' Ben muttered through gritted teeth.

'That reminds me!' cried Harry, pressing a finger behind his left ear and sloshing champagne over his shoulder. Zoë wondered whether he could be drunk already. 'I can't hear any music. Dover, get us some *tunes*!'

With a fixed smile, Ben nodded and left the room. Harry inverted the champagne bottle over his glass, looking confused when nothing came out, and then reached for another from the table.

'So! Looking forward to your tour?'

'Um . . .' Zoë wasn't sure how to reply; Louis had mentioned something about a tour but they'd both been so preoccupied with getting the contract signed that he'd stopped short of saying anything useful. Zoë was about to explain this to Harry when she felt herself being caught up in a whirl of red fabric and a cacophony of jangling jewellery.

'And *what* a story!' cried the plump, henna-haired woman at the centre of the tornado. 'What a story indeed! A publicist's dream – that's what it was. A credit to you, my dear.'

A hand protruded from beneath the layers of crimson shawls, which Zoë tentatively clasped as the woman leaned forward and smothered the air around her in kisses.

'I'm Gloria. Head of Press at Vicinity.' Following some more gushing and air-kissing, the woman went on to regale them with tales of artists whose careers they had helped to launch using 'exactly that type of PR ploy'.

'I mean, Christian and his team do a *wonderful* job, but frankly a tasty bit of press can be worth more than a million-pound marketing budget. I can see that you've already grasped that, though. No need for me to teach *you*. It's—'

'Sorry, I think there's been a—'

'I can't *wait* for our kick-off meeting.' The woman clasped her hands together in glee. 'There's obviously *so* much we can work with here. Tell me, do you have any other plans up your sleeve, just so we know?'

'The Niall King thing wasn't actually a *plan*,' Zoë explained. 'It was a—'

'Oh, marvellous! I love a girl who can be spontaneous! No forward planning, just a lunge into—'

'No, I mean, it was an accident. The paparazzi took a photo of him helping me up when I fell over and—'

'Fan-*tastic*,' Gloria shook her head in admiration. 'You "fell over", did you?' she drew quotation marks in the air, laughing. 'What a trick. *What* a trick. Well done, my dear. Now, I must dash, but let's get something in the diary. There's clearly a lot to talk about!'

The red whirlwind hurtled out, her underling in tow, leaving Zoë feeling strangely unsettled. Would she ever persuade people that the Niall King episode hadn't been a deliberate move? She tipped back her champagne flute and sighed. Perhaps it didn't actually matter either way – so long as it sold records in the long run. Zoë just hoped she wouldn't be expected to pull off more stunts in the future.

She picked up another glass of champagne, looking around at the remains of her so-called team. Edgar and Jenson had sloped off, Harry was deeply ensconced in conversation with the lawyers and Ben was practically dribbling into the cleavage of the girl from Promotions. There was something of an end-of-the-night feel in the room, as though people were only staying because it was marginally better than going back to their desks.

'Zoë!'

She turned round. Louis was beaming at her.

'Jenson's just taken a phone call,' he said, nodding towards the open-plan office. 'From Victor Ciprianni.'

Zoë swallowed. Victor Ciprianni, or Victor C as he was known, was one of the most renowned producer-songwriters of the decade. He had produced albums for the likes of The Courteeners, Jamiroquai, Alfie and Smoke Feathers and he had, according to the *NME*, been the man behind no less than fourteen number ones.

'We thought he'd be a good match for the sound you need. He's keen to meet you.'

For a moment, Zoë couldn't speak. To have someone like Victor C produce her first album would be incredible. Literally. Even with the mighty backing of Vicinity, she hadn't dared to hope for something like this.

'We'll get something set up for next week or so. I know Harry's keen to get you in the studio as soon as possible.'

Zoë's whole body was buzzing. She couldn't believe the speed at which things were moving – and the scale. Victor C was a *huge* name in the industry.

'Wow,' was all she could manage.

'Exactamundo.' Louis nodded. 'Oh, and I see you've got your invite.' He nodded at the piece of card that was still clamped firmly between Zoë's forefinger and thumb, then leaned closer.

'Good sign, that is.' He winked. 'They only invite their priorities. Now,' he brushed the crumbs off his giant shirt, straightening up. 'I gotta shoot. Enjoy the rest of the party.' He engulfed Zoë in a bear hug and held her at arm's length, still beaming. 'Congratulations, again. It's not every day you get Victor C offering to write you some songs, eh. Like a late birthday present.'

Zoë's smile fell away. 'What . . . Sorry? Did you say . . .'

Louis was already halfway through the door. He turned. 'Pardon me?'

'You said write. Don't you mean, produce?'

'Oh.' Louis waved a hand absent-mindedly. 'A bit of both. Jenson wants a few non-Zoë songs on the album, as well as your own. So I guess we're talking about the full works!'

For a moment, Zoë didn't know what to say. Louis chose that moment to disappear. It was too much to take in at once. It was great news, but it was bad news, too. Very bad. She had come to terms with the fact that as an artist, they would push her, mould her, 'brand' her like some kind of new plastic toy on the market. But to learn that the product they were planning to promote was not even going to be hers . . . That took her feeling of helplessness to a whole new level.

She grabbed another glass of champagne and tipped most of it down her throat in one go. This wasn't going to happen. She wouldn't allow it. She'd signed the contract now; she didn't need to impress them any longer. Zoë Kidd was the artist here; she wouldn't be told what to sing. She would show them. She wasn't someone who could be pushed around.

37

'Well,' muttered Zoë's mother, wringing out the dishcloth and giving her hands a final rinse. 'I think that went well, don't you?'

Various noises of agreement came from all over the kitchen.

Zoë let out a quiet snort. 'I was beginning to think the Pattersons would never leave.'

'Perhaps you needn't have been *quite* so rude about Will's piano playing.' Her mother lifted an eyebrow pointedly.

'It's a good job I was, or they'd still be here.' Zoë swept the crumbs into the dustpan and emptied it into the bin. They were referring to an obnoxious couple called Margo and Gerome, whose two teenage sons were apparently 'exceptionally gifted' and 'beyond their years' in most things. Having arrived on the dot of eleven, the loathsome pair had occupied their spot on the patio until sunset – only leaving when Zoë had started loudly stacking garden furniture around them.

Zoë looked across the room to where her grandmother was rearranging her bony limbs on the uncomfortable wicker chair. 'You okay there?'

The elderly lady nodded, her body language stating otherwise. She had turned eighty the previous week, on almost the same day that her son had turned fifty-five and her granddaughter twenty-five – hence the party. Not that Gran had garnered much of the attention today; there was too much to think about in terms of celery sticks and parasols and jugs of Pimm's.

'Shall we go and sit down?' Zoë cocked her head in the direction of the lounge.

Tamsin and Jonathan led the way, while Zoë's father insisted on rummaging around for the bottle of toxic Scottish whisky that he insisted on bringing out at this point every year.

It had been a frustrating day – more so, Zoë thought, than in previous years. She was used to nodding and smiling as various distant relatives gave detailed accounts of their daughters' or nephews' achievements. She was well versed in thinking up appropriate responses to their tedious questions about her 'high-flying job', all too familiar with the patronising smiles that greeted her when she explained that her real passion lay not in balance sheets but on the stage. Year after year, she had heard their condescending replies: 'Good for you!' 'Never give up on the dream, eh?' Every time June came around, she wished that this year would be the one when she proved them all wrong – the year she told them that actually, she *was* getting there. Her dreams *were* coming true. And now, finally, she was in a position to tell them exactly that. *Fuck you,* she wanted to say. *I'm a priority act, signed to Universal.* But she couldn't. She couldn't say that, because she still hadn't told her parents.

All day, she had been trying to find the right moment to break the news. Throughout the party, she had loitered and skulked, waiting to catch both of her parents alone together. Now, finally, the hubbub had died down and the guests had gone. It was time to declare herself an artist.

'Let's light the fire,' her father suggested, despite the warmth of the evening. He was a great believer in tradition. 'Pity James isn't here, eh?'

Zoë grunted and looked at the rug. She could see how he'd made the connection; James had always loved building the fire. He would take pleasure in gathering the timber and creating some sort of boy scout pyramid for her father to light.

'Strange time of year for rugby, isn't it?' commented her mother.

'Er . . . yeah.' Zoë glanced warily at her sister, willing her not to speak. She also hadn't told her parents about her breakup with James. She kept meaning to, but there was always something else she'd done wrong, some other disappointment for her parents to endure. The excuse for James's non-appearance today – invented under extreme pressure – was a 'rugby event', not ideal, given that (a) he didn't play rugby and (b) it was the middle of June. 'It's a . . . a charity thing. He couldn't get out of it.'

She would tell them about James tonight, Zoë decided, after sharing her good news about Vicinity. That would cushion the blow.

'Who's for a tipple?' asked her father, holding out the vile-smelling spirit.

After the fourth turned-up nose, Jonathan magnanimously obliged. If James had been here, he would have been there like a shot, thought Zoë. She had to stop thinking about him. He was gone. She had to move on.

'Mmm, delicious,' Jonathan uttered through gritted teeth.

This was her chance, thought Zoë. It was time to tell her parents what she had become.

'I think . . .' Tamsin had got there first. 'There's something you should know.' She smiled mischievously and caught her sister's eye.

Zoë grinned back. Tamsin was trying to help. She knew how important this was to her; she knew that Zoë had been bursting to share the news for the last four days.

'Oh?' Their mother looked anxiously from one daughter to the other, then briefly at her husband. She wasn't particularly fond of surprises. 'Well go on, then.'

Zoë's heart started to pound. Since the early days when Dirty Money had been little more than a bunch of amateur wannabes, she had dreamed of telling her parents that she had finally made it. She had fantasised about their reaction – one of pride, even though she knew that the reality would be different. There was always a glimmer of hope. A chance that once they realised how big she would be, they'd step up and pat her on the back.

'Jonathan and I are engaged,' said Tamsin.

Zoë's jaw hung open, like a cargo hold with a loose catch. It took a few seconds for her to work out what had happened. Her mother was shrieking and crying, hands clasped over her mouth, her father was making a peculiar, low-pitched clucking sound and Gran was staring at her granddaughter – Tamsin, not Zoë – and dabbing at the corner of her eye with a tissue.

The jubilation continued for some time, Tamsin and Jonathan sitting in the middle of it all, lapping it up with smiles and tears of their own. As if on autopilot, Zoë joined in. She reached out and hugged her sister, then her soon-to-be brother-in-law, muttering something about how pleased she was for them both.

She *was* pleased for them. Tamsin and Jonathan made a great couple and she couldn't think of two people better suited to be married. *But why now?* Why had Tamsin chosen this moment to tell their parents, when she knew how desperate Zoë was to break her own news? Why had she knowingly stolen her little sister's thunder?

'. . . then Jonathan suggested a gondola trip, didn't you?' Tamsin's eyes glistened as she relayed the full story of the proposal. 'We were halfway round Venice when he suddenly produced a bottle of champagne from nowhere and—'

'From my bag,' Jonathan explained.

'—and he poured me a glass, and there it was, staring up at me from the bottom!' Tam waved her hand in the air, the diamonds twinkling in the firelight.

Zoë added to the coos and cries, obligingly inspecting the ring. A small part of Tamsin's happiness was rubbing off on her; it was impossible not to feel emotional when your sister was sitting next to you, crying with joy. But at the same time, she felt betrayed.

It wouldn't have taken much effort to hold off for a few minutes, to let Zoë get her news out. Now, of course, she had no chance of bringing up the subject of her Vicinity contract – and even less chance of telling her parents about her breakup with James. Tamsin's engagement was the story of the night – maybe even of the month.

'Speaking of champagne . . .' Zoë's father jumped to his feet and headed for the fridge, foraging among the bottles of Cava left over from the party.

Soon, they were toasting and drinking and reliving the bended-knee moment for a second, third and fourth time.

'Now,' said their father, rather loudly and grandly. He cleared his throat. 'Seeing as we're on the subject of future happiness, I might as well tell you something else.'

The room fell ominously silent.

'Your mother and I have been talking about our assets,' he said, slowly and precisely as though he were outlining his defence to the judge. 'And in the interests of avoiding inheritance tax, we'd like to pass down a lump sum to each of you.'

The girls remained respectfully silent. Zoë had no idea what sort of sum they were talking about; she had never actually enquired about her parents' financial position.

'The transfer has to happen at least seven years before we pop our clogs,' he explained, 'so perhaps now is as good a time as any, what with your wedding plans and so on.' He smiled at Tamsin. 'The figure's in the region of eighty thousand pounds.'

Zoë gasped. Tamsin's hand flew up to her mouth.

'Each,' he clarified.

Zoë stared at him. She couldn't believe they were discussing such enormous figures.

'That would be . . . amazing,' said Tamsin, glancing at Jonathan. 'Really appreciated. I mean . . . not just for the wedding, but . . .'

'Quite.' He stiffened, suddenly. 'Yes, I should have said. I do expect this money to be used *wisely*. I expect you'll want to use some of it for the wedding, Tamsin, but . . .' He turned to Zoë. 'This is your inheritance. It is *not* to be frittered away.'

She looked at him, feeling, to her annoyance, her neck and cheeks starting to glow. She knew it would be wrong to object, but this wasn't fair. How had her parents formed this impression of her? Yes, she was different to Tamsin; she was less of a conformist, but that didn't mean she would squander her inheritance.

'We will be very disappointed if we find that it's being used as a replacement for a salary,' he went on in a clipped tone, still looking at Zoë. 'A salary that was needlessly thrown away . . .'

'It wasn't needless,' she yelped. She hadn't meant to; it just burst out. 'I couldn't go on doing both my job and my music, so I had to quit,' she explained.

He looked at her, nodding slowly as though he didn't believe a word. 'You *had* to quit your job, did you?'

'Yes!' she cried. Her whole body felt hot and inflamed. She hadn't meant to get confrontational, but this just wasn't fair. 'I had to quit one or the other, and I chose the mind-numbing, hideous one that was killing me inside.'

He was smiling faintly now; it was obviously a trick he used in court for winding people up. Well, it was working. It was fucking working. If it hadn't been for her grandmother sitting anxiously by the fire, she probably would have hurled something by now.

'It was the right choice, as it happens,' she growled angrily. 'I got signed to Vicinity on Tuesday. It's one of Universal's most commercial labels.'

She crossed her arms and watched him, waiting to see his reaction. It hadn't been her intention to spill the news in this way, but she *had* to prove her point.

One eyebrow arched, then the other one. 'Well, that's good news,' he said calmly. 'Presumably that means you won't have to fritter your inheritance away? So that's fine then.'

Zoë stared at him. That was it? That was his reaction to her news? After years of striving for this moment, of battling and juggling and leading an exhausting double life, she had emerged, victorious, only for her father to call it 'good news'.

Zoë glanced at her mother, who was being uncharacteristically quiet in the corner of the lounge. Usually happy to speak for the pair of them, when it came to important matters, she deferred to the higher authority.

'I don't get it,' she said, her head shaking violently. The sensible part of her knew that she should have stopped there, but she was too incensed to care. 'Why are you worried about me investing time and money in something I love doing, when you're perfectly happy to see ten grand spent on flowers and dresses and table decorations? Why am *I* the one in danger of frittering it away?'

In the corner of her eye, Zoë could see Tamsin and Jonathan, squirming in their seats. She shouldn't have said that.

Still completely unruffled, her father replied. 'We never said you were, Zoë. It goes for the both of you in that we don't want to see your money – *your* money – get thrown away on a dream.'

'A dream.' Zoë seethed. She was seeing everything through a haze of red. She knew what her father was getting at. He had no faith in her new career. 'It is a dream, yes,' she snarled. 'And at least I'm brave enough to try and see it through. Which is more than *you* did.'

There was a momentary flicker of confusion in his eyes, almost imperceptible, but Zoë saw it.

'You could've played rugby for *England*, Dad. What do you know about following your dreams?'

Her father didn't reply. Zoë watched for a moment as he sat there, trying to form a retort, then she stood up and left the room.

38

'Please, Zoë. Just call them.'

'And say what?'

Tamsin sighed down the phone. 'I don't know. Maybe . . . thanks for the offer of eighty grand? For a start.'

'I don't want their eighty grand,' Zoë snapped.

'Don't be childish.'

Zoë glanced at the print-out in her hand and checked the address one last time. *Barnstäd House*. The name etched onto the wooden plaque by the gate confirmed that this was the one.

'Look, I've gotta go. I'll see you tonight.'

'Okay,' Tamsin replied flatly. 'Good luck.'

Zoë slid the phone back into her guitar case and opened the latch on the gate. They'd been having this argument, on and off, for the last three days. She could see what her sister meant. It did seem churlish, turning down a sum of that magnitude just to make a point. But she wasn't going to accept their money if they continued to doubt how she would use it. And besides, Tamsin was hardly in a position to preach. *She* was the one who had pissed on her parade.

Zoë hadn't had the nerve to confront her sister over the timing of her announcement. Perhaps if she had made the challenge then this festering resentment might lift and they might stand a chance of resolving their differences over the inheritance row. But she couldn't do it. She couldn't broach the subject because deep down, Zoë knew that it hadn't been a deliberate move on Tamsin's part to steal the limelight. She hadn't meant to spoil Zoë's moment; she had just been bursting to tell her news.

Zoë made her way up the long, gravel path and pressed the doorbell. It was more of a chalet than a house – a huge, wooden chalet built into the hillside. At the back of the property, where the ground levelled off, it was just possible to make out a couple of sun loungers and the butt-end of a diving board. Beyond that was a tennis court, shaded by thick, neatly-trimmed conifers and coming from inside was the sound of a dog, yapping.

Victor C's house was enormous. It didn't seem possible that something like this could exist in the residential borough of Richmond, about a mile down the road from the concrete jungle of Kingston. This, Zoë realised, was what fourteen number one hit records got you.

The door was flung open to reveal a short, bespectacled man with a round, suntanned head, wearing khaki shorts and flip-flops.

'Hi! Hello!'

The producer's words were clipped, as though he was trying to compress each one into a single syllable. He sprang backwards to reveal the small, brown terrier trotting about at his heels.

'I'm Victor,' he declared, motioning for her to step inside. His accent was Germanic, but it was just possible to make out a Mediterranean lilt on top. 'Come, Zoë. Velcome.'

She followed the man and his dog through a vast, airy living room. The front wall was made entirely of glass, revealing a breathtaking view over Richmond Park, Kew Gardens and, in the distance, the buckling grey sprawl of West London.

'Vat can I get you? Coffee? Juice? Vaater?'

It was daunting, the speed at which Victor worked; Zoë felt as though precious seconds were being wasted on her deliberation. 'A glass of water would be great.'

He was older than she had envisaged. Most people in pop still had their hair. But then, he'd been around for a while. It felt odd, standing in the home of one of the most renowned music producers of the decade, knowing that this was the place where the hits were made.

'There. Oh, you have brought your guitar. I should have sched, no need. Ah vell. Come. Come.' He set off again, motioning for her to follow. The dog quickly overtook and led the way down the open-plan stairs.

Zoë reached the bottom step and stopped dead, her guitar sliding off her shoulder and onto the floor. The view from the window – full-length again – was much like the one upstairs, but it wasn't what was outside that had caught her attention; it was the setup inside.

This room made Clive Berry's recording studio – the place that had seemed like paradise to the girls a few months ago – look like a dusty old town hall. The electric piano gleamed white in the sunshine, expensive guitars hung on stands about the room and the walls were padded with Sydney Opera House-like baffles that absorbed all the sound. Everything, down to the knobs on the mixing desk behind the sliding glass screens, was either chocolate brown or white.

'I vas so excited ven Jenson suggested I vak viz you.'

Zoë couldn't help laughing. She was a newly-signed artist with a handful of unreleased tracks to her name, and Victor C was telling *her* that he was excited about collaborating.

'No, please. You have talent. I vatched your live schet on YouTube. Your schtyl is good. Powerful. I like to work with powerful schingers.'

Zoë looked at him bashfully. 'Thanks.'

'So.' He clicked his fingers at the dog, indicating that it should sit still – somewhat hypocritical, thought Zoë. 'Vould you mind schinging a little for me?'

She looked around, wondering what exactly the producer was

asking her to do. Did he expect her to go and play on the new-age piano? Or get out her guitar?

'Just . . . schumthing schimple. A cappella. So I can get a feel for your style.'

A cappella. She hadn't heard that term since her Grade Five music theory exam.

'What . . . anything?' She looked at him.

Victor nodded enthusiastically. 'Vatever you like.'

Was she really being asked to blurt out whatever song was in her head? Zoë was beginning to realise that preparation was something of a scarce luxury in this line of work. The whole industry ran on adrenaline and pressure; you just had to wing it, everywhere you went.

Tentatively, Zoë started to sing. She opted for a song that she knew Victor wouldn't have heard online – a song that she'd been unable to shrug from her mind for the past three days. It wasn't complete; there were only two verses and a partially-formed chorus, but it felt like the right choice; if anything represented Zoë's style, then it was 'Stubborn Silence' – the song that had emerged from her feelings over the inheritance row with her father.

Her concerns about the room's acoustics were immediately verified; it sounded terrible. The harder she sang, the more the walls seemed to suck the life from her voice, leaving nothing but a puny, soulless whine.

'Vye did you stop?' barked Victor, as she trailed off, disheartened.

'Well . . .' She shrugged. 'It was sounding pathetic, and . . .'

'Who wrote that schong?'

'I did.'

He nodded. His fingers were drumming at high speed against the desk, his eyes wandering manically through narrowed slits.

'Vat schort of schong did you have in mind, for me to write you?'

This was how it all ended, she thought. He was going to let

269

her down gently, tell her that they were thinking along different lines, artistically incompatible, etc. etc.

'Well,' she hesitated, wondering whether to be honest about her desire to write her own material. 'I guess . . .'

'Ha,' Victor nodded. He was grinning at her. 'I thought so. You don't vant me to write you any schongs, am I right?'

'Um, well, er . . .' She couldn't admit it, not when someone as successful as Victor was asking the question. That was like saying to Gordon Ramsay, 'No thanks, I'd rather make my own dinner.'

'Okay. I am right. You have a gift for schongs, Zoë. Writing them, schinging them.'

She looked at him, not quite sure where he was going with this.

'Here's vat I think,' he went on quickly. 'Jenson vants me to write you schum schongs but you vant to write about your own life, your own pains. Yah?'

Zoë nodded mechanically. Had Victor C just complimented her musical abilities?

'Okay. You tell me about yourself, and I vill write schumthing that works for you, but vith a "hook". Schumthing that will get you into ze charts, yah?'

Again, Zoë nodded.

'Tell me vatever you like. Vatever is important to you.'

Zoë began to smile, then, settling in one of the leather armchairs by the window opposite Victor, she did exactly that. She told Victor about her family and their expectations, she told him about the girls and Dirty Money, she talked about James and the breakup, her recent feud with her parents, her hopes and her dreams. She talked about how she felt trapped, guilty, lonely, despondent . . . She let everything out.

'Vell,' said Victor, when she had finished. 'Interesting.'

She looked at him hopefully.

His suntanned face crinkled into a smile. 'I vill see vat I can do.' He stood up and held out a hand. 'It has been a pleasure.'

Their meeting, it seemed, was over. Zoë thanked the producer and waved farewell as she headed back down the path, feeling as though a helium balloon had been attached to her shoulders. She checked the time and pulled out her phone. Ellie and the girls would have finished their audition by now.

'Hey, Zoë!'

'Come on – spill the beans. How was it?'

'Oh . . .' Ellie gave a nervous laugh. 'Not too bad. I think we're going through.'

'Really? That's great! Isn't it . . .?' Zoë tried to suppress the pinch of envy she felt at the thought of Dirty Money going places without her.

'I guess,' Ellie replied quietly. 'Hey, I'm just getting back now. You anywhere near?'

'Other side of town, I'm afraid. I'm just leaving Victor C's house.'

'What . . . the . . .' Ellie made a choking noise. '*The* Victor C?'

'Yeah. But tell me about the—'

'Oh, who cares about the stupid audition? It's only the first round. They let through anyone with a bit of talent or freakiness. Tell me about Victor C! What are you doing there?'

Zoë smiled. It was so like Ellie to dismiss her achievements like that. 'My label wants him to produce my album and—'

Ellie squealed so loudly Zoë had to move the phone away from her ear.

'*Victor C is gonna produce your album?*'

'Well, hopefully, but—'

'Oh my God! That's amazing! Well done, Zoë. You must've really impressed them.'

'Or not,' said Zoë. 'They also want him to *write* me some songs.'

'What . . . What's wrong with your songs?'

Zoë snorted. 'You tell me. I dunno . . . You know what I'm like, Ellie. I write my own tracks. With you, obviously. I mean, you're the only person I can work with . . .'

'I can't believe you, Zoë!' Ellie was laughing. 'Most people would die to have Victor C write a song for them, and you're trying to turn him down!'

'Well . . .' Zoë smiled. It did seem a bit ungracious, put like that. 'I didn't turn him down. He's gonna write the songs, but they're gonna be in my style . . . only more catchy, or something.'

Ellie squealed down the phone. 'I can't wait to hear them.'

'Well, we'll see. So what's next with Talent Tout?'

Ellie sighed. 'The televised rounds. They've just made us sign this thing that swears us to secrecy about everything. I'm a bit scared, to tell the truth. Meanwhile, Kate's insisting we get signed to Hot Rocks, but they want us to get representation and we're officially not allowed a manager if we go on the show.'

'Sounds like a mess, Ellie. Are you . . . are you okay?'

'We'll get through it, I guess. Keep going on both fronts, see where we get—'

'I mean *you*,' Zoë interrupted. 'Are *you* okay?'

'Oh.' Ellie hesitated. They both knew what Zoë was getting at. Nothing more had been said about that night in the caravan. Instead, they just tiptoed around the subject, talking in riddles to save Ellie from her shame.

'Yeah. I'm okay.' The words came out slowly, meaningfully. Zoë knew what she was trying to say. That that night had been a one-off; that it wouldn't happen again. That she was embarrassed it happened at all.

'Good.' Zoë hoped she was telling the truth.

'When are you playing next? I'll come and see you.'

'Well, I'm doing some sort of tour—'

'A tour?' shrieked Ellie excitedly. 'My God, Zoë. You'll be supporting U2 next! Any gigs in London?'

Zoë smiled. 'I'm sure there will be. I'll let you know.'

39

'So, what about fan mail?' slurred Ben. 'A gorgeous girl like you must get *bags* of it.' He squinted at her in a way that Zoë was probably supposed to find seductive. Either that or he had something in his eye.

'Most of it comes via email, so I just delete it.' She whipped her hand off the linen tablecloth as Ben's fingers crept closer.

'You must take a quick look, just to see what it says?' He pushed his face right up to hers.

Zoë shifted her chair sideways, avoiding the alcoholic whiff of Ben's breath.

'You do, don't you?' Ben goaded, looking up at her through heavy-lidded eyes. It was as though he was trying to melt himself over her. 'Come on. What's the worst thing anyone's ever written to you? The *dirtiest* thing.'

Thankfully, at that moment a waitress swooped in to remove their plates. Zoë took the opportunity to top up her wine and glanced again at the faces around the table, trying to catch someone's – anyone's – eye. Her table was light on celebrities compared to some of the others. Elsewhere in the enormous hotel ballroom, she'd spotted James Morrison, Sophie Ellis-Bextor, Ronan Keating, Jake from the Scissor Sisters, Amy Winehouse. From what she could tell, most of the guests on her table were low-level Universal executives, with the exception of the man to her right, who, despite the low-level ambient lighting, was wearing enormous, wraparound shades.

'Allow me.'

A coffee-coloured hand belonging to Sunglasses Man was laid over hers on the wine bottle, weighed down by a chunky gold watch the size of a side plate. She turned with a grateful smile and realised whose face it was behind the giant sunglasses. She was sitting next to Denzel White, last year's Talent Tout winner.

'Thanks. Er, hi,' she stammered as her glass was filled almost to the brim. She could feel herself blushing as she tried not to gawp at his high cheekbones and pearly white teeth. What was he up to now? Had he realised his first album? What could she say to him that hadn't been said a million times by adoring fans? Zoë immediately regretted drinking her way through the first three courses.

'Are you with him?' Denzel cocked his head towards Ben, who unfortunately interpreted the move as an introduction.

'Hi! Nice to meet you,' he cried. 'My name's Ben, A&R at Vicinity. I love your sound.' He thrust out a hand, brushing Zoë's cleavage in a move that didn't look entirely accidental.

'Oh yeah?' Denzel raised an eyebrow. His words and gestures seemed to have a rhythm to them, as though they were all part of a gangsta rap. 'Which particular sound would that be?'

'Well . . .' Ben looked up to the ceiling as if thinking through Denzel's extensive repertoire. 'I'm really digging your recent stuff.'

Digging? Zoë tried not to laugh. Ben's choice of words couldn't have been more appropriate.

'Really? That's funny. Because I ain't released my first album yet.'

'Oh, well, yeah. I meant . . . Your, um, covers . . . on the show.' Ben continued to mumble from inside his glass, but Denzel had already turned back to Zoë.

'You're not with him, right?' he asked quietly.

She shook her head, sinking into the fresh glass of wine and silently thanking Ben for making the blunder she could so easily have made. Clearly A&R reps didn't know as much about the scene as she'd imagined.

'You want me to punch him for you?'

'Er, no.' Zoë shook her head anxiously. 'Probably best not. He's the scout who discovered me.'

Denzel pulled a face. 'Oh. Jeez. That's bad news, huh. Which label?'

Zoë smiled. 'Vicinity.'

'Right,' he nodded, pushing the shades up onto his forehead and assessing the dribbling wreck. 'You just got signed?'

Zoë nodded, guzzling down more wine. He really was handsome. She could see why the nation's teenagers had gone berserk.

'Who are you with? I mean, which label,' she clarified unnecessarily.

Denzel laughed. 'Polydor. It's a kinda joint venture with the Talent Tout production company.'

Zoë leaned back as a waitress slipped a dessert plate onto the table. The ratio of dessert to plate, she noted, was very small, but that seemed to be a running theme this evening.

'So . . .' Zoë was about to tell Denzel about Dirty Money and their early-stage Talent Tout success when the hotel PA system burst into life.

'LADIES AND GENTLEMEN,' boomed the voice, which, Zoë eventually worked out, belonged to a small man standing at the front of the cavernous, curtained stage. 'AS A FITTING END TO A CELEBRATION OF A SUCCESSFUL YEAR FOR UNIVERSAL, I AM PROUD TO WELCOME ONTO THE STAGE A BAND THAT HAS SOLD OVER A HUNDRED AND FORTY-FIVE MILLION RECORDS. THEY'VE WON TWENTY-TWO GRAMMY AWARDS, TEN Q AWARDS, THREE *NME* AWARDS, A GOLDEN GLOBE . . . I COULD GO ON, BUT WITHOUT FURTHER ADO, PLEASE WELCOME . . . U2!'

Zoë immediately burst into rapturous applause, only to realise that nobody else seemed to be clapping – or at least, not with as much zeal, anyway. Perhaps that was the difference between a room full of nobodies and a room full of music executives and famous artists. Bono was just another one of them – a mate, a colleague, a signing.

'You're a fan, huh?' Denzel smiled as he topped up her glass again.

Zoë shrugged casually. She was drinking too quickly. 'Well, you know . . .'

Popping the chocolate dumpling thing into her mouth, Zoë watched on the giant screens as U2 launched into their set. Remarkably, over the course of the next few minutes, while the transcendent figures worked through their hits, people started milling about. Celebrities exchanged air-kisses and executives swapped tables, the hum of conversation rising in competition with the music.

Under the table, Zoë could feel Ben's clammy hands start to wander across her legs. She batted him away.

'You stayin' here tonight?' asked Denzel.

'Er . . .' Zoë hadn't realised that staying in the hotel was an option. She hadn't noticed anything about rooms on the invitation. 'Probably not, no.'

'You should. That's when the fun starts.' He winked. 'That's what I've heard, anyway. Every room's a party.'

It was incredible to think that a year ago, this person had been a nobody. Yet here he was behaving like a true A-lister.

'Well,' she tried to match his enigmatic smile. 'Maybe I will.'

She felt a tap on her shoulder and looked up to find Harry beaming down at her, his nose glowing crimson.

'Enjoying yourself?'

'Oh, hi!' Zoë turned in her seat. It was an awkward manoeuvre. She wanted to keep her back to Ben so as not to draw him into the conversation and because – actually, this was the real reason – she didn't want to lose Denzel's interest. Unfortunately, this meant twisting more than a hundred and eighty degrees, which was anatomically impossible and highly dangerous from a cleavage point of view, so she stood up, then immediately felt dizzy and tried to sit down again, but the chair seemed to have moved.

As she clambered out of Denzel White's lap, his arm wrapped firmly around her waist, Zoë realised there was somebody else standing next to Harry. With horror, she saw that the man was Jenson Davies, Head of A&R at Vicinity. Zoë steadied herself. There was something different about him, she thought, but she couldn't quite put her finger on it.

'*Swinging to the music! Swinging to the music!*' bawled Harry as Bono battled on.

Jenson leaned sideways against his colleague. 'All's well with Kiddo, then!'

'Zeekay,' replied Harry.

'Zedkay,' Jenson retorted, and laughed.

Zoë had no idea what the men were on about, but she had worked out what was different about Jenson. It was his eyes. They were practically shut. She needn't have worried about embarrassing herself; he wouldn't remember a thing in the morning.

'We've been thinking up names,' Harry explained. 'With Gloria.' He waved a hand in the direction of their original table, which looked like the scene of a children's birthday party. Someone was lobbing chocolate sauce at a bearded man who seemed pre-occupied with setting fire to the tablecloth. Gloria, a vision of turquoise and blue, was waving madly in Zoë's direction.

'Names for what?' she asked.

'For you!'

'But . . .' She looked at them. It seemed too obvious to remind them that she already had a name. 'What's wrong with my name?'

The men looked at one another.

'It's a bit bland.' Jenson pulled a face.

'Not *bold* enough.'

277

Zoë was too confused to feel insulted.

'We thought Zeekay was good,' said Jenson.

'But that only really works if you're American, which you're not.' Harry looked at her as though she had done them a huge disservice by being born British.

'In England it'd be Zedkay, which doesn't sound as good.'

'So, have a think, eh!'

'Right . . .' Zoë watched as the two men staggered off, trying to work out how much of what they'd said was down to the booze.

'So, you're in safe hands,' said Denzel, grinning at her.

'They, um . . .' Zoë had no idea what she was trying to say. She was distracted by the hot, firm hand on her waist and the perfect symmetry of Denzel's jaw.

'Relax,' said Denzel, moving a lock of hair from her face. 'They'll make you a star. It's their job.' He grinned. 'Not a very difficult job.'

She looked at him, determined to maintain her cool.

'People like you and me . . .' He shrugged his hefty shoulders. 'We were born for the stage. Come on. Let's have some fun.'

Before she could ask what type of fun, Denzel grabbed her hand and whisked her away through the carnage – upturned chairs, semi-conscious bodies, flying food. Zoë tried to suppress her awe as some of the world's most gorgeous women flashed smiles in Denzel's direction. It seemed impossible that one year ago, this guy had been some punter that no one had heard of.

She couldn't explain how they ended up in the honeymoon suite of the hotel. All she knew as she kneeled down at the glass coffee table with Denzel White and four other semi-famous musicians, was that her life had suddenly become a lot more exciting.

'Go on then,' said someone.

Zoë leaned forward, looking at a snowdrift of white powder in front of her. She was holding a rolled-up fifty and someone had cut her a line.

Zoë looked up at Denzel, who was eyeing her expectantly. He was probably wondering why she wasn't hoovering it up. And why wasn't she? In fact, why *hadn't* she done it before? Suddenly, Zoë felt liberated by the prospect. Here she was in one of the most expensive hotel rooms in London being offered free gak from a bunch of hot celebrities. What was she waiting for?

Zoë bent down, sealed off one nostril and snorted it back.

40

Zoë stared at the message on her phone, then closed her eyes and pressed her fingers against her temples. She could still see the pixelated letters, emblazoned on the insides of her eyelids.

> Hey sexy. U R a
> dark horse. Want
> another good time?

The message had been there for three days now. Three days. That was the limit for playing it cool, surely. Any longer and they deleted you from their phone book.

The problem was, Zoë wasn't entirely sure who had sent her the message. She was *almost* convinced that the unfamiliar number belonged to Denzel White, but there was also a chance that the whole thing was a hoax. A slip-up at such an early stage in her career could mean that instead of being known for her powerful voice, she'd be known for whatever the paparazzi set her up to do for the benefit of the nation's tabloid readers.

For the hundredth time, Zoë tried to piece together the memories from her night at the Universal ball. She had a reasonable recollection of events leading up to the end of the meal, but after that it was random snapshots: brief, mismatching images in no particular order. A bar. Somebody's room. Drinking from a test tube. Dancing on a table. Being wrapped around someone's bare chest (Denzel's?). A fruit bowl. Trying to rap. A ceiling tile. Oysters. A white-coated coffee table. A minibar in a swimming pool. Lying on the dewy grass . . . naked? Could that be right?

The following morning, Zoë had woken in Tamsin's spare room as usual, with a searing pain in her head and a mortifying sense that something very bad had happened.

Zoë sighed and reopened her eyes. Perhaps it was best to forget about Denzel White. She barely knew him. After spending a whole night in his company, all she could remember about the man was the name of his upcoming record: 'Suck It'. That, and his smile. And his calm, cool voice. And his hands. And his perfectly sculpted . . . shit. This was all getting ridiculous.

Zoë pushed aside the sea of bridal magazines on the kitchen table and opened her laptop. Maybe she had missed something in one of the pictures. That was the thing about the internet: it documented everything.

Evidently, Zoë and Denzel had posed for cameras outside the hotel at some point that night. There were more pictures too, clearly taken from outside the premises during the early hours of the morning. One shot seemed to show Zoë with a well-toned guy, standing beside the pool in what looked very much like her underwear.

Zoë squinted again at the image, her eyes flitting down to the text underneath. *Fledgling singer-songwriter, Zoë Kidd . . . Last month spotted draped over Niall King, lead singer of The Cheats, this month turning her hand to another genre . . . Seen in the arms of Talent Tout winner, Denzel White . . . Who's next, we wonder?*

Zoë closed the browser, trying not to think about all the other sites that the search engine had thrown up for her name. It wasn't *all* bad; if you dug deep in the search results, somewhere on page five or six there were some decent articles and live reviews. Her MySpace page had over fifteen thousand fans at last count, and the Greenfly gig had done wonders for her credibility as a musician. It was just a pity that all that had been dwarfed by the deluge of crass one-liners about her relationship with Denzel White.

Tamsin had not been impressed, to say the least. She and Zoë had barely been on speaking terms as it was, what with the stalemate that Zoë had prompted between herself and her father, but this had strained their relationship to breaking point.

It was becoming apparent to Zoë that she was overstaying her welcome. Her sister had been more than generous to accommodate her after the breakup, but there was a limit to how much she and Jonathan could tolerate. Their engagement seemed to serve as a signal to Zoë: it was time to move out.

Unfortunately, however, her savings amounted to little more than two months' rent, at current prices – less, now that she had started eating into them. The truth was, until she released her first record she couldn't afford to move out.

An email popped into her inbox.

Hi Zoë,
    We've had a few tracks through from Victor – see what you think of the attached.
    Harry

Quickly, Zoë clicked on the first of the two files.

It was a male voice on the recording – Victor's, she thought. He was singing it an octave down, but even at that pitch she knew what she thought of 'Suburbia'. It sounded like a song she might have written herself. Or rather, it sounded like a song she would have *liked* to have written. The fast beat and heavy bass gave the song a weighty feel, but at the same time it was catchy. Zoë hummed along. She could see herself on stage, singing this. She caught some of the lyrics. . . . *Walking down the cul-de-sac to catch the eight-oh-four / He pecks her on the cheek just like he did the day before* . . . It was about a young woman trapped in a monotonous life, with a doting partner and a perfect suburban life. It personified her feelings exactly.

'Butterflies' was lighter, more chirpy. Zoë liked it. She suspected that it wasn't the first song to have been written about breaking out of a cocoon and embarking on a life of beauty and freedom, but it had a good chord structure and the lyrics were sharp. Zoë started to tap out a reply to Harry when her calendar pinged with an alert.

11am – Gloria (Starbucks)

Zoë checked the time and pushed back her chair in a panic. How had this happened? A few months ago, her diary had been rammed full of meetings, appraisals and lunch dates and she'd never had a problem keeping to schedule. Now, she was struggling to make the single appointment of the day. Her life no longer had any structure.

It wasn't hard to spot Gloria. Draped in a selection of greens that clashed somewhat with her hennaed hair, the buxom woman was cooing from the corner of the café, oblivious to the dirty looks.

They air-kissed for some time before Gloria launched into a sensational monologue about how excited she was to be working with such a talented artist and how utterly fabulous Zoë was looking and how she couldn't wait to get 'stuck in'. Simultaneously, she managed to secure them a table and place their order for coffees.

'I'm surprised, you know. I had you down as a herbal tea girl. Latte contains a surprising amount of fat. Look at your gorgeous long legs – don't you have to watch your figure? You are lucky. Still, you're young, aren't you? Twenty-four . . .?'

'Twenty-five last month.'

'Yes . . . there you go. You can eat what you like. Lucky you.'

Zoë took her seat, watching as Gloria tucked into a raspberry and white chocolate muffin.

'Oh.' The woman flashed a guilty smile. 'I'm going on a new

diet tomorrow. Today's my last day of freedom! Want some? No, very good. Very restrained. Now. I can't stress enough the *scale* of the ideas we have for you.' She chomped down a mouthful of sponge. 'You're going to be huge. *Huge.*'

The PR executive started waving her hands about as she went on to talk through the impressive list of artists she had worked with in the past and the success stories she hoped to replicate.

'. . . which is why *I'm* handling your press. Your release is a big priority for Vicinity and I feel *certain* we can do it justice. You and me. We're a team. I'll get you the press, but *you'll* have to put in the PAs. I can't—'

'The what?'

'Oh.' For a moment, Gloria looked nonplussed. 'PAs. Personal appearances.' She brightened again. 'It's like another language, isn't it!' She gave a loud hoot and polished off the remains of the muffin.

Zoë dipped her head, trying to hide as much of it as she could inside her coffee mug.

'Now,' Gloria clasped her hands together. 'Are you happy with Zoë?'

'Er . . .' Zoë looked at the woman, trying to work out why she had suddenly started talking in the third person. 'What?'

'As a name, darling. Are you happy with it?'

'Well . . .' Zoë was still confused. 'It is my name, so yes.'

'We thought it was iconic, you know. The one-word thing. All the top artists go by a single word. Adele, Beyoncé, Madonna, Shakira . . . Zoë. It's got a fantastic ring to it, don't you think? And it's *bold*, which is key.'

Zoë nodded slowly, finally grasping what Gloria was saying. Her thoughts flitted back to the Universal ball, when Jenson and Harry had spouted their peculiar variations and abbreviations, and decided she had got away quite lightly.

'Yes. I'm happy.'

'Wonderful. Lovely. And just as well, because I think Jenson said the tour merchandise was already underway. Ha!'

Zoë gave a hollow laugh. It wasn't funny that these things were being decided in her absence – although, to be honest, the idea of merchandise did sound exciting. The idea of T-shirts and beanies and caps bearing her name sent a shiver running through her.

'Is there . . . Is there anything else I should know about the tour?' she asked.

'Oh, goodness. Well, it's hardly for me to say. I just handle the press – of which there will be *no shortage*, during those five weeks! I think you'll—'

'So, it's five weeks then?'

Gloria smiled patronisingly at her. 'Oh, dear, I assumed you knew all this. As far as I know, it's about twenty dates across five weeks, but you'd better check.'

Gloria went on at length about PAs and live sessions and local radio interviews, while Zoë tried to contain her excitement behind the coffee cup. Frankly, she didn't care that the Radio One interview would entail getting up at five in the morning, or that *Grazia* would probably airbrush her into a cartoon character. It would be worth it if her first release made it into the charts.

'I don't think it's ever too soon to go for a double page spread in one of the music mags. *Mojo* or *Q* would be ideal, but *NME* might do . . .'

Zoë's heart was pounding. Ever since she had bought her first guitar, she had harboured private fantasies about seeing her face smiling back at her from those hallowed, glossy pages.

'It wouldn't be a huge deal, financially,' Gloria quickly added. Zoë tried to compose herself. *Financially?* She was implying that the magazines might pay her to appear in them? Jesus, if that was the case then they were missing a trick; Zoë would happily pay *them* for the privilege of gracing their publications.

285

'. . . probably only a few hundred pounds, for a new artist,' Gloria went on, throwing back her coffee.

Zoë nodded mutely, trying not to get carried away. Even a few hundred pounds sounded like a fortune right now.

'Try to think of it as a profile-builder. Once the album comes out, you'll do a proper UK tour and you'll see your fees start to rise.'

'*Proper?*'

'Well, you know. Proper venues, bigger budgets. Not that there's anything *wrong* with the universities and that . . . you know what they say: today's students are tomorrow's record-buying public.'

Zoë nodded, struggling to take it all in.

'. . . and most importantly, you must *blog*!'

Zoë cringed, the word reminding her instantly of the horrible comments that were floating around the internet thanks to her recent escapades.

'Every day, if you can. On your MySpace page and your website . . . It's vital that your fans see you as something that's up to date and *happening*.'

'There's stuff out there,' she began to explain. 'Written by—'

'I know! And that's great! But we want *more*. And we want *you* to—'

'No,' Zoë butted in. 'I mean, negative stuff.'

'Nonsense!' Gloria waved her teaspoon in the air. 'Don't be silly!'

Zoë shook her head, trying to articulate the nature of what had been written alongside those photos. 'There's . . . comments. It's . . . bad press.'

'Darling,' Gloria leaned forward, pushing aside her empty mug and resting her enormous bosom on the table. 'There really is no such thing.'

Zoë tried a couple of times to articulate what she meant, then decided that the woman was either totally convinced by her own mantra or barking mad. Any mention of 'Zoë', no matter how libellous or damaging, was clearly a good thing to Gloria.

'. . . anything else lined up? Are you seeing the gorgeous Denzel again?'

It took a couple of seconds for Zoë to realise that the woman actually thought that the paparazzi episodes had been part of her ongoing publicity campaign.

'Any chance of a celebrity couple thing going on there . . .? A Denz-oë . . . Denzel-oë . . . Denz . . .'

Zoë found herself wondering again about Denzel. She was becoming more and more convinced that the message had been from him; it was too much of an elaborate hoax for small fry like her.

'I got this from him, a few days ago.' She unlocked her phone and tilted it towards her publicist. 'I haven't replied.'

'Oh, darling.' Gloria's eyes lit up as she read it. 'You must!'

'Well, I wasn't sure . . .'

Before Zoë could finish her sentence the woman grabbed her phone and started prodding at keys with her fleshy thumb.

'There!' she cried, triumphantly handing it back. 'Now, press send!'

Zoë read the words on the screen and grimaced. She really wasn't the type to send teasing notes about 'good times'.

'It's . . . Um . . .'

'Go on then.'

'Well . . .'

'What have you got to lose?'

Zoë's thumb hovered over the Send key. It was true, she had very little to lose. Less than Denzel White, probably. He was already a name, and if *he* was interested . . .

Zoë pressed down the button and forced a smile.

'You're right,' she said, nodding. 'Nothing to lose.'

41

'Vunce more, please. It is not yet perfect.'

Zoë waited for the beat and came in, for the eleventh or twelfth time, with the final phrase of 'Out of Air'. In the booth, Victor fiddled with dials and behind him, Tommy leaned against the wall, watching her through the glass.

They had arrived at Victor's studio just before eight this morning – much to Christophe's disgust. The producer worked best, he had informed them, during daylight hours, which meant that for the next week and a half the musicians would have to shift their routines to accommodate.

Zoë came off the last note and froze, looking at the producer for a sign. Was that better or worse than her previous effort? She had no idea; she'd sung it so many times now that each take sounded exactly the same.

Behind the glass, Victor turned in his seat. Tommy was bending over, saying something in the producer's ear. There was an exchange of words, then some button-pressing. The men looked at one another and nodded. Zoë wondered what was going on.

'Okay,' Victor said through the intercom, eventually. 'We have it. Ze first one was fine.'

The first one? Zoë opened her mouth to object about the half hour spent re-recording the same two lines, then thought better of it. Victor was standing up and switching off lights. Behind her, the sun was just disappearing behind the woodland of Richmond Park.

'Zat vas good,' Victor barked, emerging at exactly the same time that Rod and Christophe returned from their hundredth cigarette break. 'Two songs in vun day – very good.'

Zoë gathered her belongings, smiling to herself. The producer spoke in the same way that he worked: efficiently and intensely. Throughout the day, the musicians had taken turns to sit in the sunshine while Victor focused on some imperceptible rattle on the snare drum or the level of reverb on the bass. He hadn't, as far as Zoë could make out, taken a break all day.

'Same time tomorrow, yah?'

The musicians nodded, bid Victor farewell and trooped down the drive, Christophe letting out a stream of expletives as soon as the door clicked shut.

'Fucking bloody producer! Ze man sinks 'e knows *everysing*. Fuck him . . .'

There didn't seem to be any real cause for Christophe's discontentment; the problem was more that both men were perfectionists whose ideas of perfection were slightly different. The combination of Victor's Germanic conviction and Christophe's French, hot-blooded rage was a dangerous one.

'. . . telling me to "just tap it lightly" . . . What does 'e know?'

Christophe slammed the door shut, barely waiting for Rod to clamber into the passenger seat before reversing, at speed, from the parking space and zooming off.

'Well,' muttered Tommy as the old Citroën rattled into the distance. 'That went better than expected.'

Zoë laughed, feeling a sudden surge of affection for her guitarist. She'd been lucky with all three of them, in a musical sense, but Tommy was becoming more of a friend, too. His sense of humour seemed to resonate with hers.

'Where're you heading?'

'Towards Kew,' she said. 'I was gonna get a bus, but it's such a nice evening . . .'

Zoë smiled as they set off together, their shadows elongated on the tarmac in front of them. Her life was a long way from perfect, but for some reason, it all seemed less daunting this evening. She was spending her days making music and slowly, *slowly*, she was beginning to achieve recognition. Maybe it was the balmy summer's evening or the cheeky smile playing on Tommy's lips, but for the first time in a long time, Zoë felt happy.

'I hear you met the lovely Gloria last week.' Tommy raised an eyebrow.

Zoë hesitated. She couldn't remember mentioning the meeting to her guitarist, but even if she had, she was impressed that he'd remembered. 'D'you know her, then?'

He smiled. 'Know *of* her. Everyone does.'

Zoë nodded warily. 'I think . . . I think she might be slightly barmy.'

'Either that or just good at her job. She's one of the top PRs in the game. You watch – you'll be in the newspapers on a daily basis before you can say *that wasn't me*.'

Zoë gave a nervous laugh, feeling the first twinge of doubt impinge on her buoyant mood. She had thought it odd that Gloria had probed so deeply into her seemingly ordinary middle-class upbringing, towards the end of the meeting. Every childhood fall had been interrogated, every playground alter- cation assessed, every family row analysed. She hoped Gloria wasn't planning to stitch it all together into some sort of rags-to-riches fairytale.

'You'll get loads of shit written about you,' Tommy warned, as if reading her mind. 'I guess it comes with the territory.'

Zoë grunted. 'There's already a fair amount out there.'

Tommy looked at her as they turned onto Kew Road. 'Don't read it.'

She shrugged. 'It's hard not to.'

'Seriously, Zoë. Don't.' He touched her arm briefly. 'That's how people go mad. Just . . . ignore it. Focus on the music.'

She smiled at him gratefully. He really seemed to care. Zoë didn't have the nerve to admit to Tommy that in the last instance, she had *had* to look at the blogs just to piece together her own version of events. In fact, all of a sudden, the mere thought of her night with Denzel White made Zoë feel sullied and guilt-ridden.

'It pisses me off that the industry's become so dependent on fucking PR,' he said. 'A few years ago, it was driven by the *music*. Now it's all about who can snort the most coke or who can take their clothes off quickest for the cameras.'

Zoë nodded, saying nothing. Clearly Tommy hadn't seen the pictures of her at the Universal ball.

'It's like the tail's wagging the dog,' he went on angrily. 'The press determines whether an artist gets to go on making music, not the other way round.'

Zoë thought about this as they walked down the wide, tree-lined avenue. Tommy was right. Tommy was *always* right. He had thoughts and opinions on every aspect of the industry – deep, sensible thoughts, some of which had never even occurred to her. She was humbled by his beliefs, wondering, yet again, where his insight came from – what *had* he done, prior to his session musician days – but she realised that he had stopped walking.

'Listen,' he said, head cocked to one side. 'What is that?'

Zoë backtracked a little and stood still. Faintly, coming from the other side of the stone wall that separated them from Kew Gardens, she could hear music. Only the beat and the lead vocals were audible but there was no mistaking the sound. It was some kind of open-air concert.

'Who is it?' Tommy narrowed his eyes, trying to answer his own question.

Zoë glanced up the road to where there seemed to be a gap in the wall. 'Let's find out.'

The gap, it turned out, was a works entrance to Kew Gardens.

Inset were two wrought iron gates that were locked together with a hefty chain, but the square patch of grass in the recess made for a perfect viewing platform. In the foreground were tall, gnarled trees and well-tended flowerbeds but beyond, it was just about possible to make out the glass roof of the magnificent palace and behind it, on a grassy knoll, thousands of people.

The music carried clearly in the breeze. Zoë closed her eyes, vaguely recognising the song. She grasped the railings and rested her head on the backs of her hands, trying to put a name to the band.

'Doves,' said Tommy, leaning in next to her.

She smiled and nodded. Of course.

They stood in silence for the rest of the song, pressed up against the railings, side by side, shoulders touching. Zoë kept her eyes shut. She could picture her student bedroom – the place where she'd discovered Doves but also, in a way, the place where she'd discovered everything else: her love of the stage, her best friends, her determination to get her music noticed . . . So much had happened since then.

'Look at that,' Tommy said quietly. 'Thousands of people, united by the music. *That's* what it should be about.'

Zoë nodded, opening her eyes and slowly turning to face him. She wanted to tell him that he was right; that he was articulating her very thoughts, but something was choking her throat.

'Are you okay?' Tommy moved even closer and looked into her eyes. 'You're crying.'

She nodded again, smiling as a tear trickled down her cheek. Maybe it was the music, or the memories, or the feel of Tommy's warm, muscular arm as it slipped around her shoulder but she suddenly felt very emotional. His hand slid down to her arm, squeezing gently, his eyes looking intently into hers through his hair. Then suddenly the hand fell away.

'Is that your phone?'

Zoë jerked away. Their lips had been practically touching.

'Um, er . . . yeah.' It was actually just the sound of a text message, but there was no point in explaining that. The moment was already ruined. Zoë reached round and unzipped the pocket, feeling breathless and confused.

'I should go.' Tommy stumbled backwards, bashing the neck of his guitar on the iron gatepost.

'Yeah. Um . . . I'd better take this.' Zoë looked at the silent phone in her hands.

'See you tomorrow.'

'Yeah.' Zoë pressed the phone to her ear and pretended to take the call. As soon as Tommy had rounded the corner, she lowered it and breathed a long, shaky sigh. She could feel her cheeks burning. She couldn't think straight.

Distractedly, she unlocked her phone and read the message.

> U can see more of
> my darker side any
> time U like . . . How
> about next Fri?

Zoë closed her eyes and leaned back on the railing, confused. Denzel White was asking her out.

42

Zoë extracted a limp lettuce leaf and took a tentative bite out of the stale sandwich. It was every bit as tasteless as she had expected. Still, she couldn't complain. She wasn't yet at the stage where she could demand bowls of M&Ms with all the brown ones removed, but at least she was being offered something before the gig.

They were sitting around in what must have been one of the King's College classrooms. Banks of desks had been pushed up against the back wall, the sash windows wedged open with dictionaries. It wasn't the worst place to kick off a UK tour, thought Zoë.

'Where ees Tommy?' asked Christophe, pulling out a cigarette and ramming it behind his ear.

Zoë swallowed. 'Buying a Coke.' She could feel the blood creep up from her neck to her face as she spoke.

Christophe grunted and squinted impatiently at the clock.

It was ridiculous, this . . . this thing. Whatever it was. Her nerves flared up at the mere sound of Tommy's name. She felt paranoid that everybody knew what had happened between them, even though there was nothing to know. Nothing had happened. They were band mates. Just like Zoë and Christophe, or Zoë and Rod.

Tommy re-entered the room, swigging from a can. He hopped back onto the piled-up desks and caught her eye, smiling through his hair. She looked away. Then she forced herself to make eye contact, but by then Tommy was taking another swig, facing Christophe and Rod.

Her only hope was that by blasting through a full live set together, the awkwardness between them might be blown away. They'd spent too much time together in Victor's studio, recording and re-recording the same lines, fine-tuning chord progressions until they were perfect. It had taken ten days to record the eight tracks and by the end, Zoë could understand why bands often fell out while making an album. Only, in her case, she wasn't falling *out* with her rhythm guitarist, she was . . . well. It felt as though there were things that needed to be said. Zoë didn't quite know what, but she knew that by not talking, they were making things worse. They were playing in a band together; they couldn't go on not being able to look each other in the eye. And besides, there *couldn't* be anything going on, because in three days' time, she was going on a date with Denzel White.

The door burst open and a grubby-looking skinhead with a goatee walked in.

'That's what I'm sayin'. Do the Luton and Oxford gigs from 'ere, in the minibus. Warwick an' the rest we'll stay in the Travelodge.' He opened his mouth and belched. ''Scuse me. Ruby for tea.'

Zoë tried not to stare, but it was hard not to. The man was wearing hefty, steel toe-capped boots, a dirty black T-shirt and khaki shorts, complete with a fully equipped tool belt. He was obviously lost.

There was a polite cough from behind the bald man and Zoë realised that Harry was standing in the doorway.

'Hi, Zoë. This is your tour manager, Gary. I don't think you've met.'

Zoë jumped to attention. 'Er, no. Right. Hi. Hi, I'm Zoë.'

'Yeah, kinda worked that out, love.' He turned to Christophe and winked. 'Not that you ain't a looker yourself, mind.'

Christophe glared at the man, his fists tightening.

'Lovely dameetcha.' Gary swaggered over to Zoë and squeezed her hand in his, glancing approvingly at the sparkling black catsuit she had on. Beads of sweat glistened on his shiny forehead. 'We'll 'ave a lotta fun, we will. I tellya, I got a good feelin' 'bout this tour.' He clicked his tongue and winked again. 'The tat's flyin' off the shelves an' you ain't even started singin'!'

'The . . . what? Sorry?' It was as though he was speaking another language.

'Tat. You know.' He rubbed his fingers together and whistled. Zoë was none the wiser.

'Merchandise,' Harry explained, after a painful silence. 'The paraphernalia we're selling out front.'

'Oh!' Zoë nodded. 'Right! Cool.' She had seen the table of T-shirts, caps and bangles on her way in. The ZOË logo, such as it was, consisted of leggy silhouettes set against a block of white stage lights spelling out the three-letter word. It looked like an ad for a cheap lapdancing club, Zoë thought. But still. She had to hope the Vicinity guys knew what they were doing.

'They're fuckin' *lovin'* the badges,' said Gary, reaching down and scratching his balls. 'But that's students for you, eh. Cheapskates. Always goin' for the heebie jeebies . . .'

Zoë nodded slowly, glancing briefly at Tommy, who shrugged helplessly.

'Freebies,' Harry clarified.

Gary nodded. 'Don't worry, T-shirts're shiftin' too.'

'Right.' Zoë nodded more confidently. 'Good.' She wondered how the proceeds from the merchandise got divided up. She'd have to check her contract.

'An' you got a hot little fox as support, eh.' He nodded through the wall in the direction of the stage. 'Whippin' them up into a right little frenzy.'

Zoë smiled, trying to untangle the peculiar sentences. The support act's name, according to the call sheet, was Hazel Myers – not one that sounded familiar, but that didn't mean a lot. There were plenty of female artists trying to make it on the London circuit, as she knew all too well.

'Is it nearly time?' she asked.

'Reckon so.' Gary nodded, hitching up his shorts and letting out another burp. 'You done 'ere?' He clapped Harry on the back with some force.

'Yep,' he spluttered. 'Yes, I've gotta shoot I'm afraid. Good luck.'

'She's in safe 'ands now,' assured Gary as they trooped out of the dressing room.

As they waited in the wings, Zoë felt the adrenaline start to leak into her bloodstream. Her legs weakened, her hands started to feel clammy and the reality that this was her first date on a UK tour suddenly hit her with full force. It was petrifying – but it was also fantastic. Recording with Victor had been an intense and rewarding experience – Zoë was proud of the tracks they'd laid down – but it didn't compare to this. After nearly two weeks in the studio, she was desperate for the buzz of a gig.

Zoë manoeuvred so that she could take in the crowd, careful to stay in the shadows. She'd forgotten how much she loved students. Dirty Money had done a few university gigs around London, always coming away with a new fan-base and an inflated set of egos. Drunk, noisy and carefree, they were easily the best sort of audience to play to. They had so much energy, and they didn't seem to mind expending it on the sticky, overpopulated floor.

Gloria, to her credit, had engineered a full-page feature on Zoë in the King's College student newspaper, and someone – Gloria denied her involvement in this – had infiltrated the online message boards and plastered them with glowing reviews of Zoë's tracks. Authentic or not, they'd done the job. The auditorium was packed with inebriated, delirious undergraduates.

Zoë turned to watch the support act as she finished her final song. She had a great voice – softer and more mellow than Zoë's, but still powerful. She was tall, with neat curves that were accentuated by the fishnet tights and hot pants that made up her somewhat daring ringmaster outfit. Beneath the top hat, it was just about possible to make out the white-blonde wisps of hair.

'Thank you, everyone,' she cried as the students screamed and jumped up and down. 'And now I'm gonna hand over to the girl you're all here to see . . .'

The girl looked left and right, pausing for dramatic effect. Zoë stared. The cropped hair looked familiar. She *did* know the girl. Not from the circuit, but from one of her own gigs – the Greenfly gig at Brixton Academy. She was the fan who'd been hanging about by the backstage door, the one who had been to nearly every one of her gigs.

'Please welcome the main act for tonight, and my all-time favourite singer . . . *Zoë*!'

43

Zoë turned off Charing Cross Road, trying to ignore the fluttering in her stomach. She recognised the sensation from nearly seven years ago – her first proper date with James. It was the thrill of the unknown, the unanswered questions, the excitement of the blank canvas that lay before them . . . although in this case the canvas wasn't entirely blank. Not from Denzel's perspective, anyway. She had a feeling that he'd remember a little more about that night than she did.

She scanned the pub, breaking into a smile as she got to the bar. He was dressed in dark, low-slung jeans and a fashionably ripped top that showed off his muscular arms. Several heads turned as their eyes connected.

Zoë was determined not to let her excitement show as he kissed her on the cheek. She wasn't sure, but she had a feeling that some of the women sitting by the window were taking pictures on their mobile phones.

'I'm sorry,' he said, nodding for them to leave the pub. 'I picked a shit-hole for a meeting point. Let's go.' Denzel held open the door and then joined Zoë on the street. 'This way.'

'Where are we going?'

Denzel slowed to a halt on the pavement and turned to her. 'You look . . . gorgeous.'

Zoë smiled bashfully. Clearly the short black dress had been the right decision. She tried again. 'Where . . .'

Denzel's finger was pressing against her lips. 'You'll see.'

Zoë smiled as he took her hand and led her onto Litchfield Street. Then he stopped again.

'After you.'

Zoë looked up. They were standing outside a bar with coloured, stained-glass windows and gas lamps above the door. She looked up and read the sign. It took a couple of seconds for her to register. She'd read about The Ivy in the press; it was a celebrity hangout. She had never even known where it was before now.

'Are we . . . going in?'

'Well,' Denzel smiled. 'I suppose they might do takeaways.'

The door was opened by a man in a top hat and tails, and suddenly they were back in the nineteen thirties: green, swirly carpets on the floor, wood-panelled walls and plasterboard, art deco lampshades. Having confirmed their reservation, a stunning blonde showed them through to the restaurant.

'Look to your three o'clock,' he whispered, grabbing her hand and squeezing it.

Zoë glanced over her shoulder and found herself looking straight into Dannii Minogue's blue eyes. She managed to turn her stare into a general glance around the room. Inside, she was screaming. Dannii Minogue! The Ivy! Denzel White holding her hand!

'Crazy, huh?' said Denzel, once the hovering waiter had tucked in Zoë's chair and handed out the menus. 'People claim to come here for privacy, when they're really here for the exact opposite.'

She frowned.

Denzel shrugged and dipped his head in the direction of the other diners. 'It's got frosted windows and all that, but you'd get more privacy if you went to Mr Wu's in Chinatown, with all the paps.'

'Paps?' Zoë stared at him, alarm bells ringing.

'Yeah. You saw the car outside on the double yellow?'

'Er . . .'

The waiter returned to enquire about wines and Denzel's question remained unanswered.

'The Burgundy, please.'

Zoë smiled gratefully as Denzel sent the waiter on his way.

'So.' Denzel leaned forward and looked into her eyes. 'I Googled you.'

Zoë looked down at her lap. 'Oh. Oh dear.'

He laughed. 'What's to be ashamed of? You got a lot of hits.'

'Yeah. Mainly pictures of me in my underwear.'

'Well, yeah.' He lifted his muscular shoulders. 'Some of them were a bit blurry, but still sexy. Hey, we looked pretty cute together, don't you think?'

Zoë laughed reluctantly. Denzel lived up to his cheeky smile.

'I, um . . .' Zoë thought about how to phrase the question without sounding stupid. She wanted to know what had happened in the hotel after the Universal ball. 'I was a bit drunk, that night.'

'You were?' Denzel looked surprised. 'I wouldn't have known.'

'Really?' Zoë looked at him. Then she cringed. He was joking.

Denzel nodded. 'I had my suspicions.'

'Did I . . . do anything outrageous?'

'You don't remember anything?'

Zoë's head danced from side to side. 'Bits.'

'But you remember . . .' Denzel looked at her meaningfully. 'You know. *That.*'

Zoë gulped. She hadn't . . . They hadn't . . . Oh God. Where? How?

Denzel's expression suddenly broke. 'Hey, chill.' He laughed. 'I'm jokin'.'

For the second time, Zoë was saved from her mortification by the waiter, who made a great show of uncorking the wine and pouring it into Denzel's glass. Eventually, the tasting show was over and Zoë emerged from behind her menu, hoping the blood had drained from her cheeks.

'Are you ready to order?'

Zoë looked at Denzel, who was nodding despite not having opened his menu. Perhaps he was a regular at The Ivy, she thought. Perhaps he came with a different girl each time . . .

'I did learn a few things about you,' said Denzel, having reeled off his order to the waiter by heart. 'Once I got past the photos.'

'Oh yeah?'

'Yeah. I learned that Jenny from Milton Keynes thinks you're amaaaaazing and the Tunbridge Wells posse can't wait for you to go back to the Forum.'

Zoë smiled bashfully. 'I'm on tour. I've been doing the South East gigs this week.'

'I know.' Denzel held up his wine glass and clinked it with Zoë's. 'I'm honoured you fitted me into your schedule.'

Zoë rolled her eyes. 'It's not exactly the stadium tour you did after Talent Tout, I know.'

He shrugged. 'That wasn't such a big thing, actually. It was mainly schools and hospitals and local radio shows. Oh, and a nice little bar in Maidstone where one of the roadies got hospitalised in a fight.'

'Nice.' Zoë smiled, taking her first sip of wine. Denzel was being modest. Shannon hadn't been able to shut up about the Talent Tout tour last year and frankly, the coverage had been unavoidable. 'Didn't you end with a gig at Wembley Arena?'

'Yeah. But it was filled mainly with school kids – that's what they do.'

'Really?' Zoë was sceptical.

Denzel nodded. 'There's a lot that people don't know about Talent Tout.'

Zoë couldn't help thinking about Dirty Money and their entry in this year's contest. 'Such as?'

'Such as the fact that finalists like me don't come from nowhere. They do their time, singin' the shit bars, losin' money to thievin' promoters an' sendin' clipboards round for the fans, just like everybody else. The only difference is that people like me have the balls to go up on stage and risk it all in front of twelve million people.'

'Oh.' Zoë nodded understandingly. 'I know that much.' Maybe Shannon was right to put them forward for Talent Tout. Maybe it *was* just a question of having the balls to get up there. 'My old band's auditioning for the next series.'

'You serious?' Denzel looked at her. 'What're they like?'

'They're a three-piece girl band, but not a *girl-band* girl band. They're musicians. Gorgeous, too.'

He lifted one eyebrow. 'But not as gorgeous as they were before. What happened?'

Zoë smiled, taking a large sip of wine. 'Well . . .'

Over their starters, she explained. Initially, it was just her abridged explanation – the one she gave strangers who wanted to know about her band. But Denzel kept asking questions. He wanted to know who updated the MySpace page, how Dirty Money got their gigs, where they'd played. It felt so refreshing, talking to someone who knew about life as an unsigned wannabe.

'So, the rest of your band, they've got through to the . . . let's see, it's gotta be the bootcamp auditions, right? Without a lead singer?'

Zoë pulled a face. 'They've got Ellie.'

'Hmm.' Denzel nodded, slowly.

'What?' Zoë looked at him. The waiter silently loaded their empty plates and whisked away the wine bottle, catching Denzel's subtle nod for another. 'What are you thinking?'

'Well,' he said, leaning forward and smiling. 'I ain't seen these girls, but if they're anything like you, and they're through to bootcamp . . .'

It was as though he was leading Zoë to draw her own conclusion, but she had no idea what it was.

'I think they're in with a chance,' he said eventually.

'I hope so.'

'No.' He looked at her meaningfully. 'I mean, I think they're *in with a chance*.'

Zoë held his gaze, trying to decipher his words.

He sighed, looking up at the stucco ceiling and then back at her, leaning forward so that his face was up against hers. 'They hand-pick the finalists from day one,' he said quietly. 'Once they've decided who they're going to be, they make sure they've got plenty of footage from the early auditions. If your girls have been up in front of the producers and they're as hot as you say they are . . . then they're in with a chance.'

'Oh.' Zoë glanced cautiously around the restaurant. 'Is that really how it works?'

Denzel nodded. 'I didn't tell you that. Talent Tout launched my career. My album's comin' out in a few weeks. As far as anyone else knows, it's a straightforward talent show.'

Zoë looked at him, horrified. She had always worried that going on Talent Tout would put the band at the mercy of the editing suite, but she'd never imagined that the whole thing, right down to the choice of finalists, was fixed.

'Hang on.' She frowned. 'Does that mean they rig the phone votes?'

Denzel shook his head, waiting as their main courses were slid onto the table and a fresh bottle of wine was opened, again with great panache.

'No,' he said finally. 'No, that'd be illegal. The voting's just about the only thing that *ain't* rigged.'

'So how—'

'By the way they make the acts perform. If you're a singer and they want you off, they give you a crap song to sing. If you're a dancer, they put you in a shitty outfit so they know you'll trip over . . . That sort of thing.'

Zoë stared at him, her fork hovering.

'Anyway.' Denzel cut into his steak. 'I didn't say any of that. My album's out in October so until then, I'm Talent Tout's golden boy.'

'Right.' Zoë shelved her concerns, making a note to talk to Ellie about this. 'So . . . your album. Is it your own material?'

Denzel smiled wryly as he chewed. 'Kinda. That's the other thing about being the golden boy.'

'Oh no,' she cringed. 'It's all up to them?'

''Course it is.'

Zoë nodded unhappily. This was exactly why she'd been against Dirty Money entering the contest. Denzel had lost his artistic control.

Denzel shrugged. 'But hey, that's not where the money is anyway. Nobody gets rich from releasing records, do they?'

Zoë mirrored his expression, too afraid to admit that that was her plan.

'It's the endorsements I'm after.'

'Right.' Zoë nodded, slowly. 'Like . . . what?'

'Watches, gyms, credit cards . . . anything that fits.'

Zoë carved off a piece of fishcake. She understood what he meant now. For the big names – the Beyoncés and Eminems of this world – the money they made from record sales was just loose change in comparison to what they raked in from sponsorship deals. She tried to decide what to make of Denzel's approach. You couldn't fault his ambition; he was going straight for the big prize. Whatever the housewives of Britain thought about Denzel White, he wasn't just a pretty face. But she couldn't help thinking there was something missing from the equation. Where did the music fit into his plan? Didn't he want to feel proud of his first release?

Over the second bottle of wine, they discussed Denzel's forthcoming album. As they talked, it slowly became apparent to Zoë that she'd done the guy an injustice. He *did* care about the music; he just cared about his profile even more. Which was fair enough, she supposed. He'd done pretty well so far from being the handsome, cheeky pin-up . . . Zoë wrenched her gaze from his torso and tuned back in to what he was saying.

'That's the thing about fame. It's addictive. Once you've had some, you can't go back to the nine-to-five life.'

'Exactly!' She nodded enthusiastically. It didn't matter that she'd barely sampled a fraction of the fame Denzel had tasted the previous year; it was the principle. Denzel was practically voicing her own opinions and she suddenly wanted him to know that she understood. 'And nobody seems to realise that!' she cried. 'They wonder why you've become so obsessed . . .'

'But that's what you gotta do,' he put in. 'Become obsessed.'

Zoë smiled at him across her wine glass. The common ground was uncanny. Denzel had even divulged that at one point during the final stages of the contest the previous year, he had stopped talking to his family, following a row over his priorities.

He drained his glass and flashed her a naughty smile. 'Mahiki?'

For a moment, Zoë wasn't sure what he meant. Then she registered. Mahiki was a club in Mayfair – another celebrity haunt.

'If anywhere's good for building your profile,' he said, 'it's that place.'

Feeling merry and drunk, Zoë nodded. Given the state of her profile, a night in Mahiki could surely do her no harm. Denzel summoned the bill and she headed off to the ladies, colliding with one of the waiters on her way over.

Cheeks cooled by a splash of cold water, Zoë emerged and gratefully took Denzel's arm as they left the restaurant. The streets were busier now. Tourists swarmed, taxis hooted and theatre-goers spilled onto the pavement in front of them. Cameras flashed in the amber glow of the streetlamps and everything looked . . . well, beautiful. Maybe it was the wine, but Zoë couldn't help feeling that she was living in one of the best cities in the world, leading the best life she could imagine. She'd have to write a song about it when she was sober.

Denzel's eyes were glinting in the car headlights. Zoë was about to suggest walking to Charing Cross Road to hail a cab, but before she could get the sentence out she felt his hand in the small of her back, pulling her closer. His chest was pressing against her ribs and suddenly, they were kissing.

Zoë closed her eyes, dimly aware of the tourists' cameras flashing in the night sky but not caring. All that mattered was the bond. Never before had she felt so in tune with a man – and certainly not a man like Denzel. He knew what it meant to follow a dream. He was perfect. They were perfect together.

44

'Fan-fackin-tastic,' said Gary, walloping Zoë on the back. 'Them northern monkeys ain't gonna know what's hit 'em!'

Zoë thanked him breathlessly, throwing herself on the dressing room sofa and kicking off her silver heels. She felt exhilarated and exhausted at once. That was the incredible thing about touring: Each night, you put everything into your performance, but each night, you managed to squeeze out a little more than you had done the night before.

'Who's up for coupla Richards, then?'

Zoë instinctively looked at Tommy, even though he was even worse at deciphering the tour manager's code than she was.

'Beers?' he guessed.

It was difficult to say how it had happened, but the awkward-ness that had hung over Zoë and Tommy since that moment in Kew had evaporated during the course of the gigs. They were harmonising, improvising, trying out cheeky onstage banter. They were looking each other in the eye again.

'Spot on, mate. Come on, the lot of ya. Let's go for some Richards Geres. It's me last night of freedom, innit?'

Gary meant, presumably, that it was their last London gig. For the next fortnight, he would be taking to his minibus at the end of each night to transport them to whichever grotty motel they'd been booked into by the label. They had two nights off before they all jumped into the rusty Ford van and headed for Leicester,

Nottingham, Sheffield, Leeds, Newcastle, Glasgow, Manchester, Liverpool, Birmingham, Cardiff, Southampton, Portsmouth and Brighton. Zoë couldn't wait.

Tommy looked back at her, saying something with his eyebrows that she took to mean *I'm not drinking with that lunatic on my own.* They were warming to their Cockney tour manager, but he wasn't the type of guy they would have picked as a drinking buddy under normal circumstances.

'Yeah,' Zoë nodded. 'Why not?'

Tommy added his vote, while Christophe gave a haughty snort and Rod started rolling a cigarette.

'Lovely jubbly. I'll be back in five.' Gary lifted his leg, farted, and left the room.

After a good deal of flapping of magazines, the air finally cleared. Zoë perched on the desk next to Tommy, wondering why they hadn't just declined Gary's proposal and snuck out for a beer on their own.

Within seconds, the tour manager tumbled back into the room, elbows first, jostling as if trying to defend himself from attackers.

'Not . . . allowed . . . backstage . . .' He grunted with the effort of holding off whoever it was, awkwardly turning to Zoë. 'Jesus Christ,' he yelled as an arm lashed out at his tree-trunk neck. 'Zoë, these chicks're sayin' they know you.'

Before Zoë could reply, Shannon, Ellie and Kate tumbled into the room.

'Oh my God!' she screamed, rushing over and embracing all of them at once. She looked up, still squeezing their shoulders and realising that her eyes were filling with tears.

'Right,' said Gary in a weary tone. 'So you know 'em, do you?'

Tommy was watching from across the room. He caught Zoë's eye and smiled.

'It's . . . This is . . . Well, this is my old band.'

'Nat *your* band,' bellowed Shannon. 'Now come on, you

soppy eejits. Are you goin' for a point, or has Ellie got us here under false pretences?'

Zoë ran a hand across her streaked mascara, still smiling. Kate had tears in her eyes, too, she noticed, and Ellie was grinning like a little girl. Zoë slung an arm around her best friend, then remembered her promise to Tommy. He cocked his head as if to say, *go*.

The pub next door to the venue was an old bastion of British culture: threadbare carpets, stains on the walls and customers that looked as though they'd been there since the pub's heyday. The girls' entry must have lowered the average age in The Crown by about forty years.

'I'll buy!' cried Zoë, happy to throw away a week's food allowance on friends she had thought she would never see again. The decrepit barman served them their drinks, which they carried to a corner table, not caring about the multiple sets of eyes that were tracking them across the room.

'So . . .' Zoë looked at them. Shannon and Kate looked exactly the same as they had done six months ago. Ellie, though . . . it was her eyes. They seemed smaller – less lively. There were dark bags underneath them that hadn't been there before. 'How are you all?'

It wasn't the question she'd wanted to ask. The big question really was *how did Ellie persuade you to come along tonight?* But she feared that would trigger all sorts of rejoinders.

'We're good,' replied Ellie, nodding keenly.

'Don't you wanna know why we ended up coming to see you?'

Zoë smiled. Shannon was very astute, for someone so tactless. 'Well, yes.'

'It's my fault,' Ellie said apologetically.

'*Fault?*'

'Well, I mean, it was my fault what happened, and then what happened made them realise . . .'

'Basically,' said Kate, 'we were doing our first televised audition and Ellie had a bit of a . . .'

310

'A breakdown,' Shannon put in.

Ellie cringed. 'I'm sorry,' she said. 'It was the pressure . . .'

'And then when we asked what was wrong,' Kate picked up, 'it all came out how it had happened before, in the caravan . . . and then she told us about you, and how it wasn't all that great with Vicinity after all, but you were sort of trapped . . .'

'And we thought, fock that. We're all having a shit time, so we may as well have a shit time together.'

Zoë laughed, making a mental note to ask Ellie what had happened at the audition. She was obviously not 'fine' at all.

'But now you're doing a *UK tour*,' said Ellie, brightening a little.

'Yeah.' Shannon nodded and gulped down some beer. 'So then we thought, hang on a sec, she's not making it to fockin' stardom without us tagging along.'

Zoë laughed again, properly this time. She had forgotten how much she missed all this.

They wanted to know every little detail: whether it was true about the pool table in the basement of the Universal offices, what Victor C's dog looked like, where she'd got her Fender '65 Mustang, how much money she'd made so far, who exactly she had in her 'entourage' and why she had shortened her stage name to Zoë.

The questions made her smile, but they also made her feel sad. Six months ago, the girls had all shared the same dreams. They had all believed they'd get rich from playing music. They had fantasised together about the day they'd have an entourage and fancy stage names.

So much had changed. It was as though she had grown apart from the others – grown up. They still hankered after the golden ticket that would take them to the stars, but now Zoë *had* the ticket and she'd read the small print on the back – the bit that said, 'only in exceptional circumstances'.

'And you're going out with Denzel White!' cried Kate, pulling out an *Evening Standard* from her bag and slamming it down on the table, open at the photo of the two of them entwined outside The Ivy.

'Ugh.' Zoë flipped the paper over. She had seen a copy earlier in the day. Gloria had waltzed in with a stack of press cuttings and a triumphant fanfare as though it represented some sort of achievement. Zoë felt queasy just thinking about it. She wasn't comfortable with the idea of paparazzi photographers lurking round every corner.

'And you *kissed* Niall bloody King!' accused Shannon.

'Actually that was—'

Shannon slammed her glass against the table. 'I can't believe you did that!'

'I didn't—'

'What did I tell you?' yelled Shannon. 'He's mine!'

Zoë held up her hands. 'I didn't kiss him.'

'She didn't *kiss* him,' Ellie explained quietly. 'I told you, it was a dodgy photo.'

Shannon huffed a bit, but Zoë could tell she was messing around.

'Tell me about Dirty Money,' she said. 'Are you gonna win this year's Talent Tout?'

'Yes,' replied Shannon, just as Kate said, 'No.'

Ellie just lifted her slender shoulders as if to say, *See?*

'Bootcamp, here we come,' Shannon said proudly.

'Shh!' Ellie pulled a face. 'You're not allowed to talk about it!'

'We've signed a form,' sneered Kate. 'Although I'm not sure we're exactly spilling the beans here, are we?'

Zoë thought about telling the girls what Denzel had let slip about the fix, then remembered her promise. He had an album coming out; if the leak was ever attributed to him, the label would drop him in a flash.

'Ellie's right,' said Shannon. 'We're not supposed to discuss it.'

'It's not like we've seen anything worth discussing,' Kate pointed out. 'Four rounds of auditions and a couple of fleeting encounters with the judges.'

'Shh!' Ellie looked around anxiously, then realised that most of the clientele were probably hard of hearing. 'Seriously, Kate, I know you don't care if we get dropped, but you'll get us into trouble!'

Zoë watched them, her brow furrowed. Perhaps it was her imagination, but it seemed as though the bass guitarist had changed since they'd last met. The Kate she remembered would never have dared break the rules like that. She was nervous and fretful, strong-minded but continually worried about the repercussions. The girl sitting opposite, however, was assertive and bold. She didn't seem to give a shit about the repercussions.

'We got a call from Hot Rocks Records, a while back,' said Kate. 'Did Ellie tell you?'

Zoë squinted, implying that she vaguely remembered. She wasn't going to tell them she'd passed on the call herself.

'They're bullshitters,' declared Shannon.

'They're not,' Kate said quietly, looking at Zoë as she sipped her wine. 'They just won't take us on without representation, and—'

'It's against the show rules for us to have a manager,' Shannon explained sulkily. 'But that won't stop us having one afterwards.'

'After we've signed away—'

'Stop it!' cried Zoë. 'I'm sure you've had this argument a hundred times already.'

Ellie nodded exaggeratedly.

'Well then.' She held up her drink and smiled. 'To Dirty Money.'

'To Dirty Money,' they chorused.

'To Zoë.' Ellie lifted her glass again. 'And success on her *worldwide tour*.'

'UK.'

'Whatever.'

'To Zoë!'

45

Zoë hopped out of the minibus and watched as the combined might of Gary, Christophe and Tommy failed to make any impact on the dented back door, their exertions illuminated in the blue glow of the Travelodge sign.

'It is fucked,' declared Christophe, brushing the dirt off his T-shirt and marching off.

'Nah.' Gary took a step backwards and stared menacingly at the battered door, which had sprung open during transit as they'd pulled onto the A1 that morning and had since been held together with a spare power cable. 'Just needs a bit of a thump.'

Tommy edged away as the tour manager threw himself at the vehicle, bouncing off it with a satisfied grunt. Something went click.

'Job done,' he said, brushing his hands together. 'Let's get some kip.'

They trooped into the familiar-looking reception area, waiting as Gary embarrassed himself, as he had done for the last four consecutive nights, in front of the attractive receptionist. Following the Geordie girl's directions, they headed down the pine-clad corridor and up the stairs to their rooms. There were signs of a party going on somewhere in the building: a faint thud of music, chinking glasses, the hum of conversation. Zoë tried to imagine what sort of person would host a late-night event in a Travelodge.

"Ere you go,' said Gary, doling out the key cards at random. Every room, as they all knew, was identical. 'Up bright 'n' early tomorra – make it eight o'clock daanstairs. Gotta hit Scotland by noon.'

Zoë mumbled her goodnights and let herself into the room, which turned out to be an exact replica of the one she had slept in the previous night. The carpet, the bedspread, the lampshade . . . everything was the same, right down to the abstract picture on the wall. She collapsed on the bed, staring up at the dimpled ceiling and trying to force herself to unwind.

Sleep, she knew, wouldn't come for a while yet. It would take hours for the buzz to die down, as it had done the previous night, and all the nights before that. That was the thing about touring; your physical and mental energies got all out of sync. You finished the night feeling drained, your legs barely able to hold you up, but by that time the adrenaline had flooded your veins and your brain was too active to shut down.

Tonight had been the best gig so far. No question. The venue, an old converted bingo hall in the middle of Newcastle, was a step up from the usual tatty college hall – not just in terms of size, but in grandeur. If Gary was to be believed, they had sold over a thousand tickets – thanks, mainly, to Gloria, who had struck gold with the local press. Gary had even had to rope off an area at the front for the photographers, giving her a taste of what it was like to be a big-time act. To top it off, the hall was filled with the noisiest, craziest, drunkest kids that Zoë had ever played to and they couldn't seem to get enough of her tunes. Zoë smiled and reached down for her phone. She wanted to replay her messages, just one more time.

'Hey, it's Denzel. How's the tour? I'm missin' ya. Gimme a call when you're back from the grubby north and I'll treat you to something special. Once you've washed off the soot, that is. See you soon, sexy.'

'Zoë, hiiiiii. Louis here. Just a quickie. You're doing a *great* job

315

out there. Everywhere I look, there's photos of you and that fella . . . Now listen, Neil's getting a whole buncha bookings comin' through for early fall. Charity gigs, Reality TV shit and some Children in Need singathon whatsit. I'm sayin' yes to all of them, so don't you go bookin' any vacations, alright?'

'Zoë, hi! It's Gloria. It sounds as though all the interviews are going *marvellously*. You've been an absolute *hit* in the press – apparently Denzel White has been rumoured to be one of this year's *I'm a Celebrity, Get Me Off Ice* contestants so the newswires are absolutely buzzing! Now. Big news. I just heard back from *Q*. They want to run a feature on you! It'll be in their New To Q section, so they'll need you to do a shoot as well as an interview . . . Anyway, call me when you get a mo. Bye!'

The voicemails did nothing to suppress the buzz. Zoë dropped the phone on the bedspread, then felt it vibrate against her leg and grabbed it again. It was a text message.

Reckon that noise
means the bar's still
open? Dying for a
pint. T

Zoë grinned. It was nearly midnight, but she could still hear the thump of the bass through the floor. She pictured Tommy in his identikit room next door, bored and buzzing just like her.

Lobby in 5?

Zoë slipped her shoes back on, grabbed her wallet and crept out, feeling like a naughty boarding school pupil. It seemed illicit, slipping out in the middle of the night to meet her rhythm guitarist for a drink. In fact there was nothing more to it than that. It was just a beer. The reason Tommy had held off asking until they'd got to their rooms was only that he hadn't wanted their tour manager tagging along, turning the night into another Cockney bird-watching session. Still, that didn't prevent a little frisson of excitement running through her as she tiptoed along the corridors.

Tommy was waiting for her in the lobby, wearing a fresh T-shirt and a guilty smile.

'I found the bar,' he said, cocking his head in the direction of the noise. 'Apparently it's open late for a bunch of conference guests.'

Zoë raised an eyebrow and followed him through. It was more of a work canteen than a bar: IKEA tables, orange walls and a complete lack of atmosphere. However, it served beer.

'Just put it on the room,' said Zoë, as Tommy held out a tenner to the spiky-haired barman. Everything else in the last two weeks seemed to have been whacked on expenses; she couldn't see that a couple of beers would make much difference.

'No, my round. You can get the next one.'

Zoë frowned. He must have misheard. 'No, just put it on the room.'

Tommy thrust his note at the boy, who tentatively accepted it. Then he turned to Zoë. 'If I put it on the room,' he said, 'then you'd be paying for it.'

'No—' Zoë faltered. 'What d'you mean?'

He shrugged. 'Well, you pay for the rooms, ultimately, just like you pay for the barmy tour manager and the ads and the PR campaign and the producer and the biscuits for Victor's dog . . .'

Her eyes roamed the room, randomly, unseeingly, as she followed him over to a table in the corner of the bar. She was thinking back to her meeting with Charles McCarthy-Smith and remembering what he had said about royalties. *All fees and expenses are recoupable against your royalties. You'll only start to see an income when your debt's been paid off.* She had nodded at the time, thinking that 'fees and expenses' meant a few hundred pounds' worth of taxi receipts. Tommy seemed to be implying that it was more along the lines of *everything associated with the artist.*

Tommy pulled out an orange chair and looked at her. 'Zoë? Are you okay?'

She perched on the chair, still feeling uncertain. 'Yeah. Just tired.' She was too proud to admit her mistake, but she wanted to know for sure whether she was understanding the situation correctly. 'What, um . . . Where d'you draw the line between recoupable expenses and non-recoupable, anyway?'

Tommy laughed. 'Well, it's up to the label, isn't it? And because they're filthy bastards, they just bung the whole lot into 'recoupable'. They screw you for everything – sometimes twice over. I worked with a guy last year who discovered that his label was double-invoicing him for everything. Photocopying the receipts. It's a fucking nightmare, but there's nothing you can do about it.'

Zoë grunted, trying to do some quick calculations in her head. She knew that each album netted her around sixty pence in royalties, after everyone else had taken their cuts, and if she assumed that she was paying a hundred thousand back to the label (surely it couldn't be more than that?) that meant . . . *a hundred and sixty-six thousand*. She needed to sell that many records, just to break even. Jesus.

'Don't worry,' said Tommy, looking at her with a glint in his eye. 'It's possible.'

She pulled her thoughts back to the conversation. 'What is?'

'Making money. Assuming that's what you were thinking about?'

She smiled. Either Tommy was very perceptive or she was very easy to read.

Maybe he was right, she thought. He usually was. Making money *was* possible; she just needed to have a hit record.

'Tommy?'

Zoë looked through the hair and sought out his eyes. She had tried asking this question so many times, but he'd always brushed it aside. Tonight, she decided, she would come away with an answer. 'How do you know all this stuff? What did you do, before?'

'Oh . . .' He shrugged, sipping his pint. 'Just . . . various stuff.'

'Like *what*?'

He put down his glass. Then he chewed on his bottom lip, swilling the remains of his beer round and round until it nearly spilled out over the top. Eventually, he looked at her.

'You know the band, Gorillaz?'

Zoë laughed. ''Course.' Damon Albarn's cartoon creation was the most successful virtual group ever.

'D'you remember a copycat band that started up around the same time, called Egotist?'

'Yeah!' Zoë nodded. 'I discovered them before I even knew about Gorillaz, as it happened – I had an Egotist poster up in my room. What happened to them, anyway?'

'Well,' Tommy nibbled his lip awkwardly.

Zoë stared at him, the cogs slowly turning. 'Are you . . . Was it . . .' She couldn't believe what she was about to ask. 'Were you their guitarist?'

'Lead singer actually,' Tommy said quietly. 'And songwriter.'

'Oh my God!' Zoë shrieked, louder than she had intended. A couple of conference guests looked over from across the room. 'Sorry. I mean, wow. I had no idea. I can't believe it. You're the lead singer of Egotist!' She tried to compose herself. 'So . . . What happened?'

He tipped back the remains of his beer and smiled. 'Well, I ended up sampling the UK's Travelodge hotels and the other—'

'No!' Zoë rolled her eyes. 'I mean, what happened to Egotist?'

Tommy looked unusually serious as he prepared his response. 'We were kids, really. I was eighteen, the other three were only a bit older. We had a band – nothing special, but okay-ish. We were called The Musketeers.'

'For a four-piece.' Zoë smiled. 'Nice.'

'We thought it was really ironic.' Tommy rolled his eyes. 'Anyway, we were desperate to get signed, become rock stars, blah blah blah – the usual story. We'd had a bit of interest from labels,

319

but they could see we were just four lads messing around with guitars. Then one day, we were sitting around watching MTV and someone came up with the bright idea of making a whole band out of cartoon characters.'

'Like Gorillaz,' said Zoë.

'No. See, that's the thing. Everyone thought we were copying Gorillaz, but actually we got there first. And that was the problem. It took ages to get signed with Egotist because it was a new concept for the labels. They were *interested*, but nobody wanted to take a punt on this whacky new group that wouldn't show their faces. Eventually, we signed with Unity Records, a little indie that operated out of a cupboard in Soho.'

'But you managed to get into the charts, didn't you?'

'Ah.' Tommy gave a hollow laugh. 'We did, but not with Unity. Just after we signed, Damon Albarn was taking his brainchild to EMI and suddenly, cartoon bands were acceptable in the world of big record companies. There was all this newfound interest in Egotist, and . . . well, basically, we sold out. We signed a bigger contract with Universal, who paid huge sums to get us out of the Unity deal.'

Zoë nodded. She was beginning to see how it all worked. 'So then you owed Universal huge sums?'

'Exactly – before we'd even set foot in the studio. It was a joke. We managed a couple of hits, but nothing big enough to wipe out our debt. I was eighteen and I owed more than a hundred grand.'

Zoë gulped. She couldn't help thinking about her own situation and wondering how much *she* had racked up so far.

'The pressure to make money started driving us apart. And because I was writing the songs, I was getting all the publishing royalties, which pissed off the others . . . In the end, we severed our contract and split up, then watched as Gorillaz captured the nation's hearts.' He smiled wryly.

The Geordie barman cleared his throat loudly. 'Get non far claw sing tame, lake. If you cod stat dring-in op?'

Zoë looked at Tommy, who pulled a face usually reserved for conversations with their tour manager.

'So now you just write songs and do sessions?'

He nodded. 'That's it. My songwriting earns me a decent-ish living. A hit record would be nice, but yeah, I'm doing all right. And the playing keeps me sane.'

Zoë smiled, still reeling from the revelation that Tommy was one of the guys behind Egotist. Draining her glass, she rose from the plastic seat and followed him through the maze of strip-lit, carpeted corridors, feeling strangely excited. The story of his band was a sad one, but it gave her hope. Tommy had nearly made it. If things had turned out differently, he *could* have made it.

They slowed to a halt outside Zoë's room. Tommy leaned in towards her, pressing his mouth up to her ear. 'Don't tell the others, will you?' he whispered.

'What,' she replied softly, leaning in. 'That I used to have a cartoon poster of you hanging on my bedroom wall?'

He smiled at her for a moment, opening his mouth as if to say something and then shutting it again. 'Good night.'

He kissed her quickly on the cheek, his stubble lightly brushing her jaw. Then, one hand raised, he disappeared into his room.

46

Zoë scanned down the search results and clicked on one of the links. It was pleasing to see that following the deluge of coverage amassed during the three-week tour, the gossip sites fielding pictures of her wandering about in a coke-induced stupor had been relegated to page four of the listings, with The Ivy kissing shots even further down in the ranks. Most of the press was small-scale – local gig reviews, messageboard comments, student blogs – but the volume was impressive and, most importantly, the sentiment largely positive.

The students had warmed to Zoë. Her MySpace page had exploded with messages, fan mail and friend requests. *You f***ing rocked Sheffield,* read one posting. *Can't wait 2 buy ur album,* read another. *I am your biggest fan. Loveitloveitloveit. So unique – come back to Leeds Zoë! U R gonna be big and we'll be able to say we saw U for a fiver!* Zoë smiled as she scrolled down the page. *Love ur sound, but why why WHY did u sign to the fascists?* She closed the browser and returned to the Google hits, trying not to think about her label, fascists or otherwise. They must have received her tracks from Louis by now; she was desperate to know what they thought.

Zoë sighed. She felt inexplicably low. Not just tired, but lethargic. After an intense finale to the UK tour, culminating in a sell-out gig at the Brighton Centre and a near-death experience on the roundabout somewhere along the A27, returning to her sister's Limehouse flat felt like something of an anticlimax.

Reading the press was like looking at holiday photos. It was something to hold onto, to remind you of the fun you had had, but it wasn't anything like being back there.

Clicking on a link at random, Zoë found herself staring at the image of Denzel and her outside The Ivy. He looked like an Abercrombie model, she thought. She, meanwhile, had her eyes half-shut and was leaning rather heavily on Denzel's shoulder. She zoomed in on his handsome face and smiled. A whole fortnight had passed since that night. They had exchanged calls and messages nearly every day during her tour, but it wasn't the same. She wanted to have dinner with him again, to walk straight to the front of the Mahiki queue with him again, to get a private booth at the back of the club with him again.

Zoë's phone broke the silence, buzzing and whirring its way across the table. She grabbed it and saw, with a thumping heart, that it was Harry.

'Hi!'

'Zoë. Hi. How was the tour?'

'Great! Amazing. I think it went really well. It's—'

'Good. So I hear. I just spoke to Louis.' His tone was uncharacteristically abrupt. 'We've had a listen to your tracks.'

Zoë's heart was thumping. She managed to force out a quiet, 'Mmm?'

Harry hesitated. 'Look, um . . . There's no easy way to put this, Zoë. We've got a problem. The songs are great; it's a good album. But there are no singles on there.'

'Singles?' she echoed, even though the real question on her mind was, *why*? *What was wrong with them*? She was so proud of those tracks, of the way they'd been recorded and the way Victor, with some input from Zoë, had turned them around. What did he mean, there were no singles?

'Apart from "Suburbia",' Harry went on, 'which is perfect. But we need a couple more commercial numbers on there. We're struggling to get radio buy-in with these.'

Radio buy-in. What did that mean, exactly? Who had they asked? Maybe some junior producer who happened to prefer trash-pop to real music?

'They need a hook. And we were thinking, maybe a cover or two wouldn't go amiss?'

'A *cover*?' she said, hearing the despair in her own voice.

'Yeah, you know. Give people something they recognise. Something they can sing along to.'

Zoë grappled for words. She didn't *want* to give people something they recognised. She wanted to give them something new. Something special – from her heart. She didn't want to be a karaoke puppet; she wanted to be a *musician*.

'. . . old, like the Bee Gees or the Ramones,' she heard him say. It was difficult to concentrate. All she could think about was the fact that her label didn't like her tracks. *Bee Gees*? She suddenly registered. The Bee Gees? Had they even *listened* to her music?

She tried to imagine herself singing 'How Deep Is Your Love' while Harry prattled on. She had always found it disconcerting that any artist was allowed to cover anybody else's song and they didn't have to pay up-front for the privilege. As Tommy had pointed out, it gave songwriters like him a second stab at making the tune into a hit, but from Zoë's perspective, lining the pockets of already-minted seventies rock stars was not part of the plan.

'I'll have a think about the tracks you've given us, and take a look at what's rattling around in the old cupboard for covers. Maybe you can have a think too, and we'll catch up in a few days. Okay?'

Zoë mumbled something into the handset and threw the phone onto the table. She couldn't believe it. Her songs were powerful, sophisticated and catchy. The students had loved them. Did that count for nothing? Did the whole thing come down to whether three men in suits could get 'radio buy-in' from a couple of other men in suits? Zoë was livid.

By the time the front door clicked open, she was deep in

her own misery. She knew that at some point, she'd have to haul herself out, make a plan, but for now, she was only able to wallow, thinking dark thoughts about her label and fantasising about what she would say to Harry the next time he called.

'For goodness' sake, Zoë, you were there when I left. Have you moved at all today?'

Tamsin picked up the post from the counter and started sifting through it, her eyes migrating to the laptop screen on the table as she hacked at the envelopes. 'Are you thinking of getting it framed or something?' She nodded at the photo.

Usually, Zoë would have thought up some witty rejoinder or updated her sister with the latest development in her music career. She had been trying hard to maintain household harmony, given that she was effectively living rent-free at her sister's expense. But today, her blood was boiling with anger. Tamsin had no right to pass judgement like that.

'Shut up,' she said.

Tamsin stared, her expression morphing into a nasty snarl. *'Don't tell me to shut up in my own home.'*

'Right,' said Zoë, grabbing her laptop, wrenching its plug out of the wall and marching through the flat to her room. Suddenly, she knew what she had to do.

'Where are you going?' Tamsin barked.

'I know when I'm not welcome.'

'What?' yelled Tamsin, stomping after her.

'I can see you don't want me here,' said Zoë, grabbing her clothes off the makeshift rail and stuffing them into her suit-case. The more she thought about walking out, the more the idea appealed. 'Messing up your neat little world . . .'

Tamsin snorted from the doorway. 'What's that supposed to mean?'

'Exactly that. I don't fit into your cosy existence, so I'm leaving. Getting out of your hair.'

'*Cosy existence?*' Tamsin parroted incredulously. 'Well at least I can *afford* to make it cosy!'

Zoë rammed her remaining belongings into the case, determined not to let her sister's words sting. If she was going to cry, she could do it after she'd left the flat.

'You know,' Tamsin went on, in a more measured tone. 'I stuck up for you when Mum and Dad said you'd be a liability with the inheritance money. But now I don't know why I bothered.'

Zoë threw herself on the case, which was clearly never going to shut even if she removed all the coat hangers sticking out of it. She was trying desperately to think about something else so she didn't cry, but it was impossible to blot out her sister's words.

'You *are* a liability, Zoë, and you need to grow up. Maybe you'll realise that, when you're out on the street, not able to pay the rent. You might be a superstar in *your* world, but it's not the *real* world.'

In the end, Zoë wrapped the elastic straps around the case and tightened the buckles, towing it as quickly as she dared through the flat. Miraculously, it held together while she hauled it through the front door and along the covered walkway. Then, as she rounded the corner, it all fell apart. And so did she.

Zoë fell to her knees, picking up items of clothing and books and guitar strings from the pavement, the sobs taking over her entire body, blinding and choking her. It was starting to rain. Big, heavy droplets ran all the way through to her scalp, down her forehead and onto her face, where they mingled with the tears.

She must have been there for some time, ramming her belongings into the tatty case and trying to suppress the sobs – long enough to get completely soaked. She had no idea where she was going; her thoughts hadn't addressed anything so rational. All she could hear was her sister's voice in her head, and then Harry's, and then the sound of her world crashing down on her. *There's no easy way to put this, Zoë. We've got a problem.* You *are* a liability, Zoë. *There are no singles on there.* You need to grow up. *We're struggling to get radio buy-in.* You might be a superstar in *your* world, but it's not the *real* world. It was like torture, every line crushing her morale a little more.

Zoë looked up. She appeared to have walked to the Tube station. Zoë shivered. She was alone in East London, cold and damp, with a case full of soggy belongings and barely enough cash in the bank to last the month. She had to get a grip.

Ellie lived in a caravan with her boyfriend; there was no point in asking her for a floor to sleep on. Zoë's thumb wavered over the Call button on her phone. It wasn't just a matter of floorspace, she thought, pressing down and lifting the handset. It was friendship. She needed to talk.

The phone rang and rang. Eventually, the voicemail kicked in. Zoë panicked and cut off the call. She didn't want to talk to a robot; she wanted Ellie.

Shannon shared a flat with a bunch of random girls. They had so many people on floors and mattresses at any one time that Zoë lost track of who actually lived there. It was the obvious choice.

This time the phone rang five times and then reverted to voicemail. Again, Zoë stopped the call. She was starting to worry. Maybe the girls were out of town. In fact, had they said something about their next audition being in Manchester? And what then, if they couldn't help? She had ruled out the option of going back to her sister's place – even if it meant sleeping rough. Ditto for catching the train to her parents'; she wasn't going back on her principles just for a comfortable night's sleep. She scrolled through her address book and stopped on D.

Denzel White was her boyfriend, wasn't he? He'd seemed passionate enough at the end of the night in Mahiki, from what she remembered. And all the phone calls . . . surely he'd put her up, if she asked? Zoë considered the idea of turning up on his doorstep, wherever his was, then dismissed it. She looked like a drowned rat. And besides, it wasn't exactly celebrity behaviour to demand a place to stay at the end of your second date.

There was Tommy, she thought, turning over the option in

her mind. She didn't know where he lived, or in fact anything about his domestic situation. He'd once said something about a dog . . . that was it. Maybe he had a girlfriend? Zoë pushed a lock of dripping, matted hair off her face and called him anyway. She was desperate. Tommy would understand.

Counting the rings, Zoë's heart began to sink. Tommy wasn't picking up. She cut the call at the sound of his voicemail, panicking at the idea of leaving a message that she'd later regret. Then she tried Kate.

'Hi, Zoë.'

'Oh, hi!' Zoë's spirits leapt. 'Thank God! I was thinking you guys were all away . . .' She was breathless with relief. 'Can I ask a favour?'

'I guess.'

Zoë was thrown by her curtness. 'Are you . . . are you okay?'

'I'm kind of in the middle of something.'

'Right, okay.' Zoë wondered whether she should ask after all. Kate sounded very distracted. 'It's . . .' Fuck it, she thought. Kate was a friend; that was what friends were for, wasn't it? 'I'm a bit stuck for a place to stay, and I was wondering . . .'

'You wanna stay with us – me?'

Zoë hesitated. As far as she knew, Kate lived alone in her rented one-bedroom flat. Perhaps she had a new man. They hadn't had a chance to catch up properly since the London gig.

'Well, only if . . .' Even as she said the words, Zoë could hear her conviction slipping. 'Well, only if it's not loads of bother.'

There was a lengthy pause. 'I'm not sure that's a good idea,' Kate said eventually.

'Oh.' Zoë couldn't think of anything more to say. She desperately needed Kate's help, but there was clearly something going on that she didn't know about.

'Sorry, Zoë. It's . . . complicated.'

'Right,' she said weakly. 'No worries.'

Kate was still apologising as Zoë pulled the wet phone from her ear, feeling a fresh wave of self-pity wash over her.

The tears flowed relentlessly as she made the calls – to Ellie, to Shannon, even to Louis. No one was picking up. She left messages: desperate, pleading messages that probably made no sense, but she didn't care. She needed their help.

After ten minutes, her phone bleeped. She snatched it up to her teary eyes and realised, with dismay, that it was a warning to say that the battery was dead. She felt exactly the same: worn out, used up, spent. Wiping the tears from her face with a bare arm, she looked up, waiting for her vision to clear. The light around her was starting to fade and she suddenly realised she was freezing cold. She had to act.

Zoë swung her guitar case onto her shoulder and grabbed the suitcase. Then she turned back the way she had come and headed for the neon sign she had walked past a hundred times on the way to her sister's flat.

'Fifteen pounds a night,' said the man, pointing to the hand-scrawled note above his head. 'And you can't stay for more than a week.'

'Oh, that's fine,' she said confidently, then thought about what she'd just said. It *would* be fine, assuming someone got back to her. It was beginning to dawn on her that the line between make and break was very thin. Four days ago, she'd been strutting, diva-like, across a stage in front of a hall full of fans, flash bulbs exploding at her feet. Today, she was pleading to be let into a filthy youth hostel. All the safety nets that had cushioned her path so far had disappeared.

An hour later, she was sitting on a broken bunk bed, damp belongings strewn about the place, still crying. There were three other people staying in the room but they were all out. Zoë closed her eyes and leaned back against the brown, peeling wallpaper, reliving the row with her sister and then thinking back to the row with her parents, then the night James had told her it was over, and realising . . . *It was all her own doing.*

It was all so obvious, when you put it together like that. In the last six months, she had alienated everyone: her boyfriend, her mother and father and now her sister, and her best friends along the way – all because she was chasing her wretched dream.

It was only rarely that she stopped to question the dream, to ask herself why she was following it and at what cost. She was living in a bubble. But the bubble kept growing, fuelling her hopes as it grew and grew . . . She knew it could burst any moment and leave her with nothing, but she didn't want to think about that. She didn't want people like Tamsin pointing it out. It was *her* bubble, and nobody else's.

Zoë reached for her guitar and swung it onto her lap. *My Bubble,* she thought, trying out a few lyrics above the chords. She didn't care whether the song would make it onto the album, or whether it would get 'radio buy-in'. She didn't care whether it had 'hooks'. She only cared about capturing this emotion, distilling it and pouring it, neat, into the song. Because *that* was what music was about.

47

'Lovely, yeah. Nice and moody, that's it. Rrrr. Try a pout?'

The photographer worked his way round her silk-wrapped body, his camera flashing repeatedly from every angle while the stylist and makeup girl squinted critically at their morning's work. It wasn't hard for Zoë to look moody; she had pouted and scowled her way through the last three days.

'Great, I think we're done.' He took a final shot, nodded pleasantly at Zoë before scrolling through his accomplishments on the screen.

Zoë retired to the corner of the studio, waiting for the numerous assistants and technicians to busy themselves before pulling her jeans and T-shirt over her red silk gown. She couldn't believe that it took so many people to create something that would most likely end up covering less than half a page.

A scruffy young man dressed in drainpipe jeans and a tank top appeared in the doorway. He was stroking his patchy facial hair as he scanned the room.

'Ah, hi!' he cried, catching Zoë's eye and bounding over. 'Zoë? I'm Paul. I'll be doing the interview. Are you done here? We'll grab a coffee downstairs if that's all right with you?'

Zoë shook his hand firmly, forcing a smile. She had read enough interviews in *Q* to know that every part of the encounter, from the greeting to the way you held your cappuccino, was fair game for the journalist. A bad first impression could potentially haunt her for the rest of her musical career.

'Hold on,' shouted the photographer, looking down at the camera's display. 'I just wanna check I've got it . . . Before you go . . .'

Paul rolled up his notebook and started tapping it against his palm, grinning impatiently at Zoë.

From somewhere inside her bag, Zoë could hear her phone ringing. She ignored it, knowing all too well what the journalist would think of a newly signed artist who interrupted proceedings to take a call. The ringing got louder. People were beginning to stare.

Eventually, she dived into the bag and reached for the Reject button. She couldn't help looking at the screen as she did so. It was Ellie. She'd probably just picked up Zoë's frenzied voicemail from the other night. Zoë hesitated. The journalist was watching her. He'd hear everything. She started to press the red button, then changed her mind.

'Hello.'

'Oh my God!' Ellie gasped. 'Thank God – I thought something terrible had happened!'

'Sorry, yeah.' Zoë tilted her body away from the journalist, then felt his eyes on her back and swung round again. 'I'm fine.'

'Are you? I'm so sorry I missed your call – I was up with Sam's family . . . What happened? Tell me everything! Do you still need a place to stay?'

The photographer gave the thumbs-up to Paul, who looked pointedly in Zoë's direction.

'Um, er . . .' Zoë tried to think of a way to convey her situation without giving away to the journalist that she was homeless. 'All sorted now,' she said brightly. 'Hey, I'll call you back. I've gotta go.'

'Oh. No worries. I'm just glad you're okay.'

'Thanks, El.'

Ellie laughed. 'To be honest, it probably would've been a bit of a squeeze in our caravan anyway! I'll speak to you soon.'

'Yeah. See ya.' Zoë ended the call, trying not to think about Ellie's last remark. 'Sorry about that.'

Paul was already leading the way through the door and into the lobby. Zoë followed, surreptitiously opening a text message that had arrived while she'd been on the phone.

Hey Zo, sorry I
missed ur call the
other day. Hope
it was nothing important.
Tommy

Nothing important. Zoë thought back to the frantic phone calls she'd made to Tommy and Ellie and everyone else. It was pathetic, but she couldn't bring herself to admit that it *was* important; that she was homeless, and that she needed their help. They were her friends. She knew they wouldn't think any less of her if she came clean, but somehow, she still couldn't force the words out. Her pride got in the way.

Taking a deep breath, Zoë tried to dupe herself into a positive frame of mind. She could do this; it was just a question of eliminating all thoughts of Tamsin, her parents, her label and her dire financial situation. The problem, she suspected, would come when the interviewer started asking about such things.

'So,' said Paul as they settled at a table by the window. 'You've just completed your first tour?'

Zoë nodded. Suddenly, she felt nervous. She had managed to shrug off the gloom, and whilst that was good for her temperament it also meant that the numbness had worn off. She cared about things again. She was sitting opposite the man who would immortalise her words in one of the biggest music journals of all time and the significance was only just beginning to sink in.

'That's right,' she said, smiling as she panicked about what to say next. It wasn't like the rushed interviews she'd done before the tour gigs. They'd just been local radio stations and free news-papers – and besides, when you were about to step onto the stage in front of a thousand people, you had bigger things to worry about. This was a whole different game. She knew how hard Gloria had pushed to get her this interview; she'd probably had to promise a double-page feature on Morrissey in exchange. This was her chance to impress.

'It was great,' she said finally.

Paul jotted something down, looking nonplussed. 'Good . . .'

Zoë grasped the coffee cup, trying to hide her trembling hands. She could do so much better than this.

'Who would you say were your influences?'

Zoë straightened up. She knew the answer to this one. With a faltering start, she managed to trot off her stock response about Courtney Love, Kate Bush, Blondie, P!nk and the other thirty-odd artists whose CDs had lined her bedroom walls. She could feel herself relaxing as she reeled off the names, dropping in random facts about albums and gigs and favourite tracks.

'Wow,' said Paul, nodding and frantically trying to jot every-thing down. 'Okay . . .'

Zoë smiled. They'd got off on the wrong foot but they were making up ground.

'And your songs,' he said, looking up. 'They seem very, er, *heartfelt*. Where do they come from?'

'Well,' Zoë shrugged. Wasn't it obvious where heartfelt songs came from? With titles like 'Stubborn Silence' and 'Out of Air'? 'I draw on my own experiences,' she said. 'I can only write when things are going really well for me, or really badly, or—'

'For example?'

'Um . . .' Zoë wasn't sure she wanted to answer the question. She tried to think of a song that had derived from something not too controversial. 'When . . .' She wasn't short on examples; she just didn't want to tell the journalist.

'You do write them yourself, don't you?'

'Yes!' cried Zoë, suddenly defensive. She couldn't bear it if *Q* readers saw her as a vacuous bimbo who just sang what she was told to sing. 'There's a song about how I split up with the guy I'd been seeing for nearly seven years,' she said quickly. 'And there's one about how my parents are trying to write me out of their will . . .'

Paul raised both eyebrows and drew his head back. Zoë faltered, wondering what had prompted her to put it like that. Her parents *weren't* trying to write her out of their will. She was being melo-dramatic – which was a dangerous thing to be when your every word was being recorded.

'Go on,' prompted Paul.

'Well, there's one about how I'm sick of being put down by people trying to shatter my dreams . . .'

'People?'

'My family,' she said, before she'd had time to think. 'I mean, they're not *that* bad. They do *try* and understand . . .'

Paul looked at her inquisitively. 'But you say they put you down?'

'Well, yes. Sometimes.' Zoë closed her eyes. She was sounding flaky.

While Paul scribbled, Zoë tried to think. She needed to clarify: Either her songs were about the misery inflicted upon her by her unsupportive family, or they were about something else – in which case, what?

'Look,' she said, waiting for Paul to meet her eye. 'Can we start again? About the songs, I mean. The thing is, most of them come about from incidents involving my parents or my sister, but I don't wanna slag them off. That's kinda why I write the songs – so I don't have to.'

Paul nodded understandingly.

'I should probably explain,' she said, 'off the record, that my parents don't really understand about music. I've tried to get them involved but they're not so interested. To them, I'm a failed auditor.' She looked at him. 'This is off the record, okay?'

'Of course.' Paul smiled at her, although his hand still seemed to be jiggling behind the cups of coffee. 'No probs. So, shall we . . . talk . . . about . . . your band?' He was having difficulties multitasking.

'Please don't print anything about my family,' she said firmly.

Paul dropped his pen, holding up both hands. 'I will only include what you've said *on* the record.'

'Right,' she said anxiously. 'Okay. So . . . my band. You mean my musicians?'

'Ah, no. I mean, er,' he leafed through his notes. 'Dirty Money. That was your band, wasn't it, before you decided to go solo?'

Zoë looked down at her lap. Her split from the girls really wasn't something she wanted to discuss either. But then, if she kept ruling out topics of conversation they'd have nothing left to talk about.

'That's right.'

'What made you decide to go it alone?'

Vicinity. Louis. The record deal sitting tantalisingly on the table. The prospect of her dreams finally coming true and to hell with the consequences.

'I wanted more creative control,' she lied.

'Oh, so you didn't write the songs for Dirty Money?'

'Well, yes, I did,' Zoë stammered, realising again that she wasn't making much sense. 'It just . . . I wanted to create a *different* sound. We'd been going for several years and it felt, sort of, *tired.*' She faltered; this was coming out all wrong. 'It wasn't a bad sound; it just . . . Well, it could've been better.'

To Zoë's relief, Paul swiftly moved on to the subject of her forthcoming album. She felt guilty, talking about her friends as though they were substandard. The problem was, she could never have told him the truth. No self-respecting artist would admit that they'd put their commercial success above everything else. She had sold out, and Q readers wouldn't want to read that.

There followed a series of questions about the year ahead: the likelihood of another tour, Zoë's aspirations for her forthcoming album, plans to 'break America'. Most of her answers were stabs in the dark; she had no idea whether the rumours were true about her performing on the John Peel Stage at Glastonbury the following summer or whether there would be a collaboration between her and a certain male rapper. In fact, her A&R team would have been better placed to respond to nearly all of Paul's questions, but she didn't want to point this out.

'And finally, I have to ask about your, um, relationships. You've been spotted out with Niall King as w—'

'No,' Zoë smiled, shaking her head. 'No, that's all rubbish. We were at an after-show party and someone took a photo while we were talking. That was it.'

'Ah.' Paul wrote something down, his mouth turning up slightly at the edges. 'And it's also rumoured that you're dating last year's Talent Tout winner, Denzel White . . .?'

'Um, yeah.' Zoë nodded bashfully. The mention of Denzel's name set something fluttering inside her. 'Yeah, that's true,' she said, trying not to smile.

The journalist nodded slowly, one eyebrow raised. Then he whipped shut his notebook and looked up. 'That's great. Thanks, Zoë.'

As they were leaving the café, he stopped, waggling a finger. 'Sorry, one last question. We're asking all our New To Q acts whether they have any tips for readers in terms of hot new artists. Are there any that you'd like to mention – any you've seen on the circuit?'

'Well, there's Dirty Money,' she said. It was worth a try.

'Apart from Dirty Money.'

'Oh.' Zoë wandered onto the pavement, reluctantly thinking through all the hundreds of nearly-signed acts she had come across during her Dirty Money days. It was a small world, the gig circuit, once you reached a certain level. The problem was, Zoë couldn't remember any names.

'Nothing springs to mind. Sorry.'

Paul held open the café door for her. 'Oh. Well, maybe you could have a—'

'Except,' she said, suddenly feeling a rush of excitement. There *was* an act she could advocate. She'd only seen one live performance, and even that had been fleeting, but she'd seen enough to know that the girl would go far. 'Hazel Myers.'

Paul pulled out his notebook again and jotted it down as they reached the door of his building. 'Right.' He nodded, frowning. 'Not one I've heard of.'

'You will,' said Zoë, smiling. 'You definitely will.' She held out her hand. 'Nice to meet you.'

'And you.' He returned her handshake. 'Hope to see you again.'

Zoë turned on the step of the office block and headed towards the Tube. Unexpectedly, the interview had changed her mindset. She didn't feel upbeat, exactly, but she felt in control. There would be no more wallowing in her self-inflicted woes; it was time to act. She was going to appear in *Q*. She was going to become a successful artist. And to do that, she needed to have a hit record. If her label weren't willing to release any of her songs then she'd have to make a hit out of something else. She pulled out her phone.

'Hello?'

'Hi.' She stopped in the shade of a building, trying not to be phased by Victor's brusque tone. 'It's Zoë Kidd here.'

'Ah, yes. Hi. I vas vaiting for you to call. Harry told me you vanted to record a cover?'

338

'Yes. But there's something else, too.'

'Yah?'

'Yah. I mean yes. Another song. One I wrote a few days ago. I know Harry only wants me to think about covers, but I really think we should give this a go. I think it could be a winner.'

'A vinner, eh?' Victor let out a quick bark. 'Ve like vinners. So. How are you fixed for next veek?'

48

I wish I could tell you about the tracks I recorded today with Victor Ciprianni. I'm not allowed to say too much, but surely it can't hurt to say that the last song we laid down, which I only wrote a few days ago, might actually end up being the biggest and best of the bunch. Fingers crossed it makes it onto the album!

Oh, and I never thought I'd say this, but I feel pretty proud of the cover we recorded too. You'll find out soon enough what it is. In fact, young peeps among you won't even know it. I didn't until two days ago.

And more excitement: We'll be filming the video for my first single in a few weeks' time. There are mutterings about involving crash-test dummies and suspending me on bits of string, so I'm not quite sure how that'll pan out, but I'm sure it'll be fun(?).

Thanks for all of your lovely comments – it means so much to me and YES, I read every one of them, Gina from Basildon. Keep well!

Zoë sighed, skimmed through the piece and then clicked on 'post'. It was adequate, she decided. Gloria had been quite clear in her guidelines about what sort of tone Zoë should adopt. The daily blog was to be light-hearted but meaningful, informative yet aspirational, engaging and devoid of any reference to politics, religion and current affairs (this last point was in bold and double-underlined). In short, Zoë inferred, it was to be a trivial work of fiction.

She hadn't mentioned to her fans that she was typing the blog on her laptop outside a coffee shop, using its free WiFi and trying to avoid the waitress's eye. She had omitted the small matter of stopping off at a chemist on the way to Victor C's to buy cream to treat the mysterious bite marks that were appearing on her legs, arms and face – courtesy of the grubby youth hostel bed she was confined to through lack of funds. She hadn't talked about her row with Harry over the choice of cover, or the fact that her manager, the man who was known for turning his acts into household names, hadn't even called her back nearly a week after she'd left him a desperate voicemail.

Zoë clicked on her MySpace mailbox and started accepting friend requests. She couldn't believe the rate at which her fanbase was snowballing – and this was during a week when she didn't have any gigs lined up. She was about to close the browser when something caught her eye. One of the fans had posted a message on her profile page, complete with a photo of Zoë that had clearly been taken during one of her tour gigs.

Thanks for a great gig. It was an honour to be your support act. HM x

Smiling, Zoë clicked on Hazel Myer's profile and scrolled down the singer's page. She had a reasonable following, too – three thousand friends and a good number of postings. Zoë added her own.

Thanks for supporting. Hopefully see you backstage sometime soon. Zoë

She logged off and started to shut down her laptop, feeling more positive. Then, as an afterthought, she cancelled the shutdown and opened another browser. She knew it was unhealthy, this compulsion to Google herself every few days, but it was something she couldn't seem to shrug off.

Immediately, Zoë wished she hadn't. The number of hits for her name had soared to nearly half a million, but it wasn't the volume that troubled her; it was the nature. The pictures of Zoë and Denzel were up there at the top, and all references to her as an artist seemed to have dropped off into obscurity. Something was obviously pushing the gossip columns up the ranks.

A few clicks later, Zoë saw what it was. The contestants for *I'm a Celebrity, Get Me Off Ice* had been announced, and Denzel was one of them. Denzel mania had returned, and with it, a public backlash to his latest 'squeeze'.

'What can I get you?' The waitress was standing over her, stony-faced.

'Um . . .' Zoë couldn't tear herself away. She clicked wildly on link after link, following the trail of comments and feeling her confidence drain away. *Who is she anyway?* asked one user. *She hasn't even released an album,* commented another. *Another leggy bimbo preying on the celebs . . . Definitely anorexic. Check out her stage outfits!* 'Er, no, nothing thanks. I was just, er . . . leaving.'

The waitress hovered pointedly while Zoë gathered her belongings and hurried off, feeling hollow and shaken. Who wrote that stuff? How could they say those things? They were so ignorant; even a quick trip to her MySpace page would have told them that she wasn't just a leggy bimbo. And Jesus, she *wasn't* anorexic.

The comments troubled Zoë as she set off towards the hostel. They were floating about in cyberspace, those words, forevermore polluting the blogosphere alongside those horrible, misleading pictures, each one libellous and cruel but indelible. That was the thing about the internet; there was too much democracy. Anyone could print anything.

Zoë wandered into a small, unkempt park that presumably served as the local shooting-up spot, and pulled out her phone. She needed to set the record straight. It wasn't possible to correct all those comments for the thousands of internet users out there, but at least she could talk about them to the person who mattered.

'Hey, baby.'

'Hi!' Zoë tried to sound upbeat. 'I see you've made it onto *I'm a Celeb*?'

'I sure have. I would've told you before but it was all a bit hush-hush. Great timing for me. It airs just before my album's due out.'

'Cool.' Zoë smiled to herself. Everything in Denzel's world was about self-promotion. Well, *nearly* everything, she liked to think. 'When are you off to shoot it?'

'Not before I've taken you out on another date.'

Zoë felt her spirits lift a notch. He was smooth. 'And when might that be, then?'

'How about . . . a week Thursday?'

Zoë pretended to consult her mental calendar, although the sad truth was that aside from gigs and rehearsals, her evenings were markedly clear.

'Sounds good.'

'I haven't shown my face in Nobu for a while – you likin' that idea?'

Zoë hesitated. It sounded almost as though he was *planning* to get papped. She couldn't help thinking back to their passionate kiss outside The Ivy and wondering whether it could have been part of the Denzel publicity campaign. She wished she was more experienced in these matters. Being a minor celebrity was a whole new way of life. There seemed to be unwritten rules to which people like Denzel adhered, but nobody had taken her through the handbook. Tommy would know, she thought, awkwardly. He would know, but she didn't dare ask him. He seemed . . . Well, it was hard to say. He didn't seem to respect the showbiz lifestyle.

'I . . .' She put aside her doubts. 'That'd be lovely.'

'Where d'you live? I'll get a car to swing by.'

'Er, no,' she said hurriedly. 'I'll be fine.' The truth was that in two days' time, she would run out of time at the youth hostel and she hadn't yet plucked up the courage to ask Shannon for floor space. 'I'm . . . moving house,' she said eventually. 'Not sure yet when we'll exchange.' She hesitated. 'I mean, complete.' Shit. How did house-buying work?

'Whatever you like,' he said easily. 'Make it seven in the lounge bar.'

Zoë took a breath, determined to keep the excitement from her voice. 'See you there.'

'Lookin' forward to it.'

'Oh – Denzel?' Zoë realised she still hadn't said what she'd called up to say. 'Just one thing. You know all the press . . .'

'Yeah!'

Zoë hesitated. 'No, I mean . . . The stuff about us.'

'Oh. Yeah, that was good, too. You see the picture of me offering you my jacket? Pretty cute, eh?'

'Yeah . . .' Zoë faltered. 'But, well, some of the comments on those sites, they sort of imply—'

'Comments?' Denzel blew sharply down the phone. 'You look at that shit?'

'Well, yeah. I mean, no. No, I guess not,' Zoë mumbled, feeling foolish.

'It's all about noise, babe. Just as long as they're takin' pictures and talkin', who gives a crap what they're sayin'?'

'Yeah. Quite.' Zoë laughed. 'I just . . . you know, had a look when I was bored . . .'

'Honey, I gotta go. I'll see you next Thursday.'

Zoë stammered her goodbyes and dropped the phone into her lap, replaying fragments of the conversation in her head. It was admirable that someone could care so little about what other people thought of them. Zoë wished she had a little more of that sort of confidence herself. But deep down, she knew she could never be like that. She wanted to be liked. Was that so bad? She wanted to be liked for making good music. Denzel seemed to be content with just being *known*.

She was still thinking about this when her phone started ringing in her lap. She snatched it up, wondering whether it could be Harry with an answer on her latest tracks. It was wishful thinking, of course; she'd only sent them off an hour ago.

'Hiiiiii.'

'Oh, hi.' Zoë was disappointed and then immediately angry. It had taken her manager a whole week to get back to her.

'Just got back from the Tepid Foot Hold tour – bad timing. Y'all been having a few problems here, then?'

His flippant tone was doing nothing to stem Zoë's rage. 'A few,' she said curtly.

'All sorted now?'

'No,' she replied. There was no point in hiding how she felt. 'They're not *all sorted*. I'm currently staying in a skanky East London youth hostel and my face is covered in bites.'

Louis hesitated. 'Right. I see.'

'Really?' she yelped. 'Do you? Because I'm beginning to wonder whether anyone does. I quit my job five months ago and since then I've seen about two grand from Universal . . . How exactly am I supposed to live? Should I be flipping burgers while I'm blogging about being a rock star?'

'Hey, Zoë. Don't stress. This was never gonna be easy, you knew that. You said yourself that you're not in it for the money—'

'No, but I need to be able to *eat*!'

'Yeah. Right.' Louis sighed. 'Okay. Listen, you hang on in there. Have you signed on?'

'What?'

'Signed on – you know. Social whatever-you-call-it over here.'

'The dole?'

'Yeah.'

Zoë gulped. She couldn't believe he was actually suggesting it. She could imagine what her mother would say if she told her she was living off the dole. 'No.'

'Well, maybe you should. No harm, eh?'

Zoë was too shocked to even respond.

'Meanwhile, I'll make a few calls. No promises, but I may be able to help you out.'

Zoë grunted. She'd heard Louis's 'no promises' phrase before.

'Oh, and Zoë?'

'Yeah?'

'Sort out those bites, wontcha? Nobody likes a pop star with fleas.'

49

'I can't bloody believe you,' cried Shannon, panting as she lugged Zoë's suitcase out of the elevator and into a bright, white atrium. 'One minute you've not heard of Tepid Foot Hold, the next you're living in their apartment!'

Zoë smiled guiltily as she fumbled with the keys. A few hours ago, Shannon had picked her up from the grubby, insect-infested youth hostel, appalled at the conditions in which Zoë had spent the last week. Now, thanks to some string-pulling on the part of her manager, she was moving into the Mayfair apartment of Toby Fox, lead singer of Tepid Foot Hold. Shannon was right; it did seem absurd that her life could transform so quickly from one of destitution to one of relative luxury.

It was a quirk of fate that Zoë's penury had come about when it had. Only a few days earlier, Toby Fox would still have been using the place as a base for his UK tour. A day later and he would have flown back to the States, taking the keys with him. According to Louis, the singer had actually relished the prospect of somebody keeping it occupied during the coming months.

'Hurry the fock up,' urged Shannon, jiggling up and down as Zoë tried the second key, then the third. There was one for the private underground garage, one for the patio doors, one for the main gate when the porter was off duty . . . Clearly Toby Fox had done something right in his career.

Eventually, they were in. Shannon burst through the door, abandoning Zoë's suitcase in the hall.

'Oh . . . my . . . Lord.' She looked back at Zoë. 'I can't *believe* this.'

Zoë followed her in and then stopped. Shannon was staring at her, with good reason. The apartment was like a vast, echoing cathedral, only more modern. Its patent floors were draped in beige rugs and dotted with cream upholstery. A spiral staircase led up to a mezzanine level and the south-facing wall had been entirely replaced with floor-to-ceiling windows, giving rise to a spectacular view over St James's Park. In the far corner, next to the giant globe, was a gorgeous baby grand.

Zoë stared for several seconds. 'I can't live here.'

'Well, in that case, you're welcome to my eight-by-eight bedroom in Bayswater,' said Shannon. 'I'd be happy to swap.'

Zoë laughed. 'Seriously . . .' She prised off her shoes and watched nervously as Shannon skipped across to the stairs and swung round one of the banisters. 'Please don't break anything.'

'Jesus!' Shannon rolled her eyes. 'You're sounding like Kate. Hey, come over here. You won't believe this.'

Tiptoeing over to the middle of the room, Zoë mounted the first step and looked up. The upper level seemed to be decked out as some kind of cinema, with the end wall tilted neatly to face the projector at the back of the room and the intervening floor covered in beanbags and armchairs – all leather.

'You and lover-boy can watch dirty movies in *giant* form!'

Zoë rolled her eyes. Pornography aside, she couldn't deny that thoughts of bringing Denzel back here after their next date had crossed her mind. She was about to suggest that they check out the bedroom downstairs, but Shannon was already clambering up the stairs and pressing buttons on the remote control.

'It's V Festival!' she yelled, above the stadium-volume noise that was now pumping out of the speakers around the apartment. It sounded as though Snow Patrol had set up camp in the living room. 'Up here – look!'

Obediently, Zoë joined her friend in the private home cinema.

'Look at that,' said Shannon from her leather throne. The screen was showing the crowds in high definition, screaming and shouting the lyrics as the camera panned across the field. 'That'll be us, next year. Dirty Money on the main stage . . . and maybe you in one of the smaller tents.' She nodded with mock sincerity. 'If you're lucky.'

Zoë kneeled down on one of the beanbags, her eyes not leaving the mammoth screen. She couldn't laugh at Shannon's joke; there was something making her feel sad.

Maybe it was the music. She couldn't help thinking of her recent tour and all the tours that supposedly lay ahead, if Harry's promises were to be believed. She wanted all that more than ever, especially now that she'd had a taste of the lifestyle. But as Shannon had inadvertently pointed out, they weren't things you could enjoy on your own. If Dirty Money had stayed together, maybe they'd have a chance of realising their dreams *together*.

'D'you think it'll work?' she asked quietly. 'The Talent Tout thing, I mean?'

Shannon looked at her and shrugged. 'I hope so. Bootcamp audition in two days.'

Zoë nodded. The drummer didn't seem anxious in the least. 'What about Hot Rocks Records? Kate seems to think you'd have a better chance with them.'

'I know she does.' Shannon waved a hand. 'And maybe she's right. But you know, when you've gotta choose between a show with an audience of twelve million and a bunch of losers in Soho who claim they can get you onto some seedy, late-night chat show . . . I say go for the twelve million.'

Zoë smiled meekly, all too aware that she was heading down the late-night chat show route herself, unless she had a hit record soon. Harry still hadn't got back to her on the latest tracks.

'Is Ellie okay with it all?'

Shannon let out a long, loud breath. 'I dunno. I think so. Ellie's Ellie, isn't she?'

'Mmm.' Zoë nodded, hoping that Shannon had actually considered Ellie's feelings when making the decision. She knew what the drummer meant; Ellie never let on how she felt. Ellie would keep going and going just to please everybody else, in the hope that someday, good things would happen. Ellie was a concern.

They were still watching the festival coverage when Zoë realised her phone was ringing. She extracted it from her back pocket and motioned for Shannon to mute the TV. It was Louis.

'Hi!' she yelped. 'I was gonna call you. This place is *amazing*. Thanks for arranging it! There's, like, a cinema in the lounge and . . .' She looked around. 'A glass chimney, and a light that's kinda suspended from thin air, and . . .'

'Lemme know when you're done describing the decor in the apartment, will ya?'

'Right . . .' She trailed off. Louis's tone implied he had more important things to talk about than light fittings.

'I have some news. Two things. Firstly, Harry and co. have gotten back to us on your new tracks.'

Zoë held her breath. She could hear the pulse in her ear as she waited.

'To be honest, I don't think they were expecting the second one,' he said. 'They thought they'd just be getting the cover.'

'So . . .' Zoë waited for more. She didn't give a shit about what they'd expected; she wanted to know what they thought of 'My Bubble'.

'They seemed to like the cover. What was it? The, um . . .'

'Ramones,' she put in, pulling an exasperated face at Shannon, who was staring at her expectantly. '*I Wanna Be Sedated*.'

'Yeah, that was it. They really liked it.'

'Cool. And . . . the other one?' she prompted.

He waited a few seconds, then cleared his throat. 'THEY FUCKIN' LOVED IT!' he bellowed.

'Really?' Zoë needed to be sure.

'Yeah! *Spot on* were Harry's words. He reckons it's a single. Just the right mix of weighty and light. Great news, huh?'

Zoë leaned back, letting the beanbag engulf her and smiling up at the pristine, white ceiling as the relief flooded in. *They fucking loved it.*

'Which brings me onto the other thing,' said Louis, with a mysterious lilt to his voice.

Zoë sat up again, giving the thumbs-up to Shannon, who was making a peculiar grunting noise in her direction.

'They got you a sink deal.'

Zoë hesitated. 'A what?'

'A sink deal. You know, synchronisation? They got you a sync deal for "Bare-Faced Cheek" – some agency wants it for a TV commercial.'

'What? Which . . . what commercial? How . . .?'

'There's some new energy drink comin' out – Zest, I think they said. The agency reckons it's a perfect fit.'

Zoë shrieked. She had read about sync deals online. For some artists, getting a track played during an ad break on primetime TV was enough to launch their career.

'Harry's psyched, as you can imagine. The ad runs from October, which means you can release it as your first single and use that new one as your big-hitting second.'

Shannon, by this point, was flapping her hands about like a deranged monkey. Zoë covered the mouthpiece for a second and told her about the ad.

'. . . come in to discuss the schedule with them,' Louis was saying as Shannon started jumping up and down on the leather chair. 'Oh, and they got Victor to spice up a coupla tracks too, apparently.'

'Spice up?' she asked dubiously, trying not to think about the damage Shannon was doing to Toby Fox's upholstery.

'Yeah, I don't know the details. Those guys know what they're doing. I'll call you early next week, huh?'

Zoë thanked him and hung up, bracing herself as Shannon bounded over and leaped onto the beanbag beside her.

'You jammy cow!' she cried. 'First you get yourself a palace to live in and now you get yourself on TV before you've even released a fockin' jot!'

'You'll be on TV too,' Zoë pointed out, picking herself up off the floor. 'And anyway, I haven't seen the ad yet. It might be one of those irritating ones involving a talking animal.'

Shannon squinted thoughtfully for a second and then shrugged.

'Whatever.' She jumped to her feet, held out a hand and pulled Zoë up. 'Come on. Let's spill some red wine all over this carpet!'

50

'It's got a feel-good vibe.'

'Yeah, nice and catchy but not *too* catchy.'

'Very radio-friendly.'

Several heads nodded around the table. Zoë glanced at Harry, who seemed to be the closest thing they had to a chairperson.

They were discussing, in a roundabout way, the song that had just been promoted to the position of Zoë's first single, as a result of the upcoming television ad. Despite the label's original opinion that her first set of tracks contained 'no hooks' and 'no singles', the last ten minutes had been spent exchanging glowing one-liners about 'Bare-Faced Cheek'.

'I can see it working as a club mix,' said Darren or Dan, one of the young men whose job it was to get her tracks onto the radio playlists.

'Totally,' agreed the other one. 'I should think there'll be covers, too.'

Zoë looked around the room, willing somebody to say something constructive. The pluggers were nodding at one another. Louis was stroking one of his chins. Harry's eyes were glazed over and Ben was trying to make lascivious eye contact with Zoë, something she was trying hard to avoid.

'What about the other singles?' asked Zoë, when it became clear that the conversation had stalled.

'Oh, yeah.' Darren or Dan wagged a finger. 'Really good, both of them. Shouldn't have any problems with them, either.'

'We should be able to get the, um, oh . . .' Dan or Darren made a frustrated winding gesture.

'"Suburbia?"' Zoë prompted. '"My Bubble?"'

'That's the one. "Suburbia". We should be able to get that onto the A-lists too, I reckon.'

'And "My Bubble",' pointed out the other one.

'Great!' bellowed Louis.

Harry, who had lapsed into a vegetative state at the head of the table, jolted awake.

'Yup. That's great. So, we're all happy with the schedule?'

There was more nodding, even though they had moved on from the subject of the schedule several minutes ago. It had been agreed that the release of Zoë's first single would be brought forward to coincide with the ad campaign, which was due to start in mid-October. Then 'My Bubble', the 'killer track', would come out a fortnight after that – later if 'Bare-Faced Cheek' was still getting airplay. Victor's 'Suburbia' would be the third single and would come out in mid- to late-November, along with the album.

'So . . .' Harry looked down at his notebook, scratching his head. 'Ah yes. Video. We'll need to rejig the shoot order, in light of the new release schedule. Debbie?'

The curly-haired woman looked up and smiled. 'Yes.' She shuffled the papers in front of her and cleared her throat. 'So, we've received five treatments for 'Bare-Faced Cheek'. I think we can dismiss the two performance-based ones . . .?'

'Heavens, yes!' cried Gloria. 'No point in wasting Zoë's gorgeousness, is there?'

Zoë dipped her head as Debbie pushed two piles of paper to one side. She would have been happy to go with a performance-based video, but clearly the decision had been made.

'Okay,' she said, looking down at her notes. 'First up, we've got . . . er, yes . . . This one centres around the "cheek" element of the song. That is to say, um, Zoë's butt cheek.'

'Oh! Lovely!' chirruped Gloria. 'This is more like it!'

Zoë waited with trepidation for Debbie to go on.

'Yes, it's fairly simple really: Zoë in silver hot pants . . . Union Jack backdrop . . . mime artists in block colour doing robotic moves in the background . . . lots of cheekiness, very bold. You get the idea.'

'Hmm,' Harry said contemplatively. 'I like it.'

Across the table, Ben was nodding vigorously.

'Okay, so next up . . .'

'Hold on,' Zoë blurted out, horrified at what was being suggested. 'I don't, um . . . I don't think that works, for the song.'

Harry frowned. 'Why on earth not?'

'Well . . .' Zoë didn't know where to begin. Had they listened to the lyrics? Surely the chorus was a giveaway? *You're sounding like a little brat / How dare you speak to me like that? / Whose fault is it you're filled with scorn? / I never wanted to be born.* It wasn't about butt cheeks; it was about being brazen and going about things your own way. Zoë had written the song following a row with her mother. 'It's not a sexy song.'

Gloria hooted. 'Don't be modest, Zoë. Everything you do is sexy.'

'No, I mean—'

'Shall we whiz through them, anyway?' Debbie blinked up at Harry, who gave the nod. 'So, number two . . . You really need to see the storyboard for this one. Essentially, it's a portrayal of Zoë going in and stealing someone else's man. Big house in the country . . . Zoë in tattered ball gown . . . Storming into house, stealing man away from the girl . . . that's it, basically.'

'Could be good if it's shot well,' said Darren or Dan.

'Hmm,' nodded the other one. 'In black and white, maybe?'

'*Yes,*' gasped Debbie, jotting something down.

'Um,' Zoë pressed her fingers into the corners of her eyes.

She couldn't find the words to express herself strongly enough. 'Sorry, but this song's not about me stealing someone else's boyfriend.'

Louis let out a laugh and looked over at Harry, who pulled a pained expression.

'Not *literally*, perhaps.'

'So . . .' She didn't like the way everybody seemed to be looking at her, as though somehow *she* had missed the point. 'Does it have to come from one of these ideas? Can't we think up something ourselves? It's just, they seem a bit . . . random.'

'They probably do,' Harry agreed with a kindly smile. 'But trust me, they come from experienced directors who've worked on some hit music videos in their time.'

Zoë sighed. She wanted to protest, but couldn't think of anything more to say. It seemed obvious to her that they were misunderstanding her music, but at the same time, they did seem to know their stuff. Perhaps, she conceded, she should just put her trust in the experts.

'So, the last one's another storyboard,' Debbie went on, rustling her papers. 'Zoë gets up in the morning, applies lipstick, pulls on fishnet tights . . . some sexy hooker outfit . . . Walks through the house – a traditional American ranch farmhouse . . . Father looks outraged, mother drops a plate . . . Younger siblings eating breakfast look shocked . . . Zoë strides brazenly out of the house and jumps on a Harley Davidson . . . Then we see her dancing in a club . . .'

'Nice,' said one of the pluggers approvingly.

'I like the nod to the Yanks,' added Louis. 'That'll work well internationally.'

'So?' Harry looked around the table expectantly.

Zoë didn't know what to say. All of the concepts seemed wholly inappropriate for 'Bare-Faced Cheek', but she couldn't seem to make them understand why. And besides, she didn't have any better ideas up her sleeve.

'I'm for the ranch one.'

'Me too.'

'I wonder if we could slip the silver hot pants into the ranch video?' suggested Gloria.

'Mmm.' Debbie scribbled the idea in her notebook.

'Love it.'

'Okay . . .' Harry looked around at the nodding heads. 'Great. Well, that's easy then. Who submitted that, out of interest?'

Debbie pulled out the relevant page. 'It came from Nigel. Pretty low budget, too.'

Paralysed, Zoë sat there, thinking back to a recent conversation with Tommy. The shocking truth was that she'd ultimately end up paying for half of this American ranch scene debacle.

'How are we doing on the artwork?' Harry asked brightly.

A small chap with mousy hair jumped to attention. 'Pretty much there,' he said, sliding a piece of coloured card into the middle of the table. 'Just waiting for sign-off, really.'

Zoë leaned forward and stared. She had only just realised what it was she was looking at. The card, which looked like something you'd find wedged up against the window of a phone box, was to be her album cover.

'Wow,' muttered Ben.

'Eye-catching,' commented one of the pluggers.

'Is that Zoë's scrumptious body?' asked Gloria.

'No!' cried Zoë. She couldn't believe they were planning to peddle her music under the guise of something semi-pornographic – and more to the point, that they seemed to have reached 'sign-off' stage without her knowledge.

'It's just a stock photo,' the mousy guy explained. 'I was waiting for approval before we set up the shoot.'

'You have *my* approval,' said Harry, nodding. 'It's great.'

'Absolutely,' said Gloria. 'No objections on the PR front!'

'But,' Zoë spluttered, taking a closer look at the image. The girl's body was perfectly toned, tanned and airbrushed, positioned in a way that nudged the picture just into the 'soft' side of porn. She didn't want to be a part of this horrible idea.

Louis looked at her. 'You don't wanna do the shoot?' he asked, full of faux compassion.

'Ooh! An idea!' cried the artwork guy. 'Look – you can't see the girl's face because of her hair, so it doesn't matter that it's not Zoë.'

Harry slid the card closer and peered at it. 'Good point. The hair's the same length. We can just go with the stock image.'

'Great!' cried Gloria.

Zoë looked about helplessly. Then something caught her eye on the design.

'Why does it say, *It Goes Pop* on the front?'

The art guy shrugged. 'That's the working title, isn't it?'

'Oh.' Zoë glanced at Harry, hoping that the working title had no bearing on the ultimate album title.

'That's what we're working with, yes.'

'I like it!' shrieked Gloria. 'We should use *that* for the album!'

'It goes with "My Bubble",' Louis pointed out. 'You know . . . "pop"? Get it?'

'Has a nice ring to it,' mused one of the pluggers, nodding.

'Well,' said Harry, looking rather pleased. 'It sounds rather as though we're reaching agreement!'

'But—' Zoë curtailed her protest, aware that she was in the minority.

Harry started stroking the lank curls of hair that clung to the nape of his neck, obviously sensing her discomfort. 'No need to decide now,' he said. 'Plenty of time . . .'

Zoë glanced sideways at her manager. She had heard that line before. Louis had used it on the girls when they'd recorded their demo track. 'Plenty of time' was shorthand for 'We call the shots around here'. Zoë looked back at Harry, her memory jogged by the thought of meddling producers.

'Louis told me you'd got Victor to tweak a few things on the tracks. Can you play me the final versions?'

Harry frowned. 'Oh. I thought you already had them, to be honest. Ben, can you get them emailed to Zoë as soon as poss?'

Ben nodded, taking his boss's cue and gathering together his papers. After a few seconds, everyone seemed to be doing the same.

Like a drone, Zoë followed her manager through the door, trying to prioritise her objections, ready for a confrontation.

Suddenly, there was a yelp from back in the room.

'Ooh!' cried Harry, holding his BlackBerry high above his head as if it were some sort of trophy. 'One moment, everyone! Big news!'

The delegates stopped in their tracks, waiting for the scruffy A&R exec to elaborate.

'I've just heard . . . From an official source . . .' Harry was smiling mysteriously at Zoë. 'That the local support act for The Candy Chicks on the opening night of their UK tour . . . at the O2 Arena in October . . .' He looked around at the expectant faces. 'Will be Zoë Kidd!'

Zoë tried to react, but it just came out as a splutter. Everyone around her started whooping and cheering. The Candy Chicks were *huge*. Their gigs sold out within seconds. Admittedly they'd been manufactured on a reality TV show a couple of years ago and didn't, as far as she knew, write any of their own material, but they were proper pop stars with an enormous fan-base.

'They're on the label,' Harry explained to her, as people started drifting out again. 'Tara G's their touring support act, but you'll be on straight before her on the opening night. It'll be a great opportunity for you.'

Louis slapped her on the back. 'A *great* opportunity.'

In a daze, Zoë pushed her way through the revolving doors into the September sunshine and stopped to take it all in. Her earlier frustrations had been wrestled aside to make way for a burgeoning sense of elation. Maybe Vicinity knew what they were doing after all, she thought, picturing herself up there on the giant stage in front of a packed floor of screaming fans. Perhaps the trashy album cover and poptastic video might even work in her favour? She reached for her phone to call the girls.

51

Zoë jacked up the volume on the sound system, skipping into the echoing bathroom and assessing herself in the full-length mirror. The red cotton dress was short, but not indecent. It revealed just the right amount of leg and a hint of cleavage. She spun on the spot, wary of wardrobe malfunctions in light of Denzel's remark about getting spotted.

She danced into the lounge, reluctantly switching off the music and wondering whether it really was Denzel's intention to get 'papped' tonight. Thinking about his imminent appearance on *I'm a Celebrity,* it did seem apparent that Denzel was the type of person who rather enjoyed the attention. Whilst Zoë wanted her music to be renowned across the world, Denzel felt the same way about his face.

She was halfway through the door when she looked back and saw that her laptop was still on. Tiptoeing across in her heels, Zoë jiggled the mouse to shut it down and noticed that an email had arrived.

Hi Zoë,
Sorry for the delay – here are the re-mastered versions
of your tracks.
Enjoy!
Ben

Zoë glanced at the clock. She was already running late but she couldn't resist clicking on the files.

Her heart was thumping as she waited for 'My Bubble' to come through the speakers. The 'killer track', as it had become known, was to be her second release. That suited her fine; it was the song she felt most proud of. Heartfelt, but still commercial, it had a meaning as well as a 'hook'. She could see why the label had singled it out.

An unfamiliar sound filled the room. Zoë looked down, wondering whether Ben had sent her the wrong set of files. Then she started to recognise the bass line. An electronic whining noise came in over the top and then a throbbing, grinding beat. Zoë froze. She could hear her own voice in the mix, but it sounded completely different. The song hadn't been remastered; it had been completely re*made*.

Frantically, Zoë clicked on 'Bare-Faced Cheek', the track that had been optioned for the ad. With a plummeting feeling, she realised that it too had been sugar-coated. It sounded fizzy and sickly and oversynthesised. She tried 'Suburbia', Victor's master-piece. That too had been altered, although not as much as the others. Quickly sampling the other eight tracks, Zoë felt her optimism drain away. The album had been mutilated.

For a moment, she didn't know what to do. She scrolled through her phone book and then realised that calling off her date wouldn't help. She thought about calling Ellie, then checked the time and slammed the laptop shut, silencing the obnoxious sound and rushing through the front door.

Twenty minutes later, Zoë emerged from Green Park station, her mind overflowing with questions. How could Victor do this to her? How could Louis allow it to happen? Why would Harry *want* her tracks to sound like that? She'd written songs that were original and interesting, and now, they sounded like generic, factory-made pop. Was that what they wanted? Did they expect her to replicate this crass sound on the stage? Because if they did, then they'd be disappointed. She wasn't compromising her sound for these fools.

Zoë slowed to a halt as she turned onto Berkeley Street and took a deep breath, trying to push out the negative thoughts. All wasn't lost. She could work on the Vicinity guys, convince them that she was more than just a performing pony. She would argue her case, and she would bring them round. Maybe Denzel would be able to help her. Yes, perhaps they could have some fun tonight plotting how to win over her label.

'Evening, ma'am.'

Zoë did her best to smile serenely at the Japanese doorman. She felt out of place, all of a sudden. All she knew about Nobu was what she'd seen in the papers: photos of celebrities stepping out late at night looking glamorous. She was no celebrity – not yet, anyway.

'You have a reservation?' asked the beautiful woman behind the desk.

'Y-yes,' Zoë stuttered, glancing around for Denzel. She was twenty minutes late; even by fashionable standards, she was pushing the boundaries of politeness. 'In the name of Denzel White.'

Zoë's eyes continued to scan the room as the woman looked down her list. The place was unmistakably Japanese: black-framed artwork, cream upholstery and lampshades the shape of gnarled maple branches. A row of svelte twenty-somethings was drinking spirits at the bar and dotted about the lounge were unfeasibly attractive young couples, sipping champagne and flirting. There was no sign of Denzel.

'Ah, yes.' The women looked up and smiled. 'He hasn't arrived yet. D'you want to have a drink while you wait?'

Zoë nodded and walked over to the bar. Why wasn't Denzel here? He'd said seven; it was nearly twenty-five past.

Zoë flipped open the wine menu and tried to smile as she realised she was holding it upside down. It felt as though every eyeball in the room was looking at her.

'Can I get . . .' Zoë gulped. Having turned the menu the right way up, she was browsing the *By the glass* section. The prices seemed to start at *thirteen pounds*. Glancing around in the vain hope that Denzel had made an appearance, she returned to the menu and discovered a section further down the page in which the wines started at a mere seven pounds. 'I'll have the Chablis,' she said, opting for the standard second-from-cheapest.

As the amber liquid trickled into the glass, Zoë extracted her phone and busied herself by scrolling up and down her read messages. Simultaneously, the possibilities spooled through her mind: Denzel had forgotten, Denzel had arrived earlier and given up on her, Denzel had been involved in an accident, Denzel was lost, Denzel had started seeing someone else . . . At half-past, Zoë plucked up the courage to call him.

After two and a half rings, the call clicked through to voicemail. She hung up. There were only two explanations: either Denzel had rejected her call, or something had cut them off – like bad reception or a tunnel. If it was the latter, he'd call her back, she reasoned. If the former . . . well, she didn't like to think about that.

The minutes ticked by. Zoë scrolled and sipped, the mouthfuls becoming ever smaller as the glass began to empty, the doubts mushrooming in her mind. *He wasn't coming.*

By eight fifteen, she wasn't so much drinking as lifting and lowering the near-empty glass, like a physiotherapy patient trying to build up her strength. Eventually, she drained it and forced herself to call him again. This time, the voicemail kicked in immediately.

'Whassup. You're through to Denzel. Leave me a message and I'll see what I can do. Ciao.'

She gripped the handset and cleared her throat, grateful for the fresh flow of alcohol in her bloodstream.

'Hi Denzel, it's Zoë. Gimme a call when you get this. I'm at Nobu. Um . . . Maybe I got the time wrong. Hope you're okay. Speak soon.'

Her heart was racing when she ended the call. Her cheeks felt flushed and her breaths were coming in short, sharp gasps. Desperate to end the humiliation, Zoë slipped off the stool and summoned the bill. Reluctantly, she handed over her last note and realised that she would be left with precisely three pounds in her purse. In her life, in fact. Once that was gone, it was a case of delving into the unauthorized overdraft with no foreseeable way of paying it off.

Zoë marched herself out, forcing her head high in case of lurking paps. Not that they were likely to recognise her anyway, she thought wretchedly. Why would they? She was a nobody. Fighting back the tears, she retraced the steps she had taken an hour before.

A busker lay slumped at the bottom of the steps on the way into Green Park station. Strumming a battered guitar, the long-haired man was belting out Van Morrison's 'Brown-Eyed Girl'. Zoë tried to walk past, but she couldn't. She watched his unshaven jaw as he launched into the second chorus and felt something shift inside her.

The busker was good. He was a better guitarist than a lot of the guys on the live circuit, and yet he was sitting on a blanket in the corner of Green Park station. It was unfair, thought Zoë. Success wasn't proportional to talent. There was a factor in the fame game that nobody ever seemed to talk about: sheer fucking luck. Zoë reached into her bag, pulled out her purse and dropped her last three pounds into the busker's case.

52

'Cut! Sorry. Barbara, your timing's still off. You need to turn round as she's saying *little brat*, then drop the plate when she gets to *me like that.*'

'Right. Sorry.' Barbara nodded, nervously wiping her hands on her apron.

'In fact, can we try it without the plate-dropping? Zoë, you need to look more brazen. *Strut* your stuff. You look kinda . . . cold.'

'I *am* cold,' Zoë replied, looking down at the fishnets, hot pants and a glittery bra. 'I'm bloody freezing.'

The director ignored her and called the makeup girl over. 'Jess? Any ideas?'

Jess stepped forward, brandishing a can of spray-on fake tan. 'Close your eyes.'

'Great. Much better,' said the director, nodding approvingly as the fresh coat of greasy brown paint was applied, prompting no rise in body temperature. 'Everyone ready?'

Zoë backtracked to the kitchen doorway and waited for the music to start. For budget reasons, the American Ranch idea had had to be 'toned down', which was why she was standing around in her underwear on a damp September morning in a farmhouse just outside Bracknell. It was hard to believe that flights to Arizona would have bumped up the cost by much, in the grand scheme of things. The cast itself must have put them back thousands. Alongside the three actors playing her 'family', there was the dog, the dog handler, two camera operators, the lighting man, the stylist, the makeup girl, the director, the continuity woman, the props manager, the runner and the guy whose job it was to follow her about with a floppy, reflective silver disk.

Zoë counted herself in and then walked, as brazenly as she could, across the kitchen.

'No! Cut!' The director leaped back onto the set. 'Jack, where's your cereal?'

The eight-year-old looked down guiltily at his empty bowl.

'Jesus! Mark, can you give him some more?' The director turned back to the boy. 'Just *pretend* to be eating it, okay?'

Bracing herself, Zoë stood in the doorway, listening for the sickeningly familiar two-bar intro. She was still furious about the remastering, and hearing the same fizzed-up version of 'Bare-Faced Cheek' on loop was only aggravating her further. Talking to Louis hadn't helped either. He had promised to talk to Harry 'as a matter of urgency', but he had also explained, to her despair, that the energy drink company would be running with the remastered version. She was effectively arguing to release a song that was nothing like what people were hearing on TV – not an easy case to make to Universal's most commercial record label.

Zoë flounced through the kitchen, shouting the words to the song and timing her stride as instructed. In the corner of her eye, she could see Barbara turning, right on cue, preparing to drop the plate in horror.

'Cut!' cried the director, just as Barbara let go of the plate. 'Oh, fuck. I said cut!'

'Sorry,' mumbled the actress, stepping back as the runner started sweeping the shards of crockery into a dustpan.

'Mark, how many plates do we have left?'

'This is the last one,' Mark replied, handing Barbara another identical plate.

'Bloody hell. Look, Patrick,' he said, turning to the middle-aged male actor. 'Your horrified expression is all wrong. She's supposed to be your daughter, for Christ's sake. I know she's dressed like a hooker, but you're *perving* at her.'

Zoë looked at the floor as the actor tried out various horrified expressions.

'That's it. Okay. Everyone happy?' The director clapped his hands and nodded to the runner to switch on the music. Unfortunately, the dog interpreted the hand-clap gesture as a signal to start chasing its tail around the kitchen table.

'Can someone control that animal!'

Eventually, the handler intercepted and by some quirk of fate, on the next run, everything went according to plan. Zoë strode in, Jack looked up from his cereal, Patrick stared at her with exactly the right degree of horror and Barbara turned, gasped and dropped the plate on the floor.

'Fantastic!' cried the director. He looked at the cameramen. 'All good?'

The younger one nodded. 'Yep. Got everyone in except Barbara.'

The director's head flicked back at the young camera operator. 'You didn't get Barbara?'

'Nope. Zoë was further along by the time she dropped the plate, so she was just out of shot.'

'And Nick . . . You didn't get Barbara either?'

Nick shook his head. 'I was tracking Zoë.'

The director's screech was loud enough to wake up most of Berkshire. 'I don't believe this!'

After much debate, it was decided that the plate-dropping moment could be shot separately and inserted in the edit. Zoë was dismissed while the props manager set about rooting through cupboards in search of suitable crockery. She retreated to the makeshift green room, pulling a hooded top over her slippery, orange skin and kicking off the painful high heels.

There was one missed call on her phone. Zoë checked the

caller ID and felt something lurch inside her. It was Denzel. Her fingers shook as she dialled her voicemail, either with cold or with anticipation. It wasn't something she would readily admit, but the image of Denzel brought on a whole cocktail of emotions: excitement, fury, shame . . . Three days had passed since their supposed date, and not a word. Zoë had convinced herself that it was all over, that the no-show was Denzel's way of calling things off – albeit a harsh way. She had shed a few tears, but she had moved on. Her album was the only important thing in her life right now and she didn't need any distractions. But the truth was, she still felt a faint glimmer of hope that she'd got it wrong – that there was another explanation for events.

'Hey, Zoë. Babes, I dunno where to start. I am *so sorry*. I'm having a crazy time right now, and things happened . . . you know . . . Listen, I'll explain when I see you. If you'll forgive me, that is. Please forgive me. I'll make it up to you. Call me, gorgeous.'

Zoë smiled, despite herself. She *wanted* to take pleasure in deleting the message and removing Denzel's number from her phone, but she couldn't. There was something about his lyrical voice and the thought of his gorgeous smile . . . It was only fair to hear him out.

'Zoë, baby, I'm so glad you called,' he said, picking up the phone almost instantly. 'Listen, I'm so sorry. I don't know how to begin tellin' you how sorry I am. I got a call from the *I'm a Celeb* producer sayin' they wanted to shoot some London clips an' I thought it'd be done by, like, six, and we were still goin' at eight. By the time I got out, you were gone.'

'You could've called,' Zoë pointed out.

'Well, yeah, see, I . . . I didn't have my phone.'

'For three days?'

'Ah, well, see . . . that's the thing, baby. I *thought* I'd left my phone at home, but it turned out I'd lost it. I just got my new one through.'

The sound of smashing crockery next door distracted Zoë

from the question of how Denzel had retrieved her number from a phone that had gone missing.

'I wanna make it up to you,' he said. 'Lemme . . .' There was a smile in his voice. 'Lemme take you to Paris.'

Zoë hesitated. She allowed herself a quick daydream, picturing the two of them wandering the Place de la Concorde, stopping off in a bar on the Champs Élysées, dining out in a fancy restaurant . . . A beeping sound came on the line.

'Someone's trying to get through,' she said hurriedly.

'Lemme know, Zoë. I fly out for the shoot in a week, so lemme know soon.'

'Okay.' She switched lines. 'Hello?'

'Zoë, hi! Darling, it's me!'

'Oh, hi.' The me in question, Zoë deduced, was her publicist.

'Wonderful news,' she sang, opera-style. 'I've just picked up the October issue of Q . . . And there you are, right in the middle of it!'

Zoë's heart started pounding.

'You look utterly *gorgeous*,' declared Gloria. 'Go see for yourself. Oh, and more news: Tara G, The Candy Chicks' touring support act, has just had some kind of breakdown! So you're getting a bit of extra coverage, thanks to her!'

'That's . . . great,' said Zoë, feeling a little guilty about cashing in on another artist's misfortune.

'It's not great, darling – it's *fantastic*!'

Zoë made some excited noises and thanked her PR for the update. She could hear the director calling for her in the other room.

'I'll see you soon,' cooed Gloria. 'Stay gorgeous!'

Zoë put the phone back in her bag and carefully peeled off the hoodie, holding her breath to avoid the toxic fake tan fumes. The anticipation was making her dizzy. The Q article was out, but thanks to the country farmhouse shoot, she'd have to wait until tomorrow to read it. There had been no point in asking

370

Gloria how it looked; Gloria's vocabulary consisted entirely of glowing superlatives.

'Zoë! Harley Davidson scene!'

She stepped into the stripper shoes and headed back to the set. Halfway through the door, Zoë stopped. Her phone was ringing again.

'Hello?' she gasped, nearly tripping in the Perspex heels.

'I suppose you think you're funny?'

Zoë frowned, instantly recognising the Irish accent.

'What?'

'Taking the piss out of Dirty Money like that. Was it, some kinda joke between you and the journalist? *Ha ha, they're beneath me.* Was it?'

Zoë thought back to the *Q* interview and cringed. She could only imagine what had been written. 'I haven't seen—'

'You quit your band because it was *sounding tired* and it *wasn't as good as it could've been?*'

'Shannon, I didn't—'

'Oh, fock you, Zoë. You know, I thought we were friends again, but I was wrong.'

'I didn't—'

'Yeah right. 'Course you didn't. You're a liar, too, Zoë. I don't know why we even gave you a second chance. You know, I'm fockin' *glad* Kate's stolen your boyfriend!'

Zoë tried to yelp, but nothing came out. She stood, frozen, as Shannon slammed the phone down on her, trying to take it all in.

Kate was seeing James.

She felt sick. She could hear people calling her name, but the cries sounded distant. All she could hear was a scream, rising up inside her as she pictured the pair of them, her friend and her ex-boyfriend, together.

53

Zoë stared at the television, unseeing, unblinking. Somewhere in the back of her mind, she registered the bleep of the microwave oven, reminding her that her Pot Noodle was going cold.

For four days now, she'd been living on autopilot. Rehearsing, interviewing, blogging, arguing with Harry . . . it was all going on, but it felt as though Zoë was only half-involved. She was just going through the motions.

It would have made her angry, had she not felt so numb – the fact that revelation was having such an effect on her. James had split up with her months ago. It was no business of hers who he chose to sleep with. And similarly for Kate; her choice of boyfriend had never bothered Zoë in the past, except in a protective sense, so why did it matter?

She'd been with James for nearly seven years. She'd been band mates with Kate for the same period. Throughout all that time, she had trusted them, confided in them, poured her fucking heart out to them because that was what you *did* with your boyfriend and your band mates.

Slowly, Zoë pushed herself up from the folds of leather and headed downstairs. She knew it wasn't rational, but she felt betrayed. She understood that James wasn't right for her; it wasn't that she wanted to get back together. It was just . . . Well, it felt as though she'd been cheated of nearly seven years of her life.

She stirred the lumpy concoction and put it back in the

microwave for another two minutes. Thinking about Kate's recent behaviour, it all made sense. Her refusal to get drawn into a conversation about her latest man, her curt manner on the phone when Zoë had practically begged for a place to stay . . . Zoë felt sick.

There were other people involved, too. Shannon and Ellie must have known for a while. If Shannon hadn't blown her top about the Q interview then maybe Zoë would still be meeting up with them all, sharing jokes, buying them drinks, none the wiser. *Ellie knew*. She knew and she hadn't told Zoë. That was what really hurt – more, in fact, than the betrayal itself.

The Q article wasn't as bad as she'd feared. The piece focused mainly on her music and – to Zoë's bewilderment – her 'legendary' stage outfits. There were references to her 'turbulent family life', predictably, but the journalist had stayed true to his word, carefully quoting only from what she had stated on record. Unfortunately, however, that record included lines such as 'It wasn't a bad sound; it just could've been better' in relation to Dirty Money. Zoë flinched, just thinking about it. She hated herself for coming out with such a needlessly fallacious statement.

The microwave bleeped. Zoë removed the plastic pot, poking at the overcooked noodles. She had nothing to be depressed about, in the grand scheme of things. So many people in the world had it far worse than she did. She was living in a palace in Mayfair and she was signed to one of the most successful labels in pop. Her first single, 'Bare-Faced Cheek', was proving popular with the radio producers and had even made it onto a couple of A-playlists. The Zest ad was due to go live any day and in exactly two weeks' time, Zoë would be performing to nearly twenty thousand people at the O2 Arena. She had no right to feel low.

But the girls weren't talking to her. Unsurprisingly, perhaps, neither Ellie nor Shannon was returning her calls. Zoë hadn't had the nerve to call Kate. She wondered whether they'd ever speak again.

Denzel had called again, setting a date for their romantic

weekend in Paris – a date that was several weeks off, due to his *I'm a Celebrity* shoot in Iceland. Zoë had managed a half-decent show of enthusiasm, but it wasn't easy, thinking about romantic gestures with the image of Kate and James so fresh in her mind.

Zoë wandered over to the rack by the stereo and pushed a CD into the machine, turning the volume up to full. She stood there, looking at her reflection in the full-length window and thinking back to the first time she'd heard 'Mr Brightside'. James had played it to her after one of their first dates. She remembered wrapping her legs over his on the small student bed, falling in love with the song and falling in love with James. It was all so ironic, she thought, as the tears built up behind her eyes. The song was about jealousy and bitterness, and now here she was, feeling jealous and bitter about the very person who had introduced her to it in the first place. Zoë tried to cast the memory aside, but all she could think about was how things had changed and how she had given up everything in order to 'make it'.

The music was like a drug, pushing her emotions to the extremes. What did *making it* actually mean, anyway? When was it time to say, 'There, I've made it'? Was it when you cut your first album? When an energy drink company used your track in an ad? When people knew who you were on the bus? When you won an Ivor Novello? Or when your parents finally said, 'Well done'? It was only just beginning to dawn on her that perhaps there was no such thing as *making it*. Nobody ever managed to walk to the horizon.

The tears streamed down her cheeks as the angst-ridden lyrics blasted out. Some of the best days of her life had been spent chasing the dream, but now that the dream was starting to become a reality – the stadium gigs, the fans, the PR – it was losing its appeal. She never thought she'd say it, but she missed those nights of waiting for Ellie in backstage hovels, playing in draughty shopping centres and arguing with crooked promoters. The fun, it seemed, was all in the chase.

The song faded but Zoë couldn't move. She was lost in a world of self-inflicted, self-centred misery. She wiped her eyes, forcing her eyes to focus through the tears. Her gaze settled on the gorgeous white Fender, one of the few pieces of kit in the apartment that actually belonged to her. She wanted to play it, to pour out her feelings, but she couldn't. Ever since she'd written 'My Bubble', she hadn't been able to look at her guitar without feeling guilty.

Tamsin had bought her that guitar. Tamsin had put a roof over her head for three months when she'd had nowhere else to go. She had stuck up for her in the feud with their parents, been there to hear Zoë's petty gripes . . . she had done everything she possibly could have done. And what had she got in return? A sulky little sister who fucked off at the first opportunity and hit out with unwarranted criticism in the national press.

Zoë stumbled back to the sofa and reached for her phone. She couldn't believe it had taken this long to see it.

'Hi Zoë.'

'Hi. Um . . .' Zoë tried to assemble her thoughts. She'd been so quick to make the call, she hadn't stopped to think what she'd say. 'I'm sorry.'

'About what?' Tamsin's tone was acidic. 'The article?'

'N-no,' Zoë stammered. 'Well, everything.'

'Oh.'

Zoë drew a deep breath. 'I've been selfish and immature and you were right; I've been living in my own world. The thing is, I've been trying for so long to make a go of my music that now it's finally happening I've . . . I've lost track of everything. It's like an obsession . . . And I was so horrible to you. I think it was because you were so bloody perfect and I knew I could never be like you. But you didn't deserve it – you did everything for me and I just threw it all back in your face. I'm so sorry, Tam. I'm so sorry.'

Zoë's chest was heaving; she wondered whether Tamsin had caught everything that she'd said. Holding the phone against her ear, she waited for some kind of response.

'Zoë?' Tamsin said, after several seconds. 'What brought this on?'

Zoë moaned, looking around for a tissue. 'I just . . .' She tried not to think too much about what she was about to say. 'I found out that James is going out with Kate. It was a bit of a shock. Got me thinking, you know . . .'

Tamsin drew a sharp breath. 'I see.'

'But that's not the point,' Zoë insisted, determined not to get dragged in. 'I called to apologise.'

'Well,' Tam replied, her voice sounding a little warmer. 'Apology accepted.'

Zoë found herself crying again, but this time with relief. 'Really? I thought you'd never speak to me again.'

'It crossed my mind, when I read the article,' said Tamsin, her smile evident in her voice.

'Yeah . . .' Zoë wiped her eyes. 'I said some stupid things.'

'Well, you might wanna try talking to Mum and Dad to explain.'

'Yeah . . .' Zoë squirmed. Talking to Tamsin was one thing, but her parents . . . That was something else. She hadn't exchanged a word with either of them since the garden party back in June.

'Mum knows about you and James,' said Tamsin.

'What?'

'I had to tell her. She kept threatening to talk to him about you.'

'Oh.' A few days ago, Zoë might have exploded with rage at the idea of her family members colluding behind her back, but instead she just felt . . . grateful. Tamsin was trying to help. She should never have turned on her sister.

'Have you found somewhere to live?'

'Um, yeah.' Zoë looked around the apartment, embarrassed. 'I'm staying in a flat that belongs to one of Louis's American artists. It's—' A beeping sound interrupted. 'It's pretty nice. Sorry, I've got someone on the other line. Stay there, one sec.'

'Hi, is that Zoë?'

'Yes.' Zoë tried to place the deep voice and Irish accent.

'This is Niall King. How're you doin'?'

Zoë's hand tightened on the handset. *Niall King?* Her mind reeled back to the night of The Cheats gig and after-show party when the photographers had snapped her with Niall. She'd been drunk. Had they exchanged phone numbers?

'Good, thanks,' she replied, bewildered. It had been three or four months since they'd met.

'I have an invitation for you.'

'Really?'

'Really. I'd like you to come to the Famine Relief charity gig we're playin' at the Albion next Friday. It's a private party, guest list only. Pretty cosy. Donations welcome. I'd be honoured if you could make it.'

'Er . . . Um . . .' Zoë couldn't work it out. She'd exchanged no more than a few words with the star back in May, and that had been ages ago. Surely she wasn't considered one of the wealthy elite in celebrity circles? If it was her donations they were after, they'd be sorely disappointed.

'I've seen you here and there since we met,' said Niall. 'I saw a few pesky rumours flyin' about us, in fact.'

'Yeah,' Zoë cringed at the memory of the headlines. 'Yeah, there were a few.'

'So, shall I put your name on the door for next Friday?'

Zoë couldn't think of a reason to decline the offer.

'That'd be great.'

'I'll see ya then.'

'Zoë?' The sound of her sister's voice came as a surprise. 'Are you still there?'

'Sorry about that,' she mumbled, still reeling.

'Who was it?'

'Well . . .' Zoë racked her brains one last time, to no avail. 'It was Niall King, from The Cheats.'

'*What?* As in, the guy who sings 'Anaesthetic'? The guy who's currently number one?'

'Um, yeah. He was inviting me to that charity gig they're doing at the Albion next Friday.'

'*What?!*' Tamsin screamed down the phone. 'What, my baby sister has a personal invitation to one of the most exclusive gigs of the year?'

'Well . . . it seems that way.'

'Ha!'

'Oh.' Zoë realised something. 'Oh, but I can't go. It's the night before my Candy Chicks gig.'

'Your what?'

'I'm . . . I'm supporting The Candy Chicks at the O2 Arena.'

Tamsin made a noise as though someone was strangling her.

'Well, actually I'm supporting the support act, if you know what I mean. Sorry – I forgot you didn't know.'

'Jeeeesus.'

'That's annoying, though – I wanna go to Niall's gig.'

'Well,' said Tamsin when she'd finally composed herself. 'It sounds as though you're a wanted lady. Who says you can't do both?'

Zoë thought for a second. It was conceivable, going to the party on the Friday, the night before the biggest gig of her life. She just had to make sure she stayed out of trouble. No alcohol, no paparazzi fodder. 'Maybe.'

'Do it,' urged Tamsin. 'You've been trying for so long to make a go of this and now it's finally happening – enjoy it.'

Zoë smiled. A familiar, warm glow enveloped her. 'Thanks, Tam.'

'Don't be silly. Oh, and you know what you said earlier, about me being perfect and you wishing you were more like me?'

'Yes?'

'I've spent the last twenty years wishing I could be more like you.'

54

'Spotlights!'

Zoë blinked as a row of high-wattage bulbs above her head burst into life. It was as though somebody had taken the sun and pointed it in her direction at close range.

'And . . . play.'

Zoë stepped up to the microphone and pretended to sing. Somewhere behind the row of ferocious lights there was movement: a crane arm swinging into place, screens showing flickering shots of the mute band from every conceivable angle. Zoë felt like a crew member on board some huge, circular spaceship.

Never, in all her years of performing, had she rehearsed for a gig. She had practised, in a musical sense, but this was different. This was everything *but* the music. It was the first time she'd been asked to consider exactly where on the stage she would stand, how high she liked the microphone and how much time she took between songs. Even at Brixton Academy the run-through hadn't covered such organisational minutiae.

'Finish song . . . And full band exits, stage left.'

Obediently, Zoë led the way back to the wings and let out a sigh of relief.

'That was great. Well done.' The woman with the headset smiled primly. 'Any questions?' She barely waited for a response. 'We'll be printing the set lists this week, so no changes please.'

Zoë nodded, edging her way back to the dressing room and exchanging a fraught look with her band mates.

'It's like ze Chinese army,' Christophe spat. 'No chance for spontaneity.'

'Well,' Tommy shrugged as he picked up his bag. 'I guess at forty pounds a pop, the fans wanna know they'll get a decent performance.'

'Stop it,' said Zoë. She was already feeling queasy at the thought of the twenty thousand-strong audience.

Christophe yanked open the door and motioned for Rod to follow. The bassist slowly collected together his things.

Tommy turned to Zoë. 'You want a lift?'

'If you're going . . .'

'It's on the way,' he smiled, grabbing her guitar case and heading out.

They waited for Christophe to slalom through the smattering of parked cars and then followed at a more reasonable pace.

'Nervous?' asked Tommy, glancing sideways at her.

Zoë watched as the reflection of the huge, canvas dome receded in the wing mirror. She hadn't been nervous up until today. Excited, yes, but not nervous. Playing at the O2 Arena was one of her greatest ambitions. Only a few years earlier, she had taken Ellie to a one-off Led Zeppelin gig at the arena. The seats had been right at the back of the stadium, half a kilometre away from the stage, but she could still remember the rush she'd felt when Jimmy Page had struck his first chord. She had sat there, feeling it, grinning at Ellie, thinking, *one day*. And now that day was only a week away.

'Fucking petrified.'

Tommy laughed.

She smiled at the side of his face as the car plunged into the dark orange glow of the Blackwall Tunnel. Tommy didn't seem to get nervous. Or if he did, he never showed it. Zoë poked at the array of wires and tape reel coming out of the car stereo.

The Beetle was of an age that preceded iPod docks and, by the look of it, even CD players.

'How does this work then?'

'Oh. You have to press power and play together.'

Zoë did so. Nothing happened.

'Then hold that cable at a certain angle, that's it, then press play on the iPod . . . There.'

Zoë turned up the volume as the opening track on The Strokes' debut album came crackling through the speakers. She let her head fall back, shielding her eyes as the gloom of the tunnel gave way to the milky pink sunset up ahead. Like a gas, the vibe filled the car and she breathed it in. She could feel it, displacing the stress of the long day, working its way into parts of her brain where the nagging doubts and nasty feelings lurked.

They hit rush hour traffic but neither of them seemed to mind. Zoë peered out as they crawled along Commercial Road, passing the flea-infested youth hostel that had, until a few weeks ago, been her home. It seemed as though so much had changed since then. In reality, little had. She still wasn't talking to her parents. She was still broke. She still needed a hit single in order to make ends meet. The only difference was that her manager had wangled her a free luxury pad and her A&R rep had given her a couple of lucky breaks.

Zoë's phone started buzzing against her leg. She ignored it and turned up the volume on the stereo. It was probably Gloria. Her calls had become a frequent occurrence, thanks to the recent deluge of media enquiries. It was mainly small scale requests: tinpot radio stations, obscure publications and digital TV shows that Zoë had never heard of, but it all added up. She owed a lot to the person who'd picked 'Bare-Faced Cheek' for the Zest commercial.

The ad was running, although Zoë hadn't seen it. She had looked, of course. Six hours she had spent watching ITV the previous night. She'd even tried Googling the energy drink to see if the ad was online, but to no avail. It didn't matter, really. It was only her ego that was driving her to see it.

Tommy pulled up on Marlborough Road, leaving the engine running while he hauled Zoë's guitar out of the boot.

'D'you wanna come in?' she asked, feeling suddenly bold.

Tommy looked at her, lips puckered. 'That'd be . . . Actually, better not.'

'Right.' Zoë nodded, giving Tommy a few seconds in case he changed his mind. If nothing else, she wanted to share with him the incredible sound system in the pad.

'I've gotta . . .' He trailed off.

'Walk the dog?' she suggested, when the pause became painfully long.

'*Dog*?' Tommy frowned.

'Er . . .' It was Zoë's turn to falter. 'I thought you had a dog. You mentioned it once, when—'

'Oh.' He looked down at the ground. 'Ah. Yes.'

'What?'

'Um . . .' Tommy looked slightly embarrassed. 'Yeah, I remember saying that. But I don't actually have a dog.'

'Right,' she said, slowly. This was getting awkward. 'So why did you say you did?'

'I think,' said Tommy, still talking to the pavement, 'that was the night when we were having a drink after a gig and your boyfriend made an appearance. I . . . I hadn't realised you had a boyfriend, so I kinda . . . made up an excuse to leave.'

'Oh.' Zoë looked at the side of his face, trying to unravel the implications. As she did so, her phone went off again.

Tommy looked relieved. 'Always the way.' He smiled, swinging himself back into the driver's seat. 'See ya.'

It was Louis calling. Zoë would have gladly ignored the call for a second time, but Tommy was already putting the car in gear and revving the engine.

She leaned down and kissed him on the cheek through the open window. 'See you Wednesday.'

Tommy's strange behaviour was still on her mind when she picked up the call.

'Hi, Louis.'

'Hiiiiii. Listen, you haven't gotten back to me on this rider, sugar.'

'Oh.' Zoë sighed. She had just curtailed her conversation with Tommy in order to talk about the stupid rider that Louis had been banging on about for the last two weeks. She didn't care what they put in her dressing room before the gig. 'Can't you just put flowers or something?'

'It's kinda embarrassing, honey. The whole point of the rider is to be difficult. To check they're payin' attention. If they get the rider right, they'll get the stage equipment right.'

'Well . . .' Zoë frowned. 'I'm sort of hoping they'll get the stage equipment right anyway. It is the O2 Arena.'

'Yeah, okay,' Louis said, sounding miffed. 'But it's the principle. Come on, I'm not talking bunny rabbits here – just something challenging. Food? A special liquor?'

Zoë thought for a second, gently depositing her guitar inside the door of her flat. 'Okay,' she said, suddenly decisive. 'Put down a bottle of Extra Dry Vermouth.'

Louis made a gargling noise. 'You like that stuff? It's kinda like an old lady's drink, isn't it?'

Zoë smiled. 'Maybe. And add a bottle of Laphroaig, too.'

Louis seemed perplexed by her choice but didn't argue. He couldn't possibly know that Zoë had no intention of drinking the spirits herself – that she had decided, finally, that it was time to put an end to her ongoing feud with her parents. It wasn't even a decision that had consciously been made; it was more of a thought that had been floating around in the back of her mind ever since her conversation with Tamsin.

After The Candy Chicks gig, when all the fuss had died down

and her first single was out, she would go round and apologise. As a signed artist with an imminent album release, she would try to explain to her parents, one last time, how much this all meant to her and why she had behaved as she had done. And she'd make it clear that she wasn't just grovelling her way back into their good books to get at their money.

'I'll let them know. Oh – hey, Zoë?'

'Mmm?' Zoë was already thinking about dates and wondering whether she should ask Tamsin and Jonathan to come along too.

'Are you near a TV?'

Zoë quickly retuned to the conversation. She knew why Louis was asking. Without stopping to reply, she bounded across the room and reached for the remote.

'Oh my God!'

On the screen, two tanned, leggy blondes were swigging from bright green cans in the back of an open-top Mustang as it burned along a sun-drenched coastline. In the front seats were two perfect specimens of mankind and the soundtrack to the scene was the remastered chorus to 'Bare-Faced Cheek'. As the camera panned out it became evident that the young men were gaffer-taped at the wrists, and over the top of the last refrain, a testosterone-laden voice growled, 'Have a little Zest for life.'

'Well?' cried Louis.

Zoë laughed and muted the TV. She still maintained that the original version of the track would have been better, but it would have been churlish to complain. 'It's great.'

'They got a primetime slot, too. Right in the middle of the trashiest show ever made. Good going, girl. See you soon.'

Zoë put down the phone, glancing again at the TV. A montage of screaming fans, backstage frenzy and the familiar Talent Tout judging panel flashed up on the screen before a large, smoke-filled stage loomed into view. She was about to switch it off when the smoke started to clear and she saw the unmistakeable silhouette of the three-part band. A female band. Zoë stared. It was Dirty Money.

She unmuted the TV and watched as Shannon bashed together her sticks and kicked off the song. A moment later, Kate came in with a cheeky bassline that grew and grew until the pair of them were nearly at maximum volume. Shannon was grinning, clearly enjoying every second. But Zoë wasn't looking at Shannon. She was looking at Ellie, who was standing, staring into the auditorium, her hands clamped tightly to the strings of her guitar as she waited to come in. She looked petrified.

Eventually, the intro gave way to an explosion of vocals and harmonies and Ellie started to look more at home, her fingers working the frets, her mouth pressed up against the mike. Zoë couldn't work out how she felt. She couldn't deny that she was a little envious. Even though she didn't believe that Talent Tout was right for the girls, she couldn't help wanting to be up there with them on that smoky stage.

Zoë watched as the judges deliberated, asking the girls who had written the song, discussing the performance and pointing out Ellie's 'wooden stance'. Zoë felt like hurling something at them. *Of course she looks wooden,* she wanted to scream. *She's a guitarist, not a lead singer*! Ellie stood there, alternately blinking into the lights and looking down at her shoes. In the end, they were voted through, as Zoë knew they would be, but somehow she couldn't feel pleased. It was as though they'd been misunderstood.

Zoë switched off the TV and collapsed on the sofa. She *had* to move on. It didn't matter what the girls were doing now; they were free to make their own decisions. If they wanted to take a chance on Talent Tout, that was up to them. She didn't need to look out for them. They sure as hell wouldn't look out for her – in fact, they'd probably be pleased to see her fail, given recent events. She kicked off her shoes and pulled out the set list she'd scribbled down during the day. She had a gig to prepare for. She had to forget about the girls.

55

'Could you just check one more time?' Zoë shifted her weight onto the other foot, shivering in the cool night air and feeling distinctly uncomfortable.

'Sorry, madam.' The man shook his head. 'Your name's not on the list.'

Zoë glanced at the other tuxedo-clad bodybuilder. He was staring straight ahead, into the glare of the flashing cameras.

She couldn't turn around and walk out. She just couldn't. It had been embarrassing enough making her way up the carpeted steps in the shimmering, white sequinned affair that Gloria had convinced her to wear; there was no way she could face the humiliation of walking back down again.

'If you could just move to one side, madam,' said the doorman as Alicia Keys sashayed towards them on the arm of a tall, bronzed Adonis.

Mortified, Zoë started to retreat. It didn't make sense. Niall King had invited her. He had called her especially to say that he was putting her name on the guest list. Surely it would be too much of a coincidence to assume that one of the other Zoës in his address book had also sparked tabloid rumours about the pair of them?

She took a deep breath and prepared to slope off, casting a final glance in the direction of the party inside. Through the gap in the door she could see a jumble of silk dresses, toothy smiles, bow ties and glossy manes of hair. Blue eyes. Freckles. She squinted harder. Yes, it was definitely him. He was standing in the lobby, greeting guests as they flowed through the door.

'Niall!' she cried, instinctively. He didn't hear. Unfortunately, one of the doormen did.

'Look, madam, please—'

The next thing she noticed was a shrieking noise coming from the crowd and a rush of air, caused, she realised, by the Mexican wave of cameras. The Irish rock star was standing in the doorway, looking at her. The doorman turned his back on her, leaning towards Niall and saying something she couldn't quite catch.

'Yeah,' he said eventually, face tilted towards the doorman but eyes focused on Zoë. 'Yeah, that's fine.'

For a moment, all she could feel was a mixture of relief and gratitude. Then she realised that Niall was speaking to her.

'Apologies,' he said, smiling. 'Probably a guest list mixup. I remember you from, er . . .'

'The after-show party back in May,' she reminded him, slightly thrown by his apparently vague recollection of their encounter. Was this really the guy who had called her with a personal invitation to the party?

'Right, yeah.' Niall nodded unconvincingly. 'Well, I gotta sound-check. I'll see you later. Enjoy the night.'

Still shaking, still thinking about the peculiar state of affairs, Zoë headed straight for the glass table laden with cocktails. The whole ground floor of the Albion Hotel, it seemed, had been transformed into some kind of fairytale world. There were flowers entwined around banisters, candles flickering in corners and coloured spotlights reflecting off the polished marble floor. But she wasn't looking at the decor as she reached for the cocktail and then stopped, remembering her self-made promise. She was looking at the people.

It was like walking through the pages of *Hello* magazine. Everybody, without exception, looked as glamorous and perfect as their airbrushed, printed counterparts. The men were dressed in either black tie or a jeans-and-jacket combo, while the women were draped in ball gowns and cocktail dresses. Zoë walked through to the next room, deciding that it didn't matter whether Niall had meant to invite her or not.

The double doors marked 'Ballroom' were closed, presumably for the sound-check. Above the murmur of polite conversation it was just possible to make out the angry twang of a bass guitar.

Non-alcoholic Pina Colada in hand, Zoë roamed the ground floor of the hotel, doing her best to look glamorous. There were so many rooms in the place that it was actually possible to wander indefinitely without having to worry about coming across as a loner. Despite Niall's choice of words on the phone, the event was proving anything but cosy.

Zoë was perfecting the aloof, purposeful look as she headed back to the bar for a second time, when she felt a hand slide around her waist.

'Hello, gorgeous.'

Zoë turned, her heart fluttering and then sinking as she saw who it was. 'Hi, Ben.'

'Some party, eh?' He lurched sideways.

Zoë nodded, wondering how much he'd had to drink and how he had wheedled himself an invitation. The Cheats were signed to Polydor, not Vicinity. Then she noticed the cluster of smirking, pasty-faced young men, standing a few feet away. They were the ones she'd seen coked up at the after-show party.

'Tasty stuff,' he said, lifting his glass and reluctantly dropping his other arm as Zoë slithered free. 'Not bad for a freebie.'

Zoë nodded, trying to think of an excuse to slip away. She felt slightly annoyed; it was as though Ben's presence somehow devalued the privilege of being here.

'Hey, Zoë. Let's do some ch—'

Thankfully, just as the fumes from Ben's breath hit her nostrils, a loud gong sounded nearby, sending him reeling backwards.

'Woah . . .' Ben steadied himself, hands clamped over his ears. 'No need for that!'

The doors of the ballroom were flung open and slowly, the beautiful people filed through.

'Shall we?' suggested Ben, holding out an unsteady arm.

It wasn't an offer Zoë wanted to accept, but nor was it one she could refuse. Forcing a smile, she hooked her arm through his.

Gigs didn't come much more exclusive than this, thought Zoë, looking around as The Cheats came onstage to a patter of polite applause. There were probably a couple of hundred guests in the room but every one of them – with the exception of Ben and the pissed-up industry boys, and possibly Zoë too – had earned their place in the crowd. They were the showbiz elite.

A hush fell on the ballroom. Niall looked round and gave his drummer the nod.

'*I always said they'd be huge,*' Ben stage-whispered in her ear. Zoë cringed, pretending not to hear him.

'*I told Jenson we should get them on Vicinity,*' he hissed.

She nodded curtly as, thankfully, The Cheats kicked off with one of their loudest hits.

Ben continued to spit unintelligible words in her ear throughout the whole of the song, seemingly oblivious to the dirty looks. By the end of the fifth number, a void had formed in the crowd around them.

'*I was in a band, you know,*' muttered Ben, just as Niall embarked on a soulful acoustic track from their first album. '*I don't mind telling you, we were pretty shit-hot.*'

Zoë had just made the decision to slip out before someone threw them out, when Niall announced that the next song would be their last.

'. . . and I just wanna say thank you, everyone, for being here tonight. We've raised close to a million pounds for Famine Relief and it's not too late to donate. Please, dig deep . . .'

'*Dig deep, you rich cunts!*' Ben muttered hoarsely.

Zoë looked at the floor for the duration of The Cheats' final song. When they finished, Zoë slipped away, joining the throng as it spilled through the labyrinth of hallways and rooms, relieved to be free of the lecherous scout.

It was enlightening, watching the party through sober eyes. Supermodels stumbled in their six-inch heels, heartthrobs made bold plays for passing totty. The paps would have a field day later on.

Zoë had just picked up what she'd decided would be her last Virgin Sea Breeze when she heard a familiar voice in her ear – literally, in her ear.

'*You gotta hear this . . . It's like, amazing. Incredible . . .*'

Zoë's shoulders fell as she realised that Ben had caught up with her.

He lunged forwards, trying to grab her with both hands. '*This guy . . . Fuck me . . . You've never heard anything like it . . .*'

Zoë pulled away, watching as Ben's eyes rolled around in their sockets. He clearly thought he was telling her something interesting; his hands kept pawing at her as though he needed to express the magnitude of his revelation.

'*Seriously . . . You've got to hear it for yourself . . . Out of this world . . .*'

When it became clear that she didn't have any choice, Zoë allowed Ben to lead her through the hotel to a room at the back. She had walked past several times that evening, but what with the Arabian rugs and cushions all over the floor, the low-level lighting and the scent of shisha pipes and candles, she'd assumed it to be some kind of couples' retreat. Judging by the bodies that lay, in various states of consciousness, Zoë assumed she'd not been far off.

'*Check this out*,' Ben hissed into her ear as his hand slid down onto her backside.

Removing the hand, Zoë followed him across the dimly lit

room, suspicious that this might be some sort of drunken ruse to snare her. Then she heard it: a quiet, tuneless yowl that sounded like a young child trying to play a violin whose strings were made of elastic bands.

'*Wow*,' gasped Ben, trying to nestle his head into the crook of her neck. '*He's like . . . Mozart or something. It's like a whole nother level of music. I've gotta get this guy signed*!'

Zoë was about to advise against the idea when she saw something glinting in the corner of the room, behind the musician. White eyes, white teeth, shining out from a dark face somewhere at floor level amidst a jumble of flesh. Pale flesh. Cleavages, midriffs, legs. She felt her pulse quicken.

Ben trailed off, following her gaze and then looking back at Zoë. '*Is that . . .*'

Zoë was squinting into the darkness, desperately willing it not to be him.

'*Aren't you supposed to be—*'

'Shut up.' Zoë pushed him aside and walked over to the guy on the floor, her hope fading with every step. It was him. There was no doubt. The man who had promised to whisk her away to Paris was sprawled on some African bedspread, his hands resting, like dark, inky shadows, on the waists of two stunning brunettes.

'Denzel?'

He looked up, slowly, and smiled. *Smiled*. Still fondling the beautiful models, he looked right at Zoë and flashed his giant, pearly teeth.

'I thought you were filming?' she challenged, not brave enough to ask the question she really wanted to ask.

'Hey, honey. Oh, yeah. Well, I thought so too but they re-scheduled a few things. We're flyin' out tomorrow.' His hand moved slightly in the darkness. One of the brunettes giggled.

Ben moved closer. '*Uh-oh*,' he muttered in her ear.

'Shut up,' snapped Zoë, still looking at Denzel. Several heads had popped up from the surrounding booths, but she didn't care.

'Hey, babes, come and join us down here,' Denzel laughed. 'Lose the goofer though.'

It took a few seconds for Ben to realise he'd been insulted. By the time the message hit home, Zoë was already halfway to the door, the pressure building behind her eyes. As she walked out there was a thud, then a cry and a collective scream. She didn't look back.

Ignoring the concierge's recommendations, Zoë stormed through the hotel lobby and down the steps. A few bored-looking photographers looked up and snapped her as she passed. She didn't care. They could report that her romance with Denzel was over, that she was distraught about the breakup, jealous, deranged, pregnant, whatever. She wasn't crying about Denzel; she was crying about her life.

It was a wakeup call. Suddenly, with crystal clarity, she saw it as an outsider would have seen it: a sham. The good-looking boyfriend with whom she had so much in common, the invitations to exclusive, high-profile events, the penthouse apartment, the stadium gigs, the support from her record label . . . it wasn't real. She had believed in it because she'd *wanted* to, but in truth, it was no more authentic than the stories she read about herself in the tabloids.

For weeks now – no, *months* – she had been hiding away in this cosy cocoon, creating a life for herself that looked and felt like the one she'd always dreamed of. But it was a hollow shell of an existence that contained nothing inside – no love, no friendship, no pride, no sense of self-worth or achievement. She marched along Euston Road, the high heels rubbing blisters in the backs of her heels. She wanted out. She wanted an end to this superficiality.

Ellie wasn't picking up. Zoë left a message, then tried Kate, then Shannon. No one was picking up. It was hardly surprising;

it was one o'clock in the morning. She knew she'd do better to wait until the next day but it felt as though she needed to tell them *now*, while it all made so much sense. She couldn't have them doubting her for a moment longer. Thumbing through her address book, Zoë found the number for Shannon's house phone. Someone would be up – someone was always up late in that place.

'Hello?'

'Oh, hi. It's Zoë here – a friend of Shannon's. Is she there?'

'No,' the girl stammered. 'She's at the hospital.'

'What? Why?'

'Oh, it's not her. It's her friend. One of her band mates took an overdose.'

56

Zoë hesitated before she entered, looking through the glass panel in the door and taking a deep, shaky breath. They were both there, Shannon and Kate, hunched over on grey, padded chairs, clutching empty plastic cups. Sam was there too, a few seats away, staring into space. He looked haggard, his eyes sunken and red behind curtains of greasy hair.

They looked up – first Kate, then Shannon, then Sam. Zoë forced herself forward, one foot in front of the other. She didn't know how the girls would react. Would they acknowledge her or ignore her? Welcome her or blame her? It was impossible to tell.

Kate rose to her feet. Her cheeks looked gaunt and hollow. Zoë slowed to a halt, trying to quell the nausea inside her. Then suddenly, Kate was launching herself across the waiting room, flinging her arms around Zoë's neck.

Zoë couldn't speak for a moment; words couldn't express the conflicting emotions that were colliding inside her: self-loathing and shame, for what she had done to the girls, relief at Kate's reaction and a sickening, bottomless fear of what might have happened to her best friend.

She was still buried in Kate's hair, still trying to articulate herself, when she realised that Shannon was hovering nearby. On her face was a grim smile. Zoë felt a tear roll down her cheek as she reached out and pulled Shannon into the embrace.

Sam stepped forward as they pulled apart. They hugged, briefly.

'How is she?' asked Zoë.

'They gave her an antidote to bring her round,' he explained. 'But they're worried about her breathing.'

'It slowed down to a stand-still,' said Kate, quietly. 'That's what happens, apparently. Everything slows right down.'

'That's all we know.' Shannon looked at the floor. It was the first time that Zoë had ever heard a quiver in her voice.

Sam sat down, then stood up again almost immediately and started pacing.

'Maybe we should ask someone.'

'They'll tell us if there's anything to report.'

'It's been nearly two hours.'

Sam delved into his pocket and brought out a tin and a packet of Rizlas. With a trembling hand, he rolled a cigarette and placed it between his lips. 'Can you come and get me if there's any news?'

Zoë nodded, perching on the seat next to Shannon as Sam slipped out.

'How did it happen?'

'She took heroin, Zoë!' Kate screeched hysterically. 'What was she thinking? She's never done anything like that before!'

Zoë opened her mouth to remind them about the time she'd been summoned to Ellie's caravan, but then stopped herself. *They didn't know.* Ellie had told the girls about the incident, but she had obviously glossed over the fact that she'd smoked, crunched and snorted every illegal substance she'd been able to lay her hands on that night.

'It's my fault,' said Shannon, shaking her head at the floor. 'I think she was stressed about the Talent Tout thing.' She looked at Zoë. 'We're supposed to be flying to Norway on Monday for the overseas round.'

Kate looked up. Her eyes were brimming with tears. 'I was the one who kept telling her to pull out, so we could go with Hot Rocks. She obviously didn't know what to do.'

'Stop it, both of you.' Zoë glanced sideways at Kate and

then Shannon. 'I'm the one who should be feeling guilty. I should've seen this coming.'

'How? You're not the one who's been bossing her—'

'She's done it before.'

They both looked up.

'That night. When she broke down on me. She didn't tell you, did she? She'd taken a fucking pharmacy.'

Shannon and Kate were staring at her.

Zoë sighed, hating herself even more as the words came out. 'She hadn't overdosed, but she was a wreck. I think Sam's been taking some harder stuff lately.'

Shannon and Kate both glanced anxiously towards the door.

'I should've warned you. I should've been looking out for her.' Zoë looked down, her vision blurring as the tears formed a film over her eyes and started dropping heavily onto the floor. She felt an arm around her shoulders, which only made the sobs come thicker and faster. 'I'm so selfish.'

Kate put her head against hers. 'No, you're not.'

'I *am*.' Zoë shrugged her away. She didn't deserve tenderness. 'I've been so fucking wrapped up in my own world, I haven't had time for anyone else.'

She trailed off, looking up as Sam re-entered the room. He was wearing a different expression: something akin to a smile.

A nurse emerged behind him, looking around at the anxious faces.

'Ellie's stable,' she said. 'It looks as though there's been no permanent damage to her internal organs and her breathing is returning to normal, but we'd like to keep her in for forty-eight hours. There's a chance her lungs will suffer a relapse.'

Zoë closed her eyes, feeling a fresh surge of tears coming on, but this time they were tears of relief.

'Thank God,' Shannon sighed.

'Can we see her?' asked Kate.

'Not yet. You'll have to wait until tomorrow evening. There's

nothing you can do, so I suggest you go home and get some rest.'
The nurse dipped her head deferentially and disappeared back
down the corridor.

The tension dispersed immediately. It was as though someone
had slashed through it with a knife. There was more hugging,
more crying, laughter. Sam tried to insist that he stuck around,
'just in case', but Kate, ever practical, persuaded him there was
nothing he could do and eventually, they managed to bundle
him into a taxi.

Zoë yawned as they waited on the deserted street for another
cab. It was three o'clock in the morning. For the last two hours,
the shock and anxiety had carried her through, but now it had
all worn off and she suddenly felt exhausted.

'Haven't you got a big gig coming up?' asked Kate, yawning
in sympathy, while Shannon danced around in the middle of
the road.

Zoë blinked at her. 'Yeah.' She had actually forgotten about The
Candy Chicks gig. 'Jesus. I'm playing at the O2 Arena tomorrow
night.'

'As in . . . tonight?'

'Er, yeah.' Zoë nodded. The prospect seemed rather surreal. A
few hours ago, if someone had asked her about the next twenty-
four hours of her life, she would have gone into overdrive at the
thought of what lay ahead. All of a sudden though, it no longer
seemed important.

'Hop in!' Shannon waved them over. She had flagged down a
car that didn't look the least bit like a cab.

Squashed together in the back of the old BMW, inhaling the
secondary smoke of the driver's spliff, the girls lapsed into
silence. Zoë's thoughts drifted from her own imminent gig to
the girls' endeavours. They were due to fly to Norway in twenty-
four hours; there was no way Ellie would be in a fit state by
then.

'What will you do?' she asked. 'About the audition.'

'Fuck the audition,' Shannon replied quickly. 'That show put Ellie in hospital, for God's sake. We're not flying to Norway.'

Kate let out a sigh of relief. 'I'm so glad you said that. I wasn't looking forward to another row.'

'You know,' said Shannon, leaning forward and looking past Zoë at the bassist. 'I never thought I'd say this, but you were right. We should've gone with the record deal – not the overhyped, trashy talent show.'

Kate shook her head vehemently. 'No. *No.* I was wrong too. We all were. Hot Rocks would've been no better than Talent Tout. They would've screwed us just like Vicinity screwed Zoë.'

'So . . .' Zoë was wondering where this left them.

'So we're not doing either,' Kate said firmly. 'We're not chasing fame any more.'

Zoë let her head fall sideways onto Kate's shoulder and smiled. Perhaps it was the effect of whatever it was the driver was smoking, but she was beginning to feel wholly tranquil. As they drew up outside Shannon's flat, she watched fondly as the drummer climbed the steps to her door, turning and yelling something about visiting hours and then disappearing into the darkness.

Too tired to shift into the empty seat, Zoë stayed slumped against Kate's collarbone as they pulled away. She was just drifting into a shallow sleep when she realised the bassist was talking.

'. . . about James,' she said. 'I should've told you, not left it for you to discover.'

Zoë jolted upright and looked at her. With the emotional trauma, all thoughts of James had been pushed to the back of her mind.

'I didn't know how to tell you,' Kate went on. 'To begin with, I didn't think there was anything going on. I went round to pick up a few things from your old place and he offered me a drink . . .'

'Stop it,' said Zoë, shaking her head.

'No, not a *drink* drink—'

'No, I mean stop justifying it. It's fine.' She frowned, trying to

398

iron out her feelings as she went along. She wasn't sure whether it really was fine; it certainly hadn't seemed fine a few weeks ago. Either way, though, Kate didn't deserve to feel bad about that on top of everything else.

'Sorry.' Kate put her hand on the door handle as they pulled up outside her flat.

Zoë fixed a smile on her lips, trying not to think about the fact that James was probably up there, staying awake for her. It was too weird.

'It doesn't matter,' said Zoë, leaning over and hugging her tightly.

Kate clambered out and then ducked back inside. 'Text me when you get home,' she said, pressing a tenner into Zoë's hand and cocking her head in the direction of the driver, who was lighting an over-stuffed joint as he re-tuned the radio.

Zoë smiled, waving as Kate's blonde head receded to a little dot in the rear-view mirror. It was impossible not to think about James as she rolled around, semiconscious, in the back of the car. Kate seemed so much more confident now; Zoë couldn't help wondering whether James was good for her.

She hadn't noticed until now quite how badly matched he and Zoë had been, by the end. Years ago, they'd been perfect together, but they'd both changed. He was too reliable, too safe. He was no longer the guy who rode shopping trolleys down Lambeth Hill. She was too much of a maverick. His conformity got on her nerves and equally, her rebellious streak left him nonplussed. But perhaps James was exactly what Kate needed.

'St James's Park, yeah?' mumbled the driver, through the haze of marijuana smoke.

Zoë leaned forward and repeated the address. Then she stopped, hunched over with her head in the fumes.

'Sorry,' she said. 'Could you turn the radio up?'

He yanked on the volume knob. Zoë fell back against the seat. There was no mistaking it. That was her voice coming through on the crackly car stereo. They were playing 'Bare-Faced Cheek'.

'What station is this?' she yelled, feeling a suppressed sense of exhilaration – even though it was three in the morning.

He bent down and squinted at the controls through the haze. 'Radio One. It's all crap at this time o'night, innit.'

Zoë laughed. Until a few hours ago, she would have cared that the cabbie didn't like her song. She would have felt desperate for people to like her first single. Now, though, it didn't matter. She didn't care what people thought; she didn't even care whether it made it into the charts. It was as though she had zoomed out on the picture and seen everything in perspective. There were bigger things in life, she was finally beginning to realise, than 'making it'.

57

'I can't do it.' Zoë slumped forward, running her hands through her freshly-sprayed hair.

'Sure you can.' Louis wandered up to the minibar and squinted at its contents. 'Like I said, just pretend it's a regular gig. Everybody gets nervous; you just have to push on through.'

'It's not *nerves.*' She looked up and glared at the back of his head. Tommy caught her eye and gave a sympathetic grimace. 'It's Ellie. I need to speak to her before I go on.'

'Look, we've all got our superstitions, honey. One of my acts claims he needs to stand completely naked in a—'

'It's not a superstition!' Zoë screamed, pushing herself to her feet in the leather, thigh-high boots. Had the manager not listened to a word she'd said this afternoon? Had he somehow missed the part where she'd told him that her best friend had taken a life-threatening overdose? 'She's in *hospital.* I need to know she's okay.'

'Oh.' Louis nodded. 'Right. Why didn't you say?'

Zoë turned away from him, unable to bear the sight of his bloated face any longer. She checked her phone. There was still no word from the girls. They'd planned to arrive at the hospital at seven. It was now coming up for eight o'clock. She pressed redial and pulled the phone to her ear, letting her eyes roam the ludicrously well-equipped dressing room. It was smaller than the one she'd been given at Brixton Academy, but plusher, with comfier sofas, more realistic fake plants and a sixty-inch plasma screen TV eclipsing one wall. Kate's phone was off. So was Shannon's.

'Try not to think about it,' Louis suggested brightly.

Zoë looked at him, nostrils flaring.

'You got a big night ahead . . .' He reached down and pulled out one of the bottles that formed part of her rider, rolling the single malt Scotch in his palm.

'That's mine,' she reminded him.

'Hey, sugar! Don't stress. I know it's yours – although God knows why you didn't pick something *drinkable*.' He pulled a face at Christophe, who ignored him. 'Try to relax.'

The door swung open. 'Ten minutes,' said the woman, beaming and then disappearing again.

Zoë felt a brief flurry of nerves in her stomach on top of the sickening, dull ache of fear. Something was wrong. That was why they hadn't called. Ellie had suffered a relapse, or taken another overdose, or . . .

'Hey,' someone whispered, right next to her ear. It was Tommy. 'You okay? You need some air?'

Zoë took a deep breath and realised that she couldn't actually inhale properly. Maybe it was the PVC bodice, but it felt as though someone had placed a set of cast-iron jaws around her ribcage. She nodded.

'Won't be a sec,' Tommy muttered in Louis's direction as they left the room.

Zoë tried to suck in a lungful of air. 'Thanks.'

'Not sure we'll actually get anywhere near fresh air,' he warned, looking up and down the corridor and plumping for the route that led away from the stage.

'I don't care. I just needed to get away from that moron.'

They found themselves in a small lounge area with vending machines and plastic seats. For a minute, they didn't speak.

'Is it just Ellie?' asked Tommy, eventually.

Zoë sighed, leaning back on one of the chairs. Tommy was way too perceptive.

'I guess not.'

He didn't probe further, but she told him anyway.

'The situation with Ellie made me think about everything else. What I want. What I'm doing.' She looked at him. 'I don't know if this is right for me.'

Tommy held her gaze for several seconds, then, slowly, he moved closer, gently touching her bare arm.

'You wanna know what I reckon?'

She nodded helplessly.

'I reckon you should save your thinking for half an hour's time. You can have all the doubts you like after the show, but in a couple of minutes you're gonna be walking out in front of a lot of people. You need to try and focus.'

Zoë straightened up and wrapped her arms around the guitarist as firmly as she dared in the outfit.

'Thanks,' she said, pulling away. 'You're right.'

Trying her best to take Tommy's advice, Zoë led the way back to the dressing room.

'Hey, sweetie. All chilled-out and ready to go?' Louis's eyebrows danced up and down.

Zoë turned away, determined not to let him wind her up.

'Oh, you had a call.'

She whipped round and snatched up her phone. There was one missed call and a voicemail from Kate. Zoë's heart started hammering against her tightly-wrapped chest.

'Hi, Zoë!' Kate sounded cheerful. The hammering receded a little. 'It's me. Us. We're all here.' There was a chorus of greetings. 'We just wanna say good luck.' More shouting, most notably Shannon. 'Sorry we can't be there, but we've heard Crazy Jeff will be making an appearance, so we're counting on a blow-by-blow account on the web tomorrow morning. Have a great night!' The message ended with a curtailed cacophony, again led by

Shannon, and the sound of a nurse telling Kate off for using the mobile phone. Zoë looked at Tommy.

'She's fine.'

He grinned back at her.

'Let's show this town what you're made of!' cried Louis, shooing them out as the woman held open the door.

The next few minutes flashed by very quickly. The music faded, the lights dimmed. Zoë barely had time to get nervous. With a quick glance at Tommy, then Christophe and Rod, she stepped out, carefully but confidently, onto the hundred-metre-long runway.

She had pictured this scene, in her head. She had visualised the packed stadium floor, the banners and flags and delirious fans, but the one thing she hadn't conceived was the volume. These were girls who probably hadn't even heard of her before tonight. They had come to hear The Candy Chicks, but *fuck* they were loud. Zoë could only imagine what they'd sound like when The Chicks themselves came on stage.

She strode up to the mike, smiling so hard that her cheek muscles were starting to ache. By the time she reached the little cross on the floor, her breathing was fast and shallow, a combination of nerves and exhaustion.

'Thank you,' she gasped, turning to the left, then the right. She flapped her hands meekly, trying to quieten the din. Then she looked round at her band mates. Tommy winked at her. Rod nodded from behind his lank hair. Christophe held up his sticks. She gave the signal.

In the run-up to the gig, Zoë had wondered what sort of reaction she might receive from The Candy Chicks fans. She guessed that they would be young – and they were. Nearly all of them were in their teens, most of them female. There was no guarantee that they'd like her music; it was, after all, more on the rock side of pop than The Candy Chicks. That morning, having slept fitfully for a couple of hours, it had taken at least an hour to shrug off the nightmare that the audience had comprised angry hospital staff who had booed her off the stage.

In the event, she needn't have worried. Perhaps it was the size of the auditorium or the sheer number of fans – or maybe, she considered, they actually loved her music – but the cries of excitement were bouncing off the concrete tiers, echoing from the rafters and coming at her in deafening waves.

She ended the penultimate song and reached down for some water, taking the opportunity to catch her breath. It was only as she looked round to check the band was ready for their final song that she noticed the chanting. It was only a smattering of voices, most of them in the front few rows, but it was loud enough to be audible from the stage.

The chanting became a little louder, a little more coherent. Whole rows were catching on. Then she realised what they were saying: '*Bare-Faced Cheek*', '*Bare-Faced Cheek*'. They were calling out for her song.

Zoë turned, nodded for Tommy to begin and launched into the song. It seemed unbelievable that word could spread so fast. It had only just made it onto the radio, yet already people recognised it as one of hers. Some of them even seemed to know the *words*.

Zoë raised her guitar to the crowds, thanked them and led her band offstage. A mob surrounded her as she reached the wings: Louis, Harry, Ben, Gloria, Gloria's daughter, a couple of people she vaguely recognised from the label and a handful of strangers.

'That was fantastic!'

'Incredible.'

'You *nailed* it, Zoë.'

'You have star written all over you . . .'

Zoë couldn't stop smiling. She felt weightless, as though she might float away if she didn't hold onto something. *This* was the rush that people talked about. She batted away the compliments, allowing herself to be squeezed and mauled by various people as the adrenaline raced through her bloodstream. She made it back to the dressing room and then promptly collapsed on the sofa.

'Well done,' Tommy said quietly, as Gloria started warbling at her from the other side of the room.

Zoë sat up, making the effort to look him in the eye. 'Thanks.'

'Zoë!' There was more whooping and shrieking. 'Someone here to see you!'

She looked over and saw Tamsin and Jonathan in the doorway, proudly brandishing their backstage passes. Zoë beckoned them over.

'Amazing,' said Tamsin, shaking her head and biting her bottom lip as she squeezed onto the sofa next to Zoë.

Jonathan nodded. 'I can't believe that was you, up there.'

Zoë smiled, glancing from Jonathan's face to Tamsin's then back again. Tam's jaw was quivering. 'You're not tearing up, are you?'

Tamsin burst out laughing, or crying, it was difficult to tell which, and threw her arms around Zoë's neck.

'Okay,' Louis bellowed, to the room at large. 'Who's for a drink?' He reached into the minibar. 'This is the start of a beautiful thing . . .'

Zoë looked at him, her smile suddenly fading.

'Sorry, no.'

'Eh?' He cracked open a beer and held it out for someone to take. 'Whaddya mean?'

Ben crept forward and plucked the bottle from his grasp.

'I mean, I'm not staying for a drink, and this isn't the start of a beautiful thing.'

The room went quiet.

'Why not?' cried Louis, doing his best to keep up the jovial tone but his expression gave him away.

Zoë unzipped the long, leather boots and levered her sweaty

feet out. 'Because my friend's in hospital, like I told you. I'm going to see her.'

'Ah . . . yeah.' Louis nodded, pulling out another beer. 'Yeah, of course.'

'And as for the future,' Zoë went on, watching as her manager's grip tightened on the neck of the bottle, 'I'm afraid you got that wrong, too.'

Everybody was looking at her now. Zoë took a deep breath, looking at a spot on the wall opposite. This speech wasn't premeditated, but she knew what she needed to say.

'That was my last solo gig,' she said, still staring doggedly at the wall. 'I know it went well. And I know I could do it again and again, if I wanted to. But I don't. That's all there is to it.'

'Wait, Zoë—'

'Hang on—'

'It's just the adrenaline—'

Everyone wanted to speak at once. Louis reached over and tried to put a hand on her shoulder. She moved away. Harry kept trying to start the same sentence over and over again but Louis kept talking over him. Tamsin didn't say a word, but her horrified stare said it all.

'No,' Zoë shook her head, silencing the protests. She walked over to her belongings and pulled out her trainers. 'I'm quite serious. I've thought it all through. I'll pay back my advance – I just don't wanna do this any more. I'm not a solo artist.'

'But you *are*—' Harry was obviously thinking of the money the label had ploughed into her launch – money that would never be recouped if she didn't have that hit single.

'You can't just—'

'Yes I can,' said Zoë, sounding more confident than she felt. She hadn't had a chance to check her contract; she didn't know where she stood, legally. 'Can't I, Tamsin?' She looked at her sister. 'Tamsin's a lawyer,' she explained.

'Um, well, er . . .' Tamsin flashed her a pained expression. 'Yes,' she concluded, finally understanding what was required of her. 'Yes, I believe so.'

'So, if you'll excuse me, I've got to get to the hospital before the end of visiting hours. Jonathan, can you grab those bottles there?' She nodded at the spirits on the sideboard and started gathering her belongings.

Zoë led Tamsin and Jonathan through the maze of backstage corridors, not looking round until they'd arrived at one of the side exits.

'Jesus!' cried Tamsin, panting a little as they hit the cold air. 'Talk about putting me on the spot!'

Zoë grinned, pulling a jacket out of her bag and wrapping it around her. She hadn't felt this happy in a long, long time.

'Sorry. I should've warned you. You could've lied, anyway. Nobody there would've known.'

Tamsin's protest was curtailed by the thud of footsteps.

'Zoë!'

Tommy burst through the door, bent double and panting.

'I know you've gotta run,' he said, drawing a breath and looking at Zoë, one hand on her upper arm. 'I just wanted to say . . . Before it's too late . . . Are you sure this is what you want?'

Zoë met his eye, hesitating before she replied. A moment ago, she had felt euphoric. Her mind had been made up, the sense of liberation overwhelming. Now, she was feeling a twinge of regret.

'I'm sorry, Tommy. I've just done you out of a job. I didn't want to have to do that to you – I love playing with you guys, but—'

'No!' Tommy rolled his eyes. 'I'm not talking about my job. I'm talking about *you*. What *you* want. I mean . . . I hope I didn't put you off with all that talk of getting screwed over . . .?'

Zoë shook her head. She felt bad about ending the Zoë Kidd show, for the sake of her musicians – but for no other reason.

408

She probably *was* still high from the performance, but this decision had been a long time coming; she knew what she was doing.

'Don't worry,' she said, smiling. 'It wasn't you who put me off; it was the industry. I learned my lesson, just like you.'

Tommy nodded, eyes narrowed, as if only half-believing her.

'I should go.' Zoë started to retreat, wishing she didn't have to rush off. She wanted to tell him everything: why she had quit, what she intended to do now, how bad she felt about leaving the band that was just beginning to feel like hers. 'I'm . . . I'm sorry about the job.'

'Zoë,' Tommy looked at her, holding her at arm's length.

She met his gaze and realised he was smiling. He was *beaming*, in fact. 'What?'

'I don't need the job.' He glanced over to where Tamsin and Jonathan were standing, a few metres away. It was as though he was toying with the idea of telling her something. Then he looked back at her, decision made. 'Your friend, Niall King, has just had a number one hit.'

Zoë frowned, unable to see the relevance of this fact. Niall King had indeed spent several weeks at number one with The Cheats' latest single.

'What's . . .' She trailed off, suddenly realising. 'No way . . .' She recognised the modest twinkle in his eye. 'Did you write 'Anaesthetic'?'

Tommy didn't need to reply.

'Oh my God . . .'

'Go,' he urged, pushing her gently away. 'Gimme a call sometime.'

Zoë hugged him tightly, overwhelmed with awe and pride. Then she turned and hurried down the covered walkway.

Jonathan cleared his throat. 'Er, how were you planning to get to the hospital?'

Zoë looked out at the endless rows of parked cars, glinting in

409

the floodlights. Tommy had driven her over that afternoon. 'Tube, I guess.'

Tamsin rolled her eyes. 'You'll never get there before midnight. We'll give you a lift.'

'The only problem being . . .' Jonathan looked at her meaningfully.

'Ah.' Tam nodded, slowly.

Zoë tried to decipher their expressions. 'What's going on?'

'I'll call them,' said Tamsin.

'Call who?'

Tamsin shook her head and wandered off, phone pressed against her ear.

A minute later, two silhouettes came hurrying out of the main entrance.

'Is that . . .' Zoë stared in disbelief. 'Is that *Mum and Dad*?'

Tamsin nodded awkwardly. Zoë stood for a second, struggling to comprehend what was going on. Then she dropped her belongings on the tarmac and rushed over to meet them.

They hugged and kissed and looked at each other for a few seconds before speaking. Then eventually, Zoë found something to say.

'Is that . . . Is that a denim shirt you're wearing, Dad?'

At that point, her mum started crying too, reaching out for Zoë's arm and telling her, over and over again, how proud they both felt and how sorry they were for dismissing her music for so long.

'. . . and to think we've never been to one of your *gigs*,' she said, pronouncing the last word as though it was a worthy new addition to her vocabulary.

'Quite something,' muttered her father, nodding earnestly at his daughter. '*Quite* something.'

Quickly, Zoë explained the urgency of the situation.

'Come on!' yelled Tamsin, unlocking the Nissan Micra and waving them over. 'The sat-nav's bust, so Jonathan's map-reading. Which means you lot will have to pile into the back.'

Zoë couldn't help laughing as they writhed and squirmed, trying to find an arrangement that worked for three long-legged adults. A few moments ago, she had been staring fame and fortune in the face: the parties, the private jets, the chauffeur-driven cars . . . And she had turned her back on it all, for this.

'Don't you mind people making all that noise when you're trying to sing?'

Patiently, Zoë tried to explain to her mother the concept of a gig.

'And who's in charge, so to speak? I mean, you don't have a conductor or anything . . . How do the other musicians know what you're doing when you're facing the audience?'

'They listen. We have amps facing us, too.'

'Amps?'

Zoë groaned. Eventually, they pulled up outside the hospital.

'Oh.' Zoë remembered something as she was ejected, head first, from the back of the car. 'I got something for you. Jonathan, have you got those . . .?'

He rummaged around at his feet and pulled out the bottles.

'Oh!' cried Zoë's mother, admiring the Cinzano and leaning over to check out her husband's Laphroaig. 'What's this for?'

Zoë hoisted her guitar onto her shoulder. 'To say sorry.'

'You shouldn't have!'

'Well, I didn't, exactly,' Zoë admitted. 'It was my rider.'

'Who's your rider?'

Zoë grimaced, slamming the door shut and pointing at Tamsin's fiancé. 'Jonathan will explain,' she yelled.

'Zoë?' Her father wound the window down and stuck his head out. His breath formed a cloud around his face. 'I meant to say.' He cleared his throat, looking momentarily awkward. 'The inheritance money. I had no right to judge you on how you'd spend it. Please, take it. Use it however you wish. You were right; there's nothing wrong with taking a risk every once in a while.'

Zoë watched speechlessly as the car pulled away. She turned

411

towards the hospital entrance, feeling an irrepressible grin spread across her face. It wasn't the money; it was the words. For months now, she'd been plagued by this rift that had formed between them. Like a festering wound, she knew it was there; it kept her awake at night, but she couldn't seem to do anything about it. Now, finally, it had healed over.

'Hurry up, you lazy cow!' Shannon hissed loudly, prompting the occupants of surrounding beds to look up. Ellie had been moved to an open ward to recuperate.

Zoë bounded over, keeping the long coat wrapped around her to conceal the latex underneath.

'Sorry,' she gasped, leaning in to see Ellie's face. Her cheeks were pale and there were dark rings around her eyes, but she was smiling.

'Well, honestly, Zoë.' Ellie looked at her with mock annoyance. 'You know how I hate it when people are late.'

Zoë raised an eyebrow. 'Don't be selfish now, Ellie; you know how I hate it when people put themselves ahead of everyone else.'

58

'This is madness, Zoë.' Jenson looked at her, brow furrowed.

'Your single's still getting *major* airplay,' said Harry encouragingly.

'You know you've been asked to perform at the Universal showcase next month?' Louis pitched in.

'And The Candy Chicks have said they want you supporting on their next tour,' added Ben.

Zoë sighed as the men went on. They had been talking at her like this for about ten minutes. It was as though her explanation had passed right over their heads. They were so absorbed in their midweek chart positions and revenue streams that they couldn't begin to imagine that there were other factors influencing her decision.

'Have you any *idea* how hard it is to get into the Ones To Watch list these days?'

Zoë nodded wearily. Jenson was referring to her debut single, 'Bare-Faced Cheek', which had entered the charts at a fairly respectable number fourteen that week. She was pleased, of course, but her mind was made up.

'I just don't understand,' said Harry, tugging fretfully at his wiry sideburn. 'You've got all the ingredients. You're talented, good-looking, *very* PR-able—'

Zoë smiled, shaking her head. He was trying to flatter her.

'Thanks, but I told you. I want to use the ingredients to make something different.'

Harry looked at her, perplexed. 'But why?'

'Yes. *Why?*' Jenson leaned forward, looking directly at Louis. He obviously felt that his team had been duped into taking her on. 'And why sign a three-album deal if you had no intention of sticking around?' he asked, turning to Zoë.

She met his eye. At the beginning of the meeting, it hadn't been clear where the balance of power lay, but as the minutes ticked by, it was becoming increasingly obvious that she didn't need to worry. Jenson's fraying nerves were all the evidence she needed to confirm that this was a last-ditch attempt by Vicinity to woo her back into the fold.

'I did intend to stick around,' she explained, 'but over the course of the last few months, I've seen things that have made me change my mind.'

Jenson pressed his fingers into the corners of his eyes, clearly too furious to ask Zoë what she had seen. 'Alex,' he said, looking in the direction of the Universal lawyer. 'Presumably this is in breach of contract?'

'Well,' the lawyer pulled a face. 'Assuming the artist wishes to pursue other commercial musical projects, yes. Legally, Zoë's next two albums belong to Vicinity.'

Charles McCarthy-Smith cleared his throat.

'As my client has explained,' he said, with spectacular flamboyance, 'she has no intention of pursuing other commercial musical projects. She simply wishes to lay down her tools.'

Jenson glared at the lawyer.

'Contractually, she has an obligation to produce two further albums for Vicinity. However, I should warn you that these albums may take some time.' He looked at Zoë and smiled. 'Some *considerable* amount of time.'

Zoë managed to stay calm. Inside, she was jumping about with glee. The tables were turned. She was the one in control, while

Jenson and co. were feeling the pain of being contractually shafted.

'As they say,' Charles went on, '*you can't force Thierry Henry to play.*'

Zoë smiled, catching her lawyer's eye.

Harry appeared somewhat agitated, but he managed to form one of his grandfatherly smiles. 'How about this,' he said. 'How about you stick around to promote your first album, then we can have another little chat in a few months' time? We can talk about releasing you properly from the label, perhaps.'

'Assuming you recoup,' Jenson put in.

Zoë shook her head slowly, enjoying every second. 'Why d'you need *me* to promote the album?'

There was a polite ripple of laughter that implied they all thought she was joking.

'I'm serious,' she said, stony-faced. 'Practically everything else has been done without my input. The songwriting, the re-mastering, the album artwork, the branding . . . You obviously don't need me to shift copies.'

There was an outcry from all around the table, with words like 'valued input' and 'integral part' being bandied about. Zoë just smiled. For the past three months, she had desperately wanted to be more involved in the process, but the label had shut her out. Now, she was trying to curtail her involvement and suddenly, they were falling over themselves to bring her back.

'As far as I can see,' she said, silencing the hubbub, 'I'm legally entitled to walk through that door. So if it's okay with you, that's what I'm gonna do.' She stood up.

'You do realise you can't sign to another label?' called Jenson as she left the table. 'You can't release any material, can't play any more stadium gigs, can't appear on TV . . .?'

Zoë turned and looked at her lawyer. He nodded calmly.

'But I can still play pub gigs with my band.'

She smiled beatifically at Jenson and then swept out of the room.

It was exactly the result she'd been after. She was, in theory, still under contract with Vicinity – she would be for the rest of her life. But that meant nothing, as far as she was concerned. She couldn't sign to a label with Sony or Warner or anywhere else – not even with Dirty Money, but she knew that she'd never want to. She had seen enough of the soulless, corrupt inner workings of the industry that she no longer wanted any part of it. For her, pub gigs were enough.

Charles caught up with her as she was waiting for the lift.

'Happy?' he asked.

'Very.'

'Well, it's been a pleasure.'

'The pleasure's all mine.' Zoë grinned. 'Especially as Vicinity's footing your bill.'

Charles chuckled as they stepped into the lift.

'Actually,' said Zoë, looking up at the lawyer and waiting to catch his eye. 'Perhaps you can help me on something.'

Charles eyed her warily. 'Hold on . . . You're not planning to sign with another label? I did make that clear, didn't I . . .?'

'Perfectly,' Zoë smiled. 'No, this is something else entirely.'

59

'You reckon people will remember us?'

Zoë surveyed the familiar backstage cupboard and smiled. 'I dunno. I'm sure we'll get the usual cat-calls until you shut them up with your solo.'

Ellie looked away bashfully, then suddenly turned, letting out a little gasp of excitement. 'Hey! We could play one of *your* songs! We could play "My Bubble!"'

'We could,' Zoë mused, opening her guitar case and pulling out the beloved Fender. Since its release just over a week ago, 'My Bubble' had proved a surprise hit across the nation, with the popified track making it to number three in the previous week's charts. It was getting sickening amounts of airplay, even now. They *could* add the song to the set list. The Mad Cow crowd would probably appreciate a taste of the unsweetened version. But somehow, the idea didn't appeal.

'Oh.' Ellie looked at her. 'You don't want us covering your songs.'

'No!' cried Zoë. 'No, it's not that. It's . . .' She tried to explain. 'It's just that I'm not feeling it any more. I . . . I wrote that song when I was at my lowest point, when I was all alone and angry . . . But now I'm not. All the angst is gone and I can't get worked up about it any more. I'd rather sing *our* songs.'

Ellie nodded. A smile started to creep across her lips. 'Good thing you had all that angst while you were signed to Vicinity, eh?'

'Yeah.' Zoë laughed. 'Yeah, the label's happy.'

She hooked the guitar strap over her head, thinking about how things had panned out. Perhaps 'happy' was too strong a word; Jenson was still fuming about her premature departure. According to Louis, who was also pretty disgruntled, the A&R manager was convinced he could have 'milked the brand' for at least another two albums, following the success of *It Goes Pop*. Those words had been all the proof she'd needed to convince herself that she'd made the right decision. Zoë didn't want to be milked.

The door opened to reveal Kate, laden down with guitar, bags and a weighty-looking pile of newspapers.

'Planning to be trapped in here for a while?' asked Zoë.

Kate shrugged off her bags and stepped closer, thrusting the papers in Zoë's face. 'What is this all about?'

Zoë looked down, then up at Kate's face. Her newfound belligerence was rather intimidating.

'Ah.' She grimaced at the picture on display. 'I was waiting for someone to spot that.'

'It's not just one; you're in all of them!' Kate waved one of the newspapers in the air. 'Denzel was my everything, Denzel is a hero, Denzel walks on water . . . I thought he was a cheating bastard? I thought you hated all this stuff?' She dropped the papers on an upturned box for Ellie to see. 'They're *interviews*, not paparazzi shots. What are you playing at?'

Zoë swallowed, preparing to explain. Then the door flew open.

'Drinks!' cried Shannon, reversing in with a tray laden down with three beers and an orange juice. Since Ellie's scare, she had not only given up hard drugs, but cannabis, tobacco and alcohol too. She'd even started turning up to places on time. 'Eamonn felt bad, so he's offered us free drinks all night.'

'Bad?' Zoë frowned, aware that Ellie and Kate were still waiting to hear her explanation.

Shannon nodded slowly, meeting Zoë's eye with an awkward grimace. Eventually, she explained.

'I asked Eamonn to pretend to be Niall King and invite you to that party. I wanted to embarrass you in front of the cameras when you got turned away.'

Zoë looked at her, speechless.

'I know it was childish, but I felt so angry about that thing in *Q*, and . . .' Shannon trailed off.

Having got over the shock and realised the irony of it all – the fact that if she hadn't been fooled into going along that night then she might never have had her epiphany, never have come running back to the girls – Zoë couldn't think of anything else to do but laugh. Then Shannon started laughing too, then Ellie.

'Okay,' said Kate, when the noise had finally died down. 'So you were about to explain these?' She pointed angrily at the news-papers.

'Ah, yeah.' Zoë composed herself. Shannon was already letting off a stream of shocked expletives. 'Well . . . I did it because Denzel needed some good press. He's releasing his first single this week and he needs the public support.'

'But you hate him!'

'Didn't he just win *I'm a Celebrity*?' asked Shannon, sifting through the articles. 'Surely he can't need any more exposure?'

'He's worried the public will see him as a bit of a knob for being so competitive.'

'*Why are you helping him*?' Kate asked through gritted teeth.

There was a knock at the door and a swathe of white-blonde hair swung through the gap.

Shannon looked up from the tabloid. 'Ooh, hi. Weren't you on stage just a minute ago? I heard you from the bar. Great voice. Not your average Mad Cow performer, eh?'

The blonde smiled meekly and slipped into the cramped little room. 'Thanks.' She turned to Zoë. 'I've been thinking about what you said.'

Zoë looked at her expectantly, aware of the looks she was getting from the girls. 'And?'

The blonde was grinning. 'I'd love to sign to Kidd Records.'

'Kidd what?' Shannon screwed up her face.

'What's going on?' asked Kate.

'Oh my God . . .' Ellie clapped a hand over her mouth.

Zoë held the girl close, feeling flushed with excitement. 'Kidd Records,' she said, withdrawing and presenting her to the rest of her band. 'Meet Hazel Myers, my first signing.'

'You're setting up your own label?'

Zoë nodded. 'That's why I did the deal with Denzel. He needed the endorsement from a chart-topping artist – well, *nearly* chart-topping,' she dipped her head modestly. 'And I needed an introduction to his label's distribution arm. I've hooked up with them to create Kidd Records.'

Ellie squealed. 'That's amazing! *Well done*, Zoë.'

Kate eyed her cautiously. 'I thought you despised record labels and everything they stood for?'

'I do. But this is a whole new way of working. At Kidd Records, the artists keep all their copyrights. They can record what they like and there's no ramming into moulds. Only the genuinely talented acts get signed and they can walk away at any time. Oh, and they get a bigger share of the profits – not two per cent or whatever it was at Vicinity.'

'I'm sold!' cried Shannon. 'Great idea!'

Kate nodded, slowly. 'Is this what you're spending your inheritance on?'

'Partly.' Zoë smiled. Clearly Kate was as prudent as ever. 'Don't worry; I'm not blowing the whole lot on the venture.'

'No, I didn't mean it like that.' Kate looked over at Hazel, then back at Zoë. She laughed. 'I think it's great what you're doing. It's about time someone shook up the industry.'

There was a cough in the doorway. Eamonn was bearing down on them. 'You playin' tonight, ladies?'

Zoë checked the time. They were nearly twenty minutes late. Gathering their instruments, they headed for the stage, watching

420

from the wings as some bearded relative of Eamonn's shouted into the microphone.

'They split up for six months but then realised they couldn't be apart . . .'

Zoë looked round at her fellow band mates, feeling the familiar, anticipatory buzz. She squinted. There was somebody with them, backstage. A man. Black T-shirt, muscular arms, shaggy hair obscuring his face.

'*Tommy*?' she hissed.

He stepped out of the shadows.

'Thought you might need a roadie,' he whispered, grinning.

Zoë reached round and pulled him towards her, kissing him properly on the lips. 'You know,' she said, pulling away, 'I think I might need one later.'

'LADIES AND GENTS,' yelled the compère. 'PLEASE WELCOME OUR LAST ACT OF THE NIGHT . . . THE GORGEOUS . . . THE TALENTED . . . DIRTY MONEY!'

Backstage with Polly Courtney

Where did Zoë, Ellie, Shannon and Kate come from?
I play violin in an all-girl string quartet called No Strings
Attached, and was considering writing a novel based on our
experiences when a record producer friend introduced me to
one of her new acts, Jadylu. On hearing her story of true-surgeon's
daughter to aspiring pop star, I realised there was a book to be
written about what it means to be striving for fame and success
in today's pop industry, so I combined the two themes.

I should say that the characters are not direct representations
of Jadylu or the members of my quartet. Caroline is a perfectly
safe driver, Rebecca is not a control freak, and Celia would never
set foot in a caravan, let alone live in one!

Lots of my friends play in unsigned and recently signed bands,
so it was impossible not to weave some of their anecdotes into
the narrative too. My favourite was the one from Joss, lead singer
of all-girl rock group, Black Widow, whose drummer sent ampu-
tated spiders' limbs to record label executives in an attempt to
get the band a deal!

Is Zoë's journey based on anything you have experienced?
I'm no Zoë Kidd. I can only play one song on the guitar, so I
wouldn't make it very far on the circuit! That said, I did quit the
monotonous but well-paid city life to pursue my dreams and
become a writer, so perhaps our paths aren't so different after all.

There are certainly parallels between music and writing. In both cases, a huge significance is attached to 'getting signed', be it with a record label or a publisher, yet in reality, putting your signature on the dotted line is only the first hurdle. Once the ink dries, you realise that the challenge is not just to create; it's to get your creation picked up by fans. Writing songs or books is the easy part. In the same way that band members lead double lives – living quietly in a recording studio for months on end and then jumping on a tour bus to put on a series of lively performances – I find myself coming out of hibernation when a book is due out and switching to 'promoting mode'. Although I imagine my library talks don't quite compare to singing in front of ten thousand fans . . .

What's the best thing that's happened to the music industry in the last ten years?
The internet. With YouTube, Twitter, Facebook and so on, it's easier than ever for musicians to reach out to fans. Thanks to bloggers, news spreads instantly, and with services like Spotify and MySpace, so does the music. Tunes can be downloaded and streamed anytime, anywhere, and in some cases, artists can cross continents without even leaving their homes.

And the worst?
The internet. It's a poisoned chalice. As a fan, I love the way in which the web has made music accessible to the masses. But for artists, things have become a lot tougher. Musicians earn almost nothing in royalties, thanks to illegal downloaders and cut-price album sales. Even for those who are signed, only one in every hundred makes a penny from their music.

Fan-bases are shrinking, thanks to the flood of new artists who are thrown at the scene every year by record companies desperate to make money. There's only so much listening time to go around, so many musicians find they get literally 'fifteen seconds of fame' before returning to obscurity. It's great that such a broad range of music exists on tap, but I find it sad that there will never again be a band as far-reaching as the Beatles or the Rolling Stones.

What is the 'fame factor'?
Pop moguls might tell you that it's a special combination of talent, looks and attitude. There are certainly attributes that all the stars tend to have. But in the process of writing this book, I realised that there was another, less talked-about element in the equation: luck.

There are more wannabes out there – wannabes who tick all the boxes – than there are places on our television screens and iPods. By definition, some will go nowhere, despite possessing all the right qualities. As an artist, whether you make it all the way depends on whether the A&R rep happens to listen to your demo, which producer they have lined up for you, whether the plugger is having a good day when he plays your tracks to the radio stations . . . There are so many factors outside your control that it's down to chance, more than anything else, whether you make it through.

What advice would you give to the wannabes out there?
Think carefully about where you really want to be, and how you want to get there.